THE COUNCIL OF ATHYZIA

PART I OF THE ATHYZIAD

D.H. HOSKINS

Copyright © 2022 by D. H. Hoskins

Maps by D. H. Hoskins using Other World Mapper

Cover by Lucy Giller with Little Gem Studio

Kingdom emblems by The Noun Project

All rights reserved.

No part of this publication may be reproduced, distributed, or transmitted in any form or by any means, including photocopying, recording, or other electronic or mechanical methods, without the prior written permission of the publisher, except as permitted by U.S. copyright law. For permission requests, contact [include publisher/author contact info].

The story, all names, characters, and incidents portrayed in this production are fictitious. No identification with actual persons (living or deceased), places, buildings, and products is intended or should be inferred.

To Fred Hoskins
The Eagles Came Back

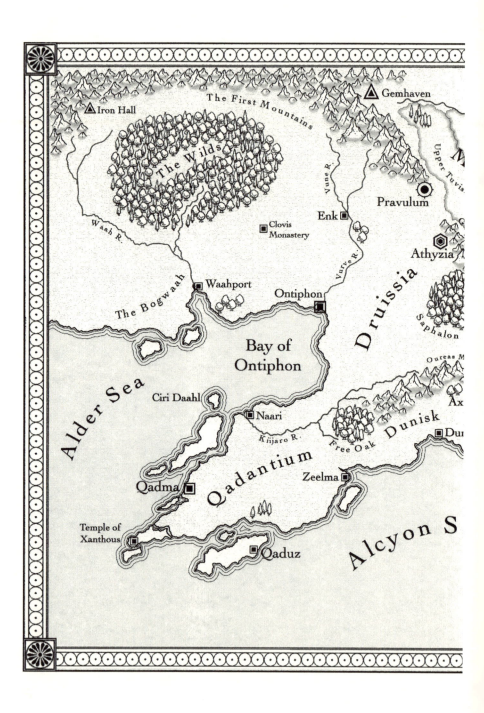

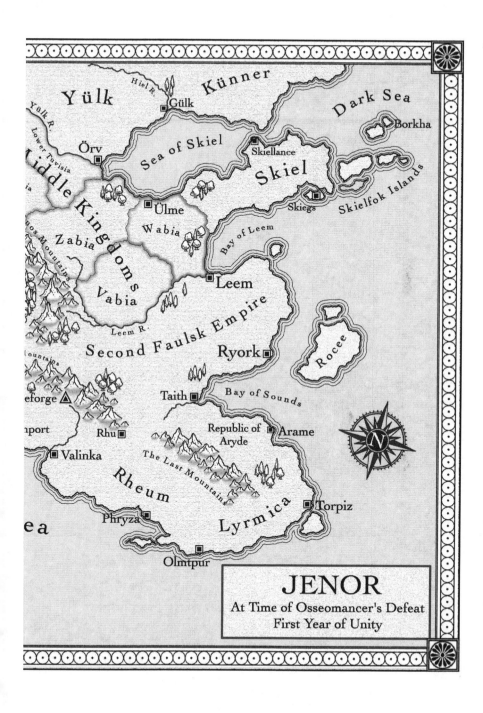

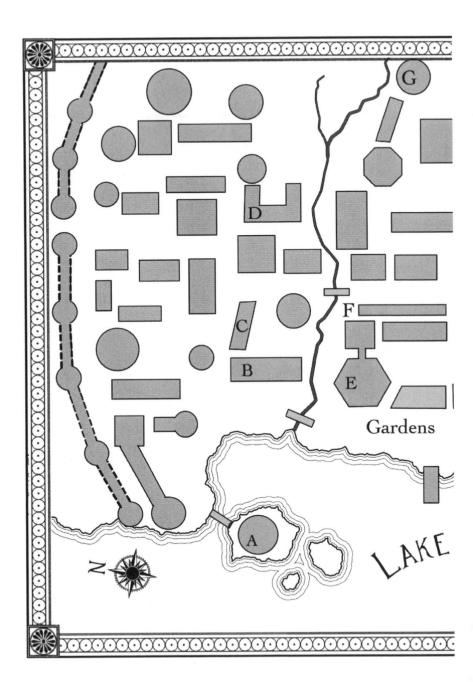

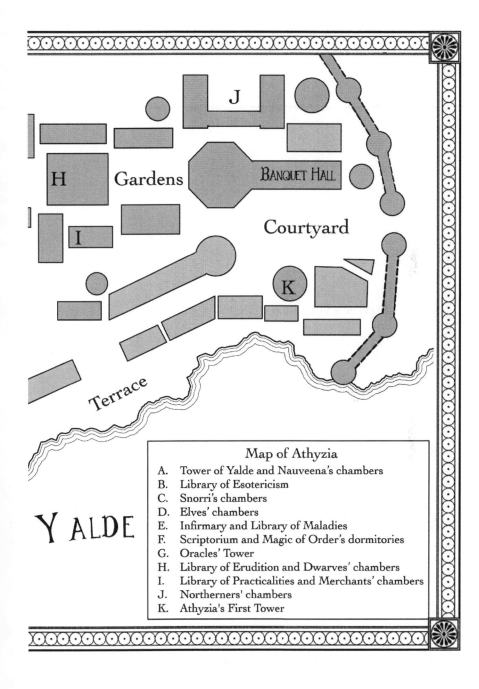

ATTENDANCE

ELVES

 Saphalon Forest - Queen Em' Iriild

 Free Oak - The poet Csandril Em' Dale

 The Wilds - Chieftain Zufaren Em' Zee

DWARVES

 Gemhaven - Lord Ferrum Rüknuckles

 Axeforge - Ambassadress Galena Quarryborn

Centaurs, Beasts of the Land, and Birds of the Air

 The Druid Malachite

Independent Merchant Cities

 Valinka - Grufton Mann, ombudsman of the Merchants' Guild

 Phryza - Mayor Ivalka Puchee

 Olmtpur - Treasurer Loblic Haleem

Oracles

 Temple of Xanthous - Kìtrinos, the High Priestess

Kingdoms of Men

 Qadantium - The Prince Regent Javee

 Druissia - King Bane VII, with the witch Venefica of Zeelma

 Dunisk - Queen Yellialah

Rheum - General Dolcius

 Lyrmica - Balzhamy, Alchemist and Vizier to King Tutus

 The Bogwaah - Wilhelm Vaah, the Burgomaster of Bogmantic

 Republic of Aryde - Fichael Porteau, Foreign Minister

 Yülk - King Ümlaut the Bearclaw

 Künner - King Caron Háček

 Skiel - Veeslau the Unbound

 Second Faulsk Empire - Fallou, the First Protector of Leem

Wabia - Falidurmus the Younger, the Protector of Ülme

 Zabia - Malidurmus, the Protector of Dracc

 Vabia - Malthius, the Protector of Vuberg

 Upper Tuvisia - Vicodermus, the Protector of Maldorf

 Lower Tuvisia - Vicodermus, the Protector of Twerdorf

CONVENED BY

 The Academy of Mages at Athyzia - Snorri the Esoteric, assisted by Nauveena of Ciri Daahl

Pronunciation Guide

Many languages are spoken in Jenor, both ancient and common. To make English speakers more comfortable, names have been translated as phonetically as possible. However, some might still prove challenging. Guidance on more difficult names is offered below.

Places
Athyzia (ah-THEE-zee-ah)
Aryde (air-AH-day)
Druissia (drew-ZEE-ah)
Qadantium (KAH-dan-tee-um)

Characters
Snorri (SNOR-ri)
Nauveena (nah-VEEN-ah)
Venefica (VEN-if-ah-kah)
Csandril (SHAN-drill)
Em' Iriild (em-AH-rilld)
Zufaren (ZOO-fair-en)
Kitrinos (KEY-tree-nose)
Javee (HA-vee)
Fallou (FAL-low)
Caeruleom (SIR-ill-ee-um)
Osseomancer (O-see-o-man-sir)

BOOK I

Chapter One
The Great Alliance

> "Magic may come from the earth. And from the blood. And from the stars. And be combined as the letters of the alphabet are combined to form words. The only limitation is the sorcerer's imagination."
> ~*Philosophies of Magic*
> Bezra Umal
> 1092 BU

After a quarter-century, the Osseomancer — that Doom Weaver and Deceiver King, that Dark Lord worshiped by all things vulgar and without shame — had been defeated. At long last, the Great Alliance had pushed back his hordes. Inch by inch, they forced them from their lands until they converged on the Osseomancer himself. In the final, terrible battle, he was vanquished. With his power shattered, he was cast from his mortal form to wander the twilight worlds weak and alone.

A quarter-century of fighting. A quarter-century of fear. A quarter-century of death.

The land would take just as long to heal itself. And only the magic of time could aid it.

For a generation, his armies had swept across the kingdoms. In each, they opened graves and tombs to swell their ranks. Everywhere they marched became inflicted with the blight. The necromancy he used to command his forces leached into the land. Fields became barren. Crops withered. Streams dried. Livestock perished. His armies did worse, devouring all before them with sword and with torch.

Each kingdom endured the onslaught as best they could, but alone. Only when they united as the Great Alliance were they able to turn the tide.

Even in defeat, his magic lingered. The land remained desolate. More monsters than before roamed undeterred, let loose by his enchantments. Travel became difficult. Crisscrossing armies had scarred the roads, leaving them washed out and eroded. Bandits became emboldened and willing — in their hunger — to rob travelers for the smallest trinket. In the ebb and flow of the war, retreating armies had ordered bridges destroyed behind them, often with magic. Now, they found the same magic could not easily repair those bridges.

It was a testament, then, that despite the dangers and the difficulties and the longing for home, almost everyone had come to Athyzia.

Athyzia.

Beautiful, wise Athyzia.

Powerful magic protected the academy's towers and libraries and gardens. Such magic had not come easy, or without cost. The same wards had shielded the nearby mountains and lake below. Everything had been preserved and kept safe.

Now, Athyzia was full again. Everywhere Nauveena looked, she found activity. Mages bustled from one library to another, eager to resume their research. Guests explored Athyzia's winding paths and towers. The smells of cooking wafted from the kitchens. Around every corner, Nauveena could hear conversation — and laughter.

Nauveena too had returned to her old routines. Once more, she walked with her graying mentor. She carried pen and parchment. She took notes. She could almost forget there had ever been a war at all. However, instead of Snorri's lessons on incantations, they discussed the council, and the council made it impossible to forget such things.

"And Skiel?" Snorri asked as they entered Athyzia's courtyard.

"It is only Veeslau and his manservant," Nauveena said. "They were easy to find accommodations for." She now stood almost a head taller than the mage. He walked slower as well. Nauveena had to shorten her strides so she would not outpace him.

They always made an odd pair — now even more so — Nauveena, with bronze skin and dark hair, walking besides her mentor: rounder, shorter, grayer. Athyzia had guests for the first time in years and Nauveena had dressed for the occasion. She wore her finest dress of purple damask, embroidered with silver stars and moons. The long fabric of the hanging bell sleeves fell almost to the ground. She had put on every piece of jewelry she owned; not much, but enough for decorum. Snorri? Snorri wore the same tired robes he always wore. He could have been in his study, not greeting every scion from Qadantium to Künner.

"Right, right. How about the merchants?" Snorri skipped from one topic to the next as each thought occurred to him. "They wished for space to work."

"It has been provided to them in the Library of Practicalities."

The members of the Great Alliance had arrived one after the other. They came from the northern kingdoms: Yülk and Künner, and the mysterious lands of Skiel. From Druissia, which had suffered the sharpest of the Osseomancer's blows, withstood it, absorbed it and struck back. From the sun-soaked vineyards of Qadantium and Dunisk and the wealthy southern ports: Phyrza and Olmtpur and Valinka. The dwarves had arrived only the other night.

The Great Alliance could not be dissolved. Not yet. Their primary goal — the Osseomancer's defeat — had been achieved. But the world was now shattered and needed to be rebuilt. A new age was before them, a new chapter to be written. And they would write it together.

Only one contingent had yet to arrive.

Snorri normally strode aimlessly, finding it easier to think while walking. Now, he went with purpose. He led Nauveena to Athyzia's first tower. It might not have been the tallest, but from its parapet they could still see far and wide.

When they reached the top, Nauveena understood why they had come. The druid Malachite waited for them. He still wore his weather-beaten travel cloak despite having been in Athyzia for many weeks. Neither had he trimmed his rust-colored beard.

"Anything?" Snorri asked him.

Malachite shook his head. "Not yet."

"Where are they?" Snorri rubbed his hands together as he looked over the ramparts.

"They will come."

"They are the last," Snorri said, "and they have the least far to come."

Typical of the elves, Nauveena thought. The young sorceress could see the elves' forest of Saphalon from the tower. It too had protected itself against the Osseomancer's curses. Now, it sat like an emerald, alone on a sea of gray.

How many evenings had Nauveena watched that glimpse of forest at the base of the mountains? A sister to herself, isolated as the tides of war struck against her and she could only muster enough magic to protect her own sphere. She protected Athyzia as the Academy of Mages went to fight in the pitched battles. Snorri had taught her all he could, and still, at times, it did not feel like enough.

She had looked at the elves' forest for strength. They too withstood the attack as surge after surge came, each somehow stronger than the last. She wondered if the forest's protector did not look longingly at her high upon her tower, alone in the world.

From the tower, Nauveena could also look north, although she tried not to. In the north lay the Osseomancer's terrible stronghold: Pravulum, the tower from which he'd commanded his forces. In the final battle, the Great Alliance had prevailed and splintered the stone fortress with their combined magic. Months later, it still smoldered, replaced with a column of ash that would remain for a generation.

"We not only wait on the Elf Queen of Saphalon," Nauveena said. "The elves from the Wilds also plan to attend. As does Free Oak."

"The Wilds are not so far," Snorri said. "The Bogwaah also lays beyond the Vurve, and they arrived three days ago."

Nauveena knew this only too well. The burgomaster and his entourage had made their presence well-known to Athyzia's kitchen staff.

"As I understand, the elves of the Wilds might have been delayed," Malachite said. "The orcs continue to be a problem."

Snorri sighed. The council was his idea. Nauveena knew how anxious he was to begin.

"The elves will want to meet separately first," Malachite continued. "To hold their own council, on matters that would not concern men."

"Which makes me wonder why they are coming at *all*." Fallou, the First Protector of Leem, appeared on the tower and approached the group. In recent days, Athyzia had been filled with much joy and much laughter, but none from him. Nauveena wondered if the First Protector had ever laughed in all his lean years. Between his gray hair and gray vestments, only one expression appeared: an ever-present glare. "The elves rarely concern themselves with the matters of man; why should they in this case?"

Fallou always managed to appear unannounced, as if out of thin air. Nauveena might have guessed by magic, but she assumed the Magic of Order precluded such uses. She knew little about the strange cult, even though it had existed in the eastern realms for more than a century.

The First Protector had a knack for appearing at inopportune moments in a conversation. It was not the first time Fallou had asked about the elves.

"That's exactly why they should," Snorri said. "What an opportunity we have before us. Never before has such an alliance formed. We are tasked with putting the world back together. Everyone who worked to defeat the Osseomancer should be involved, and we will be better off for it."

"Involved how exactly? Will there be a vote of some sort?" Fallou asked. Again, not for the first time. Many wondered about the council Snorri had planned. Fallou in particular. He asked every time he talked to Snorri and Nauveena.

Nauveena already knew Snorri's answer, but this did not stop her mentor from saying it once again. "I have thought it all through," he said. "All through. Of course, it is a most important issue. And it will be the first one we discuss. Once we have everyone together."

"It is not just the elves we are waiting for," Malachite said. "What about the island of Rocee? Or the monks of Clovis?"

Snorri shook his head. "Rocee has not returned our invitation. Fallou, perhaps you have heard from them? I know Faulsk does much trade with them."

"They have become quite isolated since the war. They wanted to protect themselves. *Many did.*" Did Fallou's words harbor a slight? Nauveena thought they might. Then he sneered, imbuing his words with their intended malice. The Osseomancer's army had conquered many kingdoms, leaving behind orphans and widows and the blight. The middle kingdoms had fallen first and remained under his yoke for the duration. Much of Faulsk fell before his armies marched into Rheum.

Yet many lands within the Osseomancer's path survived. Athyzia lay close enough that Nauveena could see Pravulum on a clear day. Still,

Athyzia remained untouched. It had not suffered the desolation of the other lands. Those kingdoms that had suffered remembered those who had shut their doors. Nauveena knew such resentment was unjustified. She had been ordered by the Academy to protect Athyzia at all costs. Many books in Athyzia's libraries contained ancient knowledge the Osseomancer coveted.

Much more would have been lost if Athyzia had fallen.

Still, she often felt guilty for having spent the war in the protected sanctuary, especially when so many others had fought and died. Could they have opened their doors to others? The war had created many refugees. Could they have offered safe haven?

"Very well," Snorri said. "All we can do is invite them. As for Clovis, the monks declined our invitation. They wished us luck and have sent a dozen hogsheads of their ale instead."

Malachite's eyes lit up. "Between that and all the Qadantium wine Prince Javee brought, we will have quite the party."

"'Party?'" Snorri said. "'Party?' No, there will be no party. We have partied since Pravulum fell. No, now is when the work begins."

As Nauveena's mentor said this, the wind shifted direction. The standards of each Alliance member had been unfurled from the tower's heights: the golden sun of Dunisk, the crimson bull of Druissia, the oracles' eye, wide and staring, and the gray letters of each middle kingdom in simple calligraphy. Each swung as the wind came from the south. From Saphalon.

A hawk swooped down to land on Malachite's shoulder. The bird put its beak to the druid's ear, and Malachite nodded in understanding.

A moment later, and Nauveena could hear a song of lutes and ocarinas upon the same wind. She saw their procession first. The Elf Queen in all her glory came forward on a white mount. Her golden hair sprayed out from a tiara of diamonds and white flowers.

On either side of her rode the other two elven representatives: one from Free Oak and one from the Wilds. Each brought a retinue that flared out behind them in separate columns. Even from a distance, Nauveena could tell them apart. The elves of the Wilds were broad-shouldered and taller than their Free Oak cousins. Their leader cut his hair into a high mohawk. He sat sternly on his mount.

Free Oak had sent the poet Csandril Em' Dale to represent them. His pointed ears poked through his long golden hair. He always appeared to be winking or about to tell some jest, and Nauveena thought he might be, even now, as he bounced in his saddle in rhythm with the elven minstrels.

After all the struggles of the war, the clashes of armies, the fall of heroes, and the wisdom of mages, Nauveena could think of no stranger sight than all three elven kingdoms riding together — and approaching Athyzia.

"Yes," Snorri repeated to himself. "Now is when the work begins."

Nauveena heard Snorri repeat the phrase to himself as they descended the tower's stairs. "Now is when the work begins. Now is when the work begins."

The refrain had been a rallying cry for him as he sent invitations across the lands. He had worked happily and eagerly, never more at peace than when he had a task before him.

But, Nauveena knew he also worked anxiously. Typically, his work involved experiments alone in his atelier. Alone in his work, he could proceed in his own fashion. The council would be another matter entirely. For the council relied on others — many others — and that introduced more variables than any experiment Snorri had ever conducted before.

"Now is when the work begins," he muttered as he rushed into the courtyard, out of breath after descending so many stairs. "Now is when the work begins," he said faster and perhaps louder in his excitement, but ultimately, not loud enough.

Because no one — besides Nauveena — seemed to hear him.

Athyzia's gates burst open. The elves' entrance became a gallant procession, a parade led forward by their music. The Elf Queen Em' Iriild rode at the head. The long trek over open country had not touched her white dress, which appeared as if it were fallen snow. The elven seamstresses had undoubtedly spun a bit of their magic into the weave, so that it changed consistency as she moved. Even her horse's caparison was made of a finer silk than anything Nauveena had ever worn herself.

Those watching from the tower — Nauveena and Snorri, Malachite and Fallou — had not been the only ones to hear the elves' approach. Practically all the Alliance members came out in one mad rush, flooding the courtyard.

The elven minstrels did not stop their songs. As the other members of the council came to greet them, their music only changed in rhythm and instrumentation. Drums struck a steady beat that one could not help dancing to, as if it were an enchantment.

If Nauveena had time to study the matter, she might have guessed that it was. Elven songs had their own history and a field of study all to themselves. At another time, she might have found the matter quite curious. But now, she found she was not immune to their effects.

"Make way, make way." Snorri pushed through the crowd. He became lost in the sea of heads, but eventually emerged besides the Elf Queen. Nauveena followed behind her mentor, fighting the urge to dance.

"We are thrilled to have you." Snorri took the Elf Queen's hand in his and shook it wildly. After a moment that was long enough to be polite, the queen removed her hand so gracefully that Snorri didn't notice. "Thrilled to have you," he said as he continued to shake his now-empty hand. "Never before has such a council been called: elves, dwarves, and men. We will create a peace like no other."

Queen Em' Iriild curtsied. "It is an honor to be invited," she said. "I believe in the aims of this council. May the dark nights of the war bring forth a glorious dawn."

"Yes, I do hope so," Snorri said. "It is always darkest before the dawn, they say. But a new day. A new day it is. And I hope we can get started right away. I know you came as fast as you could, but we can have no delay."

"You'd like us to go *right* to chambers?"

"Most certainly. Why not? Seats have already been set up on the terrace. Why delay when we can begin building this new world order?"

"A new world order can wait one day more, certainly. I have barely gotten off my horse. It has been a full day's ride from Saphalon. And I hardly imagine you can get anyone else here to focus."

As others rushed from their rooms and the kitchens and the libraries to greet the elves, a great feeling of joy swelled through Athyzia. For so long, such emotions had been stored away deep down and protected. Now, they surged out.

Snorri looked crestfallen. Nauveena knew how eagerly he wanted to begin. She remembered how anxiously he had dictated each invitation to her. Mages had many ways to send letters quickly, but that did not always mean a quick response. Snorri did not know if he would be received kindly, or rebuffed. Even for a two-hundred-year-old mage — the leader of the Academy of Mages at that — rejection was hard.

"Don't look so upset." Queen Em' Iriild comforted the mage with the lightest touch to his shoulder. "The Osseomancer has fallen; it is right to celebrate. At least for tonight. Tomorrow, we can remake our world."

The Elf Queen's touch and kind words were enough to buoy Snorri's spirits. He smiled up at the queen. She returned the smile before handing the reins of her horse to a squire. She then clapped three times in the direction of her minstrels, a signal to increase the tempo.

The poet Csandril Em' Dale took the Elf Queen's cue as well. He effortlessly scaled the flagpole in the center of the courtyard in two easy hops, until he hung well above the gathered crowd — just below Athyzia's standard of a tower on a purple field. Those gathered looked up, eager to hear what he had to say.

"Men and dwarves, my fellow elves," the poet pronounced. "All those who stood against the evil of our age. Happy are we all that you stood and fought and lived. Without your strength and bravery and resolve, Pravulum would not now be a crater, the armies of the undead would not now be vanquished, and the safety of all innocents not now guaranteed, but — and most importantly — we would not be here to have the celebration I assure you we will have tonight."

The tumultuous joy bounding over the pave stones hit a fevered pitch as Csandril finished his address. His last words were drowned out in shouts and claps. Snorri had no hope now.

The elves' music swelled to accompany Csandril as he leapt from the flagpole. He was caught by the crowd and carried forward in a sea of well-wishes and hoorays. Soon, all that Nauveena could hear was clapping and the stamping of feet against the stone.

Soon, Nauveena forgot all about her mentor and his conversation with the queen. She quickly went from tapping her toes to swinging from arm to arm, skipping to the tune and humming it herself. The elven song was indeed contagious, and soon, everyone had joined in.

Malachite, the druid, danced clumsily, his boots meant for wandering the world and not dancing. Csandril Em' Dale added his own lyrics to the song as he danced, recounting many of the battles fought over the years. Javee, the Prince Regent of Qadantium, added his famous pyromancy to the show by igniting sparks of flame whenever he snapped his fingers. In between dances, draughts of Clovis ale and glasses of Qadantium wine were handed around generously.

Eventually, even Snorri joined in, becoming the most comical of all, and certainly the least graceful. Years of study meant he did not dance often.

Only those adherents to the Magic of Order refrained. They followed the First Protector of Leem to the scriptorium to illuminate manuscripts instead.

◆

The dancing continued for the rest of the afternoon. The music's enchantments made it possible to dance without end for hours, until the sun set over the Falls of Yalde and the winter moon crested above the mountains.

As night settled in, the kitchen laid out a great feast. Everyone took turns to pause from the dancing to eat. Such a spread had not been seen since before the war: Whole wheels of cheese from the dairies beyond the Vurve. Mozzarella from Qadantium's buffalo. Pickled onions from Vabia. Herring from Faulsk. Salted cod from the Sea of Skiel. Smoked salmon from the Hiel River. Caviar from the Dark Sea. Oysters and calamari from Ciri Daahl. Goat from Zabia. A Wabian goose the size of a small lamb. Roasted game hen from Upper Tuvisia. Ham and pancetta from Lyrmica. Mutton from Rheum. Venison from the Wilds.

Desserts had not been forgotten. For this, they had apples and plums from Dunisk. Pears and blueberries and raspberries from Saphalon. Wild honey from Free Oak. The southern merchants from the independent cities had brought chocolates from the Distant Lands. Those from Valinka had even brought fruits from such orchards that only goblins could find.

It seemed anything that had survived the blight had been laid out on the central table. Everyone brought something. Even the dwarves offered cave mushrooms, although these remained untouched by everyone except the dwarves.

Candles floated above the courtyard, where long tables had been positioned around the dance floor. For the first time all year, the day's warmth lingered past evening. The end of spring. The Atmospheric Mage said summer would not be long now.

Even with the added stamina of the elven songs, the mood slowed with the coming of night and the addition of food. Accordingly, the minstrels gently wound down to a less spirited waltz. The celebrants orbited into smaller groups.

Nauveena leaned against a balustrade to sip a glass of wine and rest. After hours of dancing, she felt the need to retreat. She always felt more natural on the outside, watching. A student by nature, she couldn't help but study whatever was put in front of her — in this case, the interactions of Athyzia's guests, put together after so many years apart.

Never before had so many kings and mages, queens and lords, ambassadors and heads of state, warriors, princes, and poets gathered. Each had fought on separate fronts during the war, only coming together in the final cataclysmic battle. Now, they reminisced and shared stories.

One of the elven warriors from the Wilds regaled the southern merchants with his exploits. The merchants — in their strange southern fashions — leapt back with gasps at one point as the warrior became a bit too graphic. He had evidently shattered many orc skulls.

Prince Javee and Csandril Em' Dale sat together, smoking among the oracles of Xanthous. They animated their tales with smoke rings that transformed into scenes of battle. Nauveena could hear the oracles' laughter over the music as Csandril Em' Dale provided commentary.

As a smoke ring passed, Nauveena smelt the fragrance. Sweet and pungent, it could provide prophecy all on its own. Qadantium was known for more than just its wine.

The Magic of Order returned from the scriptorium to eat. They still kept on one side of the tables, as far from the elves' song and the drink as they reasonably could. Still, a few bobbed their heads to the music. One or two carefully glanced over at the oracles gathered around the prince and poet.

Nauveena did not pay them much attention, however. Instead, her focus had shifted to the far corner, where King Bane of Druissia sat in deep conversation with the Elf Queen and the witch Venefica. Nauveena specifically studied Venefica. The witch's black hair was weaved into tight braids, the tips of which had been dyed with the blood of scarabs. She wore a crimson dress, bright against her brown skin, and many jangling talismans: around her neck, on her wrists, piercing her ears and in her hair. The magic of witches bordered on superstition almost as much as folk mages' — except witches' magic often worked.

Nauveena was studying this group so intently, she did not notice the druid Malachite wander over to her. He carried a carafe of wine, and refilled Nauveena's glass, catching her attention.

"I wonder what they are discussing," Nauveena said, too distracted to drink.

"Do not be so suspicious."

"She supported *him*." Nauveena made sure to keep her voice to a whisper. "She served him. Now she is here."

"That was early in the war." Malachite tried to sound reassuring. "And it was a *long* war."

"They called her the Witch of Pravulum." Indeed, Venefica had been one of the Osseomancer's chief servants. She had given aid to him and done his bidding.

"She has the trust of King Bane now," Malachite said as if to end the matter. And it did. Everyone had been surprised when Venefica arrived with King Bane at the council, and more surprised when he said she would be his advisor.

Nauveena looked to the king of Druissia. His black skin had begun to wrinkle, his thick beard had begun to gray. Still, he looked formidable with his broad shoulders and ceremonial gold armor. He had withstood assault after assault from the Osseomancer. No one's trust carried as much weight.

Still, Nauveena wondered what he and the witch were discussing with the Elf Queen. Each kept their voices low. Nauveena could not hear them from across the room, especially as the conversation and laughter of the others threatened to drown out even the music.

They especially could not be heard over the dwarves and the northerners, the rowdiest bunch by far. Already, Malachite's focus had shifted to this more boisterous group.

"Have you heard what's going around?" he asked, changing topics, smiling as if he knew some secret.

Nauveena looked in this group's direction now, forgetting about the witch for a moment. The dwarves sat on ale barrels or stood on the tables to be as tall as the northerners. Each northerner was well over six feet tall, including the women. Queen Breve was at least a foot taller than Nauveena, who was not short by any means.

Of all the warriors, the northerners were the most fearsome — short of, maybe, the elves of the Wilds, who made a habit of fighting orcs. They had wild beards, braided in elaborate fashions, and terrible scarring, more likely from the wars among themselves than those with the Osseomancer. Each northern warrior wore armor encrusted with bones and gems. The dwarves too, with their armor, had an impressive showing of rubies and emeralds and gold and silver.

"No, what's that?" Nauveena asked.

Among the northerners, Malachite specifically glanced at Ümlaut, the king of Yülk, who excitedly told a story from the war. The king punched the air to mimic some fight that had taken place against the army of undead. The dwarves laughed and mimicked the action themselves.

"Seriously? You haven't?" Malachite beamed with excitement at finding someone who hadn't heard his rumor. "You see the one talking?" he asked. "King Ümlaut?"

Nauveena nodded.

"His wife" — Malachite pointed her out with his gaze — "is sleeping with the king of Künner."

Nauveena gasped. Not from the shock of it, but because she thought the northern queen Malachite pointed out *was* the wife of the king of Künner. All night, Nauveena had seen Queen Breve interact with Caron, the king of Künner. Their interactions were enough to make her think they were wed.

King Ümlaut was much older than his bride. His dark beard had been peppered gray for many years. His body ached in the cold, and it was always cold in the north.

Caron, on the other hand, was a fierce warrior. His rippling biceps and forearms were sliced with runic tattoos, dark against his pale skin, that imbued him with a ferocious power in battle. Like many of the northerners — including King Ümlaut himself — Caron was one of the legendary berserkers. Looking at him, Nauveena didn't doubt it.

"In the north, it is customary for the women to fight as well as the men," Malachite said. "The northern kingdoms formed an alliance early. They made their stand on the Yülk, where they fought the Osseomancer for many years. It is said that quite often, Caron and Breve would ride together into battle. They disrupted the enemy behind his lines, and at night, they would camp together. And the blood lust of battle would turn into something else."

"I mean, it seems very obvious," Nauveena exclaimed. "Just watch them."

As Ümlaut continued his story — now miming the act of choking some long-gone advisory — behind him, Breve traced the strange markings along Caron's muscles.

"I would have thought they were together," Nauveena said.

"Me too," Malachite laughed.

"Who knows?"

"Everyone — everyone except Ümlaut."

They both laughed now.

When they had finished, Malachite said, "That is not the only rumor I have now heard about the north."

"Oh, really? What else?"

He looked from side to side. "Maybe that, we should discuss somewhere else? And at another time."

"I never took you for such a gossip," Nauveena said.

"Someone has to be," Malachite said. Then his tone became more mournful. "Without Caeruleom."

Both glanced away. Neither had yet spoken of the blue wizard to one another, although both thought of him often. In the penultimate battle, the Osseomancer had made one last push against the Alliance gathered at his doors. He rode out against them and quickly routed those gathered on the plains before Pravulum. Many fell before his terrible power.

All seemed lost until the wizard Caeruleom met the Osseomancer in battle. The world cleaved in two as they collided. Lightning cracked, and stars fell from the sky. In the end, the Osseomancer retreated to his tower, broken, and the tide of war turned once and for all.

But when the smoke cleared, it was seen that the wizard had sacrificed himself in the cause. His staff had shattered. Vanquishing the Osseomancer had proved too much, even for his great power, and he could not remain in the world any longer.

Caeruleom had often come to visit Nauveena. He had brought news of the war and gossip and secrets and jokes. She had looked forward to his coming.

Both Nauveena and the druid grew quiet. It seemed now terrible to be celebrating when so many others could not. Over years of war, many had perished. How could they celebrate when those others were not here to take part? The celebration came from their sacrifice and felt unearned.

Just then, Snorri approached, carrying a stein of ale. "Can you believe this?" He hiccupped. "How will they be in any state to begin tomorrow?"

"How will *you* be in any state?" Nauveena laughed. She had never heard her mentor slur his words before.

"Now, don't worry about me." Snorri wagged his finger sternly. "I will be fine. Yes. I will be fine. It is the rest I worry about. But we will begin tomorrow regardless. We have many long days before us. Much work."

He took a drink from his stein, leaving a foam mustache from the beer.

"But maybe we can start in the afternoon."

Chapter Two
The Work Begins

> "Men have fought over land. They have fought over gold and they fought over magic. These conflicts might have been set aside, but they have not vanished. Now, it is the council's task to address them."
> ~Notes on the council
> Snorri the Esoteric
> 1 YU

Athyzia lay nestled between Lake Yalde and the peaks of the Gnos Mountains as a collection of spires that followed the mountains' ridge. From the tallest towers, one could see through a break in the mountains over the Falls of Yalde and out across Druissia.

Of Athyzia's towers, Nauveena had long lived in the Tower of Yalde: a tall, thin tower built on a small island on the lake and connected to the mainland by a short bridge. The tower's rooms opened to tall ceilings and wide windows, and were decorated with many colorful silken tapestries, plants, and — of course — books.

Nauveena maintained her own library from the many books Snorri had given her to study during his long absences. She found others that satisfied her curiosities: theories on magic, particular and useful spells, several romances of faraway places, and at least three separate histories on Athyzia herself, each contradictory, but no less true in Nauveena's mind.

Nauveena left her tower just after noon and met her mentor in front of the Library of Esotericism. The spring sun felt warm after the long winter. Part of Nauveena would have rather basked in its glow like Athyzia's many stray cats, which came and went and lounged lazily.

Snorri emerged from his chambers no worse for wear from the night before. His excitement eased the aches in his bones. The two walked to the council together, discussing any lingering details. They crossed a bridge spanning Athyzia's lone stream, its waterfall breaking beneath, and they continued, weaving through her many towers.

No one knew who built Athyzia's original tower. Or for what purpose. The name of the architect had been lost to the realms of time. Mages had used the tower as a retreat for centuries. Out of the way of the world, it could only be found with magic. Over the ages, mages began to meet at Athyzia whenever they sought each other's counsel. As the world increasingly tilted towards chaos, they found themselves seeking each other's counsel more frequently.

These mages soon established the Academy. Many mysteries surrounded magic. The Academy sought to answer these as best they could: to study magic's sources and uses and meaning. Each mage had their specialty, but they conferred with each other and shared their research openly.

They added buildings as needed, in their way. More towers were erected. Then belfries. A kitchen. Several libraries. Aviaries. Conservatories. More libraries. Laboratories. Workshops. Personal studies. Gardens. Dormitories. A great hall. An observatory.

Athyzia became a sprawling estate devoid of unity or cohesion, but beautiful nonetheless. Mages were well-practiced in their craft, but that craft was not decorum. The result was an endless maze of vestibules and corridors, portrait galleries and wine cellars, and almost too many libraries to count.

One such library could have hosted the council, of course — if enough bookshelves were moved. But Nauveena and Athyzia's cats were not the only ones looking longingly at the spring sun. After the long winter, Snorri thought it only fair to hold the council outside on the terrace.

Here, Athyzia's many gardens converged on a tiled patio overlooking the glistening lake below. Bumblebees drifted between the already-blooming flowers, while the cherry blossoms were in their full splendor of whites and pinks. Still, Nauveena preferred the rows of tall cypress, as these always reminded her of pointed mage's hats. Out over the lake, she could hear the honking of Künnerian geese as they flew north across the mountains.

Centuries before, one of the more artistic mages had commissioned sculptures around the terrace to represent the different magics studied by the Academy. One statue gazed upon a crystal ball, while another mixed vials together, and another studied the cosmos through a telescope. Others pondered tea leaves, runes, scrolls, and the contoured, fleeting patterns of smoke.

A series of long tables had been brought to the terrace. They formed first a center square and then an outer square around the first. Only those sitting in the center would talk during the conferences. Even with a limited number, this still might prove too many. Everyone else was welcomed to listen. A theatre might have provided a better venue, but no mage had ever seen the need to build one at Athyzia.

Around the edge of the terrace, the flags of each member of the Great Alliance fluttered in the breeze: a bear on a field of black for Yülk, a wolf on gray for Künner, a sea serpent for Skiel, Free Oak's brown acorn, the Wilds' lone pine tree, the Forest of Saphalon's silver tree upon a pure white background, a rooster on red for the Republic of Aryde, a green frog for the Bogwaah, the snorting boar of Rheum, and Lyrmica's ibis on cobalt blue. All the merchant's banners showed some image of the sea: a marlin, a ship's wheel, an anchor. Both flags of the dwarves were displayed: a gemstone for Gemhaven and crossing axes for Axeforge. In the center, Athyzia's own standard: the first tower surrounded by a soft purple.

Snorri and Nauveena found several members of the Great Alliance already on the terrace. Fallou, the First Protector of Leem, sat at one of the center tables with the Lesser Protectors flanking him. As the Magic of Order dictated, they all wore plain gray hooded robes with the symbol of their order stitched on front. With their matching haircuts and stern expressions, they could have been copies of each other and not individuals.

Only slight differences in ornamentation separated their ranks, with Obeyers wearing the simplest robes, followed by Guardians, Keepers, and then Protectors. Fallou himself wore a golden chain over his robe, signifying his position as First Protector. They valued their hierarchy only slightly more than their parsimony, it seemed.

They all sat quietly with their hands clasped together and resting on the table. Scrolls had already been flattened, while quills waited in their inkwells.

"I see we are excited to begin," Snorri said, rushing into the center. "Always so prompt, so prompt."

Then he paused. His excitement faded. Nauveena knew why. She had seen it as soon as she walked in.

"Fallou," Snorri said, "would it be possible to speak together?"

"Yes," the First Protector said. "I am always eager to speak with you."

"Privately?"

Fallou looked up and down the central table at the Lesser Protectors. "There's no need for secrets. Whatever you want to say to me, you can say to my fellow Protectors of Order."

Snorri paused, uncertain what to say. He mumbled to himself, trying to formulate a sentence.

Eventually, Nauveena couldn't handle it anymore and intervened. "Our thought was to limit the number of voices," she said. "Which is why we had limited seats in the center. All the Protectors are welcome to listen, but we worry too many voices at once might cause the council to go on forever."

"Is this what you meant when you said you *'thought it all through?'*" Fallou asked Snorri.

"Many have traveled to the council," Nauveena said. "Each king brought their court: squires, knights, advisors, family. They should all listen, but only one should speak for each."

"The invitation said all will be heard," Fallou said.

"And they will," Nauveena said. "We thought you would represent the Magic of Order."

"But each Protector has been charged with defending Order within their kingdom. I cannot possibly speak for them all."

The Lesser Protectors had all come from the many middle kingdoms, which Nauveena could never remember the names of. She knew little about the Magic of Order. But she understood that they arranged their mages in a strict hierarchy. The Ultimate Defender presided in Ryork, and right below him was Fallou, the First Protector of Leem. Below

Fallou were the Lesser Protectors, then Keepers of Order, all the way down to Obeyers of Order, who could be simple common folk without any ability to do magic.

While the Lesser Protectors came from kingdoms across the east, Snorri and Nauveena had both assumed that with the Magic of Order's hierarchy they would be perfectly happy being represented by Fallou. That had been an incorrect assumption, it seemed now.

"For this reason, I asked how we would proceed in deliberation," Fallou continued. "You rebuffed me each time. Now, I come to learn many of my peers will be relegated to the audience, when by all rights they should speak for themselves."

"I am terribly sorry," Snorri began before being interrupted. Athyzia's bells began tolling, inviting all to the council. They rang bold and clear, and Nauveena thought they likely could be heard in Druissia, although they were not deafening to those gathered in Athyzia, but welcoming.

"We should have spoken before the council began." Despite the bells, Fallou did not need to raise his voice to be heard. "Then this embarrassment could have been avoided."

"I completely agree," Snorri said. "But, of course, I did not want such discussions off the record."

"It is our hope to be as transparent as possible in all council matters," Nauveena said. "And that is where this issue should reside: in front of the council. We can let everyone decide who should have a seat in the center."

"I certainly hope so," Fallou said. "I had my reservations on the very idea of this council from the start. This is doing nothing to reassure me."

For the time being, the Lessor Protectors went to the outside square. They did so with much production in terms of rolling up their parchment and holstering their quills and capping their inkwells, all for the sake of moving ten feet. The First Protector of Leem stared sternly at Snorri the whole time, making it clear whom he considered responsible for the miscommunication and resulting embarrassment.

As the other Great Alliance members filtered onto the terrace, they were greeted with the strange scene of the gray robed men packing their writing supplies and sullenly moving to the back.

To save Snorri from any more embarrassment, Nauveena tugged on his sleeve, directing him to their seats at a center table. Snorri reluctantly sat down. Nauveena knew he had lost focus. In his mind, he had made a mistake — an assumption — and put the council at risk.

He had dictated many long letters to Nauveena to convince Fallou to attend the council. After multiple letters, Snorri had finally gotten Fallou's acceptance and, with it, that of the other nations of the east. Many of the leaders of the eastern kingdoms turned to the Magic of Order for advisory roles. Many of the common folks were adherents. It seemed natural that these kingdoms would be represented by the Magic of Order.

Snorri could not watch as the terrace filled. Nauveena knew he had been anticipating the council even before the Osseomancer fell. He had seen the need to gather all together for some time. Now, he could not even enjoy it as the council finally came together.

The dwarves arrived last. Snorri hardly noticed when they did, and all the members of the council were seated. Instead, he sat with his face in his palms, just short of convulsing. Nauveena had to tap him on the shoulder, indicating that he could begin.

When Snorri did look up, it was a sight. As he had envisioned, the council included a representative from almost every kingdom.

He and Nauveena represented the Academy of Mages. Some of the more curious mages from the Academy had come to see the proceedings and sat directly behind them on the outer square.

Malachite, the druid, also sat at their table, which formed one side of the square.

To the right of this table sat the elves: Queen Em' Iriild from Saphalon Forest; Csandril Em' Dale from Free Oak; and last, Zufaren Em' Zee — the warrior elf Nauveena had seen riding ahead yesterday — who would represent the forests of the Wilds.

Also at the table with the elves sat the High Priestess Kitrinos, said to be the most powerful oracle of her age. One of her prophecies had warned of the Osseomancer's coming.

Prince Javee sat next to the High Priestess. His tunic of golden samite was embroidered with Qadantium's flame emblem and complemented his dark complexion well, but Nauveena suspected anything he wore would have done so.

At the end of this table sat King Bane of Drussia, with his thick black beard and broad shoulders. Nauveena did not doubt the stories of his prowess on the battlefield. She didn't think any other could have held the Osseomancer at bay for so long.

Snorri had allowed the witch Venefica to sit beside King Bane. For the occasion of the council, her dark braided hair had been pinned up with elaborate golden clasps. Her crimson dress provided a casual elegance not common among witches, although her neckline plunged deeper than Nauveena would have ever dared. Nauveena continued to eye Venefica suspiciously, regardless of what Malachite had said the night before. Among her jewelry, the witch wore a rat skull with small rubies in the eye sockets as a necklace. *What wards could such a pendant offer?* Nauveena wondered.

The witch turned her head, catching Nauveena looking in her direction. For a moment, the two locked eyes. The witch's were piercing, dark brown, speckled gold. Nauveena felt they could look through her. She quickly averted her gaze, continuing to scan the other tables.

At the next table, the one parallel to the first with Nauveena and Snorri, sat General Dolcius, who continued to wear his silver breastplate. The bulbous metal sparkled in the sun without a single nick or dent. Nauveena did not believe it had ever seen battle. She expected he wished to portray a martial air, but she couldn't help thinking the general looked like a large tea kettle.

Next to the general sat the mage Balzhamy, old and gray, who advised the king of Lyrmica and would represent the kingdom at the council. Balzhamy had once studied at Athyzia before coming to advise the king of Lyrmica. His pointed hat matched his dark blue robes, which might have been a size too large. Both hat and robe had large moons and stars stitched on them, as had been in vogue years ago. Nauveena couldn't help finding them clumsy and old-fashioned, more like costumes. The star-and-moon pattern embroidered into her own dress was much more delicate and stylish.

Next at this table came a representative from each of the southern merchant cities. First sat Grufton Mann, the ombudsman and leader of the merchants' guild for Valinka. To his right sat the mayor of Phryza, Ivalka Puchee, in a dress that looked rather expensive. Rounding out the southern merchants was Loblic Haleem, the treasurer for the city of Olmtpur on the Alcyon coast. Even sitting still, his fingers moved around each other as if he were counting coins.

Continuing along the table, next came Wilhelm Vaah, the Burgomaster of the Bogmantic, as frog-like in appearance as the Bogwaah's emblem. Beside him sat thin and frail Queen Yellialah of Dunisk and then twitchy Fichael Porteau, the foreign minister from the Republic of Aryde.

The last table, at which the Lesser Protectors had tried to sit, now belonged to the warlords of the northern kingdoms: King Ümlaut of Yülk and King Caron of Künner. Nauveena noticed Queen Breve in the second row, sitting much closer to Caron.

Veeslau the Unbound, the law speaker of Skiel, sat next to the northern lords, mimicking geography. He had remained quiet since arriving at Athyzia. A dark hood shadowed his pale face. A blindfold covered his eyes. Veeslau had come alone, save for a hobbled imp who acted as his servant. The land of Skiel, shrouded in swirling mist, was as mysterious as the strange magic practiced there. Nauveena tried not to look at Veeslau for too long.

The dwarves sat at the far end of this table. Two of the three dwarven kingdoms were represented. Lord Saxum of the southern dwarves had sent the ambassadress Galena Quarryborn, while the leader of the northern dwarves, Lord Ferrum Rüknuckles, had come himself. Their entourages sat behind them. They had brought tankards of Clovis ale with them. The retinue from the northern kingdoms looked on jealously for not having thought of bringing ale to the proceedings.

The third dwarven kingdom of Iron Hall, in the far west, beyond the Wilds, had declined the invitation. The orcs in those parts were still quite strong, still emboldened by the Osseomancer, and travel was too difficult.

Sandwiched between the northerners and Veeslau and the dwarves was an unhappy-looking Fallou of Leem. Behind him sat the lesser Protectors from Vabia, Wabia, Zabia, Upper Tuvisia, and Lower Tuvisia. Again, Nauveena had difficulty distinguishing between them; the two from Upper Tuvisia and Lower Tuvisia even shared the *same name* — in case it was not difficult enough to tell them apart.

Despite everyone seated at the center tables, Snorri could only stare beyond to the outer ring, at those Protectors he had excluded. These were all kingdoms in their own right, and Snorri looked on them with a dreadful expression.

A general hubbub of conversation had built, as it would whenever a large number gathered together. Each member turned to the other and offered greetings. Plans for dinner were made. Conversations from the night before were continued. However, the commotion could not last forever. It subsided as each member settled and looked expectantly at Snorri's table.

But Snorri's mind was elsewhere. To him, the entire council was a grand experiment, and he had set the parameters wrong. What else could now go wrong?

Seeing this, Nauveena nudged her mentor to begin. At the poke of her elbow, Snorri snapped to attention. He looked around the crowd. It suddenly seemed so many. As well as each representative at the center tables, the outer rim was filled by the Lesser Protectors and Keepers and the courts and entourages of all those assembled.

"They expect you to say something," Nauveena whispered.

Snorri looked at her blankly.

"*Your speech?*"

"Yes, yes, of course." Snorri looked at the crowd. "Everyone — "

"Stand up," Nauveena said.

"Yes, that makes sense. Yes. Of course." Snorri stood. In the silence on the terrace, his chair made a scraping sound as he pushed it back. He had rehearsed his opening speech to Nauveena for many hours. Now, he seemed to have forgotten it completely. He stared blankly at the gathered council. Then he remembered he had come prepared after all. He searched in his robe until he found a folded parchment and his reading glasses. He placed the glasses on his nose, adjusting them so they were at the right angle. With some difficulty, he opened the parchment and scanned the speech for the beginning.

"Excuse me. Excuse me," he finally said. "Thank you all for coming. And welcome to Athyzia. Many of you have traveled very far. Over dangerous roads. And are weary from the long years of war."

He spoke in the Middle Qadantine that most members of the council knew well — if it was not their first language, they spoke it at least passingly — but he spoke softly. Nauveena saw many leaning forward to hear, especially those in the second row. She kicked Snorri softly below the table.

Snorri looked down, startled.

"*Speak up,*" Nauveena urged from her seat below — she mouthed the words more than whispered them.

Snorri looked back at the crowd and realized his mistake. "Oh, right. Excuse me," he began again, this time louder. "Thank you all for coming. And welcome to Athyzia. Many of you have traveled very far. Over dangerous roads. And are weary from the long years of war."

Many nodded. They could hear Snorri now. The mage continued, "In all my long years, I cannot remember a more devastating war. And I cannot help thinking how much destruction could have been avoided if only we had come together sooner. The Osseomancer saw we were divided and used our divisions against us. He had the luxury of attacking each of us individually, assured we would not come to each other's aid. How much death could we have prevented if we had simply put our differences aside earlier?

"Of course, is such a question not true for any war? Our wars between each other have been equally ruinous. And these might be even more tragic, since they could have been more easily avoided — if only we had spoken to each other first. The Alchemy Wars divided us long before the Osseomancer rose to power. Before that, there was the Eleven-and-a-Half-Year War. And there are still those who remember the War of the Three Wizards.

"Could these wars have been avoided if we had some other way to work out our differences? This is what I propose now. Our unity should not end with the Osseomancer's defeat. Let the Great Alliance continue, so we can guard against any division that might lead to our collective ruin.

"Let us trade the battlefield for raised voices. Let us discuss any matter that might divide us. Let us resolve our differences here, rather than through war. Let us determine the key matters of our age. Let us learn from the devastation of the Osseomancer, so such bloodshed will not have been in vain. Let us find ways to live in peace and harmony together."

After a rough start, Snorri finished strong. He felt passionately about the matter and hardly had to read the last few lines from the parchment. He enunciated well and took beats to look from one member to the next as he finished.

"Of course, I do not think everything will or can be decided here, once and for all. Even though some of us are gifted with prophecy, we cannot look into every possible future and see every possible issue that might arise. So, more importantly, I would like us to establish a framework from which we can address future issues without the need for war or aggression."

He remained standing for a moment longer, allowing all to absorb his speech and the nature of why he had called them together. When he felt satisfied, he sat.

Now, the druid Malachite stood. "Thank you, Snorri, for gathering us all here today," he said, and managed not to sound too rehearsed. "I think we all believe it is a noble cause. I have traveled the lands far and wide and can attest to the need for this council. We have much to discuss."

"Well-said, my good druid." Prince Javee now sprang to his feet. He seemed to produce a glass of wine out of thin air. The wind had swept his hair into just the right position. "What a great idea this council is. We will engender great relations between us all."

Next, the high priestess of the oracles, Kìtrinos spoke. Behind her sat a flock of her sister priestesses, each as tanned and long-legged and dark-haired as the next, garbed in lavish yellow robes cinched at the waist by cords of gold.

Kìtrinos spoke softly, which seemed such a departure from Prince Javee's soaring oration. "Many nights ago, before the end of the war, I dreamed vividly," she said. "In my dream, I saw a tall tower. At first, I thought it was Pravulum, for I knew instantly that something momentous would happen there. But when I woke, I realized instead of dark Pravulum, I dreamed of Athyzia. I dreamed of many coming to its towers. They will speak of what has been done here for many ages."

"Yes, they will." Now, King Ümlaut of Yülk held out a horn of ale as a toast. Apparently, someone had brought the northerners beer during Snorri's speech. "We've seen the power that comes from our combined forces. We should not let that go to waste. Even without a common foe, let us remain united."

After him, Queen Yellialah of Dunisk stood. She seemed so frail and delicate speaking directly after the muscled king of Yülk. Her fine silk gown of emerald green clung to her thin frame. In her youth, she had been known as a great beauty. Much of that beauty still remained, but a sickness had whittled away at it. Her hair had turned as silver as the Gnos Mountains above, but such color added to the beauty she had left, contrasting well with her dark Dunisk features.

"One matter interests me greatly," she said. "*Magic.* Even before his destructive war, the Osseomancer interfered in the lives of men to his own mischievous ends. And he was not alone. Magic provides great power and great temptations, especially when it is used against the common folk. I thank you, Snorri, for calling this council. I hope together, we can curb these temptations of magic."

Out of the corner of her eye, Nauveena caught Snorri smiling. Magic was a key issue for the sorcerer as well. It often divided. Many wars would be avoided if the council could address such issues instead. Nauveena smiled herself. For a moment, she had not known how the council might go. Now, it seemed everyone was embracing it.

Until the Elf Queen spoke. When Queen Em' Iriild stood, the others waiting to speak sat as if commanded. Still, Queen Em' Iriild took her time, waiting for complete silence. "This is a question I have had since receiving your invitation," she said. "Am I to understand the nature of this council is to dictate the uses of magic?"

"Well, among others," Snorri said.

"I will remind you, elves practiced magic long before man came to these lands."

"Yes, but now, we must all practice magic together," Snorri said. "Which is why we wanted you to attend this council. We would benefit greatly from the elves' wisdom in dealing with magic."

"I look around this council and I see mainly men," Queen Em' Iriild said. "Will men now tell the elves how to use magic?"

"And the dwarves?" Lord Ferrum asked.

"You will have a say in it," Snorri said.

"'*A say?*'" Queen Em' Iriild said. "'A say?' When it was ours to begin with. The elves and dwarves once lived alone in this world before man came and sullied it. They sullied not only the land, but the magic as well. Using it as their greed and temptations demanded."

"An unfortunate chapter, of course," Snorri said. Nauveena wished he had chosen his words better, but he continued. "However, I am concerned with now and going forward. We all must live together. In the past, arguments have arisen between men and elves on the use of magic in each other's realms. This council offers a forum in which to discuss these issues."

"I too have a question on this." Now the First Protector of Leem took his turn to stand. "The idea of a council is all well and good, and we can all have discussions until long into the night. But how will matters actually be decided? A vote?"

"If it comes to it," Snorri said. "Yes, a vote. I have thought this all through. The purpose behind the council is to give every perspective a voice. My hope is on many topics, we can reach a consensus satisfactory to all. We have enough wisdom gathered to do just that. But if topics cannot be decided with discussion, then we can put it to a vote. For each voice, there will be a vote. But a vote only after all sides have been heard and given their due."

"Every perspective?" Queen Em' Iriild asked. "Who, then, has a vote? Surely you must mean one for the elves. One for the dwarves. And one for men?"

Once again, Snorri hung his head. While Fallou had thought too few were being heard in his initial plan, Queen Em' Iriild clearly saw it as too many. She only wanted three votes?

"Of course, these are not the only perspectives I can think of," she continued. "What about the centaurs? What of the beasts of the land and the birds of the air? Should they not be considered? Not just for magic, but for other issues as well?"

"I have thought it all through," Snorri said. "The centaurs are well-known for their wisdom, and would of course be welcomed here. As would the animals of the world. However, they do not wish to attend. It has been decided that the druid Malachite will speak for them. He has become a friend to all in his travels."

"I wonder how the centaurs will feel about being branded with the birds and beasts?" Queen Em' Iriild asked.

"I assure you, they do not mind," Malachite said. "The centaurs are busy migrating to their summer lands. I have spoken to them at length, and they have given me their proxy. As have the beasts and the birds. And I believe they are all of one mind."

"I see the wisdom in this," Queen Em' Iriild said. "Then we shall have one vote for the elves, one for the dwarves, one for men, and one for the animals and centaurs through the druid?"

Before Snorri could answer, Fallou spoke. "I believe Snorri intended that each of us seated at the center tables should have a vote. Is this correct?"

"It was a starting point," Snorri said. "My thinking went along these lines: Our lands have organized themselves into sovereign entities: sometimes kingdoms, sometimes empires, and even this novel republic. I do not pretend to understand the differences, but they are convenient for what I wish to do here. Each nation will represent itself."

"Then it is safe to assume each of the southern merchants and Aryde will get their own vote?" Fallou asked, gazing at their members seated in the center.

"It was a starting point," Snorri conceded.

"Yet they are not magic users," Fallou said. "As you said, this council will discuss many matters of magic. How can they possibly offer guidance on these matters? I do not believe they know more about magic than Protectors of Order."

The foreign minister from the Republic of Aryde, Fichael Porteau, stood and addressed the council. "I believe I understand the rationale behind this. While I myself cannot use magic — no matter how hard I try — Aryde is proud to be home to many who can. Magic users vote in our elections and serve on our parliament, and as such, have elected me to represent them. I have a working knowledge of magic and an understanding of how our public opinion feels in most matters. I will do my best to represent them."

"My thinking exactly," Snorri said. "It is the same logic behind my decision to invite the southern merchants and the Bogwaah. They have many users of magic — sorcerers as well as folk mages — in their nations. These mages are represented by common folk at home, so they can be represented by common folk at this council."

Many nations were ruled by magic users. In that case, it was an easy matter. In other cases, rulers were advised by mages. What was important, as far as Snorri was concerned, was to have everyone — those with magic and those without — represented in some way. He could not possibly invite all to the council, but through representatives from each realm, he could try to include all one way or the other.

"I understand your goal of representation better now," Fallou said. "And it is indeed admirable. However, if this is your aim, I fear some have been excluded. Each Protector of Order has devoted their lives to matters within their kingdom. They and not I should be representing each of them. They accepted your invitation with that in mind. And the kings they represent sent them with this understanding as well."

"I see this now," Snorri said.

"And now, it is clear to me that you intend for the elves to have three votes," Fallou said. "Certainly, they have a similar hierarchy with their queen that we have with our Ultimate Defender."

Nauveena knew Snorri had intended for the elves to have three votes: one for Saphalon, one for Free Oak, and one for the Wilds. The enclaves had been independent for centuries, even if they were still ruled by Queen Em' Iriild in formal arrangements. She did not blame him for *not* saying this to Fallou, however.

"No," Snorri said instead. "I wanted to leave this for the council. Should the elves have a single vote or not? As I did not know how the council would decide, I allowed a representative from each kingdom to sit in the center."

"Is that the same for the dwarves?" the Ambassadress Galena asked. "Surely you cannot force the northern and southern dwarves to have a single vote?"

Nauveena wanted to intervene, but she did not know what she could say to end the discussion amiably. She had always imagined this might be the hardest part of the council. Before the nature of voting was settled, there was no easy way to decide on the nature of voting.

As she was deciding what to say, the witch Venefica stood and addressed the council. "The relationship between the elves and Queen Em' Iriild is of a completely different nature than that of the Magic of Order."

Fallou glared at the witch, but she continued undeterred.

"Not to mention the dwarves have never been united, and there is not one kingdom that stands above the other. They must receive two separate votes. In fact, I ask where the dwarves of the Iron Hall are? For they too should take part. As for the elves, it should be a vote for each of their forests. It is a simple matter, as far as I can tell."

"And the Magic of Order?" Fallou asked.

"One vote," Venefica said. "Another simple matter."

"A simple matter to one who does not understand the Magic of Order," Fallou said.

"Oh, I understand it *plenty*," Venefica said.

"Then you understand how critical the Magic of Order was in the Osseomancer's defeat. Each kingdom's Protector maintained order in the face of overwhelming chaos and kept the Osseomancer at bay. With the power of order, we fought the Osseomancer back and broke him. Without us, he would not have fallen."

"As if Druissia did nothing?" Now King Bane leapt to his feet. "Our lands were ravaged. How many of our young men died in the fight? An entire generation was lost."

"He was not stopped until he reached the gates of Rhu," General Dolcius barked. "And finally met *my* armies."

"We all sacrificed much," Prince Javee said.

"But not equally," Fallou said.

"And what is that supposed to mean?"

"The Osseomancer never crossed the Kiijaro."

"Not by choice," Prince Javee said. "The river will never be the same. Our armies marched to your aid as well."

"And your vineyards went untouched."

"More valuable things than land were lost during the war."

"This is not why we are here," Snorri said, exasperated. "Pravulum still smokes and already you are turning on each other."

No one heard the mage, however. Instead, arguments rippled across the terrace like raindrops onto the surface of a pond.

Nauveena shook her head. She could not stand to hear such defeat in her mentor's voice. But of course the council was already bickering. Even when threatened by annihilation, they had resolved to fight on their own. Until Snorri united them.

For it was Snorri who saw that doom awaited them all if they fought separately and alone; Snorri who urged unity; Snorri who went to the dwarf kingdoms, seeking their skill in crafting weapons and mining gems; and Snorri who put those weapons in the hands of fighting men and those gems in the hands of fighting mages.

It was Snorri who spent months in Saphalon Forest, pleading with Queen Em' Iriild to join the war; Snorri who convinced the southern merchants to provision the armies; Snorri, accompanied with Malachite, who sought the aid of the centaurs.

It was Snorri who organized the war effort; Snorri who built supply lines; Snorri who coordinated attacks so they would occur at the same time and stretch the Osseomancer's forces.

Nauveena had to say something. She stood to give herself more authority. She placed her hands on the table and leaned towards the council. Everyone stopped and looked at her. She did not know what she would say until she was saying it. "Do you all hear yourselves?" she asked. "How quickly you turn to squabbling? Already, you dissolve into the same animosity and pettiness that made us so vulnerable to the Osseomancer."

Surprisingly, everyone looked chastised by her words. Everyone except for Fallou. "The issue of voting must be resolved, one way or the other," he said. "Or there is no point in continuing. Every discussion will break down in this manner if a procedure for voting is not arrived at."

"Then accept whatever Snorri proposes," Nauveena said specifically to Fallou before addressing the whole council once more. "There would be no Great Alliance without Snorri. You accepted his guidance when all was in peril. Why forsake it now? Snorri convened this council with one goal in mind: the unity of all. He wishes nothing more than to provide solutions that are equitable and just. *But you must let him*. He has now heard all of your thoughts. Let him decide the best path forward."

When she finished, Nauveena expected all those assembled to break into argument once more. Instead, each member remained quiet, wondering who would speak next.

Finally, King Bane of Druissia stood. He commanded much respect for breaking the long Siege of Ontiphon. "I apologize to you, Nauveena of Ciri Daahl," he said, "and to you, Snorri the Esoteric, wisest of his age, for so quickly falling into the arguments of old. Of course Snorri has our best interests in mind. I will accept whatever he decides for this council."

The others came to agree quickly after the brave king spoke.

"I've always been prepared to listen to Snorri," Prince Javee said. "He's probably thought more about this council than the rest of us combined."

"The sorceress is right," Grufton Mann of the southern merchants said. "I will accept whatever Snorri proposes."

"As will I," Veeslau the Unbound of Skiel said, the blindfold over his eyes not revealing any further emotion.

"How else will we come to a decision?" the Dwarf Lord Ferrum asked. "We can stand here and argue about it all day, but we likely won't get a wiser decision than whatever Snorri proposes."

Others stood and voiced a similar sentiment: Queen Yellialah, General Dolcius, the northerners, the burgomaster of the Bogwaah. Each of the elves pledged to accept Snorri's ruling.

Nauveena turned to her mentor. She expected his lines of worry to have vanished. She expected a smile of relief. Instead, Snorri looked almost as troubled as before. She knew why. All those seated at the center tables had pledged to accept his say on the matter of voting. All except one.

"What should I do?" Snorri leaned over to whisper to Nauveena. The sorceress could feel the whole council watching them.

"It is your decision," she whispered back. "They will listen to you and you alone."

Well, most of the council would. Nauveena was less certain about Fallou. She and Snorri had never been certain about him. Even getting him to the council had been a struggle. They had written for months to convince him to come. They couldn't lose him now, when the council had just begun. The Second Faulsk Empire was too large and too important. They couldn't have a council without it.

Snorri looked to the First Protector. "Would you accept a compromise?"

Nauveena saw the witch Venefica stand to protest, but King Bane stopped her with a hand on her shoulder.

"What would you propose?" Fallou asked.

"I've always believed that one must revise one's decisions once new information has been received. I have already learned so much from this council. The Magic of Order is truly fascinating. It seems now, I have new information, and so I should revise my earlier decision."

"How would you revise it?" the First Protector of Leem asked.

"Would you be willing to accept the elves receiving three votes for their kingdoms and the dwarves two for theirs, if the same logic were applied to each Protector as well?"

Fallou thought for a moment. He put a hand to his chin.

What could possibly be his hesitation? Nauveena thought frantically.

At last, he said, "You are indeed wise, venerable mage. A lesser sorcerer might not have admitted their mistake." Nauveena sighed in relief. "I will accept such a compromise in the name of the unity we wish to forge here."

Once again, the witch Venefica made to stand. Her eyes flashed with anger. But the matter had been decided. All the council members had pledged to accept Snorri's guidance on the matter. Now, Fallou and the Magic of Order had as well.

The final representatives were determined in short order. There would be twenty-six in all.

Drussia, Qadantium, and Dunisk would each get a vote, as would Rheum and Lyrmica, and the Bogwaah beyond the Vurve. Each of the three merchant cities in the south would be represented, as would the northern kingdoms of Yülk and Künner. Skiel too would receive a vote. The Republic of Aryde would be represented by their foreign minister, while the High Priestess of Xanthous would speak for the oracles.

The Second Faulsk Empire would be represented by Fallou, the First Protector of Leem, second only to the Ultimate Defender of Ryork for the Magic of Order. Likewise, each of the five middle kingdoms — Vabia, Zabia, Wabia, Upper Tuvisia and Lower Tuvisia — would be represented by a Protector of Order, as dictated by Snorri's compromise.

Then there would be three representatives for the elves, two for the dwarves, and Malachite the druid for the beasts and birds and centaurs.

Twenty-six in all. Some were kings and queens in their own right. Many were mages who served their kingdoms as advisors on magic. The council contained many who had fought bravely against the Osseomancer. Such combined wisdom had never been gathered in such a forum before.

Tensions had risen during the meeting, but the first day had been a success, as far as Nauveena could tell. Everyone had arrived to the council. They accepted its premise and they stayed. They had determined an acceptable method to vote. And they planned to return the next day to set an agenda for the weeks ahead.

Chapter Three
The Witch and the Druid

> "Magic should always be taken seriously. Sorcerers have shown a respect and care to practice such arts. It is the folk mages with lesser skills who practice odd magics and witchcraft, where the true danger can be found."
>
> ~An Examination of Folk Mages
> The Academy of Mages
> 45 BU

Despite his excitement, Snorri was exhausted. Many council members left in conversation with each other, but he felt too drained to do so. Another feast and dance had been planned, but he could not imagine attending. Nauveena knew he was used to his atelier and his books and his experiments, not long-winded debates, even if the council had been his idea.

Nauveena escorted him back to his quarters. After two hundred years, his bones creaked when he walked. The war against the Osseomancer had been tiring. He did not have much strength left. Nauveena expected him to retire soon. Magic was for the young. But first, he would see the council through. It would be his final work. He wanted to be proud of it. He wanted to leave Jenor with peace.

"I don't think that went too badly," Snorri said to Nauveena.

"Everyone is very excited," Nauveena said as she went into the kitchen to put a kettle on. She started a flame with a simple spell, albeit one not as flashy as Prince Javee's.

"These things never go as planned," Snorri said. "How long did we plan for? I envisioned it going so many different ways. But people are unpredictable. It is not alchemy, after all. It is people. I forget."

"People are hard to predict."

Snorri's chamber had not been tidied in some time. Nauveena had offered, but he refused. There was order in his mess: books and papers strewn about, tables covered in wax and ink, half-full goblets resting on windowsills. A chess board had stalled mid-game. Rooks and knights and sorcerers faced each other in a stalemate. Snorri and Nauveena had not found time to finish. The rook pieces always reminded Nauveena of the emblem on Athyzia's flag, and maybe for that reason it was her favorite piece. Several parrots from Qadantium squawked in a cage next to the wide window overlooking Lake Yalde. Snorri had not managed to teach them any words yet.

"Twenty-six members," Snorri said. "Twenty-six. Remember when we wrote the invitations? We didn't think we would hear back from anyone. Now, we have twenty-six members. And I cannot even count how many are in the audience. It might be a hundred."

"We will settle many issues," Nauveena said. She had a few she would like to add to the list. She found it hard to imagine, but even Athyzia did not hold all the books on magic. Many volumes were said to be hidden away by mages who wanted their secrets for themselves. Could the council rule that these books must be shared? If a copy was sought, a mage should provide. In the spirit of communal learning, it only seemed fair. Such wisdom should not be shut away, out of reach.

Snorri wanted the Academy of Mages to keep a distance from the council. The Academy had retreated from the affairs of the world to focus on their magic, after all. Unlike other mages who advised kings and rulers, the Academy kept to themselves.

This withdrawal had been a disaster when the Osseomancer began his campaign. The Academy had not taken the threat seriously at first, even when the prophecy came from Xanthous. They had reacted too late. And the other kingdoms had been too divided to compensate for the Academy's delay. They quarreled with each other over petty squabbles while the Osseomancer amassed his armies. They did not unite until it was almost too late.

Now Snorri hoped the council could offer Jenor unity, to protect them if the Osseomancer ever sought to return — and from each other.

When the kettle began to whistle, Nauveena prepared two mugs for tea. Snorri sank into his armchair and pulled a large quilt over himself. He felt colder recently.

"Twenty-six," he muttered to himself. "Twenty-six."

An aggressive knocking came on the door. Nauveena put the kettle down and rushed to it. The knocking felt like it might break the door unless she hurried. She opened the door to find the witch Venefica waiting there.

Venefica immediately swept into the room with her billowing crimson gown flowing behind her. Her eyes were on fire with rage. "That was nothing short of disaster."

Snorri almost fell out of his armchair.

"What do you mean?" Nauveena asked, forgetting the tea.

"You don't see it?" the witch asked. "How much power have you handed that vulture from Leem?"

"Fallou?" Snorri asked.

"Yes, Fallou."

"Each Protector has much to add."

"They will add whatever Fallou wants them to add," Venefica said.

"Fallou made it clear that they act independently," Snorri said. "Otherwise, why would he ask for them all to be on the council?"

"You old fool," Venefica said. "The reason is simple and plain to see, if you were not blinded by your need for this council to go well. How many votes does he now control?"

"'Control?' I wouldn't say 'control.'"

"What word would you use? The Magic of Order has a clear hierarchy. Fallou is second only to the Ultimate Defender of Ryork. Obviously, Ryork has entrusted Fallou to act for the whole order at this council. Each of these Lesser Protectors and Keepers are beneath Fallou. They will do nothing without his say."

"They must have some independence," Nauveena said. "They advise independent kings, after all. These rulers wouldn't want their advisors subservient to Faulsk."

"Yet they are," Venefica said. "Through the Magic of Order, the Emperor of Faulsk has the control of the middle kingdoms he has long wanted to reassert. The Magic of Order has such a complete hold over these realms, their rulers can do nothing without the Magic of Order's approval."

"It can't be that bad." Naúveena had heard some of the rumors from the east, but none were this bad.

"The armies of Faulsk marched across the middle kingdoms to engage the Osseomancer at Pravulum. Those armies still occupy the middle kingdoms. If those kingdoms ever want Faulsk's armies to leave, they must follow Faulsk and Fallou."

Now it was Snorri's turn to be dismissive. "You are too suspicious," he said. "I admit the Magic of Order is strange in their ways. They reject many of the traditional magics. But you are too focused on the vote. What is important is the *conversation*. We will hear all sides. Only then will we vote. I trust we will be of one mind when we get to it. Now, if you will excuse me, it has been a long day and I believe tomorrow will be even longer."

Nauveena escorted Venefica from Snorri's chambers. It had been a long day for him. She could see him moving slower in his old age. He had returned from the war with less energy. He had the same curiosity, but he could not sustain it for as long. He needed his rest if he was to preside over the council tomorrow.

The sorceress and the witch walked together. Athyzia had many winding paths, and two lost in conversation could easily become lost themselves. Nauveena would not have expected to find herself speaking with the witch so privately, so intimately.

Witches — like many folk mages — did not approach their magic with the same discipline as sorcerers. They practiced no formal training or apprenticeships, but instead passed their traditions down orally, from mother to daughter and from aunt to niece. They were said to know many things that could only be whispered about in the night, in secrecy and ritual, that were not fit for written page. They communicated with lost and forgotten gods and knew well the dark corners of graveyards and woods where the spirit world could be contacted.

The common folk often went to them in times of need, not always understanding their incantations and knowledge of strange herbs. They would confide in the witches secrets things — unwanted pregnancies, unrequited loves, economic hardships. Nauveena doubted how effective such magic was and wondered how much was simple superstition or tricks seen as magic by easily swindled common folk.

Witches remained eager to increase their power. They could be tempted by methods that sorcerers would have found too dangerous, especially for those not trained in the art. Witches often sought patronage from more powerful entities, including the Osseomancer himself, who came to offer them power beyond their wildest dreams if they would support him and hold him in their hearts.

If the rumors were true, Venefica had been chief among his supporters. But now, she was at the council. King Bane trusted her. As did Snorri.

"What issues are you concerned with?" Nauveena asked. "We have not even set an agenda."

"Many important issues will be on the table. We are doing nothing less than regulating the uses of magic. And possibly the sources. You have admitted your skepticism of the Magic of Order. They believe order alone should be the source for magic. If they gain a majority, they can pass resolutions that would be unfavorable for the rest of us."

"But they will not gain a majority," Nauveena said. The two had stopped on a balcony with a panoramic view of the mountains and lake.

"They have a good start," Venefica said. "Faulsk is one. The middle kingdoms — there's Vabia, Wabia, Zabia, Upper Tuvisia, and Lower Tuvisia — are five." She counted on her fingers. "That is already six."

"Six out of twenty-six is far from a majority."

"But it is a formidable voting bloc. And reliable for Fallou to begin building a coalition. We cannot have many more go with them. How comfortable do you feel with the other votes?"

"I am not sure. Snorri does not want discussions outside of the council. He worries that would inspire politics and conspiracy."

"What do you think Fallou is doing right now?"

"This feels premature," Nauveena said. "An agenda has not been set. How will we know how the others feel about issues that have yet to be determined?"

"We should have an idea, especially on the matter of banning certain types of magic."

"Banning? No, I can't imagine it will come to that."

"The matter will most certainly be brought up. Some have discussed outlawing necromancy now, and other magics used by the Osseomancer."

"Well, that might be reasonable," Nauveena said.

"Ban necromancy and then what is next? Blood magic? Bone magic? Voodoo? And Fallou will want to ban much more than this. The Magic of Order is very strict."

"Are you sure these are not just rumors?" Nauveena asked.

"I wish that they were."

"How do you know so much about the Magic of Order?"

"I have my ways. Now, we need to begin securing votes."

"It is much too early for such conspiring. The council has only just begun."

"And already Fallou has a six-vote head start," Venefica said. "We should know where the other twenty stand."

"I have hardly spoken to the other members. At least not on these matters. Snorri wanted all discussions to happen in council."

"I have with a few. I would have Druissia. I'd imagine Qadantium is safe. From my talks with their queen, I believe the elves would never support restricting magic. I can also secure Dunisk. I am less familiar with the dwarves and the northerners. And I do not know how the merchants will side. I have no idea how Rheum will go under General Dolcius. And there is no telling Aryde either. Ever since they gained independence from Lyrmica, they have been ruled by the mob. It is the eastern kingdoms in particular we must worry about. Faulsk's influence is greatest in the east. And, of course, we have Snorri and the Academy's vote."

"The Academy doesn't get a vote," Nauveena said.

"What do you mean 'The Academy doesn't get a vote?'"

"Snorri wants us to remain independent. The Academy is insular. We have retreated to our studies. We represent no one but ourselves."

"But that is quite a lot to represent." Venefica had gone pale.

"Of course, we will vote if there is a tie," Nauveena said.

"Let us hope it does not come to that." Venefica looked off at the mountains and lake below them. "What about the druid?" she asked.

"I know him well," Nauveena said. Malachite was the only one of his order Nauveena had ever met. The few remaining druids rarely left their forests. "He is very wise and reasonable."

"I have yet to speak to him at length," the witch admitted. "I imagine he would be useful to have on our side. He has relationships with many of the council members."

"I do not understand why you choose to see sides," Nauveena said. "We have come together in unity so there will not be sides. It is a dangerous mindset to bring into the council."

"It would be dangerous to not bring this mindset into the council. Where is the druid currently?"

Malachite had been at Athyzia for some time. He often left the grounds, however, to wander into the forests in the high mountain passes. As they waited for others to arrive at the council, Nauveena had often gone with him. After having spent so long in Athyzia, unable to leave, it had felt liberating to hike into the pine groves.

Nauveena knew many of the spots that Malachite frequented and led Venefica there. If the grounds of Athyzia were winding and twisting, the forest's paths were worse. Neither the witch nor sorceress were dressed for hiking, with long, flowing dresses and heeled shoes. The hems of their gowns snagged on branches, and they tripped on the long gnarled roots of the ancient trees that guarded Athyzia.

The druid did not appear at his usual clearings or springs. Evening crept through the low branches, purple and gold in the late spring. Nauveena had almost given up when Malachite appeared before them.

He sat on the trunk of a fallen tree covered in a moss that matched his weather-beaten cloak. On a branch not far from him, a robin sat perched, relating to the druid in birdsong.

As the two approached, Malachite said something to the bird, who flew off the branch and landed on Nauveena's shoulder. The bird hummed a pleasant song that reminded the sorceress of dawns from when she had been a child, when she first arrived in Athyzia. The bird stayed for a moment longer, serenading the sorceress. When it had finished, it flew off into the forest.

"How strange," Nauveena said.

"He was thanking you," Malachite said.

"Thanking me? What for?"

"I told him who you are. And that you protected Athyzia and these forests from the Osseomancer. This forest is rare now. All around is devastation. You have created a sanctuary for many. It has not gone unnoticed."

"I did not know," Nauveena said. Her purpose had been to protect Athyzia. She had not known she was protecting the neighboring forests as well.

"What did you think of today?" Venefica asked.

"Today was the start of a long process." The druid chose his words carefully. "The war forced us to forget our differences with each other. I do not think it will take us long to remember them."

"I am worried what happens when we remember as well," Venefica said. "What are your thoughts on the Magic of Order?"

"I have not traveled to the eastern lands since the war began," Malachite said. "But even before, my travels took me there rarely. The animals coming from the east speak of it changing. And not for the best. The Magic of Order demands all those living in their lands follow their beliefs."

"Fallou will steer the council in his direction," Venefica said. "I worry about the votes he already controls. It is too much power."

Malachite thought for a moment. Then he stood and began walking through the forest. Nauveena and Venefica followed him.

"Yes, I was surprised Snorri relented so quickly in allowing each of the middle kingdoms a vote. I would have preferred another compromise. Faulsk has a strong influence over those lands, and it has only grown stronger since they liberated them from the Osseomancer."

"I do not believe it is too early to begin securing votes," Venefica said.

"Votes for what?" Nauveena asked again. "When the agenda has not yet been set."

"Does Snorri know we are having this conversation?" Malachite asked both Nauveena and Venefica.

Both shook their heads.

"He wanted transparency between all council members," Malachite said. "Now, on the first day, two are meeting in secret — with his own apprentice — discussing votes."

"I've only come to convince Venefica that none of this is necessary," Nauveena said.

"Do you really believe that?" Malachite asked. "Or do you see the witch's logic? Fallou showed his cunning today. He is well-trained in the art of negotiations. The Magic of Order has prepared him for it. Many decisions are reached in their cult through currying favor and bartering. I worry what we saw today was only the beginning of his cleverness at work."

"But for what ends?" Nauveena asked.

"That, I wish I knew," Malachite said.

"I imagine you could guess," Venefica said.

"Yes, I suppose I could. Even with how little I understand the Magic of Order. And after the protracted battles with the Osseomancer, he might not need much cunning to bring others to his side."

"That is why we have come to you," Venefica said. "I spent much of the war in Ontiphon, under siege. I do not know the other members of the Alliance as well as you. You have traveled to the north and lived among the elves."

"And I wish I knew them better. The Blue Wizard knew them best of all. His counsel, I miss dearly. He would have had many thoughts on how today proceeded."

"But he is not here, so we must make do," Venefica said. "Does it not make sense to go now to the dwarves and the northerners and begin to understand their minds?"

"We should, yes, but not tonight," Malachite said. The end of twilight had come, leaving the forest in a dim half-light. If the druid had not been there to lead them out, Nauveena and Venefica would surely have become lost.

"If I know them, they will have already begun to unwind since the end of the council. It would be no use speaking to them. We must begin much earlier in the day if we want to have any constructive talks. Our best course of action now is to see what tomorrow brings. We will set the agenda, and Fallou might reveal his aims."

Chapter Four
Alchemy, Calendars, and Scales

> "Auras rank chief among the sorcerer's arsenal. The force of the magic is impenetrable — perfect shields during battle. But the force is even more deadly once the sorcerer learns how to direct it and use it as a projectile."
>
> ~*Magical Tactics for War*
> 120 BU

The Osseomancer longed for Athyzia's knowledge. He thirsted for it. He wished to come upon her books and drink from them, leaving them empty husks and himself sated and gorged. He sent his armies to conquer her. They came crouching and slithering. They came as rattling bones. They came howling and cursing, saying wicked things.

At first, the mages of the Academy resolved to remain in Athyzia, to shut themselves away until the threat ended on its own accord. But as the early years of the war passed, it became clear that the Osseomancer would not be so easily defeated.

Snorri convinced the Academy to join the fray. The Osseomancer's forces seemed everywhere, never ending, never giving quarter. Many mages left to offer aid where they were needed most. But they would not leave Athyzia undefended. Athyzia had her own protections, ancient and deep, built into her very foundations. But the mages devised their own magics as well: clever charms, protective wards, invisible snares. The mages placed powerful spells over Athyzia so the Osseomancer's armies could not reach her.

And they left Nauveena.

Nauveena's parents had not been magical. Instead, they were simple, common folk, without any idea of magic, but that had only made her more remarkable. Her family harvested oysters on the island of Ciri Daahl, a meager life filled with the smell of the ocean's salty brine and threatened by the turn of the tide. Nauveena taught herself to read from the few books on the island. She managed to stretch pots of seaweed stew for weeks. She even found ways to pull oysters from the bay without the need to go in the water.

Nauveena did not know what she was, but her parents did. Her mother had heard stories of Athyzia and the Academy of Mages. She saved her coin and sent a letter, describing the abilities of her daughter. Unable to write, she dictated to her young daughter, unaware of the magnitude of what the letter was asking.

Not many in Athyzia cared when a letter came from a family of poor oyster farmers. Many royal families and those with ancient magical bloodlines sent their children to Athyzia with quite large endowments. They did not often take pupils from such a poor background.

Only Snorri found the letter intriguing. His curiosity brought him to the island to see the girl's skills for himself. He brought Nauveena back to Athyzia only a few years before the war began.

When he was forced to leave, he felt confident leaving Nauveena behind. She could tend to the defensive magics left by the mages. She had her own powers too. She could pulse magic and flare its force, creating defensive shields that the Osseomancer's forces could not penetrate.

Snorri taught the child ways to concentrate such force, ways to maintain and strengthen it. The power came from magic welled deep inside her and projected outward. Auras were a more physical magic than those spells recited from books; the breaths between each word were as important as the incantations themselves.

With the mages' charms and Nauveena's skill, the Osseomancer and his armies were repelled again and again. Defeated, they slunk back. They had come often at first, early in the war, but soon attacked less frequently, seeing the folly in such attempts and having the temptation of much easier targets.

Nauveena's time within Athyzia became long, dull stretches punctuated with these terrible assaults. Snorri and the other mages continued to fight elsewhere. The war volleyed from one theater to the next. Snorri returned as often as he could, usually with Malachite and Caeruleom the Blue when they needed to research for the war effort and to confer and plan with one another.

In between these visits and the battles, Athyzia could become quite lonely. Nauveena only had Athyzia's stray cats to keep her company and these were not very social. She continued to feed them, but they did not seem very appreciative. They kept their distance and one even hissed when she tried to pet them in a moment of loneliness.

The buildings themselves were not any better. The hallways felt empty. Nauveena's echo followed her from one room to the next. She took the time to explore each library, becoming lost in the endless volume of books. How many years would she wander the empty rooms — alone — wondering how long the war would last and how it would end? Her own mind and the possibilities she conjured seemed just as expansive as Athyzia's myriad levels.

Now that Athyzia was full again, those empty moments seemed as if they had happened to someone else, as if she had just watched. She could not return to that other time, or to that other person. The council's bustle felt so removed from those quiet moments of loneliness.

The council would start early, of course. Snorri saw to that. Already, the bells were pealing. Nauveena's chambers in the Tower of Yalde remained out of the way, and so it would take her some time to descend the tower's stairs, cross its narrow bridge, climb more stairs, cross another bridge, and then wind through the many crisscrossing paths of the gardens before reaching the terrace where the council took place.

It would take even longer if she wanted breakfast.

Nauveena had to rush to tease her hair, to arrange the few simple pieces of jewelry she owned and to trace her eyelids with a layer of kohl. She would never have fussed with such ornamentation when she had been alone, but the ceremony of the council seemed to call for it. Still, she would feel plain compared to many of the queens — and even some of the kings — in attendance.

This left barely enough time to eat breakfast before proceedings began. Going forward, the council would begin at this early hour. Snorri preferred the morning. He wanted to use the day as wisely as possible, and the only way he knew how to do this was to begin early.

The morning did not suit everyone. Many arrived bleary-eyed. The desire for merriment that persisted ever since the Osseomancer's defeat would not retreat quickly. Although, after a few more early mornings, it might.

To accommodate all twenty-six members — and Nauveena, Snorri, and Venefica, who advised King Bane — more tables had been added to the center. Five might have been enough, but Snorri preferred symmetry, and had opted for six tables instead. The tables now formed a hexagon, which he thought held magical connotations. Nauveena wasn't so sure about that, but she reasoned six gave everyone more room, at the very least.

"Before we begin, there are a few items to discuss," Snorri began after everyone was seated. "The first involves the actual process for setting the agenda. It is my belief that every relevant issue should be discussed. But how do we determine what is a *relevant* issue? I have my rubric, but I do not want to sway the direction of the council. I also know how excited everyone must be and how many items each wants to add. To discuss everything brought forth might take years. And as excited as I am to share everyone's company, I do not imagine that after twenty-five years at war, you want to spend another twenty-five in discussions."

Snorri paused for a laugh that did not come. Only Malachite chuckled sympathetically.

Undeterred, he continued. "We must then have a process for adding items to the agenda. My proposal is that if seven of the council are in agreement on an item, it will be added. Why seven? I have no particular reason, but it feels right. We have twenty-six members in total, I do not think it will be difficult to get seven votes, but it should be restrictive enough. Today, we will only be adding items to the agenda, not debating them. We may debate whether to add an issue, but we will save the actual merits of the issue for the day we set aside to discuss it."

Snorri had rehearsed this speech almost as often as he had the one from the day before, to the point that Nauveena could recite it from memory.

Snorri could too, and with less nerves, did not need to read from any parchment.

"I also acknowledge that we might think of other issues after today," he continued. "I therefore think it is reasonable to allow issues to be added as the council progresses. If — after today — you have additional topics to add, please bring them to the council's attention, and we will vote at the beginning of each session. Does that work for everyone?"

Lord Ferrum took a rather loud sip of coffee. Beyond this, everyone either nodded in agreement or at least made no outward sign of protest.

"The next topic I need to discuss," Snorri said, "is how the actual voting will be conducted. Once an item is added, we will assign it a day when we will discuss it in this council. If multiple days are needed, we will allow for it. During discussion, we will provide all views and propose resolutions for the issue.

"Our task is to find consensus with our collected wisdoms. I do not believe that will be a challenge. I have no doubt that there are many difficult matters, but through discussion and debate, we should be able to find a solution pleasing to all parties. However, if a consensus is not met and we still have divisions, then we will hold a vote.

"We have determined the twenty-six representatives of the council. Only they will vote. I believe it best for the vote to be anonymous. I do not believe that voting will become contentious, but I believe anonymity best insures each member's independence. And limits any *uncomfortable* conversations. Now for the fun part. Well, I think it is fun at least. Maybe a bit dramatic. And theatrical. But from time to time, that is acceptable. When it is time to vote, each council member will receive a piece of parchment."

As Snorri said this, a piece of parchment fluttered into place in front of each council member. The mage could manage impressive feats of magic when he wanted.

"You will write your vote on the parchment. Make sure no one sees it. Fold it and then — one by one — place it in the fire." When Snorri said "fire", flames ignited in the center of the six tables. Hot and blue at first and then a slower burning orange. No brazier had been placed in the center. Instead, the fire simply floated above the pave stones. "Once all votes have been cast into the fire, the smoke will transform into smaller clouds and float to that scale."

The fire illustrated Snorri's words as if following instructions. The sudden flames woke a few members, and they followed the smoke attentively. A scale appeared on the table beside Snorri.

"Each cloud will solidify into stone, and land on either side. One at a time for each vote cast until all have come from the fire and one side of the scales weighs more than the other."

"Interesting." Lord Ferrum stroked his beard, impressed by the showmanship.

"A majority will be needed to pass each resolution." As Snorri finished, the fire, scales, and smoke all disappeared.

With these matters taken care of, Snorri opened the floor for discussion.

Nauveena watched Fallou and the other Protectors of Order. Most Protectors had come to occupy the additional fifth table with Fallou. Nauveena couldn't help noticing how many there were now. Sitting with the other members, they made a formidable bloc: six including Fallou. More than any other group.

Even more sat in the second row. These were the Keepers and Guardians and Obeyers of Order — what might otherwise be thought of as apprentices and pages. As she studied them, Nauveena noticed how young many were. *Too young*, she thought, to have devoted their lives to something as strict as the Magic of Order. Their youth was completely hidden beneath their boring robes and strange haircuts.

She wondered if the rumors were true. That adherents to the Magic of Order were required to remain celibate to conduct magic. Some rumors even spoke of castration among their ranks. *All in order to do magic?* Nauveena had never heard of such a thing. Or read about it in any of Athyzia's books.

Was that what Fallou would propose to the council? A vow of celibacy to do magic? Surely he could not expect that to pass. Venefica would not need any backroom conspiring to recruit votes against such a measure.

Likely, the First Protector of Leem had something even worse planned. Or Venefica's paranoia had become contagious. Nauveena continued to watch Fallou, waiting for him to stand and address the council, but he remained seated.

Instead, the Burgomaster of Bogmantic, Wilhelm Vaah, stood. He had a generally toad-like appearance. His breeches and overcoat were a size too tight, and the top button of his shirt strained to hold it closed.

"One issue is of particular importance to the Bogwaah," he said. "Our region is well known for the production of ingredients used in magical potions and spells. These ingredients make for the best magic. Potions using ingredients from other regions often misfire or do not achieve their aim. It has come to our attention that other regions are packaging inferior products and selling them under the name of *Bogwaah*."

Many spells — made by witches, folk mages, and sorcerers alike — required natural ingredients for potions, most often when they needed to affect the body: reduce headaches, fatigue, or cause sleep. Nauveena had learned many such potions, but she could not attest to the quality of the Bogwaah's products. The Botanical Mage grew many of the ingredients found naturally in the Bogwaah.

"We would like to move to end this practice immediately," Vaah continued. "It is an ill for both the consumer as well as the Bogwaah itself. Our reputation as fine producers is sullied. I would even move to *only* allow those ingredients produced in the Bogwaah to be used in magical spells."

In response to Vaah, the merchant leader from Valinka stood. Grufton Mann wore the strange three-sided hat that many sailors and merchants wore in the south.

"The proper labeling of magical ingredients is a fair concern," he said. "But outright limiting ingredients to those produced in the Bogwaah is a bit much. Many products of similar quality are produced throughout Jenor and even in the Distant Lands. And even those of lower qualities are not an ill if the buyer is aware of what is being sold and the price reflects the quality."

Leave it to the common folks to discuss issues of trade and commerce, Nauveena thought. They had the ability to discuss any issue and they could only focus on markets. Fortunately, they didn't need to debate the matter now. Which Snorri reminded them.

"I appreciate the conversation," the mage said. "But now is not the time. Now, we are only adding topics to the agenda, not debating them. Do we have seven who believe this is worth adding?"

When it came to adding agenda items, Snorri saw no reason for anonymity. Instead, he took a simple tally with the raising of hands. More than seven accepted the proposal, and the item was added to the agenda.

Nauveena did not look forward to spending a whole day on the topic. And she did not take much interest in the next topic either.

Grufton Mann, the Ombudsman of Valinka, continued to hold the floor. "There's the matter of alchemy," he said. "Transforming base metals to gold or silver, either for a limited time or permanently, can destabilize local currencies."

He was quickly interrupted by the mage Balzhamy of Lyrmica. "That is largely unfounded."

Prince Javee chuckled. "If my history is correct, rampant transmutation led to the Alchemy Wars."

"That's not—"

Before Balzhamy could continue, Prince Javee had cut him off with more laughter. "It was called the *Alchemy* Wars for a reason. Lyrmica suddenly paid all their debts. Only much later did the gold transform back to lead."

"And the southern kingdoms went to war to stop the flood of new gold," Grufton Mann agreed. "I propose a ban on the use of alchemy for such purposes."

"I second it," the dwarf Galena said, raising a stein of beer in salute. "Lyrmica is still rich with the alchemist's gold, while the gold we mine has lost value."

"No alchemists remain in Lyrmica," the mage Balzhamy protested. He seemed quite defensive on the matter. Of course, he had been advising Lyrmica during the alchemy fiasco, and had suffered quite the humiliation over it. "Lyrmica has accepted the doctrines of the Magic of Order. The alchemists of the old regimes have been driven from the kingdom. Such magic is no longer tolerated."

The Magic of Order? Nauveena tried to hide the look of surprise on her face. Why was Balzhamy speaking of the Magic of Order? He had studied at Athyzia, after all. She knew the Magic of Order's influence had grown in the east, but she had not expected Balzhamy to recite its doctrines.

"No alchemists remain, but their gold does," Galena said. "Why does Lyrmica remain so rich? The gold of its alchemists is indistinguishable from what we mine. Even the most learned dwarves cannot tell them apart."

"The Magic of Order preaches harmony," Balzhamy said. "Keeping gold unnaturally conceived would be disorderly, and so the Magic of Order forbids it. The king of Lyrmica has turned over all the alchemist gold to the Magic of Order."

"Lyrmica saw the folly of their ways," Fallou said. "Their pursuit of gold brought war upon them, a direct result of their dance with alchemy. They see the gold is cursed. They do not hold any more."

"That is all well and good," Grufton Mann said. "Lyrmica's king amplified the problem by coining the alchemist's gold, but other small-time counterfeiters still exist and are creating such gold every day. We must put in laws to stop them."

"You will have no objection from Lyrmica," Balzhamy said.

"Or the Magic of Order," Fallou said.

"Or the dwarves," Galena said.

The matter hardly needed to be put to a vote, either in terms of being added to the agenda or passing laws. But in this case, Snorri added it as an agenda item. Now Nauveena could look forward to a full day hearing each council member abhor alchemy when they were all still clearly employing alchemists themselves.

The next discussion did little to wake the council, either. In fact, it might have caused even more to nod off. Fichael Porteau, the foreign minister from Aryde, stood to address the council.

"What I bring up might seem a small matter," he said. "However, I believe the ramifications are quite wide. Each kingdom uses a different calendar to understand the year. Qadantium uses one based on the sun and solstices. The northern kingdoms follow the seasons of animals. And Druissia marks time based on the movement of the moons. While our small republic has adopted a hybrid of these.

"None of these calendars are synched, which causes confusion between kingdoms. We do not align on feast days and harvests. We can get along on different cycles, but in the spirit of unity you want to evoke, Snorri, might it be helpful to align on one calendar?"

Nauveena saw several members' eyelids droop.

When no one spoke, Falidurmus, the Protector of Wabia, cleared his throat and filled the absence. "The Magic of Order's calendar is composed of ten months divided into six weeks of six days with a five-day period set aside for fasting during the winter solstice," he explained. "Perfectly harmonious and not submission to celestial bodies."

"I hardly see how this is a matter for this council," King Caron of Künner said. "How can calendars possibly be this important?"

"Oh, I think calendars are *very* important," said Snorri, the only one excited by the issue. "Very important indeed. I am very interested in this hybrid system Aryde has developed, but I have also been working on something myself. Astronomy is an ancient magic. Our lives are dictated by the sun and the moons and stars, and the schedule of our lives should reflect that. I'll add it to the list — no need to vote, no need."

Since the war had ended, Nauveena had been looking forward to the council. Now, she could not believe that all any of its members could think to discuss was alchemy and calendars. At least alchemy had been the cause of wars in the past and justified discussion. She had never given calendars a second thought, despite studying astrology for years.

The morning yawned on. Other topics added to the agenda were not much more engaging: the standardization of the length of apprenticeships, a discussion of the proper remedies for maladies and diseases, establishing uniform taxonomies for magical ingredients.

Finally, Snorri adjourned the council for a much-needed lunch break.

Chapter Five
Elf Laws and Necromancy

> "All those with elven blood are required to report to their village's highest-ranking official once per month to submit a written account of all activity."
> ~*Guidance on Elven Behavior*
> Statute II, Article I

When the council returned from lunch, Nauveena could feel a renewed energy. The sun had climbed high, breaking above the mountains and warming the terrace with the embrace of spring. The Elf Queen of Saphalon began the council's second session. Her eyes, which were already fairly intense, shone even more fiercely than normal.

"I believe it is time we dealt with a *serious* issue," Queen Em' Iriild said after rising to address the council. On either side of her, the other two elven representatives looked around apprehensively. Nauveena found it strange that Zufaren, the large elven warrior from the Wilds, could look nervous.

"This council wishes to promote friendship and unity," she said. "We have seen the power of the Great Alliance in the Osseomancer's defeat. An alliance of elves, dwarves, and men, fighting as equals. And now, we must live as equals too. To do so, adjustments must be made in the treatment of elves across Jenor. In many lands, laws prohibit the roles elves can have in society. We are not allowed to trade. We are not allowed to own property. What we do come to own is taxed at a higher rate. How can we have unity when we are not treated fairly?"

"Well-said." Prince Javee clapped quietly. "These so-called 'Elf Laws' are an abomination. I see no reason for them."

Many nodded in agreement, both at the central tables and those on the outer rim. Snorri, Malachite, Nauveena, Venefica, the dwarves, oracles and other elves all nodded enthusiastically, as did those from the northern kingdoms. Only the men of the east and south — where the laws were the strictest — remained motionless.

Of these, General Dolcius of Rheum stood in rebuttal. His wide breastplate glittered in the sun. Nauveena always found him so boisterous and prideful. The war had created many heroes, and now, not all those heroes would leave. Dolcius had been Rheum's top general. When the Osseomancer marched on Rheum, its king became paralyzed with fear to the point that some wondered if a spell had compelled the king to inaction. Only Dolcius had saved the realm, leading a horde of common folk against the Osseomancer. Now, he had disposed Rhuem's king and ruled instead.

"No men live in the elves' kingdoms," he said. "And the elves seem content with this. They isolate themselves until it is convenient for them not to."

"Before man came to these lands, our forests stretched from the Wilds to Lyrmica," Csandril Em' Dale said. "Now, men tell us how we can live in lands that were once our homes alone."

"The elves are perfectly content to keep to themselves," Dolcius said. "Your forests are peaceful sanctuaries, from what I've been told. Which begs the question: Why would any elf leave the comfort of your alcoves? Is it because they are not welcome there?"

"All elves are welcome in our forest," Queen Em' Iriild said.

"Yet those who leave are not the most honorable," Dolcius said. "They are often tricksters and thieves. They are malcontents. And they do little to assimilate into the worlds of man and our customs."

"Watch yourself." Zufaren stood and pointed intimidatingly at the general. The elf wore a menacing blade slung across his back. It would be a simple matter to unsheathe it.

"You must admit, that is a terrible prejudice," Nauveena said.

"You are painting with a rather wide brush," Malachite added.

"These are simply our experiences," Dolcius said.

"The elves in your kingdoms are not immigrants," Csandril Em' Dale said. "They existed in your lands long before you. They did not leave our '*alcoves*', as you call them. Your lands are their homes."

Nauveena had always found the laws unjust. She had thought it would be a simple matter for the council to undo them. Especially after the elves' bravery against the Osseomancer. *How could there be such resistance?*

"These laws are abhorrent," Nauveena said, surprised by her own intensity. "How can they continue?"

To answer, Fichael Porteau, the foreign minister of Aryde, stood, not General Dolcius. "Aryde does not have many elves," he said. "But we have Elf Laws nonetheless. Many in our government would like to see them changed, but democracy is a slow process. If the council rules that we must reform, it is not something that can be done overnight. Opposition will persist."

"Opposition to fairness?" Nauveena asked.

"Enough to slow the wheels of democracy," Fichael said. "I have come to this council willing to accept its wisdom, but I still must return to my parliament for ratification. I know of a few ministers who might take issue."

"The same is true in many kingdoms of the east," General Dolcius said. "The common folk fear the elves. These laws were put in place to protect *both*."

"What do they have to fear from the elves?" Zufaren asked. The Wilds were far removed from the lands of the east. Already Csandril Em' Dale and Queen Em' Iriild knew the answer.

"The elves have shown themselves to be wily," Dolcius said. "Swindlers. Capable of magics the common folk do not understand."

"These are stereotypes," Nauveena said. She had lived so close to the elves, she did not know how the gross caricatures of the east were possible.

"I have heard plenty of stories," Dolcius said. "Of elves bartering cows that later ran dry, chickens that lay eggs that only contained sawdust, and even human infants being stolen from their cribs."

"Outrageous!" Zufaren exclaimed. Both Csandril Em' Dale and Queen Em' Iriild exchanged a glance. They wished not to call attention to the claims. "What use would elves have for human children?"

"It is well-known that elves can not have children easily," Dolcius said. "They hope through a blood magic to create their own."

"Is this really what the common folk of the east believe?" Nauveena asked.

Malachite, beside her, nodded solemnly.

"I am afraid it is," Snorri said. "These are longstanding prejudices."

"General Dolcius does have some truth in his words," the mage Balzhamy said. "In a way, the Elf Laws protect the elves themselves."

"Please explain?" Nauveena asked. It was one thing for General Dolcius to support the laws, but a *mage?* She could not believe it.

"If the common folk believe elves have taken advantage of them — in business, trade, other opportunities — they might take matters into their own hands. In the past, this could get violent. The Elf Laws place a lid on a boiling pot."

"By making them second-class citizens?" Nauveena asked.

"I will admit that in some instances, these laws go too far." Balzhamy's tall pointed hat drooped over his face, and he had to adjust it to see. "However, the alternative might be worse."

"I would love to find compromise," Fichael Porteau said. "Queen Em' Iriild, Csandril, Zufaren, I have loved being in your company. Getting to know you has been an education. I will be a champion for the elves when I return."

"I too long for unity," Dolcius said. The very act of sitting and standing again every time he addressed the council exhausted him, and he panted between sentences. "Unity can be achieved through Order. *An Order in which everyone has a place.* A place these laws are meant to maintain."

The undercurrents of such words were too much. Before he had finished, the three elven representatives had all stood, as well as their retinues behind them. Venefica had also stood. Fire burned in her eyes. Prince Javee began to stand, and only the oracle forced him back into his seat.

Nauveena too felt the need to stand. She had many words to say to Dolcius's assertion, but Snorri wanted to remain neutral. She could not inflame the current tension any further.

Snorri maintained his neutrality. He stood as well, but in such a slow manner that everyone could sense his words were meant to inspire diplomacy.

"I see we have found our first truly contentious issue," he said. "The course of today was to add to an agenda. I see no reason to vote. We will set aside several days to discuss the matter."

Nauveena wondered if Snorri did not automatically accept the item because he was afraid of who might refuse to vote for it — and how many.

"I have an issue I hope this council can address," Queen Yellialah of Dunisk said, standing to address the council. She looked quite regal in her silk gown, even if she looked frail and brittle as well. "We have discussed the great power held by those who wield magic. This power is even greater from the perspective of the common folk — those incapable of handling magic themselves. Rulers without magical abilities have welcomed mages in governing their realms. And other common folk seek their advice and abilities.

"However, in some instances, these abilities are used against the common folk — against their will. I can think of several examples of sorceresses enchanting common men for their purposes, either with charms or elixirs. Under their spell, these men are powerless and must do their bidding. Women are not immune to such enchantments either.

"Would it not be appropriate for this council to discuss this relationship between magic users and common folk? Could this council not offer some protection for the common men and women of Jenor? During the war, the common folk suffered more than anyone else. And often without knowing why. Many now live in fear of magic. Can we offer something that would allow them to heal?"

"The Osseomancer has fallen." Venefica placed a hand on the woman's arm. "You no longer need to fear him."

"The common folk do not just cower from the Osseomancer," Queen Yellialah said. "Some even fear this *place*. I had many in my court who advised me against coming, so great is the fear of magic now."

"We welcome the perspective of the common folk," Snorri said. "I had not realized how great their superstitions have become."

"With all respect," Ivalka, the mayor of Phryza, said, "these are not superstitions, but legitimate fears."

Snorri looked humbled by this. "Of course," he said. "Of course. I misspoke."

"Qadantium has more magic users than any other kingdom," Prince Javee said. "We live well with the common folk, but it has not always been this way. We have protections put into place — out of a mutual respect. Perhaps we would all benefit from adopting these."

"One magic is not feared by the common folk," one of the Lesser Protectors — either Vicodermus of Upper Tuvisia or Vicodermus of Lower Tuvisia — said. "The Magic of Order requires the will of the common folk and for that reason, they have been taught to understand it."

"The common folk understand many magics," Prince Javee said, "not just the Magic of Order."

"But only the Magic of Order gives them a place within the magic," said the other Vicodermus.

Nauveena wondered if this fear might explain the sudden rise of the Magic of Order. Were the common folk turning to it to be incorporated into magic, and therefore, gain some semblance of control? She had not thought of that perspective before, but then, she did not think of the common folk or the Magic of Order very often. For so long, her mind had been on the Osseomancer and the war.

"I am happy for this council to offer guidance," Snorri said, "but it is a long-held belief by the Academy that magic should not be used in such ways. Even without this council, the common folk have little reason to fear us and Athyzia."

"Many mages might behave respectfully," Queen Yellialah said, "but all it takes is *one* to change the fortune of the common folk. And one is too many. The common folk should not live in fear of what might be done to them."

"We do not have such issues in Skiel." For the first time, Veeslau the Unbound, the Law Speaker of Skiel, addressed the council. He possessed a singular paleness beneath his dark hood. "Our common folk live alongside our mages. They respect how useful magic is for their protection."

"Many common folk find ways to use magic," King Ümlaut said. "With amulets and gems and other such trinkets. It does not need to flow through them."

"Even if they find ways to use magic, the issue is about magic being used against them," Grufton Mann said. "In this, we have little control. Enchantments are one thing. I have heard of common folk being transformed into mice and frogs for the entertainment of folk mages."

"Certainly, these are old wives tales," Snorri sputtered.

"I have not heard of such things in many years," Malachite said.

"A more recent, relevant example might be necromancy," Loblic Haleem, the leader of the merchant guild for Olmtpur, said. Until now, he had not said much, allowing the other two representatives of the merchant cities to speak instead.

"Necromancy?" Nauveena asked. "How does that apply?"

"In necromancy, are the dead not revived against their will?" Loblic asked. "Are they not then commanded without their consent? And we have no idea what becomes of their souls. Even the wisest mages do not know."

"Respect for the dead is one of the oldest of laws," Queen Em' Iriild said. "What is dead must stay dead, or the world can be tipped into imbalance."

"That seems to be a separate issue entirely," Veeslau said. Nauveena wished she could read his emotions better, but his thick blindfold covered his eyes.

"If so, I would like it added to the list," Loblic said.

"There is no reason it shouldn't be," Balzhamy of Lyrmica said. "Necromancy is one of the darkest magics. To reanimate a life that has been snuffed out goes against order. It threatens imbalance. The world pivoted on a dark axis when the Osseomancer awoke the dead in such numbers."

"But there are uses for the art," the oracle Kitrinos said. Everyone looked at her, puzzled and wondering what she meant. "The dead often have prophecies delivered to them alone. If we did not consort with them, we would lose many understandings of what is to come."

"But in such seances, are the dead not *willing*?" Csandril Em' Dale asked. "To me, that seems to be a key issue."

"To this, you make a good point," Nauveena said. "One which we can take up in due time. It seems we now have several issues to add to the agenda. The relations between magic users and common folk may take days to discuss. And necromancy alone, a week."

Snorri held a vote, although he did not need to. On the first issue, everyone raised their hands to add it to the agenda. On the second — on necromancy — almost everyone did, but four: King Ümlaut, King Caron Háček, Veeslau the Unbound, and King Bane. At first, King Bane raised his hand, but the witch Venefica gently restrained him.

◆

King Bane VII of Druissia stood to address the council. His broad shoulders and black beard exuded power. But now he seemed slumped, weary, tired from the exertion. He had held the Osseomancer at bay, and it had almost broken him.

"Many wars between nations are not begun over magic," he said, "but magic does exist in our world and plays a role in how wars are conducted. A powerful-enough sorcerer can defeat scores of common folk with conventional weapons. A key strategy in every conflict, then, is getting the strongest mage to your side, whether that be through persuasion or gold. And when both sides employ this strategy, the only result is escalation."

"What are you proposing?" Csandril Em' Dale asked.

"That magic not be used in war," King Bane said. The announcement received a number of gasps from the council.

"Yet you consult the witch," said one of the Lesser Protectors. Nauveena could not tell which.

"'Consult?'" King Bane said. "Yes, I consult Venefica. And I would not deny another king to seek the counsel of a mage or wizard or even a witch. They offer much wisdom. And if war broke out between nations, yes, I would go to her. I would be easily defeated without magic on my side."

"Then how do you ask us to prohibit its use?" asked the same Protector.

"I would only use magic out of fear of my enemy using it against me. But if we could come together now and restrict it from the battlefield, our wars — when they do come — could be much less costly in terms of human lives."

"What type of magic would we be restricting?" King Caron of Künner asked.

"Any, I suppose."

"Shapeshifting?" Caron asked cautiously.

"Magical weapons?" Lord Ferrum asked.

"Fire magic?" Prince Javee asked.

"More importantly, how would this be enforced?" Fallou, the First Protector of Leem, asked.

"That is part of the matter I would like to discuss," King Bane said.

"I see few ways to restrict the use of magic before it is done," Fallou said.

"I would think we would need punishments, known to all, to act as deterrents."

"Who would decide the punishments?" Fallou asked. "Would it vary depending on the scale of the magic used? What if a small kingdom is defending itself from a larger, more aggressive one? Would they receive the same punishment?"

"Why are you so curious?" Venefica asked. "Are you anticipating future wars?"

"I think for such a proposal, it is important to understand how it will be enforced," Fallou said. "The same goes for the other concerns of this council. We cannot preemptively stop these uses of magic, and so punishment must be meted out after — but by whom? Will you, Snorri, take on that task?"

"I did not anticipate such a responsibility," the mage said.

"Yet you must have seen that as a possible outcome?"

"The council would need to settle such matters."

"This council of twenty-six?" Fallou asked. "Will Athyzia become the site of tribunals? Will the Academy build prisons to hold offenders?"

"This is a topic we will discuss in the days to come." Snorri had not expected such a line of questioning, Nauveena could tell; she only hoped the rest of the council could not.

"I can see this council convening to settle large matters such as magic's use in military operations," Fallou continued. "But every infraction would be quite time-consuming. Is this council to meet every time a philter is used inappropriately? How many folk mages are in Jenor? The council cannot oversee all of them."

"No, of course not." Snorri huffed. "But we can offer wisdom and guidance."

"Wisdom and guidance that can be cast aside whenever it is convenient," Fallou said. "I have another proposal."

"And what would that be?" Venefica asked.

"We have great power assembled here," Fallou said. "Together, we have put forward many issues that have vexed our kingdoms separately. Together, we will find solutions for them. Let those solutions be *binding*."

"'Binding?'" Csandril Em' Dale asked. "What exactly do you mean by that?"

"A pledge," Fallou said. "A vow. An oath. Sealed by our combined magics."

"A horkos?" asked Queen Em' Iriild.

"A binding spell?" Nauveena had read about such magic before. Such spells were ancient and mysterious.

"No, no." Snorri shook his head. "No, I would not recommend that under any circumstance. I am surprised at you, Fallou, First Protector of the Order of Leem, to suggest a magic so old and — and — unpredictable. No. I dare not. No."

"It is a suggestion," Fallou said.

"It is a suggestion I dare not take." Snorri had gone pale. "How does the Magic of Order include such spells?"

"There is *order* in upholding a promise," Fallou said. "There is nothing to be scared of if each member of this council honors their commitment. Be done with false promises. Let us bind ourselves to each other and the outcome of this council."

"No. No," Snorri muttered. "I could not ask that of this council. We are here to offer guidance. And guidance not followed voluntarily is something — is not the purpose of this council. No. I will not hear of this again."

"Very well," Fallou said. He bowed deeply and sat back down. The matter seemed put to rest, but Nauveena had a sinking feeling it would not be the last time she heard such a suggestion.

Chapter Six
Borkha

> "Skiel's coasts have an odd foulness in the air that is not just the stink of low tide."
> ~*Navigations and Currents*
> Captain Kru
> 51 BU

Once again, Snorri left the council drained, exhausted, leaning on Nauveena to get to his room. The day had left her worried. Snorri had expended much energy and, with the list of items to discuss, the council might take months. She did not know how he would last.

As they neared his room, Nauveena looked behind her and found Venefica trailing closely. She had expected the witch to appear. She too wanted to talk with her, but not now. She did not want Snorri to know about her conspiring.

As Snorri fumbled to open the door to his chambers, Nauveena looked back to Venefica and shook her head subtly. They would talk later.

As she had the night before, Nauveena helped Snorri into his room and made him a pot of tea. Despite not wanting to influence the council, he had done much talking. Whether he had done it consciously or not, he had steered the conversation several times, cutting it off when tensions rose too high.

Snorri faded into his armchair with a blanket brought up over his stomach. He reached for his reading glasses and the book, *Philosophies of Magic*, that he had left on the side table.

He went to read for a moment and then stopped himself. "*A binding spell?*" He looked over his glasses at Nauveena. "What foolishness. And from someone as learned as Fallou. They talk of the discipline of the Magic of Order, but then they are so foolish as to suggest something like that."

"I have not read much of such spells," Nauveena said. "What makes them so foolish?"

"They are not just foolish," Snorri said. "They are dangerous. It is a fickle magic. And volatile. The spell must be specific. Even the wisest mages can make mistakes. Maybe it can be done over a simple contract — a negotiation between neighbors. But something like this, with twenty-six members. No. Too dangerous."

"What makes it dangerous?"

"A pact is made and bound by magic. And if the pact is broken, the magic punishes accordingly. It is dangerous to personify magic. To give it agency. Because even the most well-constructed spells might be misinterpreted. And may not specify the penalty for breaking the vow. The magic is ancient, from an unknown source — who knows how it will punish? I hope more do not listen to Fallou."

He already has six, Nauveena thought, but decided against saying anything. She brought Snorri tea, but by the time she came back to his chair, he was already asleep.

Nauveena lifted the quilt further up Snorri so he was covered. Then she took his glasses off and placed them on the side table. He preferred sleeping in his armchair recently. He found it was where he got his best sleep.

Then Nauveena crept quietly from Snorri's room.

As she expected, Venefica waited for her outside. But she was not alone.

The queen of Dunisk, Yellialah, stood beside her. The two were talking in hushed tones, although Venefica increasingly raised hers.

"I understand your fears, but there was no need to bring that before the council," Venefica said.

"How could I not?"

Queen Yellialah wore the type of fine dress Dunisk was well known for. Matching gloves went up to her forearms. Her earrings sparkled with glittering diamonds. She was a thin thing, and frail, and Nauveena wondered how her head could hold the weight of such jewelry.

"You do not know what you are doing."

"I am not asking for much," Yellialah said. "Not after what I have been through."

"And do not forget what *I* have been through," Venefica said.

Queen Yellialah had paused, pondering her next words, when both women noticed Nauveena. They ended their conversation and looked to the sorceress.

"Sorry, am I interrupting?" Nauveena asked.

"No, not at all," Queen Yellialah said sweetly, her voice a completely different tone from before. "We were only discussing the council. Snorri did such an excellent job."

"Yes, and it took much out of him," Nauveena admitted. "He is resting now."

"The discussions were quite long. And I did not understand all of them. I hope we will have rest days in between, for all of us."

Yes, Nauveena thought, that might be necessary.

"I will leave you both," Queen Yellialah said. "I need rest of my own."

"As always, Yellialah, it was great to speak with you," Venefica said.

Venefica waited for the queen to depart. Then she looked to Nauveena. "*A binding spell?*" She narrowed her eyes as if to ask, "What was that?"

"I don't know what to make of it either," Nauveena replied.

"He would not suggest it unless he believes the resolution would pass."

"What resolution, though?"

"I do not think he has proposed it yet," Venefica said. "And maybe he will not until his numbers are confirmed. Items can be added to the council at any time. He will have no problem getting the seven votes to add a measure. He can wait until he has the advantage."

"But the binding spell?"

"I don't know."

Venefica began to walk. Nauveena followed. They crossed over one of Athyzia's bridges. The waterfall below surged with the melting snow from the mountains above. The two took a similar path as the night before. They passed a statue of the mage Bezra Umal, scattering a number of Athyzia's cats: tabbies and calicos and Tuvisian bushtails. One hissed at Nauveena for the disturbance.

"Maybe he is laying the groundwork," Venefica continued, ignoring the felines. "Testing the response of the council. You saw Snorri. On this, he will not budge. Maybe Fallou will abandon it now."

"Abandon what?" The druid waited at the balcony the two had shared the night before. Nauveena imagined that he had been instructed to wait for them there.

"The binding spell," Venefica said.

"What a strange suggestion." Malachite watched a hummingbird buzz among the wisteria crawling over the lattices. "Of course, this is not the only troubling development from today."

"What else?" Nauveena felt her heart sink.

"Maybe this will not come as a surprise, but I believe Rheum has aligned themselves with Faulsk and the Magic of Order."

"Of course," Venefica hissed. "What can you expect from that dolt Dolcius?"

"He thinks the Magic of Order will give him legitimacy," Malachite said. To defend Rheum, Dolcius had led a coup to depose Rheum's king. The king had since died in his own dungeon, leaving no heirs. After leading the defenses, Dolcius enjoyed tremendous favor, but held no legitimate claim to the throne. Nauveena wasn't surprised that he was willing to align himself with Faulsk to hold power.

"The Magic of Order holds much influence in Rheum," Malachite said. "The Ultimate Defender will claim Dolcius did more than anyone to uphold order and thus legitimize his rule. So long as he continues to be their ally at this council."

"Rheum would mean Fallou has command of seven votes." Nauveena couldn't believe how much she sounded like Venefica.

Malachite nodded in confirmation.

"Is it too late to talk with the northerners?" Venefica asked. With the council having begun early in the morning, it had adjourned a few hours before dinner. Unlike the previous day, it was only late afternoon. Ideally the kings of the north would not be too far gone.

"I believe their servants brought them beer for the afternoon sessions," Malachite said.

A flush of disappointment crossed Venefica's face. "Whenever can we talk with them, then?" she asked. "Will we have to ambush them before breakfast?"

"It might be too late for their kings," Malachite said. "But their *queen* is another matter."

"Queen Breve?" Nauveena remembered the blonde queen from the feast. She wore fierce armor and appeared as intimidating as the men from her homeland.

"I spoke to her during the intermission," Malachite said. "She is also interested in hearing your thoughts on the council. She knows the minds of the two northern kings. We can learn where they stand from her."

Malachite left the balcony, and Venefica and Nauveena followed.

"I could not help but notice your king's vote today," Malachite said to the witch as they walked.

"King Bane voted for many issues to be added to the agenda," Venefica said.

"I am talking about the one he did *not* vote for."

"Yes?" Venefica asked, not seeing his point.

"You must see the wisdom in debating the topic," Malachite said. "The Osseomancer swelled his army with the dead. We have seen the devastation it unleashed."

"I had no doubt it would be added," Venefica said. "I only wanted to offer my reservations."

"You know what many on the council think of you," Malachite said. "This may only confirm their suspicions."

"I care not for my reputation."

"You should, if you want to build a coalition to rival Fallou's."

Nauveena felt suddenly excluded from the conversation, as if what they were discussing was just outside her grasp. Considering she did not wish to have such conversations outside the council, it felt very odd how badly she wanted to be included again. She found a pause to interject herself. "Necromancy is a dark magic. How can you defend it?"

"I do not wish to defend necromancy itself," Venefica said. "But I see it as the beginning of a dangerous decline. What may follow such a ban? Let us discuss it and provide guidance against it, but let us not do so blindly."

Since their arrival, the kings of Yülk and Künner and their warriors had taken residence in a series of adjoining apartments in one corner of Athyzia. They had arrived a week before the beginning of the council. In such time, they had made themselves at home. Elk and yeti furs covered the floor. Shields and armor and very sharp weapons leaned against the walls. Horns of beer covered the tables. One barrel of Clovis ale had been rolled into the center courtyard connecting the apartments.

The northern warriors had taken seats and couches from the apartments and brought them outside, placing them around the barrel. They formed a ring, in the center of which a warrior from Yülk sparred with a warrior from Künner. Their brothers on both sides cheered them by stomping their feet and clapping and yelling and toasting with their horns, sloshing much ale onto the cobblestones.

At least a few dwarves sat among the northmen, whooping and hollering at equal volume. The warriors fighting in the middle ducked and dodged each other. They fought shirtless, exposing rippling muscles threaded with intricate, runic tattoos. They expertly swung long staves as if they were swords.

On occasion, the staves made contact, and for the briefest moment, the struck warrior changed. The one from Yülk would grow, becoming giant and covered in the thick black fur of a bear. The warrior from Künner would similarly transform, his face becoming long and his canines longer, transitioning into fangs.

Neither showed any actual malice for the other. When they were struck, after the instinctual shift, they smiled, laughed, and lunged into the fight again. A round of applause and laughter from the crowd signaled that the violence was for nothing other than their pleasure.

Nauveena could not find such pleasure in the performance, though. As skilled as each fighter was, the world had just experienced too many years of pain and violence for it to become entertainment. She looked around for Queen Breve.

The queen sat behind her husband, King Ümlaut, and not far from King Caron. She seemed to enjoy the match as much as any of the men. She leapt from her seat when the warrior from Yülk made an athletic parry and delivered a blow. When she sat back down, she caught Caron's eye and smirked at him.

Then she caught sight of the druid, and behind him, the witch and sorceress. Without bothering to announce her departure, she left her seat and came over to the guests.

"Just a friendly game." Her northern accent made the words sound disjointed. "Come, follow me." She led them back into the apartments and away from the spectacle in the courtyard. "We have much to discuss," she said as she moved weapons off the few chairs remaining in her apartment. A shirt of chainmail hung over a marble statue in one corner of the room.

Queen Breve was stunningly beautiful. Nauveena had been unable to look past her armor and her animal furs. But now, sitting beside her, face to face, she could not help but notice the queen's exquisite nature: her high cheekbones, full lips, and dazzling blue eyes. And Queen Breve could likely have fought and beaten both of the warriors who had been sparring before.

"It is my wish to begin a dialogue with the northern kingdoms," Venefica said. "Many important issues will be discussed and possibly voted on. We should see where we each stand on them. In some matters, we might be strong allies."

"But" — Queen Breve looked at Nauveena before she began, her icy blue eyes piercing — "the old mage. Does he not wish for no talks outside the terrace?"

Nauveena nodded, understanding now why Breve had looked to her.

The queen continued. "We wished to follow the old mage's wishes, even if we did not think anyone else would. We know how the others think of us. How they see us. They do not think we can follow such directions. We wanted to show that we could. But then we also worried — *what if we miss important talks?* The most important discussions might not take place on the terrace."

Despite the queen's thick northern accent, her words were quite insightful.

"It is completely reasonable to worry," Venefica said.

"Our lands are far away," Breve said. "We are already so alone. We feared we might be left out further. I was so pleased when you mentioned wanting to talk," she said to Malachite. "Both kings want to respect the old mage's demands. They will not talk with the others — not away from the terrace. *But me?* I am not held to the same pledge. I am free to learn what I can and bring it back to them. Then, they will not be alone."

Nauveena could see the queen's logic, but she still couldn't help feeling that she was betraying her mentor. Snorri desired transparency. Discussions on all matters should be held in the council, for all to hear. Separate conversations between smaller groups would lead to divisions. The council's purpose was to spread unity. This did the opposite.

Queen Breve had offered a back channel, but this still broke the spirit of Snorri's wishes, if not the letter. But the conversations would happen with or without her, Nauveena told herself. And as of now, they were preemptive and, therefore, not nefarious. As long as she was present, they might remain that way.

"What are your thoughts on the Magic of Order?" Venefica asked Queen Breve.

"I do not know them. Nor does King Ümlaut. Nor Caron. They have sent missionaries over the Yülk, but they have received an icy reception." The woman tossed a thick blonde braid behind her shoulder. "We in the north love magic. We respect it. We know where it comes from. From the earth and from blood. Our greatest warriors harness it. And allow it to harness them. We do not fear it like these men in the south. Weak." She practically spat the word. "Man must live free. Magic comes from freedom."

"I am suspicious of their intentions," Venefica said. "I believe Fallou is attending this council for his own aims."

"They want no other magic," Breve said.

"We do not know *that*," Nauveena said.

"Their missionaries come to us and tell us our magic is vulgar," Breve said. "Our magic is savage and brutal. Only their magic is rational and modern and harmonious. Let our magic be savage. Savage is beautiful. Magic is beautiful. Let me ask you: Have you seen a man transform into a wolf? Into a bear? A sabertooth? They become primordial. They become gods. Those in the south have lost the ability. Their order will not return it."

"I have seen it before," Malachite said. "It is remarkable."

Nauveena had only read about such shapeshifting. She wondered what Breve transformed into. Would it be a bear with matching blonde hair?

"What do you believe this Fallou is plotting?" Queen Breve asked.

"We can only guess," Venefica said. "Based on their relations with other magic in their kingdoms, I fear he might move to limit what other magic can be done. To bring in an *age of order*."

"That man is frail," Breve said. "I could crush him." She squeezed her hand into a fist to indicate how she would.

"That is not how we want this council conducted." Malachite offered a steadying hand. "If it comes to those extremes, we must be ready. We must win in the council."

"Which is why we want to understand where your votes would go," Venefica said.

"The Magic of Order will *not* cross the Yülk."

"We can count on you to not vote for restricting magic?" Malachite asked.

"At least not in the ways the Magic of Order might demand?" Nauveena clarified.

"We stand with you," Queen Breve said. Then her tone changed. "Now, there is another matter from today that worries me. Separate from the Magic of Order. And I know it worries both kings."

Something about her tone made Nauveena think back to the day's events. She remembered who else had not voted to add necromancy to the agenda alongside Venefica. Two had been the northern kings.

"Let me not say what the issue is," Breve said. "Only that we have not practiced it in our lands for some time. But we know of those who still do. And it interests us that they continue."

◆

"What exactly is the issue?" Nauveena asked when they had left Breve's chamber.

"I think I know," Malachite said. "But it might take some time to explain. I am growing hungry. Let us sit for dinner, and I will tell you what I know."

The three went to the feast halls and found a table out of the way. They had bowls of ginger ramen and a bottle of Qadantium wine brought to the table. Nauveena would have preferred to talk in private, but she too had become hungry. She slurped up the wide noodles with as much ferocity as the northern berserkers.

"While some of what I am about to say is true, other pieces are speculation," Malachite said between his own slurps. "The first is definitely true. Plenty of accounts from sailors verify the claims. In the Skielfock Islands, north of Slier, lies an island known as the Seat of Borkha."

"The dragon?" Nauveena asked.

"I see you have heard of her," Malachite said. "That makes things easier. Borkha has made her home in the Skielfock Islands for as long as anyone can remember. She is a rare specimen. Eldest of the dragons. And one of the largest too. She can fly, although she chooses to swim."

Nauveena had read many accounts of dragons. Great beasts made by a different power than the one that made elves and dwarves and men, they lived in caves along mountain passes, devouring victims who made the mistake of coming too close. Above all else, they coveted treasure: gold and gems and all things shiny. Bestiaries detailed their abilities to breathe fire and fly with massive wings. They possessed claws and fangs larger and sharper than any weapon Nauveena had seen in the northerners' chambers.

"She haunts the waters of the Dark Sea," Malachite said. "Any ships passing in sight of her island risk being seized, capsized, and sunk to the ocean floor, where she can collect their treasures at her leisure. They say her hoard is the richest of any dragon who has ever lived."

The druid slurped some noodles before continuing. "The trade along her route is quite lucrative. The northern dwarves are known for the gems and gold they mine. What they do not keep, they trade to the northern kingdoms, who, in turn, trade further afield. Their only route to trade is to go further north, where civilization is sparse, or pass through the Dark Sea to trade with Lyrmica and Dunisk and the merchant cities, and even Qadantium and Druissia. But that route is quite dangerous. Borkha does not strike every ship, but of those she does, none survive.

"So far, everything I have told you is true. It is here where the account delves into the world of hearsay. Of course, after our conversation today,

I no longer doubt it. The kingdom of Skiel controls Skiellance, a strategic trade port on the Strait of Skiel. This position has forced the northerners to do much trade through Skiel. Skiel gets a cut of every good the northerners move. However, this cut might not only be because of Skiellance. It is said Skiel has found a way around the dragon."

"Really?" Nauveena had not heard of such.

"Well, not exactly *around* the dragon. Borkha gets her cut as well. But they have found a way to make the passage less dangerous. For many years, no one would volunteer for the journey due to the likelihood of meeting Borkha. They tried slaves, but even they refused. They feared the dragon more than the whip."

"What are you getting at?" Nauveena asked.

"Oh, isn't it obvious?" Venefica asked.

"It is?"

"I have heard rumors of the mages of Skiel using necromancy, I just never knew to what end," Venefica said. "I always assumed they were just that — rumors. Skiellance is quite wealthy, with their trade. They keep to themselves, and the eastern kingdoms have come to mistrust what they do not know, but now, I understand."

"What?"

"The ships are sailed by the dead."

"The northerners must unload their goods at Skiellance, where they are reloaded onto a ship crewed by the dead," Malachite said. "The dead then sail through the Skielfock Islands to Skiegs, where the goods are offloaded to a living crew to take them the rest of the way."

"If Borkha only takes one out of every ten ships, the gold and gems are lost, but not living sailors," Venefica said. "How clever."

"Why would the northern queen tell us this?" Nauveena asked.

"She is confiding in us," Malachite said. "Although she remained vague. Taboos exist against the use of necromancy. Especially now."

"She wants our help stopping any bans against it," Venefica said.

"How convenient for you," Nauveena said. "You have found allies in your fight."

"My resistance has nothing to do with necromancy itself," Venefica said, although Nauveena did not believe her, "but with what might be banned next. Now the northerners might not be against banning some uses of it, but I imagine they would like this specific use carved out. I see no other way around the dragon."

"There are the *dead* to consider," Nauveena said. "And also, why should we help them on this matter? You heard Queen Breve's thoughts on the Magic of Order. If they try anything extreme, she will vote against it. We do not need to help her on necromancy for her to vote with us."

"She brought it up for a reason," Venefica said. "We know the importance of the issue. If Fallou makes an exception to it, he could win them."

"That seems unlikely," Malachite said. "And ultimately, even if we tried, we could not get the votes to stop a ban on necromancy. The elves despise such magic. I doubt the dwarves would care to learn how their gems are moved out of the Sea of Skiel."

"Do not underestimate the dwarves," Venefica said. "Dwarves, more than any other race, know about the greed of dragons. I would not be surprised if they have guessed how Skiel deals with Borkha. We might not be able to get the votes, but we should feel the temperature for a possible exception."

"I joined you to stop Fallou's scheming," Nauveena said. "Which, so far, has been nothing but hypothetical. But now, we must do the work of the northerners to allow something as vile as necromancy to be practiced in Skiel?"

"Not practiced without reason," Venefica said. "Do you not sympathize with them? Let it be known how valuable those gems were against the Osseomancer. Not to mention the weapons they craft. These could not be moved past Pravulum. They had to be moved through the Dark Sea. And so, they only came to our aid through necromancy. We would not have won the war without it."

"We should make a sign of good faith to see how the others feel," Malachite said. "At least to keep a dialogue open with the northerners. But even if we cannot get them an exception, I imagine they will vote with us."

"How many do we have secure?" Nauveena asked. "On the chance that Fallou proposes something we do not agree with."

"I speak for Druissia," Venefica said. "And can secure Dunisk. These two, I am certain of."

"And of course, there is my vote," said Malachite.

"Queen Breve speaks for Yülk and Künner," Venefica said. "That is two. I imagine Skiel would be a third, although we should confirm with Veeslau."

"That's six," said Malachite.

"Certainly, Kitrinos and the oracles would vote with us," Nauveena said. She knew the oracles respected all forms of magic. They would not fall under the Magic of Order's influence. "And Prince Javee."

"Eight," said Venefica. "The elves would be eleven. They will not side with the Magic of Order. We have more than Fallou, but we must have thirteen to be certain. With thirteen, there will be a tie, and then the Academy votes."

"And Snorri will not vote on anything outrageous," Nauveena said.

"We should speak with the dwarves next," Venefica said. "They hold another two. That would be thirteen."

Thirteen, Nauveena thought. *Is it really that simple?* They need not even make concessions on necromancy, and they would likely have the northerners. The threat of the Magic of Order had always been overblown. They would never be able to gain enough to sway the council so completely.

"We should never count our dragons before they hatch," Malachite said. "Let us be certain of this number as much as possible."

Chapter Seven
Songs of Lament

> "When the elves conceive, it is cause for great celebration. All across their forest, beautiful music is played, and elves come from far and wide to enjoy the festivities. But a melancholy remains beneath all the happiness: an understanding that such celebrations are becoming less and less frequent."
>
> ~*Seven Years in Saphalon*
> Pitrinois
> 274 BU

The three conspirators resolved to talk to the rest of the thirteen. The talk with the northerners had gone well and they had not known what to expect. Nauveena expected it would be even easier to speak with the elves, dwarves, oracles, and Prince Javee to confirm their loyalties.

To make matters even easier, they had barely finalized their plans when Prince Javee himself sauntered over to their table and took a seat next to Nauveena.

"You three must be having the most interesting talk." He carried a bottle of wine. "To have placed yourself in the corner, away from the merriment and dancing." He pulled the cork out with his teeth and refilled the three's drinks.

"We have been reviewing the day's events," Nauveena said.

"I was right, then." Prince Javee's eyes lit up. "A very interesting discussion indeed. What a day it has been. The morning began slowly, but the afternoon more than made up for it."

"There were some developments," Venefica said.

"You could say that again," Prince Javee said. "Now, can anyone explain to me, what is the deal with this Magic of Order? We do not have them in Qadantium. I don't think we'd put up with that sullen lot for long. Their wardrobe leaves much to be desired."

Prince Javee wore a long silk robe, gold in color and embroidered with the flame emblem of his kingdom. Qadantium — how Nauveena longed to travel through the kingdom. Growing up on Ciri Daahl, she could see Qadantium from its shores, but still, it had always felt far away. The kingdom boasted the largest collection of artworks, sculptures, frescoes, and monuments in Jenor. Its cities teemed with museums and galleries and libraries. Many thought of Qadantium as the seat of civilization and enlightenment — the well from which all sophistication and man-made beauty had sprung.

"That's exactly what we were discussing," Venefica said.

"Could someone please explain it to me?"

Prince Javee flashed a smile. It was a smile he was well-known for — and not just because of his good looks. His spirit had remained throughout the war. It had buoyed Qadantium when others had faltered. It had not been broken, even during the war's darkest moments.

Javee had been quite young when he rode with his father to break the Siege of Ontiphon. King Jarul was as renowned for his fighting prowess as Javee was for his smile. He dispensed many of the Osseomancer's legions, casting them down and even thwarting his generals. King Jarul had threatened to break the siege — until the Osseomancer himself faced him.

The king fought well and could command fire, but he was no match for such a wizard. He should have retreated — he should have turned and fled. *But he did not.* He stood his ground. For some time, he held the Osseomancer off while others raced for safety. But it could not last. The Osseomancer struck him down, blinding him with a curse.

Prince Javee, fighting nearby, rushed to his father's side. He found the king raving with madness. Javee dragged his father from the field of battle and lifted him onto his steed to ride to safety. The day had been lost. The king was blind and mad. All around Javee was death. As his warriors fell, the Osseomancer added them to his hordes.

Javee had no choice but to retreat. As they neared Qadantium, he left his father and went to fight in the rear. The Osseomancer's army threatened to ride into Qadantium after them. The prince made his stand along the Kiijaro River, lighting it on fire so the Osseomancer and his hordes could not cross.

When Javee reached Qadantium, his father's curse had only gotten worse. The king became inflicted with fever and nightmares. He raved with madness. The greatest mages of Qadantium and beyond could not cure him. The king could not rule in such a state. Sovereignty passed to Javee, who became Prince Regent in his father's absence. If it were not enough that he should grow up without his father to guide him, he had to rule a kingdom without his father's guidance as well — and during war.

Now, he had come to Athyzia to represent Qadantium.

"I wish I understood it myself," the druid said. "But from what I understand, the Magic of Order derives its power from an unusual source."

"Order?" Prince Javee guessed.

"Yes, order, and a strange order at that," Malachite said. "I did not believe magic could come from such a source. But the Protectors speak of a secret book — *The Book of Order* — that only they can read, which explains how this is possible. They wield a powerful magic if everyone in the kingdom adheres to the order they prescribe. An order in which the king is king and must be listened to. Order has entrusted the king to rule, and the hierarchy follows from that. The common folk must know their place and not challenge it. The more who follow their order, the stronger the magic."

"Well, the Emperor of Faulsk must *love* that," Prince Javee said. Night had crept into the feast hall. He snapped his fingers to light the candles on the table. Nauveena knew it was a simple spell, but the handsome prince added such flourishes that she did not mind. "I see why the Magic of Order is spreading so fast."

One might not consider the length of a century fast, but in terms of movements and cults, for the Magic of Order to have spread from Lyrmica to Upper Tuvisia in that time was a remarkable feat. Nauveena did not fail to see the opportunity the Magic of Order offered Faulsk. For many years, they had wished to reestablish the borders of their first empire. Now, they had in all but name.

"We fear the Protector of Leem has his own designs for the council," Venefica said. "He might not have revealed them with a proposal yet, but we believe it will come. When it does, we want to have the votes to stop it."

"I have a vote," Prince Javee said coyly.

"That you do," Venefica said.

"Would you like my pledge to not vote with Fallou?" he asked.

Very easy, Nauveena thought. Why had they been so frightened of Fallou? He controlled the votes of the Protectors of Order, but his influence stopped there. The other members of the council had little use for the Magic of Order.

"Very much," Venefica said. "If you will give it. Although it does not sound like you would be voting with Faulsk anyways."

Javee shook his head. "Qadantium. Druissia. Faulsk." He raised a finger for each as he spoke. "The three great kingdoms of Jenor. When one grows too powerful, the other two strike it down. My father said this provided a certain balance. But what if one becomes more powerful than the other two combined? Once, Jenor looked to Qadantium for guidance. Now, they look to Faulsk."

"And the Magic of Order," Malachite said. "Fallou likely wants to use the council to expedite the process."

Prince Javee poured more wine. "That strange fellow is sadly mistaken if he thinks he can push the council in such a direction. My father told me it is not the people who serve the king, but the king who serves the people. His power comes from them. Not the other way around."

"Our task is to ensure as many votes as we can against Fallou," Venefica said. "We needed to talk to you, but also the oracles, elves and dwarves."

"You will have open ears," Prince Javee said. Then he looked at Nauveena. "Did your teacher not specifically prohibit talks such as these? A naive request, of course, but I would not have expected *you* to be involved in them."

"He did not anticipate Fallou's behavior," Nauveena said. "Which, I might remind you, is still purely hypothetical. We are criticizing him for something he has not yet done."

"But surely he has a mind to," Venefica said.

"We can gather votes as a precaution," Nauveena said. "But there is still a chance we have misjudged him. We all admit we know little about the Magic of Order. For the sake of unity, we should keep an open mind."

"Keep an open mind," Malachite said. "But also a cautious one. I would be surprised if Fallou is keeping as open a mind as you. Although I respect your wisdom."

"Who would you suggest we speak with next?" Venefica asked the prince. "The oracles? You seem to have grown close to the High Priestess since this council began."

"Kìtrinos often talks in her sleep," Javee said, hinting at how close he and the oracle had become. They would be in Athyzia for months, Nauveena reasoned. How else were they supposed to pass the time? "It is difficult to tell if it is babbling or actual prophecies. Only last night she spoke of something strange: *'What was protected by fire will be destroyed by water.'*"

"What could that mean?" Nauveena asked.

"Who knows?" Prince Javee shrugged. "I asked Kìtrinos when she woke. She only said not all prophecies make sense. Or come true. But it is quite the thing to hear and have to ponder while trying to sleep. But no, Kìtrinos has already gone to bed. And either way, I feel confident in saying her vote is yours, at least as far as Fallou is concerned. The elves are in their chambers now. I was planning to visit later tonight. But I could visit them early. And take you."

The elves played a sad song. Their sitars cried, while their ocarinas and gemshorns weaved melancholy notes between the chords. Csandril Em' Dale stood on a raised dais, singing of lost forests and forgotten realms. The elves had once been a mighty race, alone in the world, but they had diminished. The years lengthened between each new child, and soon, they believed, they would have none at all.

The other elves sat and listened. The music did not inspire dancing, but only the need to sit and listen and contemplate. One could only delve deep into their own mind — deep enough to find hidden fears they did not know existed.

A long pipe passed from elf to elf. The perfumed smoke further aided each adventurer as they wandered into the crevices of their mind.

Nauveena had no wish to smoke any. The music was enough. Already she doubted herself. She had remained at Athyzia while others fought.

Why had Snorri ordered her to remain behind? Did he not believe she could fight against the Osseomancer? Did he think she would be corrupted by the Osseomancer's power? If the Osseomancer had come to her, would she have been easily tempted? He possessed an extraordinary library at Pravulum. If offered, would she refuse to read his books?

And now, she had come to betray her mentor. She had made herself one of the conspirators and gone between council members, currying their favor. How would Snorri handle the betrayal? She had corrupted the council itself.

When Csandril Em' Dale saw Prince Javee and the other three enter, he finished his song. Nauveena felt the song had no ending and no beginning. It could not come to a close, but only be interrupted, paused for a short time.

"I see you've brought friends," Csandril Em' Dale said to Prince Javee. "Was your feast so boring you all wanted to come hear our songs of lament?"

"The music is beautiful," Prince Javee said. "Although I prefer your others."

"You are in luck," Csandril said. "We were just ending."

As he spoke, the tempo changed, ascending into something more enthusiastic and exuberant. Nauveena doubted that their timing had been so convenient. Only the elves could listen to their dirges for any length of time without being driven to madness.

"A happier song," Csandril said. "Which I hope you have brought wine for."

"Of course." Prince Javee seemingly produced a bottle out of thin air. Csandril matched him by producing crystal chalices equally from nothing, and the Prince poured the dark red wine into each.

Taking his chalice, Csandril Em' Dale guided them to a far corner. The music continued, far more upbeat, but not to the extent that Nauveena felt the need to dance as she had when the elves first entered Athyzia.

Csandril Em' Dale arranged seats for himself, Prince Javee, Venefica, Malachite, and Nauveena. When they had all sat, Malachite turned to the elf. "We have been discussing the nature of the council. How do you believe it has been going?"

"The ways of men are very queer," Csandril said after a moment's thought. "They often do not say what they mean, but hide their true intentions in politeness. I have never heard such polite scorn before."

"Certainly, you have come across such passive aggressiveness before," Prince Javee said. "You are a frequent traveler in Qadantium."

"Yes, but today has made me appreciate the men of your kingdom all the more," Csandril said. "Our elves live so freely in your kingdom, side by side with you, that I believe we have influenced your speech and manners. And, might I say, for the better."

"Maybe *we* have rubbed off on *you*," Prince Javee said. "Are you not concealing a criticism within your compliment?"

"I do not know what you mean." Csandril Em' Dale's laugh was as contagious as his music. Nauveena, with the rest, laughed easily.

When the laughter had died down, Venefica leaned in and said, "We were specifically wondering what you thought of the Magic of Order."

"The elves have long left men to govern their own affairs," Csandril said. "We have learned after our experiences with the dwarves, not all appreciate elven wisdom — especially in terms of how magic is managed."

"Do you find the Order of Magic strange?" Nauveena asked, maybe too directly.

"Not any stranger than a bear might find a squirrel gathering nuts. Or an eagle might find a salmon swimming upstream."

"You do know men though," Prince Javee said. "You must admit, even for men, these Magic of Order folks are odd."

"Certainly, you must think so," Csandril said. "I value your opinion greatly. If you think they are odd, then odd they must be."

"Have the elves discussed the council at all?" Nauveena asked.

"We felt tonight required quiet contemplation. Long, drawn out discussions are depleting. After so many external conversations, we can only renew our strength by looking inwardly."

"There was no discussion?" Malachite asked.

Nauveena peered around the chambers. She saw the warrior leader of the Wilds, Zufaren, smoking from the pipe. But she did not see Queen Em' Iriild.

"Where is your queen?" she asked.

"Each elf must renew themselves in their own way," Csandril said. "Many partake of the song of our histories. And the herb that grows wild and free in our forests. But Queen Em' Iriild is depleted more than all. She spoke openly at the council of concerns that have troubled her for many years. I do not believe she received the response she expected."

"Where is she?" Nauveena asked again.

"She has retired to her chambers for the evening."

"Could we speak with her?"

Queen Em' Iriild did not appear at once after Csandril Em' Dale went to speak with her. While she agreed to meet with them, she had prepared herself for the night, and it would take her time to prepare herself for visitors again.

While they waited, Csandril Em' Dale told of the elves' histories. How, at the start of the world, their cousins had been corrupted to become the orcs. Since then, both had been cursed with a fate of war against each other. Generations had been engulfed in terrible violence that could not be undone. Zufaren joined and nodded along.

Eventually, Queen Em' Iriild emerged. The music changed to her coronation tune: triumphal and boisterous. Two elven attendants swung the doors to her room open and she stepped out. The room became brighter from a hidden illumination. Her long gown brushed against the floor, concealing her feet and giving the appearance that she was gliding and not walking at all. Everyone stopped to watch her.

She approached the group and had a cushioned seat brought for her. "You have requested my presence?" she asked.

Nauveena did not believe she had been sleeping. Her hair had been expertly coiffed in a way that would have taken Nauveena a full morning to achieve. Her skin glistened like fresh dew. Her eyes sparkled with curiosity.

"We thought it wise to learn your thoughts on today's council," Venefica said.

"This was so urgent as to disturb me?" The queen shot Csandril a sideways glance.

"We are sorry for waking you," Malachite said.

"I was not sleeping. No, I was deep in reflection, wandering backwards through my own memories. But once that process is begun, it is not easily reversed and halted. I have hundreds of years of memories to garden. I must tend to each."

"Our needs are urgent," Venefica said, "although if we knew how deeply you were in reflection, we might not have forced Csandril to retrieve you."

"I am here now," said the queen.

"As I explained the other night, I am suspicious of the Magic of Order," Venefica said. "Today's events did nothing to dispel such suspicions. Fallou was deceitful in his grievances about the middle kingdoms' votes. They will vote as one, but receive six votes: a powerful voting bloc."

"It was not my decision to empower these smaller kingdoms," the queen said. "I believe that decision was made by your master." She looked to Nauveena. "Do you believe he made a mistake?"

"In the moment, I do not think Snorri had many options," Nauveena said. "He wants to unite all the kingdoms at this council. Fallou knew what he was doing when he threatened to leave. I do not envy Snorri's decision."

"But the decision was made," Queen Em' Iriild said. "And not by me. I do not see how I can help you now."

"Your help is invaluable," Venefica said. "As well as yours and yours." She looked to Csandril 'Em Dale and Zufaren. "Fallou and the Magic of Order now have six votes. Seven if Rheum is aligned with them. Twenty-six sit on the council. A tie will be decided by Snorri. We must know where the other nineteen lie. If Fallou can bring another seven to his side, he can push whatever he likes through the council."

"Do you wish me to pledge myself to you?"

"At least when it comes to Fallou," Venefica said. "We do not know what he will propose. But he does nothing by mistake. His fight to add the middle kingdoms was by design. He has some proposal he is working toward. When that comes, we would like your support against it."

"I cannot tell you what I will decide on a topic I do not know."

"We can guess what Fallou is after," Venefica said. "The Magic of Order does not allow for other magics. If he works to restrict these, would you vote against it?"

"I cannot make a decision until the time comes."

"But you believe in the principles of free magic?" Prince Javee asked.

"Not all magics are adored by the elves. We find many abhorrent, especially those that blend the veils between life and death."

"I can't imagine you voting to uphold the Magic of Order above all others."

"As a matter of course, I do not make commitments I cannot honor, and so I will not here. All I can offer is to speak with you if and when the First Protector reveals his intentions."

Nauveena sighed in relief. For the Elf Queen, this felt like a victory. She would continue communications. They would be able to know her mind before any vote.

"Thank you," Venefica said. "It is our desire that we work together. To know where each stands on the issues."

"Fallou has come to this council with his own designs," Queen Em' Iriild said. "And so have the elves. I added an item to the agenda today. You have not addressed this."

"Curse the Elf Laws," Venefica hissed. "They are a vile stain across Jenor."

"You have nothing to fear there. We stand with you," Malachite said.

"You have been counting votes. Where does the rest of the council stand on this?"

"We have only spoken to the northerners, and only on the Magic of Order," Malachite said.

"'*Curse the Elf Laws*,'" Queen Em' Iriild said, mimicking Venefica. "But I see where your priorities lie."

"My queen, we must have patience with them," Csandril Em' Dale said.

"'Patience?' You preach patience, poet of mirth?" The lights suddenly dimmed, and the queen became quite frightful. "For a thousand years, my children have been ridiculed, jailed, and degraded. How much longer can we stand by and wait?"

While Queen Em' Iriild ruled over the Forest of Saphalon, she was queen of all elves, a tradition as old as the elves themselves. She had been tasked — through her lineage — to be their mother and guardian, a role she took quite seriously. But the elves' power had dimmed. Fewer now roamed Jenor, especially compared to the progeny of man, who multiplied like rabbits. The elves could not possibly challenge the kingdoms of men.

"We have support at the council," Csandril Em' Dale said.

"We can begin a campaign for you," Venefica offered. "In the same vein we are arming ourselves for Fallou's challenge. We would need thirteen, and we can challenge the Elf Laws."

"You have my vote," Prince Javee said. "Qadantium has always been home to the elves. May it always be."

Nauveena counted in her head. Could the same votes they had already secured be used for the elves? They had not brought the issue to the northerners. Where would they stand?

"We cannot thank you enough," Csandril Em' Dale said.

"Enough with these councils," Zufaren said. He swung his thick hands wildly as he talked. His brass earrings jangled along the ridges of his pointed ears. "Be done with these long talks, these polite greetings while insults are bandied about behind backs. Let us confront man in the field. Our warriors are the most powerful. Without us, the orcs would have swung down from the mountains across the Wilds and overrun the homes of man. Why should we continue to fall in battle while man remains safe?"

Nauveena sensed the elf had been meaning to discuss this for some time. *Could it be a matter for the council?*

"Add it to the agenda," Nauveena said. "A call to arms. Certainly, we are war-weary, but we cannot allow the threat of orcs to continue. The armies of man are still mustered. Let them march against the orcs. Let the Alliance continue."

"Qadantium will answer the call," Prince Javee said.

"As will Druissia," Venefica said. "I can convince King Bane of it."

"The orcs are the fate of the elves," Queen Em' Iriild said. "And the fate of the elves alone. Only the elves could have turned them from evil and we failed. Now, we are cursed with battle against them."

"There is no reason we cannot come to your aid," Prince Javee said. "You need only to ask."

"What I ask is for my children to be treated fairly," Queen Em' Iriild said. "You have now heard me. Is this discussion satisfactory? You know what my designs are. And I know yours. I hope we can work together. But for now, the night is fading, and I must tend to my gardens."

Chapter Eight
Philosophies of Magic

> "Books are more than their parchment and ink. They are a magic unto themselves. Much can be learned of the time and place in which the text was written. They exist as manuals and artifacts and mirrors of ourselves."
> ~*Inscription on the Library of Esotericism*
> 374 BU

The night had indeed faded. No time remained to seek others' counsel. Further discussions would need to wait. The council would begin early the next day, and Nauveena needed to return to her tower if she wanted any hope of sleep.

She did not get any. The sad song of the elves lingered. She could only think of the elves' decision and their curse — to fade from the world, in constant turmoil with the orcs whom they had once loved. When she closed her eyes, she could only picture distant lands and bitter wars and the heads of elves on stakes. Carrion birds flew above.

When she did not think of the elves, she thought of her own scheming. She replayed conversations in her mind. And she had the horrible thought of Fallou doing the same, sneaking through shadows and spreading whispers, offering bribes of gold for votes.

The dawn came mercifully between the half-drawn curtains. Nauveena lay in her bed, feeling the sheets' warmth for as long as possible, not bothering with breakfast, until the bells began to toll.

Everyone at the council looked equally tired, their eyelids heavy. They peered into their coffee as if the drinks were instead lifesaving elixirs. They stifled wide yawns.

Everyone, that was, except for Snorri.

The mage looked youthful, enthusiastic, well-rested. He practically skipped onto the terrace. He grinned from ear to ear as he watched the council members fill their seats.

"Welcome back. Welcome back. I, for one, was cheered by our conversation yesterday. So much exuberance. Such thoughtful discussion. We have many topics to discuss."

Nauveena studied the faces of the gathered council. Already, many topics had been discussed. Queen Breve looked thoughtfully towards her. Csandril Em' Dale smiled whimsically. Prince Javee sat next to the High Priestess, Kitrinos. The oracle too looked well-rested. Had Prince Javee learned any more prophecies the night before?

Snorri continued. "However, before we begin, I would like to review the agenda topics from yesterday again."

An audible groan escaped the council. Snorri wished to discuss the agenda again? How could that be, when an entire day had already been spent on it?

"I would like us to elaborate on one of the issues further. And until we do, I cannot create a schedule for this conference. And I imagine I will need a day to create the schedule — at least. Today, let us conclude our conversations from yesterday. And tomorrow, let us suspend talks to give time to schedule the rest of the council."

The groans quickly reversed themselves. Not only would the council close early, but there would be no talks the next day. Smiles appeared on everyone's tired faces, except for those of the Magic of Order, who looked more agitated than normal.

"Do you expect to cancel any other days?" General Dolcius of Rheum did not bother standing. "We are sacrificing time away from our homes to be here. Rheum looks to me for guidance. They suffer in my absence. Should we not use all the time available to us, so we can return?"

"Of course, of course," Snorri said. "I have thought it all through. We cannot go on and on without break. Some of us are very old and grow weary quickly. I imagine we should schedule a rest day between each topic. It is only right to allow time for rest and reflection."

Many on the council started to clap, but Dolcius stopped them. "I remember when the industry of man was much stronger. Rest days are for idlers. The Magic of Order does not need them."

"I think it is a great idea," Queen Yellialah of Dunisk said. "Snorri is right. Some of us are indeed old and can use the rest."

"We can start fresh on the next topic and make sure nothing lingers," Csandril Em' Dale said.

"Do we all really think so lowly of ourselves that we must schedule days to rest?" Dolcius asked. He received murmurs of approval from the Protectors of Order.

Malachite had been correct. Dolcius had indeed aligned himself with the Magic of Order.

"I only wish today were a rest day." Prince Javee leaned back in his chair.

General Dolcius scoffed. "That is only because you share the affliction of your kingdom of staying up to all hours."

"The rest day can be taken to prepare for the following session," Kitrinos said. Next to her, Prince Javee shrugged in a way that only irritated the general.

"It looks like you are all against me." Dolcius threw up his hands in surrender. "Is it even worth voting?"

"On this matter, no," Snorri said. "Now, back to the discussion. This morning, I woke early and read passages from *Philosophies of Magic*. The text never ceases to fascinate. I learn something new every time, and this time was no different. I gained a new perspective on our conversations from yesterday."

Philosophies of Magic remained one of Snorri's favorite works of the ancient mage Bezra Umal. Nauveena imagined he could recite it by heart.

"Yesterday, we discussed the use of magic against the common folk. We rightly pointed out that while necromancy is a form of magic used against common folk, it should exist as a separate issue. Magic used against the dead is different from magic used against the living.

"Magic used against the living, however, can be further divided. I can think of two broad categories. First are instances when the body is controlled through magic against the will, such as voodoo. But another category controls the mind, as we see with love potions and songs of enchantment. In one, the mind might resist what the body is being ordered to do, while in the other, the mind might willingly accept its commands, but is being influenced. I do believe these are separate issues and should be treated as such."

"It has been many years since I read Bezra Umal," Malachite said. "But I remember his essays on magical taxonomies."

"He is always worth the read," Snorri said. "I highly recommend you read him again if you have time. We have several copies in the library."

Malachite nodded politely and — looking for a way out of the conversation he had inadvertently stumbled into — said, "That sounds wonderful."

Satisfied, Snorri continued. "After pondering the matter further, I believe we must dedicate two different sessions to these matters. If we do not, it is likely conversations could get confused as we try to reach a consensus on two different issues."

"I must apologize," Queen Yellialah said. "I have not read these *Philosophies*. But if we treat these as two separate issues, could we then reach two separate decisions?"

"I believe we should allow room for two separate decisions, yes," Snorri said.

"Whether a person's mind or their body is controlled," Queen Yellialah said, "if it is against their will, it should not be tolerated."

"In some instances" — Venefica now stood and looked directly at Queen Yellialah — "when the mind is controlled it is more difficult to determine if it is magic or persuasion or something else."

"And in some cases, when the mind is controlled, it is worse than the body being controlled," Queen Yellialah said.

"No one said it was not," Venefica said.

"We should speak no more of the *Philosophies of Magic*." Fallou, the First Protector of Leem, took his turn to stand. "Only one book has the authority to be discussed here, and that is *The Book of Order*."

"We should be open to all books," Nauveena said as heat rose to her face.

"*Philosophies of Magic* wastes much time with the taxonomies of magic," Fallou said, "but it does little to understand how it should be derived."

"There is a whole chapter devoted to that." Nauveena had not meant to raise her voice.

"But it is outdated and has no place in the discussions of learned men." Fallou spoke much more eloquently than Nauveena, who had practically shouted. Compared to her, he seemed more rational and thoughtful.

Nauveena worked to control herself by clenching her fists.

"We are not here to pass judgement," Snorri said. "Any book that helps us reach a decision is valid."

"Only *The Book of Order* addresses these questions directly," Fallou said.

Nauveena sat down. She could not refute him. She had never read *The Book of Order*. Only Keepers and above were allowed to read from the book. Only one copy existed in Ryork's great citadel of Vaul Ess, and additional copies were not permitted, although they quoted it frequently enough in their sermons and laws.

"*The Book of Order* offers a way for common folk to exist with magical users," Fallou continued. "The common folk produce the Magic of Order through adhering to the order outlined in the book itself. And in return, they are a part of that magic. And magic worked upon them is a process of that order."

"Qadantium does not follow the Magic of Order," Prince Javee said. "Yet we have much peace between magical users and the common folk."

"At least that is what you are led to believe," Fallou said. "How many common folk find their way into your princely presence?"

"I spend much time in the taverns," Prince Javee said.

"I am sure you do," General Dolcius muttered just loud enough to be heard.

"If this council truly wants to unite the lands, they should look to the Magic of Order," Fallou said. "Only order provides a rational life for the common folk and a rational source of magic. We should be governed by *The Book of Order*."

"And what exactly does this book say?" Prince Javee asked.

"The book," Fallou said, "posits that true, rational magic can only be the product of the masses' dedication to the order laid out by the book — the one true book. If order is maintained by all, then magic shall flow through those mages who have devoted their lives to the protection of that order: Keepers, and Protectors, and the Ultimate Defender."

As Fallou spoke of the Ultimate Defender, all members of the Magic of Order briefly bowed their heads in reverence.

"Magic derived from anything else is inherently evil," Fallou said. "Blood magic, death magic — these dark arts can only corrupt. Even the magic of nature grows feral and untamed. Those worshipers of the horned god can easily be lead astray. Delving too deep into these other forms of magic can only lead to madness. Let Pravulum smoke for eternity as a monument to this madness. Never again, I say. Let us be done once and for all with the wickedness of other magics, when order offers a path forward."

Nauveena shook with anger. Venefica's premonitions were proving correct. Fallou wanted to assert the Magic of Order upon the council. She moved to stand, but Snorri placed a hand on her shoulder. Across the terrace, Venefica readied herself to stand as well, but he equally placated her with his eyes.

Snorri stood instead. "Are you finished, First Protector of Leem?"

Fallou did not respond.

"I respect the wisdom brought by the Magic of Order," Snorri said. "We are lucky to have different perspectives on how magic should be handled. We each offer a different perspective that, combined, will give the full picture. We discussed what is valid for this council earlier. I will tell you what is: only those perspectives that can exist alongside others. Magic has always been inclusive. Some derive their power from the stars. Others from the plants of the earth. Some from within.

"None of these invalidate the others. Wars have been fought over the questions we will discuss here. My goal in this council is to replace war with raised voices. Let that be all this council brings."

※

Snorri dismissed the council well before noon. Nauveena had not expected such a simple issue to have gotten so contentious.

As an hour remained before lunch, everyone returned to their quarters rather than proceeding directly to the feast hall. They left in silence, hardly looking at one another.

Only as they wandered farther from the terrace did they splinter into huddles to discuss what had occurred. Nauveena formed hers with Snorri. Both bowed their heads towards the other as they walked. Nauveena was still shaking. She could not believe what had been said about *Philosophies of Magic*.

"If their own book is so great, why do they not let anyone read it?" Nauveena asked.

"There are many ways to read a book," Snorri said. "And interpret its lines. Readers can even arrive at a conclusion different from the one the author intended. Sometimes it is a very dangerous thing to let others read a book. You do not know what they might find."

Just then, the two heard a voice behind them. "Excuse me."

They turned to discover Fallou waiting there.

"Oh, well, yes," Snorri said in surprise. "Hello, there."

"I only wanted to approach you both and apologize if you misunderstood my aims in council earlier. On subjects I feel passionately about, my words can become quite heartfelt and might even come off as fervent."

Of course, during his entire diatribe, while Nauveena had felt heat rise to her face, Fallou had remained as stoic and rigid as ever. His voice had never wavered, as if he were simply reciting a recipe.

"This council invites such passions," Snorri said. "They are, of course, welcome."

"I made such a speech because I believe education is necessary. In many parts of the world, the Magic of Order is still persecuted. We have suffered great injustices ever since our Witness began extolling his wisdoms."

"I can only imagine." Snorri shook his head.

"Our missionaries have tried bringing the gift of order to other kingdoms, and have been rebuked. We find ignorance in many places. I believe we heard it in council today. This young prince from Qadantium. Surely he means well, but he might be showing off, acting brash for the oracles."

"Prince Javee has been Regent of Qadantium since he was a young man," Nauveena said.

"And he has led the kingdom well. Few kingdoms came out of the war unscathed. We must give him credit. But he has been so busy running his kingdom, I imagine he has not had time for his own education. Qadantium was once the leader in thought, but now, other lands have supplanted it."

"Much knowledge still flows from Qadantium," Snorri said. "I thought the Prince Regent showed much curiosity today. He only wanted to understand the Magic of Order better."

"If only all were as curious," Fallou said. "I have heard disturbing rumors."

"What types of rumors?" Snorri asked.

"I remember your directive to have all conversations out in the open, out in the light. This has been respected by the Magic of Order. I do not believe it has been respected by others."

Snorri cocked his head to the side. "I have heard no such rumors."

"It brings me no joy to share this news with you, but indeed, some council members have been meeting privately to discuss council matters. They are participating in conspiracy and the exchanging of favors. They are even intimidating and bullying other council members."

"Certainly, that cannot be," Snorri said. "I specifically instructed them not to."

"Maybe I am mistaken," Fallou said. "But I have heard it from so many sources."

"Who is having these discussions?" Snorri asked.

"Oh, I'd rather not say."

"Please, confide in me. I am overseeing this council. I can speak to the members privately and ask that they stop such activity. Certainly, it is a misunderstanding. They only share an enthusiasm for the topics and want to continue conversations after hours."

"No, that cannot be it," Fallou said. "For these conversations were quite deliberate and intentional."

Nauveena felt her hand swell with magic. She had used such magic to beat back the Osseomancer's armies. Normally, she used gemstones to concentrate and expand it, but she could flare a powerful-enough blast unaided. It coiled inside her, ready to strike. She wanted to flare her magic at Fallou. It took much willpower to control it.

"If that is the case," Snorri said, "please tell me the parties involved, so I can ask their sides of the story."

"I hesitate to tell you, because the perpetrators are well-respected, and one is even close to you."

"I would rather know than live in the dark."

"If you insist, then I can withhold the information no longer," Fallou said.

Nauveena's heart pounded. How would Snorri react when he heard her listed among the conspirators?

"It has been brought to my attention that three have been meeting secretly with council members: the witch from the south, the wandering druid, and — it pains me greatly to say — your own apprentice."

Snorri stepped back as if the news had been a heavy weight tossed to him. "This does not sound anything like Nauveena," he said. Then he turned to the sorceress. "Please tell me this is not true."

Nauveena's heart felt like it might burst out of her chest. Her mouth fell open into an expression that could only reveal herself. But she could not admit to Fallou's accusations.

"No, no," she said. "I do not know what he is talking about." Her voice fumbled out, clumsy with lies that felt like cotton in her mouth. She needed to think of something more. "I have spent nights with Venefica and Malachite," she admitted. "Both saw fighting during the war. I remained in Athyzia. I only wanted to know what the war was like."

Fallou turned to Nauveena to accuse her directly. "Did you not visit with the northerners yesterday afternoon? Have dinner with the Prince Regent of Qadantium and then visit the elves at night?"

Nauveena could not deny it. "Yes, I did. These are guests of Athyzia. It has been so long since I have had the chance to speak with those from different lands."

"I do not know how the Magic of Order feels about socializing," Snorri said. "But the Academy of Mages sees nothing wrong with it."

"And you did not discuss any council matters?" Fallou asked.

Nauveena shook her head. She felt sweat on the back of her neck. She could continue the lies, but she couldn't think of them fast enough. She had been lucky to spit out what she already had.

"Everyone is eager to share stories," Snorri said. "Nauveena has been in Athyzia all the long years of the war. You can not begrudge her the need to find friends."

"I should have seen the futility in bringing these charges to you," Fallou said.

"I will speak to Venefica and Malachite as well," Snorri said. "I know the druid quite well. I cannot imagine he would betray the council in such a way."

"The witch was a known agent of the Osseomancer," Fallou said. "If she is involved, it can only be for ill. Many witches supported the Deceiver King during the war. Many still do. They desperately wish for him to return."

"I believe those rumors are overblown. Venefica eventually fought against the Osseomancer."

"What concerns me the most is that I don't think your apprentice would act without your approval," Fallou said.

"She is not my servant," Snorri said. "Her assistance in preparing for the council has been monumental, but she is free to come and go as she pleases. I cannot prohibit her from making friends."

"And maybe she made these friends at your orders?"

"Are you trying to insinuate something?"

"Only how quick you are to come to her defense."

"I said I would speak with the others. Nauveena does not deny who she met with, only the nefarious motives you have ascribed those meetings. You have said you do not enjoy prejudices; why do you exercise your own now?"

"What is the purpose of this council?" Fallou asked. "What is the Academy of Mages plotting? You gather us here, extoll the virtues of transparency, and then have your underling do your dirty deeds."

"I am not sure I like what you are saying."

"Already today, you cut me off as I tried to educate the council on the order that can mend their well-being."

"Is that what you were doing?" Snorri asked.

"And how quick you were to interrupt me. The council sees who you favor. And they follow accordingly. Is this council nothing more than a way for the Academy to force its will upon Jenor?"

"This council was meant to bring the kingdoms together. It was not meant to be a forum for you to evangelize the Magic of Order. Speak of its perspectives and its usefulness, but do not seek conversion."

"If I had been able to speak freely, the conversions would have come naturally."

"We will see about that," Snorri said. "I appreciate your concern. As for these accusations, I appreciate you bringing them to me. I will deal with them as I see fit. You only need trust my decisions on the matter."

Fallou, sensing he could go no further with Snorri, bowed deeply, pivoted on his heels, and turned down the corridor. He walked briskly, with his long gray robe flowing behind him. Snorri watched him proceed down the hall.

"It's not — it's not..." Nauveena stuttered once Fallou had stormed out of view.

"'It's not' what?" Snorri asked. "Come, let us speak together."

Snorri started for his chambers and Nauveena followed reluctantly. He had defended her in front of Fallou, but certainly, he did not believe her meek lies. He knew the truth.

They slipped into Snorri's room. He let Nauveena into the room first, while he held the door open. He shut it behind them.

Nauveena looked to Snorri, waiting for him to speak. But he only stood behind the closed door. "I don't know what he is saying," she said finally.

A raised eyebrow.

"I don't."

"You don't?"

"Seriously." Nauveena bit her lip.

"There was no truth in what he said?"

"No." Nauveena stopped. She couldn't. Snorri knew. Her lies were futile. "No. It is — it is true."

"I thought as much."

"Venefica approached me after she stormed in here. She worried what the Magic of Order might do. I tried to reassure her that the council sought to mend us, not divide us — or whatever she thought Fallou might do. I brought her to Malachite, hoping he might dissuade her, but he only confirmed her fears."

"And you met with those he said?"

Nauveena nodded. "Not to intimidate them or force them to vote a certain way — like Fallou said. Only to understand how they might vote if something came up."

"I see." Snorri strode by Nauveena towards his large window. The parrots in their cage squawked when he came near. He looked out the window.

"You heard Fallou today," Nauveena said. "And General Dolcius. He has clearly aligned himself with Fallou. They have already begun to lay the groundwork for something. I don't know what. They want the supremacy of the Magic of Order."

Snorri sighed as he looked out the window. Nauveena only wanted to run to him. To scream and tell him that she had been wrong. To beg for his apology.

"I know what they say about the witch," Nauveena continued. "But she has been right so far. Fallou was deceptive when he got a vote for each of the middle kingdoms. He is planning something."

Snorri turned from the window, and Nauveena could see the sadness etched into his face. "I only wish that you had come to me," he said. "You must know you can confide in me, don't you?"

"Yes, of course. But you said not to have these conversations. I thought I had betrayed you."

"Betray me? No, you could never betray me. You did what you thought was right. When I made that rule, I envisioned the council going differently. Now, we are not even three days in, and I fear I must abandon my lofty ideals."

"No, the council is going well."

"But it is not a bad thing to understand where the votes lie. The council has already gone in surprising ways. I would like fewer surprises going forward."

"So, you are not angry?"

"No, no — angry only at myself. I thought I had thought it all through. But when Fallou challenged me the first day, I had not foreseen it and gave in. My lack of understanding of the Magic of Order failed me. The rumors of their radicalism might not be unfounded. I fear he might try to bend the council to his will."

"I fear it too."

"But if he thinks the council will bend so easily, he is mistaken. Fallou might think he can manipulate me after the first day, but I will not tolerate it any further. If any proposals become too extreme, I reserve the right to — well…"

"'Well,' what?"

"Veto, I daresay. It is my council, after all. It is not the council of the Magic of Order. We will not leave here as adherents to their cult."

"You can do that?"

"Of course I can. Which I imagine Fallou has guessed at, which is why he has suggested the binding spell. My veto might invalidate the conference and dissolve it prematurely, but I would rather that than anything prohibiting other magics be passed." Snorri shrugged.

"But let it not come to a veto," he continued. "Let us first hope that Fallou will wilt now that he has felt resistance. Talks of intimidation and bullying? He is the bully. Now, he knows he cannot force his will as he does in Leem. Maybe he will never propose anything. But if he does, let us have the votes."

Nauveena need not have worried. She took a sigh of relief, while Snorri continued.

"Let us have the votes." He began pacing as he thought out loud. "Yes, we must. Now that there are votes to be had, we must have them. An unfortunate inevitability, perhaps. Of course, this is why I hesitated to have a vote at all. I wished for the council to reach a consensus that pleased and included all. Now, rather than trying to persuade all, we will only barter and trade for the votes of fourteen."

"Then why leave it to a vote?" Nauveena asked.

"The practicalities of the world exist outside those of the Academy. Initially, I conceived of this council as one of discussion. We could come together to share our perspectives and slowly get closer to a universal that might be accepted. But such discussions might take years.

"We might talk and talk for months and have nothing to show for it. Some, such as you or me, might have looked forward to such discussions. But others do not have the patience. If the council is to sacrifice their time to convene, they must leave feeling that a satisfactory conclusion has been reached, and that can only be done with a vote."

"I see."

"But let us not lose that initial sentiment of mine — as naive and idealistic as it might have been. Let us ensure we have a vote if the worst comes, but before this, let us try to change minds. Look at what has already been proposed and added to the council schedule. Limiting magic at war time? Eliminating the Elf Laws? Protections for the common folk?

Even a standard calendar across all the kingdoms? We can accomplish so much.

"But even if we do accomplish much with a vote, let us accomplish more with persuasion. The council might end with a decision, but we still want each council member to go home and adopt those decisions willingly. Think of the Elf Laws. We might achieve the necessary votes to abolish these laws, but let us also shine a light on why they were wrong in the first place."

Snorri might have been more open to private discussions, but in many ways, he remained as idealistic as before. Nauveena remembered the conversations on the Elf Laws. She could not envision General Dolcius abolishing the laws willingly.

But that did not seem important now. She was still too relieved that Snorri did not feel betrayed.

"Convince everyone in the council," Nauveena said. "But in the meantime, make sure we have the votes in case Fallou tries anything?"

"Yes, yes, of course." Snorri spun around, snapping out of his thoughts. "If Fallou is going to accuse us of conspiring, we might as well do it. Tell me, what votes do you have?"

Nauveena thought for a moment. How many votes did she actually have? After all the nighttime conversations, how many had been secured? "Malachite receives a vote; that is one," she said. She could be sure of him at least. "Venefica is advising Druissia, so that vote is safe. She also feels confident about Dunisk."

"We can count on Malachite to vote wisely," Snorri said. "And Venefica is advising King Bane. She has his ear. Why does she feel so confident on Dunisk?"

Nauveena shrugged. She did not know. "She only says she can deliver the votes."

"I believe she once served there," Snorri said. "Before she came to Druissia. That is a possible three so far. Who else?"

"Prince Javee does not trust the Magic of Order either."

"He has said as much?"

Nauveena nodded. "He also said the oracles feel similarly."

"Prince Javee said this?" Snorri asked. "Did you speak to the High Priestess herself?"

"No, only Prince Javee."

"Hmmm." Snorri thought to himself. Nauveena knew her mistake. Trusting Venefica on Dunisk might be one thing, but she could not take everyone's word. "The Priestesses of Xanthous are known to speak in riddles. I would hate for Prince Javee to have misunderstood."

"I can speak to her too."

"In either case, four with Prince Javee. Five after you have spoken to the oracles to confirm Prince Javee's accounts."

"Yes," Nauveena said. She should have known Snorri would be much more skeptical in his approach. The other night, they had easily counted to thirteen, and Malachite had even warned them against counting their dragons before they hatched. Now, under her mentor's scrutinizing lens, Nauveena could only confidently say she had four.

"If we are to secure votes beforehand, we should not take half-measures," Snorri said. "As with all matters of logic, we must not make assumptions. Establish what is absolutely known and build from there. Only count a vote when they have given you their word. We cannot rely on hopes and guesses."

"Of course, of course."

"And you spoke to the northerners and the elves?"

"We did. Neither gave complete assurances." Nauveena thought it best not to divulge the use of necromancy to skirt the dragon Borkha. "The northerners have the same reservations about limiting the use of magic. They would be unlikely to side with the Magic of Order."

"They would make seven with their two votes. If we are counting the oracles."

"We have not spoken with them yet, but based on our conversation, Skiel would go with the northern kings," Nauveena said. "We, of course, will speak with them to confirm."

Just the night before, she had felt so confident about Skiel, but she had not even spoken to Veeslau the Unbound. In front of her teacher, she felt suddenly less confident. What had he taught her? To question everything. Nothing was secured until she had actually spoken to anyone.

"And the elves?" Snorri asked.

"They would not commit to anything ahead of time." Snorri looked disappointed. How far had Nauveena actually gotten? It had felt so easy the other night. "But I cannot imagine they would side with the Magic of Order."

"The minds of elves are hard to guess at," Snorri said. "Who knows what they might do? I am not surprised they would not commit. We then have four we feel certain about. Then another seven we at least don't think would go with Fallou easily. Only eleven if everything goes well."

"We planned to speak with the dwarves."

"Another two. That gets you to thirteen. Out of twenty-six, with our vote if there is a tie. Fallou has six. Unless we think there are any we can pick off from the Magic of Order?"

Nauveena shook her head. The Protectors and Keepers traveled in a tight formation at all times. When they were not in the council, they were studying treatises on *The Book of Order*. She doubted she could even talk to them separately, let alone convince them to defect.

"Fallou has more than six as well," she said. "He has seven."

She expected Snorri to look surprised, but he took the news in stride. "Right. Clearly, General Dolcius is looking to Faulsk to solidify his claim to the throne. Since the war, he has been popular, but has no legitimacy. I am sure the Magic of Order has claimed they can give him this."

Nauveena nodded.

"Another approach might be to think of whose votes Fallou can gain," Snorri said.

Nauveena saw the wisdom he offered. "Who else would follow the Magic of Order?"

"Lyrmica for one."

"Lyrmica? Why would you say them? They are represented by Balzhamy. He trained at Athyzia."

"Yes, he might have trained here, but Balzhamy has never been a particularly good sorcerer."

Now, Nauveena's face registered surprise. She had never heard Snorri speak so critically of another, especially a sorcerer who had once studied at Athyzia.

"Yes, Balzhamy's always been something of a fraud." Snorri sighed. "Wrote one treatise on alchemy that was — if I can say — mostly plagiarized. To avoid controversy, he chose to leave Athyzia, and Lyrmica had an opening. They were in need of an alchemist, it seemed...

"And I am not sure he is that much better a court mage than he was a scholarly one. If he had more resolve, maybe the whole Alchemy Wars could have been avoided. But indeed, he was the court alchemist before and during the wars. He still is, although he claims not to transform base metals into gold, but who believes that? It has been a stain on Athyzia — the part one of our mages played in that war. Balzhamy does not seek to advise, but to serve. King Tutus might enjoy this, but it is not the role of a mage. A sorcerer should work to give those he advises what they need, not what they want."

"And why would the king of Lyrmica want to align with the Magic of Order?"

"Lyrmica has been weak ever since the Alchemy Wars. Faulsk is a close neighbor, and a strong one. I could see the king of Lyrmica sending Balzhamy here to gain further allies. And I question Balzhamy's resolve. He will do what his king wants him to, and nothing more. Even if that might not best serve Lyrmica."

Nauveena nodded in understanding. She didn't want to interrupt the spell that had caused Snorri to share his feelings so openly.

"Then five of the twenty-six are unspoken for," Snorri said. "The three merchant cities: Valinka, Phryza, Olmtpur, then Aryde and the Bogwaah. In addition to the dwarves, you should talk to them."

"But we might already have thirteen."

"*Might*. And we only need thirteen, but let us hope for more than just the majority. Let us hope to influence minds as well. We still have a chance for it, I hope."

Chapter Nine
Prophecies and Metallurgy

> "Doom gathers like shadows before the night, like scavengers to the carcass. The day nears when bones will dance and the living will exchange places with the dead. He will have many names. He will be the Dark Lord. He will be the Last Tempter. He will be the Doom Weaver, and you will cower before him."
> ~Kitrinos, the High Priestess of Xanthous
> 27 BU

"Where have you been?" Venefica asked. She and Malachite waited on the bridge leading across the lake to Nauveena's Tower of Yalde.

"Fallou." Nauveena looked around. They were alone, but she did not like being in the open. "He accused Snorri of conspiracy. He knew the three of us met with the northerners and Prince Javee and the elves."

"How curious," Malachite said.

"How could he have known?" Nauveena asked.

"Spies," Venefica said. "He is more cunning than even I gave him credit for. He must be watching us carefully."

"Who would these spies be?" Nauveena felt exposed on the bridge. Could someone be watching them right now? She thought they were alone. "I doubt any among the elves would enter his employ."

"Maybe an Obeyer is following us," Venefica suggested.

"He accused Snorri of conspiracy," Malachite said. "How did Snorri react?"

"Snorri denied it; he said he had heard nothing of the sort," Nauveena said. "Of course, he had heard nothing of the sort. So it wasn't a lie. He defended us against Fallou, but afterwards, I could not hide our dealings from him. I confessed when we were alone again."

"I am sorry, Nauveena," Venefica said. "You told us of your hesitations."

"No, he understands it was naive to not secure other votes. And after Fallou's actions today, he encouraged us to continue. He insists we speak to every member of the council — short of the Magic of Order."

"Well, he has also bought us time," Malachite said. "Although I do not know if that was by design or not. We have the rest of the afternoon and tomorrow. Snorri also controls the schedule. I trust he will put more contentious issues towards the end. And if Fallou adds anything now, it most certainly will have to wait until the other points have been discussed."

"There is more," Nauveena added. "Snorri does not think we can count on Balzhamy of Lyrmica's vote."

"Wasn't Balzhamy trained at Athyzia?" Venefica asked.

"Yes, but he has been in Lyrmica for a long time," Nauveena said.

"I feared this," Malachite said. "Snorri is probably correct. I suspected Balzhamy — and, more importantly, Lyrmica — might align themselves with the Magic of Order. Now, it seems they might have already. I have only recently received news that the Emperor of Faulsk plans to marry his son to a Lyrmican bride, a cousin of King Tutus. The marriage signals a stronger alliance between the two realms."

"Snorri believes Balzhamy has been ordered to follow Fallou's wishes," Nauveena said. "If that is the case, then Fallou would have eight votes."

"We must speak to the dwarves today," Venefica said.

"Yes, and I have been giving this some thought," Malachite said. "While Prince Javee believes the oracles' vote is safe, we might wish to speak to them on another matter. We wish to understand Fallou's intentions. Could Kìtrinos's clairvoyance not aid us there?"

"You would like a fortune?" Nauveena asked.

"It is worth a try. The druids also know means of divination, but I have not practiced them in many years. Kìtrinos is much more gifted in the art."

After speaking with Snorri, Nauveena did not want to make any more assumptions. She couldn't accept Prince Javee's confidences alone. "And we should meet with Skiel, Aryde, the merchants, and the Bogwaah."

"Very well," Malachite said. "We can meet with Kìtrinos and the dwarves before dinner. Then, I will approach the others about meeting tonight and tomorrow."

The oracles had taken residence in one of Athyzia's highest towers, with the hope that the position might bring more clairvoyance to their dreams. Reaching the tower required a walk up Athyzia's sloping rise. Athyzia had been built on the side of the mountains, and the further one went from the lake, the steeper the spaces between buildings became. In many places, stairs led from one level to the next.

The oracles currently lounged on the top of the tower. Sheets had been hung to provide shade during the warmer part of the day.

Kìtrinos, the High Priestess of Xanthous, wore the flowing yellow stola of her order. Her rank was distinguished by a golden braid worn as a belt. She lounged on a wide mattress overlooking the lake below. Her fellow oracles lounged in similar positions, surrounded by silk sheets and pillows. They had decorated the tower as if it were their temple on the faraway island of Xanthous, on the far tip of Qadantium.

"I hope we are not disturbing you," Malachite asked. Tradition had long held that males could not enter the oracles' residence, but these had been relaxed in recent generations.

"You are welcome, druid." Kìtrinos waved the three over from her position on the mattress. Her long limbs were tanned from the southern sun.

Malachite, Venefica, and Nauveena weaved their way through the assembled pillows and mattresses to the High Priestess in the far corner. Many wealthy patrons insisted that the oracles of Xanthous want for nothing.

"In the early morning hour, I dreamed of three clouds converging on a barren field," Kìtrinos said. "When they converged, they began to rain, and many clovers and roses and lilacs sprouted from the field, soon covering it. You seek my help?"

"Maybe we could speak privately?" Nauveena asked, still worried about Fallou's potential spies.

"I do not understand," Kitrinos said. "You are in the company of the Priestesses of Xanthous."

Nauveena looked around her. On each cushion lay similarly tan women in yellow. Nauveena worried about Fallou's spies, but infiltrating the Temple of Xanthous would have been quite an achievement.

"It is fine." Venefica had the same thought. It hardly seemed the other oracles were listening, anyways. Many had drifted off to sleep.

"Thank you for meeting with us," Malachite said.

"Javee said you have been very busy with meetings. I am glad to be worthy of one." Kitrinos motioned for them to sit down on her mattress and pillows. Malachite did so awkwardly, worried of his muddy boots on the clean silks. He had more trouble than Nauveena or Venefica sitting in a crisscross position.

"We need your counsel," Malachite said. "In today's meeting, Fallou, the First Protector of Leem, stated he only wants one magic — the Magic of Order. We wonder if he intends to add this matter to the agenda. And if so, does he have the votes to achieve it?"

Kitrinos ate red grapes from a ceramic bowl positioned so she could reach it with the least amount of movement possible. "You wish to see the future?"

"At least as far as Fallou is concerned," Malachite said.

"We worry he will add the item once he has the votes," Venefica said.

"The matter of prophecy is not as simple as you have been led to believe," Kitrinos said. "The future does not carry on a conversation. You cannot ask questions of it and have it answer. The third eye must be opened, and it cannot be opened with the weight of such questions. It can only be opened with an acceptance of the possibility of all futures, all outcomes. Only then will the future communicate."

"I'm open," Venefica said. Nauveena doubted it was as simple as saying it out loud.

Kitrinos's expression confirmed the matter was not as simple. She looked from Venefica to Nauveena to Malachite. "Divination can be achieved in many ways. My third eye has opened to the point where I do not need to rely on tea leaves or crystal balls. However, everyone's future is their own. And to see another's future, they must be open. Since the

First Protector is not present, his future might be blocked from me. But if you are open to sharing your future with me, I might see yours. And if the First Protector features in that future, I might understand his. At least insofar as the role he plays in it."

"That would work," Malachite said. "We are open to trying anything."

"The sun is high, and the time is not strong for divination, but I will try. Come close."

Kitrinos closed her eyes and reached out her hand expectantly. Malachite looked to Venefica and Nauveena, unsure what to do. Kitrinos remained motionless, as if she were a statue, her eyes closed and her hand out.

Eventually, Malachite inched closer and reached out his hand. He placed it in Kitrinos's. The High Priestess clenched his hand tightly.

For a moment, a cloud crossed over the noon sun, and the light atop the tower dimmed. Kitrinos breathed deeply.

Then she released her grip. Malachite pulled back his hand, rubbing it as if it had been injured.

Kitrinos opened her eyes and blinked. "A long journey," she said. She stared deeply into Malachite's eyes to confirm what she had seen. "A long journey is ahead of you. One you must make quickly. Many will wait eagerly for you to return."

"To where?" Malachite asked.

"The future is cloudy. I cannot speak on the specifics. Only that it will not be your choice to make this journey."

"Is Fallou there?" Venefica asked.

Kitrinos shook her head. "He is not. He did not appear in the future of the druid. At least, not in the pieces of his future I could see."

"How about me?" Venefica reached out her hand

Kitrinos closed her eyes and took the witch's hand. Once again, the oracle breathed deeply and gripped Venefica's hand tightly.

After a few moments, she released Venefica's hand and looked up. She said nothing.

"Yes?" Venefica asked. "What did you see?"

"I'd rather not say."

"But you saw something? Why will you not tell me?"

"Because the details are indeed foggy, and with such fog, what I saw would only worry you."

"You must tell me what you saw," Venefica said.

"You conceal yourself from me. Or I could see more. There is much you do not want me to see."

"I am open. As I have said before. If you cannot see my future, it is your own skill. Now tell me what you saw there."

"Do not doubt my skill in the matter," Kitrinos said. "If you insist, I will tell you what I saw, even if you might not like it."

"Tell me," Venefica insisted.

"A betrayal waits for you."

"'A betrayal?'"

"That is all I could see," Kitrinos said. "You have gone to great lengths to conceal yourself to others, and it has clouded your future. I cannot see easily."

"So maybe you are mistaken on the betrayal?"

"The betrayal, at least, was very clear," Kitrinos said.

"And no Fallou?" Venefica asked.

Kitrinos shook her head.

"Of course," Venefica said. "Try Nauveena next."

Venefica nudged Nauveena to offer her hand next. Reluctantly, she held out her hand, which the oracle seized.

Immediately, a cloud again passed across the sun. The tower became very dark, as if it were night. Nauveena walked alone along a dark tunnel. She could only see ahead of her from a lantern she carried. The light cast forward twenty feet, and she followed it ahead.

The tunnel twisted and turned. One hallway led to another. Down stairs and through more doorways. The end of a corridor would branch into multiple passageways. Nauveena was not wandering a tunnel, but a maze.

A strong breeze rushed down the corridor. The flame within the lantern was snuffed. The light was extinguished, casting the tunnel into darkness. Nauveena felt blindly against the walls. She could not see. She felt the cold bricks and she called out in the dark, but no response came.

Kitrinos released her hand, and Nauveena pulled it back quickly. Her vision returned. The cloud passed, and the tower returned with the young oracles lounging on their cushions, eating their grapes.

Kitrinos saw the look of panic on Nauveena's face. "You saw then?"

Nauveena nodded.

"It was quite vivid. You are very open, to have such a clear vision at this hour."

"But what does it mean?" Nauveena was still shaking from the vision.

"What did you see?" Malachite asked.

Nauveena wished she could describe it to him.

"The sorceress was lost in a dark hallway," Kìtrinos said. "A labyrinth with many forked paths and only a single lamp to guide her. But this could not last, and soon, she did not have any light, and the confusing place became one of blindness as well."

"Where was I?" Nauveena asked. Athyzia did not have any rooms like the ones she had seen.

"Only time can reveal the truth of the prophecy," Kìtrinos said. "Have you had visions before? You might have the gift of scrying."

"I haven't," Nauveena said. "Not that I can think of."

"Is there any way for you to see into Fallou's future?" Venefica asked.

"Tonight, in my dreams, I will focus on the council," Kìtrinos said. "I will share any visions you might find relevant."

Venefica's questions on Fallou had brought Nauveena out of her trance. She now remembered Snorri's suggestions. "Perhaps there is another future matter you could shed light on," Nauveena said. "Without the need for prophecy?"

"And what might that be?" Kìtrinos asked.

"We believe Fallou might propose something to the council," Nauveena said. "A vote to ban all types of magic except his own. If such a proposal is made, how would you vote?"

"My prophesies are not derived from order," Kìtrinos said. "It would be a simple vote. You do not need the tarot to know which way I would side."

Since her vision, Nauveena had felt uneasy. Now, she felt the uneasiness release. As she had guessed, the oracles would not side with the Magic of Order.

Like many kingdoms, the dwarves of the north and south had lost communication with each other during the war. Between them lay a continent in turmoil. Now, they looked to the council as a time to reestablish those lines that had been severed.

When the council was not in session — and the dwarves were not enjoying the entertainments of the northerners — they met in the Library of Erudition. Out of all of Athyzia's libraries, Nauveena listed the Library of Erudition as one of her favorites — in the top five, at least. Tall stained-glass windows depicting the mages of old illuminated the thousands of volumes housed within. Bookcases rose so high that their top shelves could only be reached with ladders and spiraling stairs.

Among the library's collections were many works on mining, metallurgy, prospecting, and engineering, which interested the dwarves greatly. They raced up and down the library's ladders, finding books and stacking them unopened in the center. If the collection were not enough excitement, for the first time since the war began, the northern dwarves had access to coffee. The drink only energized them further.

They pulled more books from the shelves than they could possibly read. And they collected more than books related to their craft. Many were in more archaic Literary Qadantine which the dwarves could not read, but which contained detailed illustrations of anatomy that the dwarves found humorous and couldn't help showing to each other.

By now, the stacks had grown so high, they concealed the dwarves behind them. *It will take forever to put them all back correctly*, Nauveena thought as she, Venefica, and Malachite wandered through the stacks, searching for the dwarves' two leaders.

They found them in the library's center. They only struggled to locate them because of the quantity of books forming a maze throughout. More books were probably now stacked in the center than were sitting on the shelves.

"We must send aid to Iron Hall sooner or later." Lord Ferrum slammed his fist onto the table. The volumes stacked on the table bounced with the force, threatening to topple.

"You know we would if we were not recovering from the war," Galena, the representative of Axeforge, said.

"Gemhaven is recovering too."

"But we are not fighters. We will not have many to send."

"Ummm, hello." Nauveena needed to move several books off the top of a pile so she could peer over it at the two dwarves seated below.

"Hello, yes, sorceress," Lord Ferrum barked. "We told you before, we will put them all back. We know where each goes."

"No, no, it's not all that," Nauveena said. "Although, yes, I do hope you know where these go?"

"Of course we do," Lord Ferrum said. "Us dwarves have memories as hard as steel. And as deep as the mines of Gemhaven."

"We hoped to speak to you about the council." Venefica appeared on the other side of the table. She pulled a large encyclopedia from a wall of books and peered through it.

"Ahh, is that the witch?" Galena asked.

"Yes, it is." Venefica tilted her head so more of her face appeared through the opening.

"Welcome, then. What of the council do you wish to speak of?" Galena asked.

"I am here too." Malachite stood on his tiptoes to appear over a stack in the center.

"Druid, welcome," Lord Ferrum said. "We are quite glad to get the day to ourselves. We have many matters to discuss. But the council is also quite interesting. We are happy to discuss this as well."

Up close, Nauveena could see Lord Ferrum's nose in closer detail. In a battle with a cave troll, he had suffered a terrible blow from the troll's mallet. He'd survived with a concussion and a broken nose, but the nose had never settled correctly. The top half and the bottom half now ran in two different directions.

The Dwarf Lord took a long sip of coffee, then held the mug aloft. "Have you tried this stuff? Great for our studies and getting through the conference. Would you like some?"

Nauveena noticed a mad gleam in the dwarf's eyes. How many cups had he had? She, Venefica, and Malachite shook their heads.

"Our primary questions concern the Magic of Order." Malachite had gotten tired of standing on tiptoe, and now began reassembling the books around him to clear a view. "What do you make of their proposals?"

Lord Ferrum rubbed the portion of his nose where the two different halves collided. "A strange question. A stumper. I have not given it much thought."

"Oh, knock it off. You have thought of it," Galena said. "Of course, the southern dwarves have much more contact with them, being so close to Faulsk and all. I can't say I am much surprised. The common folks of those lands have suffered through wars of magic for almost a century now. I expect they are sick of it."

Many rumors spoke of dwarf women having beards similar to their men. But these were only rumors. Galena looked very much like any human woman compressed into a four-and-a-half foot frame. Broad shoulders. Dark, jet-black hair. And glittering diamonds studding her clothing.

"They did not even make that proposal, though," Lord Ferrum said.

"No, but I wonder if they did not put that queen up to it," Galena said.

"And how would you vote on the matter?" Venefica asked.

"I don't see why it is much of our business," Galena said. "If a sorcerer wants to control a common folk and that common folk is too dumb to stop it, then let it happen. As long as they are not enchanting me."

"Dwarves are not easily enchanted." Lord Ferrum tapped his temple with a stubby finger. "Too clever for that, we are."

Nauveena got an idea. "And on the restrictions on necromancy? Some kingdoms are not keen on that idea, either."

"Ahh, I can guess who you've been talking with," Lord Ferrum said.

"What do you mean by that?" Galena asked. Lord Ferrum leaned over to whisper in her ear, and her face registered shock at what he had to say.

"Would you side with those kingdoms on the issue?" Nauveena asked. She, of course, saw the rationale for restricting necromancy. But if she could get more votes for the northerners' issue, they might be more likely to stand against Fallou.

"Aye, I don't care much either way," Lord Ferrum said.

"I can't say I do, either," Galena said.

"But I do believe your mines benefit from its use?" Venefica asked.

"They might," Lord Ferrum said. "I never said they didn't. But I don't bother much with our gems after we trade them. What Ümlaut and Caron do with them after is their business. I don't mess with the sea for a reason. Do you know some of the crews have escaped? Turned to pirating those straits too, in case the dragon alone were not bad enough."

"Have they, now?" Galena asked.

"The crews?" Nauveena asked.

"Yes, the crews."

"What crews?"

"The dead ones, of course. Skiel employs all types of necromancers, and some are not particularly good at it. The spell should wear off after they've passed the dragon and gotten to Skiegs. But sometimes it doesn't. Those reanimated dead get lost, gain consciousness, and then what are they supposed to do?"

"So, they are just out there?"

"Yup, and with a ship. There's a whole lot of them. So the dragon isn't the only issue."

"That sounds like quite the problem," Nauveena said.

Lord Ferrum nodded. "All's I care is the dragon stays at sea. Does not get any ideas of coming to my mountains. As long as Skiel keeps paying her tax, she will. If they want to use the undead, that's their business."

Nauveena would need to report to the northerners. She had brought the issue up and possibly found votes to carve out certain uses of the magic. "We can count on you to vote against any major restrictions on magic?"

"Is that what you think the Magic of Order will propose?" Galena asked.

"We are still speculating at this point, but yes," Nauveena said.

"I wouldn't want to see too many restrictions," Galena said. She looked to Lord Ferrum.

"Me neither. Leave each other alone as much as possible," he said.

"But while we're on the subject," Galena said. "Of the Magic of Order that is. There's something that might interest you."

"What is that?"

Galena leaned forward to whisper. "A messenger from Balzhamy, the mage from Lyrmica, approached us the night before the council was set to begin. He came to tell us that the king of Lyrmica is considering allowing dwarves to reenter the mines of the Last Mountains."

"Convenient timing," Malachite said.

"What did they ask in return?" Venefica asked.

"He said we could operate at the previous tax rate — forty percent."

"A tax? They did not ask for your vote?"

Galena shook her head.

"And what did you say?" Venefica asked.

"Forty percent? Absolutely not. They would gain more from the arrangement than us. Once, the dwarves found that tax rate acceptable. But no longer. We remember when the men of Lyrmica became unhappy with the arrangement. They wanted more than forty percent. But we refused.

"In response, Lyrmica kicked us out. Violently. They blockaded the mountains. Starved us. Smoked us out. The injustice has not been forgotten. Then Lyrmica tried to work the mines. Soon, they found they could not mine as quickly as the dwarves. Receiving forty percent of what the dwarves mined proved to be more than keeping all of what they could mine themselves."

"The sudden decrease in production sent Lyrmica's treasury into a spiral." Lord Ferrum chuckled. "They had no other option than to turn to the alchemists. And we all know how that went."

"They knew they couldn't return to the dwarves," Galena said. "But they are now. Just not at the same rate. Which is not acceptable. We have not mined those mountains in almost half a century. We are due back payments."

"Those mines have been unproductive that entire time," Lord Ferrum said. "It would take much work to make them operational again. And anything over twenty percent would be more gold than the Lyrmican treasury is currently receiving."

"If that was the rate, would you accept the offer?" Malachite asked.

Galena nodded. "The dwarves have long looked to the Last Mountains, thinking of their potential. We long to return. But the rate cannot remain the same."

Chapter Ten
The Witch of Pravulum

> "The Deceiver King is worshipped by those we call witches. They seek refuge in him, hoping he will allow them to continue their abuses of magic. He seeks to shelter them and allow them to continue their perversions beneath his dominion."
>
> ~*A Treatise on Witches*
> The Ultimate Defender of Order
> 20 BU

Athyzia's banquet hall had transformed into a tavern. At any hour of the day, at least half the tables would be filled with the knights and servants and squires who had traveled with the council members. The barrels of Clovis ale had yet to run dry, and many expected they never would.

Nauveena, Venefica, and Malachite finished with the dwarves well before dinner. The day had been productive, but they still needed to talk with six other realms: the southern merchant cities of Phryza, Valinka, and Olmtpur, as well as Skiel, Aryde, and the Bogwaah.

"I do not think we can just show up unannounced," Malachite said as they left the Library of Erudition. "Let me go and talk with them. Perhaps I can schedule meetings for tonight or tomorrow."

With Malachite gone, Nauveena and Venefica found a table in the corner. They had two steins of ale brought over, then leaned towards each other to speak in more hushed tones.

"Very clever how you brought up necromancy," Venefica said.

"I didn't want to just say Skiel is employing the art," Nauveena said. "It wouldn't be right. But we will have to broach it with enough members to get an exception for it. I thought the dwarves would be the most receptive — at least the northern dwarves, since they stand to benefit from it. And it seems they already know."

"We will have to talk to the dwarves further. I would like to get their thoughts on the Elf Laws. We need to build a contingent on that as well."

"Yes, then we can at least satisfy the elves and the northerners that we are working for their causes too. At the very least, it does not seem the dwarves would vote with Fallou. With them and the oracles, do we have thirteen?"

"I wouldn't count the dwarves so fast," Venefica said.

"You wouldn't?"

"The messenger from Lyrmica."

"What about it?"

"I think we are seeing the beginning of Fallou's scheming."

"But they did not ask for their vote."

"Not yet," Venefica said. "But they established that the mines of the Last Mountains are on the table. Only at an unfavorable tax rate. The dwarves do not particularly care how men handle their own magic. They might think their vote is a small price to pay for the Last Mountains."

"But it is Lyrmica who approached, not Fallou."

"You heard Snorri and Malachite today. Lyrmica is doing Fallou and Faulsk's bidding. Faulsk has been propping Lyrmica up since the Alchemy Wars."

"I see." Nauveena felt suddenly uneasy.

"Malachite was right. Balzhamy is aligned with Faulsk to some degree; otherwise they would not have approached the dwarves with such an offer."

"Fallou keeps gaining influence," Nauveena said. "And he is trying to gain more with this offer to the dwarves."

"I, for one, am just happy we are finally seeing some of Fallou's plan in action. Our suspicions are being proven correct. That oracle could not tell us much, but the dwarves could — even if they did not know it."

"But we cannot count the dwarves in our thirteen?"

"They are a tenuous number, at least," Venefica said. "But better to know their price than to think we have it. You are right; we must talk to the remaining members. We must hedge our bets. Get insurance."

"Malachite. Druissia." Nauveena began to count on her fingers. "Qadantium. The oracles. Four we have confidence in."

"Do not forget Dunisk."

"Yes, Dunisk." Nauveena had forgotten. "But I have not spoken to Queen Yellialah yet. The dwarves bring up a good point — did she not propose the issue that is leading to restrictions on magic? The slippery slope as you say?"

"Trust me on this. I have Dunisk," Venefica said.

Just then, Malachite entered the hall from the far end. Venefica waved him over.

"I have spoken to the southern merchants and Aryde." He sat and looked around for a servant to bring him a stein. "They are willing to meet with us tomorrow."

"Thankfully, Snorri gave us the day," Venefica said. "We might be able to talk to everyone before the next session."

"There is only one thing," Malachite said.

"What is it?" Nauveena asked.

"The southern merchants — they are unwilling to meet with — " The druid looked at Venefica. "To meet with you."

"Me? Why?"

Malachite's face hardened. "Don't make me say it."

Venefica slammed her stein on the table. Nauveena expected her eyes to erupt in flame as they did whenever she became angry. Instead, her features simply sharpened. She fought to contain herself, but not from flying into a rage. She worked to conceal her sadness.

"After everything, they still do not — " She could not finish.

"Many in the east and south do not understand," Malachite said. "They will learn eventually. Don't take it personally."

"Fine." Venefica pushed back from the table. Her demeanor softened, and she returned to her previous calm. "Fine. Meet with the southern cities. Meet with Aryde, too. I can meet with Skiel and the Bogwaah. Divide and conquer."

After not sleeping the night before, Nauveena quickly fell asleep when she returned to her room. But her sleep was not restful. She quickly began dreaming.

She entered the long corridors she had seen when the oracle touched her hand. The hallways stretched before her. She wandered forward and the path split, adding more and more layers, more and more options.

The darkness remained ever-present, as it had before. She had only her lantern to light the way. But now, she knew it would extinguish soon. She hurried to find the end before the lantern went out. She wished to see more of the corridors before she was cast into darkness.

As she hurried, she heard footsteps behind her. An echo. Could they be her own? She wanted to stop and listen, but she had to rush on.

The footsteps came behind her. The pace quickened. She paused where the path split, deciding on a direction. The sound of walking continued. Heels clicking on cold stone. They continued for seconds after she paused. Then they paused as well. A long echo.

She hurried on. She hiked up her dress so she could move along the corridors faster. She held the lantern high to light more of the path before her. In front, she saw only more stone bricks. The walls did not change, no matter how often she rounded a corner or changed direction.

The footsteps following her became louder, closer. They were not hers. She knew that much, at least. At every fork, she heard them continue a moment longer than an echo would.

The sounds came closer now. They had to be right behind her. A forked path. She paused and turned around to find the sound. Who could be behind her? She feared what she might find.

As she spun, the sudden motion snuffed the light. Right before darkness consumed everything, she saw a figure watching her from the other end of the tunnel.

Then darkness. She was alone in a sea of black.

Nauveena woke in a cold sweat. She clutched the sheets to her. The room was dark but familiar. *It was a dream,* she told herself, panting. What had the oracle said? Did she have the art? Where were the corridors? Where had she been wandering?

When she had calmed her breath, she reached for the candle next to her bed. She lit it and let the flicker of light bounce about the room. She had been right. It was her room.

She lay back down and got further control of her breath, but she could not sleep again.

Nauveena did not sleep the rest of the night. She feared becoming lost in the labyrinth again and hearing the strange pitter-patter of whoever was following her. But most of all, she feared finding her way out of the labyrinth and learning what might wait there.

She met Malachite after breakfast. He sat on the terrace, some way from the tables. Without the council, the terrace was quiet and peaceful.

A squirrel stood on the druid's knee, speaking to him in warbling squeaks. As Nauveena approached, she heard the end of their conversation.

"Yes, of course, quite unfortunate," Malachite said.

Squeaks from the squirrel.

"Most certainly. I will bring it to the council."

The squeaks became more excited.

Seeing Nauveena, Malachite said, "I must be going. We can speak again."

The squirrel jumped from Malachite's knee and gave the squeak equivalent of a goodbye. The druid nodded politely, then stood and went to the sorceress. He led Nauveena off the terrace.

"What was all that about?" Nauveena asked when they had gotten out of the squirrel's earshot.

"He speaks of an oak tree felled by the Osseomancer's army."

"Oh, dear," Nauveena said, concerned for the small animal.

"The oak produced the best nuts in the whole forest, and now, it is gone. He wants me to ask the council to put it back."

The druid represented the centaurs, but also all the beasts and birds of Jenor. Many had come to find him with issues he could present on their behalf. However, in the grand scheme of council subjects, the druid seemed at a loss to bring up the felling of a single tree — even if it might seem a great deal to the squirrel.

"I tried to explain that we can plant a new oak, but it will not produce nuts in his lifetime. He asks why we cannot return the tree with magic.

But trees will be lost. If not by the Osseomancer, then by storms and the passing of time. The council cannot reverse this."

Nauveena looked back at the squirrel. Sitting next to the stone bench, it looked very small. The single tree might seem a small issue, but to the squirrel, it was everything. She felt sorry that nothing could be done.

They planned to meet with the independent merchant cities first. But as they walked, something weighed heavy on Nauveena's mind. As heavy as the lost oak had weighed on the squirrel's.

"Can I ask you a question?"

"You certainly can," Malachite said.

"It concerns Venefica."

"Let me guess: you are curious how she came to serve him."

Nauveena nodded. "I had not expected to work so closely with her during this council. And now that I have, I believe I have actually grown somewhat fond of her — in a way. And so I do not understand how she could have once done his bidding."

"She has become quite an ally, hasn't she?" Malachite mused. "I will try to shed what light I can on her, but who can ever truly know what is in the hearts of others? Still, I know some of how she came to be in his thrall, and maybe that tale will put you more at ease to trust her."

Malachite and Nauveena walked along a tree-lined path overlooking the lake. The merchants had taken residence in one of Athyzia's central libraries, close to the terrace. The two had time before they were set to meet them.

"The witch has not spoken to me about it directly," Malachite began. "I imagine she will not. But I have learned what I can from others. During the Alchemy Wars, King Hylium of Dunisk wished to sail against Lyrmica. Dunisk too had been hurt by Lyrmica's false gold. The king amassed a great army. He planned to join the coalition aligned against Lyrmica, to seek vengeance for the alchemist gold they had received as payment for debts.

"But they could not sail. The winds of the Alcyon Sea stood still, and Dunisk's fleet remained in the harbor. King Hylium tried everything. Sacrificed oxen. Consulted seers. Consulted mermaids. Consulted mages. Nothing worked. When the king had almost given up, the Osseomancer appeared. He claimed he could move the wind. He would only take a small token as payment."

"The Osseomancer?" Nauveena gasped. "And the king agreed?"

"You must remember, this was many years ago. He was not known as the Osseomancer then. He was not the Osseomancer or the Doom Weaver or any of his other names. Only Comus. A powerful wizard, but not much was thought of making a deal with him. His true deviousness was not then known. He was not then corrupted, or — more likely — he was, but he concealed it."

"So the king made the deal?"

"He did. King Hylium thought nothing of it and agreed. The winds moved, and Dunisk went off to war. They fought Lyrmica and won. Only after King Hylium returned home did the Osseomancer appear to ask for his prize."

"What did he want?" Nauveena asked.

"The king's daughter," Malachite said.

"Queen Yellialah?"

"She was Princess Yellialah at the time."

"What did the king do?"

"What could he do? He had no choice but to accept. He had struck a deal with a powerful wizard. Betraying him would be worse. Some wonder if the Osseomancer had not manufactured the still winds in the first place. Princess Yellialah's beauty was known throughout the southern kingdoms, and the Osseomancer had long wanted her for a prize."

"So the Osseomancer took Yellialah?"

Malachite nodded. "He did. Once the king agreed, the Osseomancer vanished with her, bringing her to Pravulum. King Hylium's wife fell into a terrible depression. She would not leave her room. She refused to eat. She cried and wailed for her daughter to be returned.

"Of course, King Hylium could not bear to tell his kingdom what had happened. There were rumors, but the court managed to squash these. The whole kingdom was told that the princess had died. After five terrible years of war, the loss of the princess was too much. She was known as the sunlight of Dunisk. She had kept spirits raised during the war. The kingdom succumbed instantly to mourning and quickly became a grim place. The court wore shrouds of black.

"Princess Yellialah had been engaged to Prince Jarul, heir to the throne of Qadantium — the future king and future father to Prince Javee. This engagement had to be called off. It would have forged a powerful alliance between Dunisk and Qadantium. Instead, Jarul married the cousin of King Bane, linking him to Druissia.

"King Hylium blamed himself for trusting the wizard. He shuddered to think what Comus planned for her. He drank heavily and plotted ways to bring his daughter back. In secret, he sent messengers to Pravulum, telling the Osseomancer he could name his price in exchange for the princess. He offered land. Gold. Titles. But each, the Osseomancer turned away. King Hylium would need to do something else to rescue his daughter. Finally, he settled on a plan. In his court, at the time, was a young witch from Zeelma."

"Venefica?"

"Yes. Back then, she worked in a simpler capacity. She prepared potions for lethargy, impotence, and insomnia. She predicted horoscopes and acted as a midwife. But the king went to her with an urgent mission. By now, the Osseomancer's penchant for beauty was well known. If a young, beautiful witch were to arrive at Pravulum asking for his advice and seeking to read in his library, the Osseomancer would not turn her away. Once inside Pravulum, King Hylium only hoped Venefica could find a way to rescue Yellialah.

"Venefica accepted the challenge. She was younger then, and courageous in a way. But I do not think she knew what she was up against. She rode to Pravulum. One of the Osseomancer's generals met her outside the gates. She explained she wanted an audience with the wizard, to learn from him. Curious, the Osseomancer welcomed her in. She charmed him and asked him questions and dined with him, and slowly gained his trust. She used a skill that was not quite magic — she laughed at all his jokes and thought all he said was interesting.

"But all the while, she was planning and plotting. She was learning the layout of Pravulum. How to leave without being noticed. And most of all, she was looking for the young princess. Of course, Yellialah was not difficult to find. The Osseomancer made her quite visible. Royalty. Serving his wine. Even then, he could not contain his vanity.

"Venefica remained at Pravulum for many months, slowly gaining the Osseomancer's trust so she could move about the citadel with ease. Only when she had lulled him into a false feeling of security did she make her move. Late at night, when the Osseomancer was sleeping, Venefica slipped from his bed and went to the servants' quarters.

"She found Yellialah there, asleep. She clasped a hand over the princess's mouth, so when she woke, she would not make a sound in her fright. Venefica shook the princess awake and whispered to her, explaining who she was and why she had come and that she planned to rescue her.

"Venefica had planned well. They could slip out the western entrance behind the mountains. There, King Hylium's men had been camped for months, waiting to escort them away safely once they escaped. But Princess Yellialah refused."

"Refused?"

"Yes, refused," Malachite said. "She would not go with Venefica."

"But why?"

"Physical bonds alone did not hold Yellialah in Pravulum. She had been bewitched by the Osseomancer's charms. She wanted to stay. She loved him, even though he made her serve wine like a common wench. When Venefica took her hand off Yellialah's mouth, the princess screamed so loudly, she woke all of Pravulum."

"No." Nauveena covered her own mouth with her hand.

"Pravulum's guards rushed to Yellialah's room. Venefica fought them off, but then the Osseomancer arrived, and Venefica was outmatched. He spun bonds of magic upon her and placed her in his dungeon. And there she remained for many weeks while the Osseomancer thought of what to do with her."

"I cannot believe the princess would not leave," Nauveena said.

"The Osseomancer's enchantments were very strong. And while the princess was of royal blood, she was still quite common and unable to do magic. She had been at Pravulum for many years, and all the while, the Osseomancer spun spells against her. She did not stand a chance.

"For all Venefica's slyness and daring and planning, she had overlooked this matter. She had always assumed Princess Yellialah wished to escape. But she had seen the young princess serving wine cheerfully at each dinner. Yellialah's mind belonged to the Osseomancer."

"I might have made the same mistake," Nauveena said. The morning had stretched on, but now she needed to hear the rest of the story. They would be late to speak with the merchants.

"At last, the Osseomancer went to the witch. Despite her betrayal, he meant to release her. He would only hold common folk in servitude. He would not hold a witch in such a way. It was then that Venefica made her last gamble. She had thought of it long while she had been imprisoned. She still wished to free the princess."

"After all that?"

Malachite nodded. "At first, I am sure she was angry and cursed the princess. But being locked away in the dungeon for weeks softened her. She understood the princess was young and innocent and defenseless against the Osseomancer. Venefica made one final offer. An 'equal exchange' she called it."

"No." Nauveena already guessed the offer.

"Yes," Malachite said. "She offered herself for the princess. As beautiful and royal as the princess was, she was common. Would a witch not be more useful as the Osseomancer's servant? The Osseomancer considered this. He had seen Venefica's potential. The thought of a witch, capable of magic, in his employ intrigued him. He had made many servants out of the common folk. Even a princess was less intriguing than a witch, willing and able to serve him. She would be his crown jewel.

"He accepted Venefica's proposal and released the princess. Even then, Yellialah refused to leave. She had to be carried away against her will. For many years, the Osseomancer's spells lasted. Yellialah had to be watched carefully by her governesses and servants for fear of her running back to Pravulum. Many mages worked tirelessly to reverse the spells. Some think these efforts are what have weakened her now and left her sickly."

"And in exchange, Venefica became his servant?"

Malachite nodded.

"So she did serve the Osseomancer?" Nauveena's heart sank. She knew the rumors, but after getting to know Venefica, she had wished they might prove false.

"Yes, although now you know the circumstances. At first, I am sure he used her as a common folk maid, but soon, he came to rely on her powers. She worked as his attendant. Venefica learned much under his tutelage. She remained his servant for years during the war before escaping."

"How did she escape?"

"That, I wish I knew myself," Malachite said. "Only that she did. But now, we are running late for our meeting, and we should not keep capitalists waiting. They value hours almost as much as they value coin. I only hope I did not leave you with more questions."

Chapter Eleven
Merchants and Ministers

> "The yoke of oppressions has been thrown off. We have awoken to a glorious day of self-government. The people will now determine the direction of their lives, and not tyrants."
>
> ~*Aryde Proclamation of Freedom*
> 28 BU

"And this is why the merchants will not meet with Venefica?" Nauveena asked.

Malachite nodded. They now walked with purpose towards the library housing the merchants.

"But she only served the Osseomancer to save another."

"I doubt the cities of the south know the full story," Malachite said. "She served the Osseomancer for many years. Years during which his treachery increased. Before he went to war, the Osseomancer sent Venefica as his emissary to many kingdoms and cities, offering them much riches if they joined him — and threats if they did not. This is her lasting image to many. They called her the Witch of Pravulum. They remember her well as the Osseomancer's messenger. Then she remained by his side for the first decade of the war. Everyone has forgotten why, only that she did. Especially the common folk; they have short memories."

"This is why Queen Yellialah has pledged her vote to Venefica, then," Nauveena said.

"I believe so," Malachite said. They had reached the arched entrance to the Library of Practicalities. Out of Athyzia's libraries, it was one of the smallest, and Nauveena hardly ever visited it. But the merchants had chosen it as their offices while away from their home.

While the independent merchant cities of the south — Phryza, Valinka, and Olmtpur — had separate charters and operated independently, they had much in common, and often met with each other to regulate trade and tariffs. They, of course, had lobbied for a vote for each of them. They were as skilled in negotiating as Fallou, if not more so.

Despite their separate votes, Malachite expected the merchants to vote as one. Their interests were aligned on most issues. As such, he had set up a meeting with Grufton Mann of Valinka. If they could persuade him, they likely could persuade the other two in turn.

The library's ceilings were low, with thin windows, and only enough room to stack coins atop each other. The merchants had collected many coins, which they had brought bankers to count. These bankers weaved their own magic of usury and profit margins: the art of making small portions of numbers proliferate into vast sums. The bankers moved about the library, transferring coins, stacking them, counting them, writing arithmetic on parchment, and trading stocks and bonds with the merchants in their strange three-sided hats.

Nauveena saw the treasurer of Olmtpur, Loblic Haleem, eagerly counting a stack of coins in a back corner. She did not see Phryza's representative, Ivalka Puchee in the library. She would later learn the mayor had been visiting the dwarves, taking their orders for more coffee.

The merchants had not expected Athyzia to be so profitable. But they had also not expected the dwarves to be so fond of coffee. Now that they'd found an underserved market, they had already sent word back to their home cities. Soon, merchants would be sailing across the Halcyon Sea to the Distant Lands to find the finest coffee beans they could. The dwarves would be only too willing to part with their gold and gems.

Many had come to Athyzia to meet, and so had supply and demand. A supply of coffee from the merchants and demand from the dwarves. A supply of gold from the dwarves and an even stronger demand from the merchants.

"You're late." A secretary sat a small table at the front of the library, waiting to welcome — or perhaps scold — the merchants' visitors. "Ten minutes." He tapped a strange mechanical contraption on the table next to him.

Nauveena had read about these devices, manufactured in Olmtpur to replace sundials and sand glasses. They provided accurate measurements of time down to the second. Not even the Temporal Mage could do that.

"No worries." Grufton Mann, the leader of the Merchants' Guild, intercepted them. "No worries at all. Come in, and we can talk."

Grufton led them through the small library to a corner room he used as an office. They passed the bankers and merchants at their work transforming smaller numbers into larger ones.

"You wanted to see me?" he asked when they had all sat down. He took off his three-sided hat and laid it on the desk.

"We come out of curiosity," Malachite said. "Some of it, I told you last night. The council is going differently than we expected, and so we want to gauge how everyone is feeling. Of course, we are doing this off the books, so we appreciate your discretion."

"Of course," Grufton Mann said as if it were the simplest concept in the world. Of course, while secrecy might not be foreign to him, magic was. "I must admit, this whole council is all quite strange to me," he said. "I am out of my depths in many ways. I do not use magic and know few who do. Having said that, I am thankful to have been invited. I have heard of similar councils in the Distant Lands, to balance the relations between magic. I think it is a good idea in concept. Valinka is glad to have a seat at the table."

A city of canals and shop keepers, Valinka was perhaps the wealthiest city in all of Jenor. That wealth had given them independence, alone to do business as they pleased, without a king or ruler, only an oligarchy of their wealthiest merchants.

"And we are glad to have you," Malachite said. "A council of only mages would not work. The common folk must have a voice, and we appreciate you giving them one."

"We are also happy to offer any needed context," Nauveena said. "If a topic is over your head."

"Well, that, I might have to consider," Grufton said. "As for a voice of the common folk, I have never considered myself very *common*. Neither have many in Valinka, or the other cities, as far as I know. We are less reliant on magic there, so perhaps the difference does not seem so stark to us. We care more for skills of sailing than weaving spells."

"And what of the Magic of Order?" Malachite asked. "Is it prevalent in Valinka?"

"There are those who practice it, yes," Grufton said. "I do not pay it much mind. Their Obeyers do not interfere in business, and so we do not interfere with them."

"In particular, we are concerned the Magic of Order might propose a ban on other forms of magic," Nauveena said, feeling the need to be more direct.

Grufton Mann nodded, thinking. "And you'd like to know if I would support that?"

"Yes," Nauveena said.

"It would depend on the types of magic, I suppose. We have seen how destructive magic can be. I do not think I would be against limiting some of its use."

"What about all magic besides that of the Magic of Order?" Nauveena said.

"Is this on the table? Is this what you would propose?"

"No, no, not at all," Nauveena said. "We hope it is not proposed. But if it is, we would like to know which way the votes would go."

"I see." Grufton Mann looked around his desk as if an answer might lay there. Instead, there were only scrolls with orders and receipts written on them.

Nauveena too looked at his desk, hoping to find clarity there. He did not seem to understand. Did he think she and Malachite wanted to ban other magics? His unfamiliarity with the subject was greater than she realized.

"We hope to settle many issues at this conference." Nauveena tried to be clearer still. "In the hopes that magic may continue to be practiced freely by all. After several sessions with the Magic of Order, we fear this may not be their desire. And that they might propose very large restrictions. We ask that, if those proposals are made, you vote against them."

Grufton Mann narrowed his eyes and tapped his chin with his finger, an indication that he was considering Nauveena's words.

Then Nauveena remembered her conversation with Snorri. "Let us hope to influence minds as well." It was not enough to ask for the merchants' vote. She needed to show him why as well.

"If you would like, I can bring you books on the topic, explaining the merits of free and equal magic — to educate you."

Grufton Mann thought a moment longer. After another long moment, he said, perhaps out of politeness, "That would be appreciated. As I said, I do not know much about the matter."

"I will bring books," Nauveena said. "And we can continue to speak. We do not need an answer right now. A proposal has not even been added. But please, consult with us. Come to us if you have any questions."

"One thing I will say is this," Grufton Mann said. "You have asked for the voice of the common folk. I do not love the term. But I hope I can provide the voice of the merchants. And what the merchants care about is what will be good for business. Will the free use of magic be good for business?"

The question stumped Nauveena. She felt as if she and the merchant were speaking two different languages. How could magic be quantified in such a way?

Fortunately, the druid answered. "I do not think it is or it isn't. Magic has little place in business."

"I know what was *not* good for business," Grufton Mann said. "The war with the Osseomancer. Traders from the Distant Lands feared coming to Jenor. We could not trade through the rest of the continent. I do not know what type of magic the Osseomancer practiced, but it was certainly bad for business."

◆

Malachite and Nauveena left the Library of Practicalities and crossed Athyzia to the apartments where the Foreign Minister of Aryde was staying.

Nauveena felt relieved to be out of the cramped, low-ceilinged library. There was hardly enough room for all the merchants and bankers rushing about with stock orders scrawled onto parchment. She didn't see how anyone could work in there.

"They do not understand magic," Nauveena said as she and Malachite crossed Athyzia's courtyards.

"What did you expect?"

"They were invited to a council that will discuss magic, and they do not know the first thing about it."

"Didn't you know that when you invited them?"

"We thought they would know *something*. We thought all in Jenor knew at least a little."

"You have been in Athyzia too long," Malachite said. "You do not know what it is like to live without magic. One must turn one's focus to other pursuits."

While Nauveena had not always lived in Athyzia, she could barely remember her previous life. Her parents had not survived when the Osseomancer froze the Bay of Ontiphon during the war. She hadn't been able to cry when she read the news, even though she felt like she should. That life had come to feel so far away from her. She couldn't remember what it was like to be common. She couldn't remember her life without magic.

She tried to push away such thoughts. While she hadn't cried when the news came about her parents, she always became sad when thinking about that previous life she had left behind, as if she had abandoned them.

Now, she needed to focus on her meeting with the Republic of Aryde. Aryde had once been a small region within Lyrmica, but they had always been fairly isolated by the Last Mountains, and had developed their own culture. They'd protested as Lyrmica increased their use of alchemy, and protested more when Lyrmica went to war with its neighbors. Aryde wanted no part of a war it had not begun. Towards the end of the Alchemy Wars, they'd rebelled. Lyrmica, weakened from years of war, could not prevent Aryde from proclaiming their independence and creating their own government.

Initially, Balzhamy and Lyrmica had protested Aryde being included in the council. After all these years, they still refused to recognize the republic's independence. But almost every other kingdom did, and so Snorri felt it only right to invite them. They too had fought against the Osseomancer, and fought well for such a small nation. Still, Nauveena wondered if Snorri had not felt obligated to give votes to the smaller middle kingdoms when pressed by Fallou because he had done the same for Aryde.

The foreign minister of Aryde, Fichael Porteau, stood outside his chambers. Even in the warm morning sun, he wore a thick cloak. He worked to light a rolled paper with smoke leaf inside. The leaf differed from that grown in the elven forests and Qadantium. As far as Nauveena could tell, it did not provide foresight or clarity, but only lightheadedness, which was a strange thing to want.

Fichael Porteau struggled to light the paper. His matches kept breaking. Nauveena offered her hand. He nodded towards her. She placed her index finger to the tip of the rolled paper and produced the smallest, softest lavender-colored flame. Porteau breathed in until the leaf lit.

"Thank you," he said after exhaling a pale smoke. "I hope you do not mind meeting outside. I do not like to smoke in my apartment. The smell lingers."

"Why do you smoke at all if you do not like the smell?" Nauveena asked.

Porteau shrugged. "Habit? Especially when I am stressed."

"Is now still a good time to speak?" Malachite asked.

"It is as good a time as any," Porteau said. "Do you mind if we walk?"

Without waiting for a response, he began to wander. His apartment lay on one of the higher levels, with a view of the lake below. "This place is very beautiful," he said. "No one in Aryde will believe me when I tell them about it."

Nauveena followed the foreign minister's gaze. He was not looking at the lake, though. Or the mountains. He was looking at Athyzia's many spires — rising above and beside each other, always appearing as if they might collide.

"They won't?" Nauveena asked.

Fichael Porteau shook his head. "We do not have much magic in our land. Did you grow up here?"

"Not always," Nauveena said. "My parents were oyster farmers on Ciri Daahl."

"They were common folk?"

"Yes."

"You are lucky, then. To be able to do magic. And to be brought to this world."

Despite the wide view from his apartment and the many paths that would have provided similar views, Porteau led into an alley between two large buildings. The alley was only wide enough for the three to walk abreast of each other. Porteau might have called it a walk, but it was more like pacing.

"We have found it useful to meet in smaller groups to discuss how the council is proceeding," Malachite explained. "In the course of discussions with the larger group, it is difficult to gauge where everyone is at."

"Believe me, I understand," Fichael said. "If you think this council is contentious, you haven't seen the parliament of Aryde. Afterwards, everyone is tripping over each other to talk privately."

"Then maybe you can offer your perspective?" Malachite said. "We are worried Fallou has a hidden agenda for the council. Do you get that sense from him? You have much more experience with these matters."

Fichael took a deep drag. "I don't think the agenda of the Second Faulsk Empire is particularly hidden."

"What is that agenda, then?"

"To become an actual empire again. They took the Leemstein shortly after the war began and declared themselves an empire. But that is not enough. They want all the lands of their First Empire, and then some. They've got the middle kingdoms through the proxy of the Magic of Order, but it won't be enough."

"What will be enough?" Malachite asked.

"All of Jenor."

"All of Jenor?" Nauveena gasped.

Fichael nodded and took a long drag. "They will conquer the whole continent, one way or another. What they cannot invade, they will control with Order. They wish to eliminate their age-old rivals: Druissia and Qadantium. These always acted as a check against their ambitions. In the process, they will happily march into Aryde and end our experiment with democracy."

"We fear Fallou wants to prohibit other types of magic," Nauveena said.

"I'm sure he does. The Magic of Order has provided Faulsk a unique tool: a state monopoly on magic. They want to eliminate all rivals."

"If he makes such a proposal, can we count on you to vote against it?" After her difficulties communicating with Grufton Mann, Nauveena wanted to be direct.

"Vote against Faulsk?"

"Yes. It would stop them from expanding their influence."

"Have you ever looked at a map?" Fichael Porteau asked. "Ever since Aryde gained independence, our existence has been threatened. We sit between Lyrmica and the Second Faulsk Empire and the sea."

"So you cannot let Faulsk gain any more power."

"It is not their power over magic that we fear. It is their armies. And they will see any provocation as an excuse to use those armies. Every day since I arrived here, I have received letters asking me to return home. Our generals speak of troops amassing at our borders. I am asked to return and open communications with Faulsk."

"Can you not open them here?" Nauveena asked. "Add a proposal: to recognize Aryde's sovereignty."

Fichael's hand shook as he inhaled the last remaining nub of his smoke leaf. "I have had my own meetings with Fallou and Balzhamy. They have only made it clear that they expect Aryde to vote with the Magic of Order. And that I am not to speak to you."

◆

"Let's hope we do not need any of their votes," Nauveena said at lunch. They once again sat in the back corner, away from everyone else, so they could rehash the day's conversations.

Nauveena did not feel much like eating. Her mushroom soup sat in front of her, getting cold. Malachite always managed an appetite though. He had almost finished his tomato-and-mozzarella sandwich, and he began eyeing Nauveena's soup. She pushed it towards the druid.

"It just means thinner margins. Maybe if I bring books to the merchants, I can educate them. But it will take time, and it isn't certain."

Malachite dipped the ends of his sandwich into the soup, sopping up the broth.

"Maybe I am sheltered. I stayed here through the war. I forgot all the trivial things the common folk think about: profits and politics. I guess if you do not have magic, what else can you fill your days with? But I would think you would want to educate yourself on magic. It is a whole world they are closed off to. Maybe I should write a book. Explaining magic to the common folk. It might do much good."

Malachite nodded as he finished his sandwich and held the soup bowl to his mouth.

"But obviously I do not have time for that now. Who knows about the merchants? They don't seem to care either way. But you can't count on that. A shame, since they hold three votes. Aryde is a lost cause, though. They are being extorted. Certainly, we should do something. They shouldn't be threatened by force like that.

"And clearly, Fallou is having his own meetings. I bet he's met with the merchants. Grufton didn't blink when we said we wanted discretion. He's already had similar meetings with Fallou. Or one of Fallou's representatives. So, who do we have? The northerners? The elves if we can get more against the Elf Laws? The dwarves if Fallou does not hand them the Last Mountains? I thought we were pretty strong. Now, I am not sure."

"Let us see what Venefica has to say." Malachite looked up from his soup as the witch approached. "Maybe she had better luck."

Venefica heard the end of his statement. "You hope I had better luck?" she said as she sat. "So it did not go well for you?"

Both Nauveena and Malachite shook their heads. "How about you?" Nauveena asked. She did not want to relive the earlier portion of the day. "Did you talk to Skiel and the Bogwaah?"

"Yes, I did," Venefica said. "I did not think I had much luck, but after seeing both your faces, I do not think I did so bad." She flagged a server to bring her wine. "Skiel is the same as the northerners. Veeslau was even less explicit. At last, I finally had to come right out with it and say we knew about the necromancy. They worry how the rest of the council will feel, but they want some exception carved out for them."

Venefica stopped talking as a goblet of wine was brought to the table. Malachite ordered fried potatoes. When the server left, Venefica began again. "Push comes to shove though, we have Skiel."

"And the Bogwaah?" Nauveena asked.

Venefica waved her hand dismissively and took a swig from the goblet. "Their Burgomaster just rambled on about their bleeding thistle and frog mint." She rolled her eyes. "It was all he wanted to talk about. I could hardly get a word in. If we really need them, we can try again, but I'd rather not."

"So how many is it?" Malachite asked again.

"We've at least talked to everyone who isn't with the Magic of Order," Venefica said. "You can't say we didn't do due diligence. But where the votes lie? I am not sure."

Nauveena counted on her fingers again. "We should have thirteen. I think. Even if Aryde and the merchants go with Fallou. We will just need to stay on them, keep communicating in case anything changes. If — for instance — Lyrmica makes a better deal about the Last Mountains."

"Yes," Venefica said. She had almost finished with her wine. "I think you are right. Keep checking in. Try to see where everyone is at. But besides that, all we can do is wait."

"Wait for what?"

"Whatever Fallou has planned."

Chapter Twelve
Blood Magic

> "Who will stand before him? You? You, who even now feels fear in the very marrow of your bones? Why choose such a fate? Why choose such destruction for yourself and all you hold dear? Why, when he would offer you all the riches of this life? Why, when he would offer you a world without end?"
>
> ~The Witch of Pravulum
> 24 BU

The early weeks of the council would become known for their long discussions. Each member was given time to speak for as long as they desired. The rest were given time to respond in turn, and so all perspectives were indeed heard.

After multiple requests, Snorri extended the first session, providing opportunity for more issues to be nominated. And many were. Now, Nauveena pushed to nominate the issue of the free sharing of books.

Athyzia stood alone for its Academy: sorcerers who studied independently from each other, but still shared freely their research and private collections. They collaborated often, and their apprentices worked to copy rare and unique manuscripts, swelling Athyzia's libraries.

But such communion was indeed rare. Many mages — and even cities and entire kingdoms — treasured their knowledge so highly, they came to hoard their manuscripts and grimoires. Their libraries remained hidden behind lock and key, and often magical wards, dangerous to break.

Nauveena wished to extend Athyzia's model across all Jenor. The notion would be within the spirit of the council, she argued. Communal learning could offer a foundation for the unity the council wished to engender.

The war had also shown the dire and urgent need to share such knowledge. The Osseomancer's advancing armies razed each village they came upon. Carcasses littered their tracks. And they left entire cities as mounds of ash to be dispersed by the wind. Libraries had not escaped their fury.

Falidurmus, the Protector of Ülme, recounted the burning of the famed Library of Ülme. "Oh, woe is us, woe is us," he said in lamentation. "Their forces overwhelmed the city's defenses. We were driven back. We could only watch as they set everything alight, including that most beloved of libraries."

Nauveena envisioned flames hungrily licking shelves of manuscripts before consuming them in great, sputtering inhales. The flames leapt higher and higher each time she pictured them.

Ülme's archive was famous for containing many ancient works, some the sole copies in existence. Prized among them had been *Praqnechne's Grimoire*: the first collection of spells in Jenor, written by mages more than a thousand years before.

Nauveena longed to understand where her magic came from, where all magic came from. She read what she could. Many theories cited *Praqnechne's Grimoire* for support. But she had never read the volume in full. Now, she never would. She could not let other texts suffer the same fate.

Ülme's library took such pride in holding a text so ancient and important that they had refused requests to share it or to make copies. Others could only see it by making a pilgrimage to the library itself, where it remained in a glass case. Many mages coveted their collections with the same guarded jealousy. It had been the undoing of Ülme. It had been the undoing of *Praqnechne's Grimoire*.

Was it not the council's purpose to safeguard Jenor's vast knowledge?

Snorri wished to refrain from the Academy adding too many topics of their own, so Malachite graciously added the matter on Nauveena's behalf. Now, she could only wait to discuss it.

Once the list of initial topics was decided, Snorri set to work creating an agenda. He did not explain his reasoning for the order, but Nauveena suspected he placed more contentious issues later.

He also did not assign a number of days to any topic. Each, he reasoned, would take as long as was needed to have a full discussion, where all voices were heard, before they moved to the next.

"It will take weeks," Nauveena said after reading the schedule the next morning.

Snorri was unperturbed. "If it will take weeks, then weeks we will give it."

The council discussed Pravulum first. Guards had been stationed at the ruined citadel since the Osseomancer's defeat, but a more permanent garrison was needed. Enchantments encircled Pravulum for many leagues in all directions. The Osseomancer might have been cast from his physical form and weakened, but all feared he could return, especially if he found strength in these enchantments.

The Alliance had learned early the need to clear the battlefield of their fallen. They worked now to exhume all graveyards near Pravulum. As they explored the tower's ruins, they found catacombs filled with bones — legions that would serve the Osseomancer were he to return. They began the work of removing all of them and sanctifying the land, and it needed to continue.

The area around Pravulum was partitioned. Those who could not provide warriors would provide funding and provisions instead. The dwarves volunteered to send a team of craftsmen and builders to clear rubble and build a defensive barrier around the ruins.

In the coming weeks, the council moved to other matters: How to split the costs of the war. How best to rebuild the cities and replant the fields.

They discussed establishing consistent taxonomies of magical substances as spring entered her final stages. Melting snow swelled Athyzia's river, causing the sound of rushing water to be heard throughout. The summer moon appeared in the night sky to chase the winter moon away.

The council arrived at the topic of standardizing the lengths and requirements of apprenticeships. Nauveena kept finding that each topic took longer than she expected. Her initial estimate that the council might take weeks now felt optimistic.

As the sessions flowed one into the next, and the days flowed into weeks, she found herself developing habits around the structure of the council's proceedings. The council had become her life, and her routines began to orbit around the council as a planet orbited a star.

Each session would end with a short speech from Snorri. Then each member would drift away from the terrace, some quickly, while others lingered, hoping to catch a whisper with each other. Nauveena would escort Snorri to his chambers. She would boil a pot for tea. She would retrieve whatever books he might need. Then the two would discuss the day's events until Snorri drifted off to sleep. Nauveena found him falling asleep earlier and earlier; the council tired him more with each session.

Once Snorri was asleep, Nauveena would slip from his chambers and proceed to the banquet hall. There, she would find Venefica and Malachite deep in conversation. She would join them in tilting their heads toward each other and sharing their observations from the day.

Nauveena was always amazed at how much their accounts of the council differed. Venefica, in particular, observed much that Nauveena missed. The witch kept one eye suspiciously on the Protectors of Order, but few escaped her scrutiny.

"General Dolcius looked a bit too pleased with himself," she would say, or, "Did you see the look between Galena and Balzhamy? Could it be about the Last Mountains?"

Nauveena came to learn that the witch could read a face in the same way she might read the page of a book, and that the raising of an eyebrow or a smirk or a glare might hold as much information as an entire chapter.

When they finished eating, they would make their nightly rounds with the council members. They went alone or together, depending on what the night called for. Nauveena would meet with the southern merchants and Aryde's foreign minister as often as she could, while Venefica and Malachite continued to meet with Skiel and the Bogwaah. They frequently met with the dwarves and northerners together, so much did the two groups enjoy each other's company.

Then, the three would reconvene in Nauveena's tower. On certain nights, Malachite would journey to the forest, meeting with the stags or some other contingent, leaving Nauveena and Venefica alone.

Venefica received much news from the east, and she grew increasingly worried. Nauveena had read much about the mistreatment of others. The world appeared such a cruel place. But it was one thing to read about such issues and another to hear them spoken about out loud. She found the same experience with the elves, who discussed much of the unfairness of the Elf Laws. Even these had come to be enforced more regularly and harshly since the end of the war.

Now, as Venefica explained the grim news coming from the east, Nauveena felt consumed with worry. "The noose continues to tighten," Venefica said as she poured each a glass of wine. "Witches are being jailed. I have heard talk of executions."

"Jailed? Executed? That can't be true."

"Tales came periodically throughout the war, but now, many are fleeing into Druissia. They bring with them ill tidings."

"But what are they accused of?"

"Violating order. Practicing magic which is not allowed by their book."

"That damn book. How can they try to control magic in such a way — and so harshly?"

"Does your Academy not wish to control magic as well?" Venefica asked. "Sorcerers wish for all magic to be kept in books."

"Where else would magic be kept?" Nauveena asked. "And at least the Academy allows others to read their books. The same cannot be said about *The Book of Order*."

"The Magic of Order will come first for the witches, because the sorcerers and academics have left them vulnerable, but do not think they will stop there. Folk mages will follow, and then sorcerers and mages themselves."

"No, we will stop them," Nauveena said. "If Fallou attempts such a vote — to restrict magic in such a way — we will have enough to block it." After her nightly meetings with the council members, she had renewed confidence in the vote.

"Yes, of course," Venefica said. "Maybe we can stop them from enforcing their will upon the council, but the Magic of Order controls so much territory already. There, they can enact whatever laws they want. Why, we could enact a proposal to make all forms of magic protected, but the Magic of Order could still return home and punish witches for violating order."

Nauveena took a long sip of wine. After all their long nights courting votes, it felt futile to think that any member of the council could return home and ignore everything that had been agreed upon.

"Maybe there is something the council can do." Nauveena had a sudden thought. "Soon, we will vote on the sharing of knowledge. It is the next issue after we discuss calendars. It was not my intention when I initially pushed the topic, but there could be another benefit. I wish to make all knowledge free, shared upon request, and to encourage the copying of manuscripts for their preservation. Why, such a measure would include *The Book of Order*, wouldn't it?"

Venefica considered the matter a moment before saying, "I suppose it would."

"They would be obligated to share it like any other text."

"It would not stop them from enforcing the book's rules, of course, but at least we would actually know what it says."

"Of course," Nauveena began, preparing to say more. To her, simply being able to read the book would solve so many issues. They understood so little about the Magic of Order; the book would illuminate so much.

She was about to say this when Venefica tilted her head back and laughed.

"What is so funny?"

Venefica composed herself enough to say, "At the very least, it will be worth the look on Fallou's face."

Nauveena couldn't help but laugh too.

"Do you have the votes for it?" Venefica asked when she had finished. "Fallou will see the issue as well. He will try to block you."

"I've discussed book sharing when I've met with the others, if not *The Book of Order* explicitly. None have raised objections, though. Yes, I think I could get it passed."

Venefica continued laughing as she poured more wine. They discussed the matter long into the night before turning to other topics. But inevitably, the moment came when the witch stood to return to her own chambers. Nauveena had come to fear her departure. She wished for Venefica to stay. She enjoyed their talks. It had been so long since she had confided in another in such a way. But more than this, she did not wish to be alone.

She had come to fear sleeping. Would it have been easier to sleep with another in her tower? Would that have stopped the nightmares? No, but at least someone would have been there when she woke. It had been so long since she had woken to another. For so long, she had been alone.

First, through the war. Now, it continued. Now, she tried not to fall asleep.

Maybe she was overtired. Between the day long sessions and meetings at night, she got little rest. When she did sleep, the same vivid dream from the oracles' tower returned. It was the same tonight.

Nauveena wandered down dark hallways. She held the lantern ahead of her. The dim light bounced off the brick walls, illuminating a path. Now, she could see the corridor split. She could look down each yawning tunnel, with the light revealing the choice, but not much more.

In each dream, the sound of a stranger walking the corridors could also be heard. She swung the light, hoping to reveal the interloper. But whenever she turned, the light would go out and she would be cast into darkness.

She came to understand that the stranger was not meant to be there. That he had come from another dream and broken into hers. For what purpose, she did not know — only that he was greatly curious in what her wanderings through the maze might reveal. And so, he followed her, hoping to find it first.

Most nights, she woke in a cold sweat shortly after the light had gone out. She lit the candle beside her bed and let the flickering light cast strange shadows across the ceiling. She came to take comfort in the shadows. They were real and not a part of her dream.

◆

Nauveena would need to wait to discuss the issue of books. Next on the agenda was calendars. Like the other issues being discussed, this too occupied many days, and soon, discussions bled into a second week. Timekeeping had always been a pet topic of Snorri's. As such, Nauveena also harbored an appreciation for it, but she could sense the other council members getting restless, wishing to move on to other topics. She saw many yawning. Others closed their eyes, their heads drooping. Queen Yellialah even looked like she was sleeping with her eyes open.

But Snorri's enthusiasm could not be curtailed. He appreciated the art of geometry and the calculus needed to track the movement of celestial bodies. He remained fascinated by how each realm had managed to devise a different calendar for themselves, each unique and divergent from the rest.

Qadantium and Dunisk used a calendar based strictly upon the sun, although they somehow managed to have two different ones. Skiel worked off the tides. The northern kingdom of Yülk used the hibernation cycle of the bear for theirs. Similarly, Künner had developed a calendar based on the breeding and migration seasons of the wolf. The Bogwaah marked seasons by the flooding of the Waah River. Drussia alone based their calendar off the cycles of the moons. The elves followed the patterns of the stars and wandering planets, allowing for much longer eras and epochs. The oracles used the zodiac. The dwarves did not keep a calendar. They had never seen a reason to, and they quickly became confused by the whole exercise.

And the kingdoms that followed the Magic of Order had their own unique idea: a strict regimen of weeks and months, a mathematical equation more than anything else.

Each began their years at different times: on the summer solstice, the winter solstice, the anniversary of the Witness writing *The Book of Order*, when the lunar cycle began fresh, when the bear first woke from winter.

They defined their days differently too. Künner's coincided with the hunt of the wolf, which was anything but consistent. Others began at sundown, sunrise, or the middle of the night. They could last twenty-four hours or twenty-six or have no set length at all. Even the length of an hour was not consistently recognized across realms.

Only the Republic of Aryde and the merchant cities had tried to reconcile all these differences. Aryde, the most recent realm to develop a calendar, used a hybrid system. Valinka, Phryza, and Olmtpur, in a similar vein, did not keep their own, but simply kept track of the calendars of all surrounding nations.

Snorri wanted to explore each calendar in turn, a task that served no other purpose than his curiosity. He gave each realm a turn to explain how their calendar functioned and had been developed. The council explored the differences between a sidereal lunar month and a synodic lunar month at length. For the council's education, Snorri recounted the process of intercalation in minute detail.

He even invited the Temporal Mage to give a two-day long lecture on the history of time. Nauveena wasn't certain, but felt the Temporal Mage exerted some of his power to elongate the day and increase the hours in which he could talk.

Ultimately, a compromise calendar using the positions of both the sun and moons was agreed to. And most likely because no one could bear to discuss or present on calendars any longer.

In most lands, the original calendar would be retained, but set alongside the universal one to make trade and communication between kingdoms easier. Not surprisingly, the compromise calendar bore many similarities to the one Snorri had developed. The mage believed that, given time, the new standard would come to replace the regional varieties. Of course, even he did not want them to be fully abandoned, as he maintained an academic curiosity.

Now, another related issue developed: how to number years.

Many kingdoms of men began their count on the approximate year when man first landed in Jenor: 1,538 years before.

Of course, using such a date as year zero was intolerable for the elves and dwarves.

"The year *who* landed in Jenor?" Queen Em' Iriild asked.

The elves began their era with the creation of the known universe and the planting of the first tree in Jenor, more than six millennia before.

The elves and dwarves were not alone in taking umbrage with the proposed year zero.

"The kingdoms of the north were discovered at least three hundred years before settlers reached Lyrmica," King Ümlaut said. "My ancestors crossed the frozen tundra of the north long before yours dared sail over the Forever Sea."

Ümlaut's claims were fairly dubious, as far as Nauveena was concerned. But everyone at least agreed that the northerners arrived by a different route than the settlers in the south — and possibly earlier.

The Magic of Order likewise objected.

"In the middle kingdoms," Falidurmus of Wabia explained, "we begin counting years upward from the year our great Witness wrote *The Book of Order*."

"So, it is what?" Nauveena asked. "Year one hundred and fifty?"

"Year one hundred and fifty-six to be exact," Vicodermus of Upper Tuvisia said.

"I was born before then," Snorri said. "How old would that make me?"

Prince Javee spit out some of his wine in laughter. The council on the whole — except those of the Magic of Order — found the proposal ludicrous, and an audible chuckle followed Snorri's remark.

Snorri ended the session without a resolution once again. Nauveena left with the unenviable thought of returning tomorrow to once again discuss calendars.

She found herself in Snorri's chambers after.

"We must find yet another compromise." Snorri, as he often did, paced the floor of his chambers. "I had given much thought to the mechanics of the calendar, ensuring that it lines up with the actual movement of our sun and moons. This is just — "

"Politics?" Nauveena offered.

"I'm afraid so. There is no algebra or magic which can deliver an answer. We just need something we can all agree on."

"And there is not much the council agrees on," Nauveena said.

"I'm afraid there isn't. Things were much simpler when we had the Osseomancer to unite against."

Snorri's words ignited an idea in Nauveena's mind. "That's it."

"What's it?"

"Leave it to me," she said, too excited to explain. "You should rest. I think tomorrow will be our last day talking of calendars."

Nauveena left Snorri's chambers and went immediately to the elves. She had become a frequent guest of Queen Em' Iriild. She spoke with the queen and the other two elven representatives, Csandril Em' Dale and Zufaren.

"How must I compromise now?" the queen asked. Nightly, Nauveena and Venefica had advised the elven queen to be more accommodating. In such a way, she might gain allies to eventually overturn the Elf Laws.

"A minor compromise, but one that will win you many friends. They will thank you for putting an end to these sessions."

Nauveena explained her idea. She saw the same spark pass to the elves as they digested the idea and realized it was the obvious path.

"Clever," Csandril Em' Dale said admiringly.

"I suppose that will work," Zufaren said.

"You will present the idea tomorrow?" Queen Em' Iriild asked.

"No, I will not." Nauveena saw the look of confusion on the elves' faces. "No — the idea should come from you. I ask Csandril to make the proposal tomorrow."

The poet would speak more eloquently than Nauveena ever could. He smiled, seeing her plan.

Next, Nauveena went to the northerners. Along the way, she explained her designs to Venefica and Malachite. With the northerners, she shared her thoughts and gained agreement.

The dwarves were next. And in the matter, they cared little. They did not understand calendars, and they only wished to know when another offer might come about the Last Mountains. Nauveena wondered it often too, but not tonight.

Venefica spoke with Skiel, Malachite with the Bogwaah. Nauveena visited the merchants and Aryde. Late that night, they met with Prince Javee. The High Priestess Kìtrinos was fortunately already visiting him.

For each, Nauveena did not offer anything. Ending the session on calendars would be enough. And they all liked the idea on merit alone. If it had been presented fresh in the council, they might have voted for it without needing convincing. But to each, Nauveena expressed that the idea had come from the elves, and the council members appreciated being included.

The next morning, Snorri began the session. He summarized the previous two weeks: how each realm kept track of time, another brief history on the tradition, and the current issue facing the council — when to begin counting years.

Nauveena waited patiently. Most mornings, she had needed coffee to stay awake, but now, she had no trouble.

After Snorri finished, Csandril Em' Dale took the floor to speak. "For many days, I have sat on this terrace, surrounded by beautiful gardens, with a pristine lake below me, and listened to each of you speak about the most boring topic imaginable."

While Snorri huffed, the rest of the council — including a few from the Magic of Order — laughed.

"We have discussed lunar cycles and seasons and planetary orbits and the tilting of the axis. And I have almost fallen asleep. And I have seen many of you fighting sleep as well." Again, a round of laughter. The sun shone brightly. Already, Csandril had raised most of the council's spirits.

"But the matter at hand is more important than these academic queries. Dates and weeks define the passing of time, and therefore our lives. They tell us when feast days come. They tell us when the week begins. They allow us to record important events: birthdays, marriages, anniversaries, deaths.

"And in this way, they bring us together. A shared calendar forms the basis of a shared experience. We exist in the same flow of time. I can communicate dates easily. Set appointments. Tell you when I will see you next. With each realm working with a different calendar, we were divided. We existed in separate spheres of time.

"Now, we come together to unite, to develop one single calendar that we can share universally. If I tell you, 'Let's meet next Tuesday,' we all will have the same Tuesday to meet on. This calendar will be symbolic. It will be the ultimate uniter of us: of the Great Alliance.

"And because of this, there is only one year that should begin our calendar. One year when all the lands of Jenor united against overwhelming odds, against annihilation, against certain doom, and overcame them through unity. One year when the Osseomancer fell. Let the year that Pravulum fractured mark the beginning of our calendar. Let this be year one."

Thunderous applause. No one could speak to a crowd better than the elven poet. Nauveena saw that even the Magic of Order had been moved to accept the proposal.

The vote was unanimous.

As an added bonus, Nauveena had maneuvered to give the elves the credit. In the eyes of the council, Csandril Em' Dale had made the proposal and given an inspirational speech about unity. United, men, elves, and dwarves. How could the Elf Laws be continued after such calls to unity?

Pravulum had fallen conveniently the day after the winter solstice. Its anniversary would now mark the first day of each new year.

Snorri conceded to Nauveena after the session had ended. "Well done, but I still do not know how old this makes me."

Nauveena laughed. "We can figure that out later. For now, welcome to year one."

The unity would continue through the rest of the day and the next, when Snorri called a recess between sessions. Athyzia celebrated with drinks and feasting.

But, of course, the unity could not last.

Finally, the council moved to the topic of books. Nauveena planned to address the council on the matter. She had written her speech weeks before, when the topic had just been added, and she did not alter it now. While she had a secondary motivation, she did not want any to know.

She stood to address the council. "I do not need to reiterate everything that was lost during the war. So I will not here. But there is one thing we lost that is not often mentioned. And maybe it is secondary in nature, but it is valuable nonetheless. How much knowledge was destroyed that we will never recover?

"We might not have been able to stop the Osseomancer from burning such important texts, but we could have guarded them in another way. For long, we have guarded our books by keeping them close to us and not letting others have their knowledge. It is essential now that we should make more concerted efforts to copy our texts and share them with each other.

"The knowledge contained in *Praqnechne's Grimoire* was lost primarily because other copies did not exist. My understanding is it was kept in a sealed case in Ülme's library. I understand the desire for such protection, but the true protection would have been a copy on strong parchment. And not just one copy, but many, distributed across Jenor."

Prince Javee agreed to the matter first. He had long desired to share such collections Qadantium held exclusively. He had feared the Osseomancer breaking through their defenses and ravaging the kingdom, eliminating such volumes.

King Bane likewise maintained no opposition to the notion. He had protected what works he could during the Siege of Ontiphon, and likewise, Druissia's other cities had gone to great efforts to hide their volumes during the war.

The dwarves kept robust manuals on the mining of gems and metallurgy. They saw no risk in being overtaken in the skillset. Much of their knowledge came instinctually, and they would share what knowledge they had in exchange for copies of the many volumes they had read at Athyzia.

Others came to share their support: Dunisk, the northerners, the Bogwaah, Skiel, and Lyrmica. Grufton Mann spoke of new, emerging technologies in his city, which soon might be able to reproduce manuscripts much quicker. The technology had only been delayed during the war.

Finally, Fallou, the First Protector of Leem, stood to address the council. Nauveena wondered what he might find objectionable about her motion. Would he demand *The Book of Order* remain private?

However, he did not immediately object. Instead, he said, "I cannot commend your words enough, young sorceress. Or the notion behind your speech. The loss of Ülme and other such libraries still hurts, and I do not know how we will ever recover. I too would love to aid in the sharing of knowledge, and I will provide no hindrance."

Then he continued. "But I do have some practical concerns, and I would be remiss not to address them. What would passing such a notion look like? Will we really prioritize the copying of manuscripts, when so many other issues exist? We must till the soil. We must rebuild whole cities that were razed to the ground. It may take a scholar a hundred hours to copy a single manuscript. Is this where we wish to deploy our manpower?"

"The idea is more a commitment to unity," Snorri said before Nauveena could respond. "We would not put a timetable on such matters. We know there is much we must address first."

"You will excuse me if I did not realize the purpose of this council was the voicing of platitudes and feel-good notions, when much more practical matters need to be addressed."

"No, it is not that at all," Snorri said.

"The agreement would also stop the hiding of certain texts," Nauveena said. "There have been occasions of sorcerers hoarding manuscripts, keeping them for themselves. If we agree to the free sharing of knowledge, then I would like to see an end to such practices."

"A most noble belief," Fallou said. "One I hold as well. But are there not concerns with practicality here as well? What if a mage refuses? Will you besiege a keep? Will you storm a castle for a manuscript?"

"Well, no, I suppose — " Nauveena began.

"We are asking for a commitment to goodwill," Snorri said. "Certainly, you can see that?"

"This entire council is a commitment to goodwill," Fallou said. "Why have a separate one on books?"

If Fallou thought it was such a waste of time, and that it could not be enforced, why not just vote on it? Nauveena wondered. He was wasting more time by poking petty holes into the motion. But he continued such dialogue until late into the day. Snorri did not hold a vote, and the council adjourned, prepared to discuss the issue further the next day.

"He is dragging his feet," Nauveena said to Venefica when they were alone within the Tower of Yalde. "He also has seen the implications of the measure."

"It is as we expected," Venefica said, pouring two glasses of wine. "But he cannot block it. I have spoken to Skiel. They too see the need for the freedom of knowledge. Fallou can delay, but we will have the vote."

Just then, a knocking came at the base of the tower. Nauveena rushed to see who had come. She found Csandril Em' Dale waiting at the bottom.

"My queen wishes to have a word with you," the poet said simply.

Most nights, Nauveena had gone to meet with the elves. She had not planned to this night, not thinking any of the council's issues needed to be discussed. She returned to her tower to fetch Venefica and her hood.

Csandril escorted them both to the elves' chamber, where they found Queen Em' Iriild waiting for them patiently.

"You wished to speak with us?" Nauveena asked hesitantly.

"Yes, sit down," said the queen.

During the day's discussion, none of the elves had said much, Nauveena noted. She took a seat on the wide couch beside the queen.

"You must understand," Queen Em' Iriild began, "I think your cause is noble. The elves possess certain tomes we would be willing to share, and will gladly bring to Athyzia. We only hope men will learn from what these works have to offer."

"You have no idea how happy I am to hear this," Nauveena said, but the Elf Queen held up her hand to silence her.

"There are other texts that must remain for the elves alone. They are accounts for the elves, and no one else: not man nor dwarves nor orcs."

"But —"

"The time of the elves is drawing to a close. Although it is still too far in the future for any oracle to see, the elves will eventually wither and fade. You are welcome then to pick our texts from the ashes of our forests and make what sense of them you may. But only then and not a moment sooner."

"What are you saying?" Venefica asked. "You will vote against the matter?"

Nauveena counted quickly in her head. She had spoken to several on the issue. She had the votes, even without the elves. But she could not imagine forcing the elves to give up their books, their secrets. She thought of Fallou's words: "Will you besiege a keep? Will you storm a castle for a manuscript?"

Would she come against Saphalon for such works? She couldn't imagine it. Over the course of the council, she had come to think of the elves as her friends. She would not betray them in such a way.

"We can make an exception?" Nauveena said. Venefica turned to her in surprise. "Your books are your own. When I brought the issue to the council, my concern was only the knowledge of man. You might not think it very great, and maybe your own is much vaster, but for that reason, it is imperative we share with each other."

"Some matters must remain for the elves," Queen Em' Iriild said. "I thank you for seeing this as well. You have been a friend to the elves throughout this council. One day, perhaps, you can come visit us in Saphalon."

"I would like that very much," Nauveena said.

Queen Em' Iriild thanked them and then retired for the night. Csandril Em' Dale remained behind. Nauveena and Venefica spoke with him for some time, and he told them stories of the elves and the founding of Saphalon. Nauveena wished to visit the famed forest. Few besides elves were welcome there. She wondered if the Elf Queen's offer was genuine, but she could not imagine it was not.

Once again, Nauveena did not wish to return to her tower. As they left the elves' chambers, Venefica turned towards her own chambers, but Nauveena stopped her. "Would you not come back? We have not drunk our wine?" It had been so long since she'd had such company. She looked forward to her nights with the witch.

"It is getting late, and I imagine tomorrow will be busy as well," Venefica said. Nauveena saw no way to protest. She feared going to bed. She continued to have her strange dreams, being followed through the endless maze, unable to find her way out. She feared being lost. She feared who followed her.

The two parted, and Nauveena returned to her tower. The wine waited for her, and she intended to drink a glass herself, but another waited for her too — Snorri. The old mage sat in an armchair across from the couch.

"What are you doing here?" Nauveena asked her mentor in surprise. "And so late?"

"Yes, it is much later than I would like." Snorri stifled a yawn. "But I have been having some meetings of my own. We must talk."

"Who have you met with?" Nauveena sat and took one of the glasses of wine.

"Fallou has come to me," Snorri said.

"Fallou?"

"Yes, Fallou. And it concerns your most recent notion: the sharing of texts."

"You spoke to him outside the council? Does that not violate your own rules?"

"We both know my idealism needed to be discarded long ago. I cannot begrudge the First Protector seeking a private audience."

"And what did he want?"

"He will support this movement — the free sharing of books — as long as one exception is granted."

"*The Book of Order*?" Nauveena guessed.

Snorri nodded.

"We do not need him for the vote to pass," Nauveena said. "I have spoken to the other council members. They will vote for it. We do not need to grant his exception."

"I told him we would."

"You did what?"

"I told him we would exclude *The Book of Order* from such an amendment."

"But why? Why give such amnesty? Certainly, you wish to read the text as well?"

"I will not hide my curiosity on the matter. But the book is sacred to them. I am only just beginning to understand it. They wish to safeguard the uses of magic, and so do not wish for any but the most learned to interpret their book."

"Can they even do magic?" Nauveena asked in a fit of frustration.

"'Can they even do magic?'" Snorri repeated. "Or course they can. I fought alongside the Ultimate Defender and Fallou in the Leemstein. It is a peculiar, but effective magic. All creatures have at least some magic in them. The common folk have such trace amounts they cannot do anything with it. But if all that magic can be focused and yoked together, it can be quite powerful. It is not unlike how some gods in the days of old derived their power."

"Either way, we do not need them for the vote," Nauveena said. "I have enough to pass the measure. I have Drussia, Dunisk, and Qadantium. The dwarves have no issue with it. Neither do the southern merchants. Or the northerners or Skiel. And I have just spoken to the elves. We would have their vote too. Let us press forward. We could force them to share the book. We can have a better understanding of what they allow."

"Have you not granted similar exceptions already, then?"

"I —"

"Will the elves be allowed to keep some of their own books secret?"

"Yes — how did you know?" Nauveena sputtered.

"I know Queen Em' Iriild well enough to know what it means that you have gained their vote. We cannot make exceptions for the elves and not the Magic of Order. It is not the role of the Academy to play favorites at this council."

"But are these not different matters?"

"The Magic of Order worships their book as fervently as the elves worship theirs. Who is to say one is beneath the other?"

"The elves do not try to force their beliefs onto others. Look what is happening in Faulsk and the middle kingdoms. They are dictating how magic is used. A stone shroud has descended over the east. Instead of peeking beneath it, you would give them the means to bolster it."

"There are other considerations we must make," Snorri said. "Perhaps you can collect the votes to pass such an amendment, but at what cost? We will risk losing the Magic of Order entirely."

"You are too willing to bend to them," Nauveena said. "You should not have given them so many votes."

"It only seemed fair to respect their wishes. They fought against the Osseomancer as well. We ask them to be active members of this council, and so we should listen to them and hopefully learn from them."

"They are up to something. You have heard the way Fallou speaks in the council. I do not know what he plans, but he will spring it soon."

"Then that is all the more reason to be conciliatory now," Snorri said. "I believe you are right. We cannot continue to debate matters like calendars. Soon, more contentious issues than books will be discussed. If we must anger the Magic of Order, let us do it then. We have the potential for a unanimous vote on this topic. We might not have many more. Why forsake such unity over a single book?"

A single book? How did Snorri not see that it was so much more? Nauveena wanted to argue further, but it was no use. He had made the decision without her. Just as he had spoken to Fallou without her. She could not change his mind.

The next day, Snorri had his unanimous vote, and the council appeared unified. Books would be shared, and soon, many kingdoms would begin the exercise of making copies of rare texts and sending these to each other, hoping that such multiplicity would protect the valuable knowledge in the future.

But even as the session adjourned and Snorri and others celebrated, Nauveena could not help feeling her spirits dampened. Her notion had been defanged, muted, diluted. And she could not help but wonder what was in that sacred text of the Magic of Order that they could not let any others read.

The day had been long, and the discussion drawn out. Over the course of a week, the council had reached the consensus that limitations must be developed on alchemy's use, but little agreement could be found on how strict those limitations should be.

The debate became circular in nature. It twisted back on itself, covering the same ground, becoming cannibalistic. Discussions had already spanned nine days. Now the tenth was ending. And clearly another would be needed. Alchemy proved a complicated matter with many subtopics falling beneath it and very precise uses that needed to be discussed. But such precision did not make the labor of debate any less painful.

With the coming of summer, the days had gotten longer too. The summer solstice approached. With more sunlight, the council could linger longer. They made a habit of stopping before dinner, but often when discussions became heated, they forgot. Evening offered a clearer ending, and today's felt delayed in coming.

At last, Snorri stood. King Bane and one of the Protectors of Magic — either Malidurmus of Zabia or Malthius of Vabia — had been mid-discussion. They paused when Snorri stood. They understood he meant to close the day's discussion.

"Another thrilling debate," the old mage said. "As always. The passion. The intellect. The spirit of cooperation. I thank you all. But the day is drawing to a close, and I do not see us arriving at a proposal to vote on soon. I believe it best to push the matter to tomorrow.

"Let us go to dinner. Let us think the matter over. Much has been proposed and argued and explained. I have much to contemplate. I can think of several works from ancient alchemists I will consult before our next session. I look forward to discussing the issue with you all further, but not tonight. I am old, and I must have dinner and I must sleep."

As had become customary to close the day, Snorri finished his short speech — which all bore a very similar tenor — and bowed. Many in the council sat back and took a sigh of relief. Nauveena felt her body relax for the first time in hours. She thought of the Clovis ale waiting for her in the banquet hall. She had little need for politics tonight. On this matter, there were few hidden agendas. She knew where many stood. The debate swirled around fractions and definitions, rather than core principles and concepts.

Those who had brought instruments to take notes began to pack these. Others stood and pushed their chairs in, eager to finally eat. The council had gone long after the typical dinnertime.

In the midst of these preparations, a young Obeyer of Order — a page by any other name — rushed across the terrace to hand a scroll to the First Protector of Leem. Fallou produced a long blade to slice the wax seal. He then unfurled the scroll and began reading. He narrowed his eyes and creased his forehead. His features — which in general were grim and frowning — only became more so: scrunched and full of concern.

Nauveena could only watch Fallou, intrigued by whatever the message said. What could cause his face to become even sterner?

At last, he breathed deeply. He rerolled the parchment and clutched it close to him. He then stood and looked over the council. While many had stood to leave, everyone still remained on the terrace.

"I apologize," he said. The council turned to listen. "But I must demand your attention a moment longer. I have just now received alarming news. If you would all have a seat, I will share it, because it concerns all members of this council."

Fallou remained standing while the council, rather begrudgingly, returned to their seats. The First Protector of Leem waited patiently. When everyone was once again seated, he began.

"An urgent message has come this hour from our sentries stationed at Pravulum."

A gasp ran through the council. Any matter dealing with the dark citadel was assumed instantly to be of ill fortune. The message Fallou had received was indeed disturbing.

"As this council suspected, it was indeed prudent to assign a permanent force, gathered from our collective kingdoms, to watch over the fallen tower. Earlier today, on the eastern ring, manned by forces following the Magic of Order, a figure was seen leaving Pravulum."

"'A figure?'" King Bane asked. "What does that mean?"

"Our guards saw it from their watch towers around the perimeter. They rode out at once to inspect the figure. They saw it wandering. An old man they did not recognize. Beaten. Battered. Bruised. They questioned the man, and he responded in riddles and confused speech. He claimed to not know who or where he was."

"Where is this man now?" Prince Javee asked.

"They asked to escort this stranger back here, to Athyzia, to our council. At this, he" — Fallou needed to unfurl the scroll to get the right wording, — "'*smiled wickedly.*' And then he resolved to leave. A blinding light. The guards were thrown from their horses. And when they could see again, the stranger had vanished."

"No. It cannot be." King Bane clenched his hand into a fist.

"The Osseomancer? At Pravulum?" Balzhamy of Lyrmica said.

"But we saw him cast out, ruined, a wraith," Lord Ferrum said. "How could he so quickly return to our world?"

"No, no, something is not right here," Csandril Em' Dale said. "I know the magic used in the last. Even a wizard as powerful as he would not recover so quickly."

"I can only read the report," Fallou said. "I do not doubt the sentries. If not the Osseomancer, who?"

"Of course it is the Osseomancer," General Dolcius of Rheum said. "It was naive to think we were done with him so easily."

A sudden gasp seized everyone's attention. They all turned in time to see Queen Yellialah faint and fall to the ground. Her knights rushed to her aid. Others crowded around to see the figure.

"Give her room, give her room," Venefica urged. "She is in shock."

"Who can blame her?" Malthius of Vabia said. "This is terrible news indeed."

"It's sensationalism, is what it is," Venefica said.

One of the queen's knights cradled her head, which rolled limply to the side.

"Is she..." Lord Ferrum said. "Umm... you know?"

The knight holding her head shook his. "No, only unconscious."

Snorri pushed through the crowd. "Get her to the infirmary at once. She needs her rest."

Two more of Dunisk's knights came forward to help carry the queen from the terrace. Venefica stepped forward and placed a hand on one knight's shoulder. "Tell the Medicinal Mage to place a sprig of elm beneath her pillow."

The knight nodded as if he understood what this would accomplish, then turned with the other knights and carried the queen away.

The council watched her leave. When she had been carried off, an even more somber mood filled the terrace, but beneath it was the same panic as before.

"Have you or your oracles seen any coming of this?" Prince Javee asked Kitrinos after a moment.

The High Priestess shook her head. "No, nothing in my dreams. But the tarot has revealed many cards of rebirth. I thought it might be because of spring."

"What can we do?" Ivalka Puchee, the mayor of Phryza, asked.

"We must ride out and destroy this menace," King Ümlaut said. "Now. At once."

"Reinforcements are necessary, of course," Fallou said. "But he knows now of our force occupying Pravulum. He has escaped our guards; he could be anywhere."

"We will scour the lands around Pravulum," Galena said. "How far could he have gotten? We must take our strongest mages and ride out tonight."

"There is another issue I have hesitated to bring to this council," Fallou said. "Although it is quite egregious. Only out of decorum did I not voice these concerns earlier. But now, upon hearing this news from Pravulum, these matters can no longer wait."

"What is it?" Wilhelm Vaah, the Burgomaster of Bogmantic, asked.

"I believe there are many who wish to see the Osseomancer return."

Another gasp ran like a shudder across the council.

"Who?" many asked at once.

The sun had finally fallen. Lanterns lighted on cue. Snorri instructed candles to appear on the tables. Their flickering light made the conversation that much more foreboding.

"Not all who practice magic do so with good intent," Fallou continued when the shock had subsided. "In Faulsk alone, I have received disturbing reports. The common folk come to their Protectors and Keepers often with accounts of their neighbors' misdeeds. I dare not describe them in this council; they are quite stomach churning."

"Please do, First Protector," Venefica now said. Her eyes reflected the flickering candlelight as she stared boldly at Fallou.

"I would rather not," Fallou said. "And spare the council the awful details."

"I insist," Venefica said.

"Please, Fallou; we can handle it," Snorri said.

"Very well. It is only the most perverted magic," Fallou said. "Accounts differ, but common among them is the ritual. Adherents of this sect, those who wish to be reunited with their Osseomancer, will gather. They select a house. And they bring to it young girls, stolen from neighboring villages. And infants, unwanted foundlings, seized from orphanages. Into the house they go. They extinguish the lamps once they enter, so they cannot see their own crimes. They choose to do their work in darkness. Must I continue?"

"Yes, if you wish the council to fully understand your accusations," Venefica said.

"I had hoped to keep these reports to myself to insulate the council from their disturbing nature. But if we are to make decisions accurately and with full facts, I fear I must divulge them. When the lights are gone and darkness covers the house, these adherents will fall upon the girls they have brought there. They will have their way with them, so the house can be filled with not just darkness, but lust and wantonness and all things vile.

"Only when all their wicked desires have been sated will they bring forth the infants they have procured. If their designs for the girls are twisted, they have saved the evilest fate for the babes. For they will then proceed to cut the hearts out and the entrails, often while the infants are still alive.

"They catch the dripping blood in bowls. They pass all around — heart, insides, blood — and, with the lust still upon them, eat and drink each in turn. And when they have had their fill, they recite a pledge to the Osseomancer to follow him and do his bidding. And they plead with the Osseomancer to return and throw down the just rulers, to overturn order. They believe this ritual summons him. If enough make such transgressions, it can provide him strength and return him. Now, we have seen the result."

Throughout Fallou's recounting, gasps and shudders ripped through the council. Everyone waited for him to finish. Now that he was done, the council became a hubbub of conversation. Nauveena was glad that Queen Yellialah had fainted and already left, so she need not hear such things.

"What wickedness?"

"How can there be such evil in the world?"

"No wonder the Osseomancer has returned."

The conversation continued, rising and falling in the natural progression of those who have been startled and want to make sense of what has startled them.

After a moment, Venefica stood and spoke louder than the rest. At her new height, the candles' flames became magnified in her eyes. "Lies. Superstition. The fears of common folk. Do you all believe this tripe?"

Prince Javee snickered. Malachite nodded in agreement. Nauveena felt the spell of Fallou's speech break. The reports had been sensational, outlandish.

"Let me guess the name of these adherents you speak of," Venefica said. "*Witches?*"

"Indeed, many go by that name," Fallou said.

"Then please do not hold back in your accusations."

"It is all the followers of the Osseomancer we must fear," Fallou said. "They give him strength. And tonight, he has risen from Pravulum."

"What can we do?" Falidurmus of Wabia asked.

"It is a simple solution," Fallou said. "One I wanted to wait to bring forth to this council. But the course of tonight's events have forced my hand."

"What would you suggest?" Vicodermus of Upper Tuvisia asked.

"There are many sources for magic," Fallou answered. "It can be derived from chaos. From blood. From nature. From death. But only one source offers stability. Only one source cannot be abused. Only one source has not and will not lead to ruin. And that is order. Only magic derived from this should be practiced, or no magic should be practiced at all."

"Of course." General Dolcius slapped the table. "The Magic of Order is the only way."

"Now, let's wait a minute." Csandril Em' Dale held up his hands. "There's a lot of room between the Magic of Order and eating babies."

"Yes, let us not do anything rash," Zufaren said. "Let us worry about Pravulum first."

"Of course elves would find nothing wrong with such magic," Falidurmus of Wabia said.

"It is not only these witches' rituals," Malthius of Vabia said. "All magic not derived from order can be corrupted."

"We must register all magic users," Balzhamy of Lyrmica said. "It is the only way to have a full accounting and be protected."

"I object to that notion," Snorri said. "And I am surprised at you, Balzhamy, to suggest such a thing."

"Order is what the common folk want," Fallou said. "When those with magic wage war, it is the common folk who suffer. Wizards and sorcerers can protect themselves in their towers. It is the common folk who are slaughtered, raped, hunted in the night. When crops fail, who starves and suffers?"

"Why, then, would they want order?" Prince Javee asked.

"The common folk want the Magic of Order because they are included in it," Fallou said. "The Magic of Order derives from the hierarchy. When they work in their fields and pay tithes to their lords, the magic — wielded through the Protectors and Keepers of Order — becomes stronger. From all other magic, they are excluded, and because of that they are often the victims of it. Only the Magic of Order is acceptable to the common folk. All others must be outlawed."

"'Outlawed?'" Snorri leapt to his feet. "I will hear nothing of the sort. We already have set aside time to discuss the uses of magic. This would cover any magic used for ill. But the uses of magic and the sources of magic are quite different things. I will not entertain any debates on the sources of magic."

"And these are nothing but superstitions," Venefica reiterated.

"You do not believe them?" General Dolcius asked.

"No." Venefica laughed. "No. Not in the least. They are outrageous. The common folk were superstitious long before the Osseomancer, and they will continue to be now that he is gone. We should not let their narrow views of the world dictate how we act."

"I am not surprised you hold these views," Fallou said.

"I have never tried to hide my views," Venefica said.

"We are here to make a peace for all," Snorri said. "The common folk must be considered."

Venefica turned towards the old mage. "'Considered?' Sure. Pitied? Most certainly. I do not envy their short, toilsome lives. So I say, yes, let's pity them, and consider them. But let their views and opinions shape the outcome of this council? That is a bridge too far. I have met the common folk. Spent time around them. They are stupid and crude and plain. There is much of the world they do not understand. You would shun all the mysteries of the universe because serfs may have nightmares? Please tell me this is not why we are here."

"Do you hear her?" Fallou turned to the non-magical users on the council: Fichael Porteau, Grufton Mann, Ivalka Puchee, Loblic Haleem, the Burgomaster of Bogmantic Wilhelm Vaah. "Do you hear the way she speaks of you? Would you suspect any less when she aligned herself with the Osseomancer?"

Venefica would have been the first to explain that there was a distinction between common folk and the *common* folk. "Common" denoted an inability to do magic. In these regards, those Fallou called out were common. But these were nobility, high-ranking officials, representatives of government. They were not the true common folk: serfs, peasants, slaves.

Venefica might have said that and dispelled Fallou's remarks. Instead, she said, "Be thankful I did not remain by his side. Or you would not stand here now."

Now, King Bane of Druissia, who sat next to Venefica, as he had every day, leapt to his feet to hold the witch back. "This is not the best way to make your point," he told her.

"And how do we know your allegiances are not still to him?" Fallou boomed over the council.

King Bane took his turn to become angry. He turned from Venefica to face Fallou. He appeared to grow in size. The king ordinarily looked war-weary and tired. Now, he became fearsome.

"How dare you?" he bellowed. "The witch stands beside me, and you will not question her. Do you not know what she has done? She came to us on the eve of battle. Riding as if death were behind her. I almost did not let her into the city. I too doubted her.

"But we would not have survived without her. The Osseomancer's forces surrounded the city. He froze the bay so we could not be resupplied. For ten years, we were under siege. After ten months, we were without food. Starvation surrounded us like the Osseomancer's own army. We could see his generals outside our walls, pacing, wishing to have at us. Surely we would not last, not hold out.

"Except for her. Every sixth day, the witch slit her wrists and drained herself. Then, in that weakened state, she used her own blood to make a potion — a potion that sustained every last man, woman, and child within my walls. Kept us strong until the following week, when she would do it again."

Nauveena knew Venefica had been at the Siege of Ontiphon, but she did not know the part she'd played there or how monumental it was. Everyone in the council looked at the witch with new admiration. Even some of the Protectors and Keepers of Order.

But not all.

"Blood magic, then?" the mage, Balzhamy, said when King Bane had finished. The king almost leapt across the tables in response.

"You call it blood magic," he said. "I call it salvation."

"Blood magic used for good," Snorri pointed out.

"Yet look how closely it is tied to the Osseomancer," General Dolcius said. "To evil."

Venefica fumed. "This has always been your plan, hasn't it?"

"'Plan?'" Fallou asked.

"Do not play innocent. How convenient for that note to come. How ready you were to reveal the accounts from your common folk, to feed into the hysteria."

"'Convenient?'" Fallou appeared hurt. "I thought it my duty to share the dire news with the council. Did you wish me to withhold it?"

"You have been looking for an opening, and you took it."

"I have not been looking for anything."

"Let us vote." General Dolcius slammed his fist on the table. "Right here. Right now. We all understand how grave a matter this is. Let us see if we have the seven. We must vote to outlaw all blood magic."

"Yes, yes, a vote," said several of the Protectors. They would no doubt have seven.

Nauveena looked to Snorri. He had repeatedly bent to the Magic of Order, first in granting a vote to each Protector, then in the matter of book sharing. Would he now?

No. Instead, defiance flashed across her mentor's face.

"Absolutely not," Snorri said.

"No?" Fallou asked. "But if we have seven who want it added to the council agenda, should it not be added?"

Snorri shook his head. "A matter such as this will not be brought before the council."

"How can that be? I thought the Academy planned to abstain from influencing the council. Now you will not allow the council's own members to add a topic for discussion? We are following the rules you made."

"I said my piece." Agitation had grown on Snorri's face. "This still remains my council. The sources of magic will not be discussed. And that is all."

The head of the Academy of Mages turned from his seat and left.

Chapter Thirteen
A Spy in Athyzia

> "I have now been to the island and can attest to the girl's talents, especially for one who comes from common folk. I do not imagine she has any means for payment, but the choice of apprentice is my own. I have made the decision that she will return with me to Athyzia. It is only a matter of speaking to her parents."
> ~A Letter from Snorri the Esoteric to the Academy
> of Mages
> 27 BU

"Wait, wait." Nauveena pulled up her dress hem to race after Snorri. The old mage stopped and waited for her some way from the terrace.

"You will not allow a vote?" She could not believe what Snorri was suggesting.

"I said it before," Snorri said. "I will not let Fallou use this council for his own devices. I've compromised on other matters, but I will not on this."

"If the vote does not go forward, the Protectors of Order will leave. We will lose half Jenor. The council will not continue."

"Then the council will not continue. It will end."

"*End?*" Nauveena could not believe it. They had stopped in front of the statue of Bezra Umal. She raised her voice. She did not care who heard her now. Fortunately, no one was in sight. They were far enough from the terrace that no one was around.

"Yes, end." Snorri appeared frustrated. He had not expected Fallou's proposal.

"End the council? After all that? What about what has already been decided? The calendar? The sharing of knowledge? The protections around Pravulum? Will you abandon them? Or will they still stand?"

"That will be for every council member to decide themselves."

"But we have the votes." Nauveena was surprised by her own intensity. "We have the votes," she said more softly. "Let the vote go forward. It will be struck down, and Fallou and the Magic of Order rebuked forever."

"No, no." Snorri dismissed her. "No. To even have the vote would be to validate Fallou's superstition and prejudice."

"How?" Nauveena asked. "How would us voting against him validate the stance?"

"To hold a discussion on banning blood magic in Athyzia would suggest it is an issue worth discussing. And at least eight votes will be cast against the magic. The common folk will then know where those kingdoms stand on the issue. Witches are already persecuted. The common folk will gladly take up arms against them. You heard Fallou. Trials. Witch burnings. They would go forward regardless. They would be emboldened."

"Athyzia will show we stand against them."

"We can count on eight votes for the ban: Faulsk, the middle kingdoms, Rheum and Lyrmica. Eight votes from the kingdoms of men. That is a majority of their kingdoms. The common folk of those realms will not care that the elves and dwarves voted against it."

Nauveena understood Snorri's point, but that only made her more frustrated. She wanted the vote to go forward, regardless of what he said.

"I have been courting votes." Nauveena had never raised her voice to her mentor before. Now, she had multiple times in the same conversation. "Night after night, I have met with the council's members. For what purpose? To ensure we have the vote. And I had the vote, but you let the Magic of Order keep their book secret. I have the votes now, when they move to ban certain magics, but you will not let it go forward. You would rather dismiss the council? I have the vote. We can protect these magics."

"No," Snorri said. "We cannot vote on it."

"Why not?" Nauveena could not contain herself. "Do you have such little faith in me? You did not trust me to stand against the Osseomancer. You did not trust me to leave Athyzia during the war. Do you not trust me to deliver the votes now?"

Snorri's eyes welled. He looked like he might cry, and Nauveena regretted everything she had said. It had come bursting from her, hot and feverish. She wished she could take it back.

"No, no." Snorri searched for words. Then he turned and began walking away. "No, no," he mumbled to himself. "Not here."

Nauveena followed.

Snorri did not lead to his chambers. Instead, he followed a path that wrapped around Athyzia's western edge. The lake below reflected the summer moon. They often walked the path in deep conversation. Now, they walked in silence, both contemplating their next words.

Nauveena often wondered what would have become of her had she not come to Athyzia. Only a few sea witches in Ciri Daahl's western coves practiced magic in any meaningful way. Would she have joined them? What else would have become of her? Her parents had not survived the war. Would that have been her fate?

Only one mage had found Nauveena's letter intriguing. One mage, who was then the dean of the Library of Esotericism. Not the head of the Academy as he was now.

Snorri paused. He had been thinking during the walk too, searching for the words to articulate his thoughts. "I am sorry. You are right."

"I did not mean — " Nauveena began, but did not finish. She let her mentor continue.

"No, you are right. There is another reason why I asked you to remain in Athyzia during the war. But it was not my confidence in you. I know you are capable. You could have fought in the front."

"Then why have me remain behind?"

After receiving Nauveena's letter, Snorri had journeyed to Ciri Daahl himself, braving the ferry ride full of common folk to do so. He often told Nauveena the story of when he had taken the ship from Naari. He must have cut a peculiar sight in his long robes, surrounded by fishermen and kelp farmers returning from selling their goods on the mainland.

He had not known what he would find on Ciri Daahl. Not the young girl: bright, clever, curious. She had already read the few books on the poor island multiple times. But these only contained logs of the tides and almanacs and recipes for crab and squid. She needed more.

Snorri brought Nauveena back from Ciri Daahl. He enrolled her at Athyzia. But she did not immediately fit in. The other students had not come from a poor island. They came from more sophisticated cities: Ontiphon, Zeelma, and Dunport. Nauveena was thrust into a strange world, far from her parents. Snorri cared for the girl after she arrived. She came to his office to read when she felt alone. He let her cry when she missed home. And he also learned from her: patience, tenderness, love.

"Few could have protected Athyzia from the Osseomancer. But still, you could have fought, and done well. But I made you stay here. I wanted to protect you."

"Protect me?" Nauveena asked. "But if you thought I was capable, why protect me?"

"I was not protecting you from physical harm." Snorri walked a bit forward. He continued speaking as he walked. He often spoke better while walking. The words came more naturally. "Worse things can happen in war, especially this war. The dead were unearthed. Terrible magic was wielded against both sides. Friends fell. I wanted to protect you from —"

"From what?"

"From seeing it."

"But —"

"I know," Snorri said. "But I still see you as that child who came to Athyzia. The one who read in my office at the Library of Esotericism. The war would have changed you. You were so young when the war began. It was such a long war, I did not realize you grew up during it. I should not have protected you like that. You were old enough to make your own decisions. I should have at least explained why."

Snorri had tears in his eyes. Nauveena wanted to tell him she understood. To apologize for the whole thing. It had been unfair to accuse him.

Snorri paused. He stopped walking. He looked behind him. His eyes flickered over the path they had just walked. "Do you hear something?"

Nauveena listened.

Footsteps.

Someone else was on the path.

The footsteps continued a moment more, then stopped.

Nauveena remembered her dreams.

She had heard the same footsteps every night for weeks. And when she stopped in the dark corridor, they stopped too. They sounded just the same, and they stopped just the same.

They were being followed.

Snorri's entire demeanor changed. He no longer appeared the old man who had looked over Nauveena as she grew up. Instead, he had become stern, serious, strategic. She wondered if this was how he appeared on the battlefield.

She wondered if he had wanted to protect her from seeing this side of him.

"Continue walking," he said. They both picked up their feet and continued along the path. "No, I do not think we will continue with the council. It is too dangerous."

At first, Nauveena did not know why he had returned to the previous conversation. But he spoke so loudly, she realized he wanted to be overheard.

"Fallou's deviousness cannot continue," Snorri said louder still. "Even if that means ending the council." Then he leaned in and whispered, "Keep talking as if I am here."

Snorri stooped and hid behind a statue. Nauveena paused, unsure what to do. But Snorri mouthed "*Keep walking.*" She moved along the path, stepping with purpose so her heels clicked loudly on the stones. She felt silly, but she continued the conversation as if Snorri were there.

"But the council can accomplish much good," she said loudly. "We can vote against the Elf Laws. We can strike down bans on magic. We have the votes. Let Fallou's prejudice be struck down and recorded, so everyone knows where Athyzia stands."

Nauveena still felt silly, walking alone on the path, clicking her heels loudly and speaking as if her mentor was there.

"We have the elves. Venefica speaks for Druissia and Dunisk. We have Malachite. That is six votes. Then Prince Javee and the oracles are eight. The dwarves are ten. The northern kingdoms and Skiel will not vote against blood magic. We are safe at thirteen."

A good explanation, she thought. She would need to repeat it when Snorri was actually there.

A figure rushed by her. Hooded in gray, it almost knocked her over. She leapt out of the way. In the commotion, she did not see their face or features.

Snorri ran along the path next. "Hurry. Do not let him get away."

Nauveena recovered her balance and gave chase. She hitched her dress so she would not trip over the long hem. She had run like this many nights in her dreams. Then, she held a lantern ahead of her. She had tried to see the figure that stalked her in her dreams. Now, she might reveal the spy for real.

Snorri raced ahead with much more speed than Nauveena knew he possessed. They saw the hooded figure duck behind a building and then speed toward the middle courtyards. Here were many buildings where they might hide.

"Fan out," Snorri huffed. "Spread out so we can corner him."

Nauveena sprinted in the other direction. She knew Athyzia well. She would not let the spy escape. She rushed by the Library of Speeches. Then the Library of Reason. The Library of Lost Things. Ahead, a figure appeared. It had been running. It paused, and, from a distance, Nauveena could see it looking around, not having expected to find her cutting off its path.

"Stop," Snorri called out from behind. The old mage sped up, gaining on the figure. The figure looked back and then at Nauveena. "Watch out," Snorri shouted.

The figure sprinted for Nauveena and bowed its head. Its hood came down to cover its face, so she could not see who it was. The figure ran right towards her, stuck out it arms and pushed her down. She did not have time to react. She did not have time to flare out with her magic.

Nauveena collided with the ground. She looked up, afraid the figure would leap upon her. Instead, it continued sprinting. Whoever it was had not expected Snorri to ambush them along the path. Now, they only wanted to escape.

Snorri rushed over and offered his hand to Nauveena.

"No, go, keep chasing him," Nauveena urged. She jumped back to her feet just in time to see the figure reach Athyzia's central tower. The figure looked backwards, then leaned against the door, pushed it open, and disappeared inside.

Snorri was already at the door by the time Nauveena rushed forward. The mage went inside. She reached the door only seconds after him and followed him inside. Out of breath, she hurried up the tower's spiral stairs. She took two at a time, up and around and around and up, until she began to get dizzy.

She collided with Snorri at the top. The mage had paused to catch his breath. "What are you waiting for?" she asked.

"Turn back," Snorri said.

"What? Why?"

"He is trapped. He has nowhere else to go. I will hold him on the tower. Go get help. Get Malachite. Get King Bane. Get the other mages of the Academy. I will hold him."

Nauveena now saw Snorri in a light she had never seen before. He did not seem fat and jolly and anxious any longer, but deadly serious. She dared not argue with him. She knew only to get help as quickly as she could.

Snorri opened the door and went to meet the figure.

Nauveena turned and rushed down the stairs even quicker than before. She took the steep, twisting steps three at a time now and almost tripped in the dark.

She got to the bottom and rushed outside, prepared to yell for help as soon as she caught her breath. "Help! Venefica! Malachite!" she yelled.

She heard a crash from above, an electric sizzling like lightning. Then a shout. She looked up too late.

A body fell from above. There was a low whistle as it displaced the dark night air. It came heavily, gathering speed.

With a massive thud, it landed on the cobblestones at Nauveena's feet.

BOOK II

Chapter One
The Library Beyond the World

> "Everything must be in balance in the glorious hierarchy. Lords must obey their kings and serfs must obey their lords and slaves must obey their masters. Just as wives must obey their husbands and husbands must obey their Protectors."
>
> ~*The Book of Order*
> The Witness
> 152 BU

Nauveena's screams alerted everyone within earshot. She fell upon Snorri's body, grabbing his robes to see if he had any life in him.

A figure ran towards her. Coming out of the darkness. Prince Javee. He had remained on the terrace to organize the force to be sent to Pravulum, and had already been attracted by Snorri and Nauveena's earlier shouts.

"What is it?" But then he saw. He had no other words.

The others came soon. Most had not gone far from the terrace.

Venefica. Malachite. Csandril Em' Dale. Zufaren.

As soon as they understood what happened, Zufaren and Prince Javee rushed up the tower. The elf warrior unsheathed his fearsome-looking blade. Prince Javee produced an orb of fire, which he cradled in his outstretched palm to light the way and act as protection if something were to come upon them suddenly.

Csandril Em' Dale and Venefica knelt on either side of Nauveena. Csandril rubbed her back. The witch offered a silk cloth for her tears.

Malachite watched over the three. He spoke to others as they came, attracted by the commotion and Nauveena's screams. More came: The dwarves. The northerners. The Protectors and Keepers of Order.

Even Queen Yellialah returned from the infirmary, recovered from her spell. She was surrounded by her knights, and it appeared that she might faint again as she learned the news of what had happened.

The elf and prince returned from the tower, shaking their heads. The figure — the spy from Nauveena's dreams — had disappeared, escaped.

Everyone had an explanation. A guess. Nauveena was lifted and brought into a sea of apologies and explanations and questions.

"Did you see a face?"

"What was he wearing?"

"What did he look like?"

All it took was one to suggest it, to remember the report Fallou had read not long before. How could anyone have forgotten? It began as nervous whispers and then became simple truth.

"The Osseomancer?"

"Is he back?"

"And in Athyzia itself."

Those of the Magic of Order turned to look at the First Protector of Leem. They had learned to look to him in moments of emergency.

Fallou had no trouble accepting the responsibility. "I fear the reports from Pravulum came too late," he said, confirming others' suspicions. "The Osseomancer has returned."

"The Osseomancer?" Nauveena said in disbelief.

"I am afraid so. The wizard seen by our guards around Pravulum. He must be regaining strength and seeking revenge."

Nauveena's tears had not yet dried. "No. It was not him."

"How do you know? You said so yourself — you did not see a face. Only the figure. The Osseomancer knows many tricks to conceal himself."

"But it wasn't." Nauveena looked at the body of her mentor. She already felt lost without him.

"What should we do?" Falidurmus, the Protector of Ülme, asked.

"We must lock down Athyzia at once," Fallou said. "Station guards at every tower. Impose a curfew. We must not let the Osseomancer strike again."

"No, no, it wasn't him," Nauveena said, but nobody heard her. They were too busy preparing the defenses. The Academy of Mages became involved. They quickly organized. Spells would be cast over every building. Spectral guards placed at all entrances.

"No," Nauveena continued to repeat.

Only Venefica heard her. "Do not rush to conclusions," she shouted, quieting the rest. "We have no evidence this was the work of the Osseomancer."

"And who else's work would it be?" General Dolcius of Rheum asked.

"Many others stood to benefit from Snorri's demise," Venefica said. "He had ambushed a spy. We have been suspicious of one for weeks, long before reports came from Pravulum."

"Who else might you be suggesting?" Dolcius asked.

"Only just tonight, Snorri prevented a resolution from being added," Venefica said. "He would rather end the council than let it go forward."

"I do not like the sound of these accusations." Now, the general leapt aggressively towards the witch. He thrust his stomach out, pushing her backwards. "Perhaps you are deflecting. We all know your association with the Osseomancer."

"We should hold her until we know more," Falidurmus shouted.

King Bane had arrived some time before. Only now did he insert himself. He came between Venefica and Dolcius, pushing the latter backwards. "You will not lay hands upon her," he thundered. "Any aggression towards her is aggression towards Druissia."

"Our tempers are flared," Prince Javee said. "It has been a long night, and hot. We began by arguing, and now, one of our own is dead. Let us not tear each other apart. Snorri, most of all, would have wanted us to put aside our differences and carry on. Now, more than ever, the Alliance must hold strong."

The hostility broke momentarily. The Academy took over. The Temporal Mage began assigning sentries.

Venefica escorted Nauveena from the scene. The witch did not want her to look upon her mentor any longer.

Venefica brought Nauveena to the Tower of Yalde and sat with her on her bed to let the sorceress digest what had happened. Nauveena had suffered a shock, and the witch did not want to pester her with questions.

When Nauveena seemed recovered — recovered enough to talk — Venefica asked her questions, gently and not forcefully and with time between each so Nauveena could collect her thoughts and respond.

"If you did not see his face, there must be other details you remember?"

Nauveena wished that she could. The attack must have come from someone in Athyzia. If she had any more details, they could apprehend them. But she did not. Everything had happened so quickly. She had the image of Snorri's lifeless body etched into her memories, but the image of their assailant eluded her.

Except for the sound of their footsteps. She knew the pattern so well, even if the padding of the shoes and the firmness of the stone beneath had changed. The striding was the same. The same sneaking nature. The one from her dreams. The intruder who had followed her. But who had come into her dreams? And who had followed her and Snorri? She had never been able to see the intruder in her dreams, and now, she hadn't seen them when they appeared in real life either.

"It was... the one from my dream," Nauveena began. Venefica did not respond. Nauveena knew she must have sounded mad. She had not shared anything about her nightly dreams with anyone, let alone the witch, even if she had become very trusting of her. If only she had. Maybe this could have all been avoided.

Venefica did not express her confusion, but her face gave voice to it all the same. Nauveena had no trouble reading this. Nothing she said would make sense. She began to cry again.

Venefica asked no more questions, but held her and spoke calmly when she thought it would help. The witch burned juniper and balsam. The calming smoke wafted through the tower. She brewed tea, although Nauveena did not drink any.

Eventually, when she could not cry any longer, Nauveena fell asleep. Venefica covered her with a blanket and then went to rest on the couch, close enough so she could hear her if she needed anything. She could not do much else.

Nauveena did not dream. For the first time in many nights, she did not wander the dark corridors. She did not carry a lantern and hear the footsteps behind her.

Now, she knew the dream had come true. The light that had been guiding her had gone out and she was lost in darkness.

The dwarves acted quickly and without being asked. They knew what to do. They gathered their mining equipment, shovels, and pickaxes, and went into the mountains. They brought surveying maps of the geology. They found a vein of marble. They dug deeply, extracting a large piece in the size and specifications they all seemed to know without discussing.

They constructed a system of pulleys and ropes, a conveyer belt through the heavily wooded forest. With great care, they transported the marble back to Athyzia. They found space in a mage's workshop that had not been used for years.

The dwarves cleared space. They put curtains over the windows so no one could look in. Then their artisans set to work. They began with hammers and chisels. Slowly, they chipped away the edges. The rectangular block took on features, changed in shape. It lost its hard edges and softened. It formed contours and dimensions.

A body emerged. A head. Shoulders. Arms holding objects against a torso. A generously slim waist. Then legs leading down to a pedestal, where an inscription would be carved at the end.

More sculptors added their touches. Details began to emerge. The folds of robes. The process of making something as hard as marble look like soft cloth was not easy, and took years of practice and focus.

They worked in shifts over three days. And through the night, using candlelight.

The arms came to hold a book and a scroll. Appropriate objects. The features came last. Here, the most skill and patience was needed. To add the eyes, the nose, the mouth, but also the expression: the care, familiarity, curiosity, and the joke waiting behind every smile.

They polished the marble. Washed away the dust that had come from the process. They added a gloss that made it shine and reflect the light.

Last, they added the inscription:

Snorri
Wisest Sorcerer of His Day
Head of the Academy of Mages
Convener of the Council of Athyzia
Writer, Scholar, Teacher, Friend
211 BU – 1 YU

With even greater care, they loaded the statue, shrouded in sheets, upon a dolly and brought it to Athyzia's courtyard. There, they waited for everyone to gather.

At last, they pulled away the sheets.

Nauveena, in the crowd, looked upon Snorri's likeness and wept.

◆

Snorri was buried outside the Library of Esotericism, on the western side, facing Lake Yalde. The dwarves' statue was placed on top of the burial mound. Over this, wreaths were placed. Fresh roses, orange and red and gold, poppies, and sprouts of clover.

The elves planted a perennial native to their forests: Lanterns of Evening. The flowers would appear tulip-shaped when they sprouted at the end of summer. They bloomed in the evenings and remained through the early night. They absorbed the illumination of the sun and continued to glow faintly, a greenish-white, until midnight.

"Snorri acted as a light to the world," Queen Em' Iriild said, explaining the flower's selection. "Let him continue to be one."

The flowers did not grow outside of elven forests. Not even the gardens and conservatories of Athyzia grew such rare flora.

Malachite provided a eulogy. He spoke well and eloquently and from the heart, but Nauveena could not listen. He explained how he had first met Snorri. That the then-dean of the Library of Esotericism had offered Athyzia as a safe haven for the wandering druid, but still, Nauveena could not listen.

She could not bear to think of Snorri having a special place in others' hearts. She grew selfish and covetous. Now that he was gone, there was so little of him to be shared. He felt stolen from her again when others spoke of memories with him.

The elves began their music next. Not their Songs of Lament, reserved for the elves alone; but soulful and pensive, just the same. They began with chimes and then their harps. Their pipe instruments sounded like the wind itself cried for the lost mage.

Csandril Em' Dale added lyrics, but in a language so old, Nauveena did not even know it. It was just as well, because she did not know what words could capture the sad expression of the music.

The music trailed off and became silence, which felt complete and as if it existed on its own. Everyone stood with their heads bowed for some time.

Slowly, each drifted off and departed. Each took as long as they felt necessary. Then they retreated with one last word of remembrance for the old mage.

A feast had been prepared in Snorri's honor in the banquet hall. As each left the funeral, they went to have food and drinks.

Finally, only Venefica and Nauveena remained.

"Come. There is food. You should eat." The witch led Nauveena away from the statue and the mound of dirt and the dead flowers and the seeds that had not yet taken root.

The banquet hall was already calamitous, boisterous, a million miles away from the sad silence on the western edge of the Library of Esotericism. Nauveena knew everyone mourned in their own way, and that some might mourn with cheer, but she had not expected it to happen so quickly.

The elven warriors from the Wilds and the dwarves and the northerners were having a drinking contest. Each would submit one contestant, then they would each see who could chug the longest. When the other two bowed out, everyone smashed their horns and tankards together with belches and a massive cheer of "*Snorri*!" Then it was begun again. It was not very complicated.

Venefica sat Nauveena down. "Wait here. I will make you a plate."

Nauveena watched the feast further. Only the Protectors and Keepers of Order were not present. They seldom ate during the day, choosing instead to fast in the scriptorium.

The southern merchants sat on the edge of the drinking contest, watching it curiously, not wanting to get involved, as they were certain they would lose. The other elves spoke and joked among each other. A few of the musicians played a heartfelt song, sweet and true, but no longer as sad as it had been before.

Prince Javee and the oracles sat near the elves. They began to intermingle, exchanging jokes with each other. Maybe they were sharing funny memories of Snorri, Nauveena thought. But even if they were, she could not imagine laughing.

She thought of when Snorri had first brought her to Athyzia. He had shared its history. He had showed her each library. And he had told her that each belonged to her. She could go wherever she pleased and read whatever she liked. Athyzia belonged to her. And she belonged to Athyzia.

The crowd around the drinking game became louder, which had not seemed possible. The contingent from the Bogwaah, led by the Burgomaster, Wilhelm Vaah, approached. The Burgomaster meant to challenge the elves and dwarves and northerners, and they all erupted in laughter at the thought.

As Nauveena watched the game, she made eye contact with Queen Breve, who smiled at her. Then the queen stood and approached her.

Nauveena stood when the queen came around the table towards her. Without saying anything, Queen Breve wrapped her arms around Nauveena and hugged her tightly, lifting the sorceress off the ground as if she were a small child. When the queen let go, Nauveena saw tears in her eyes.

"Do you know what the north believes happens after you die?" Queen Breve asked.

Nauveena had read the myths of the north, but she simply shook her head. *No.*

"A warrior, who fought bravely and fought well, is brought to the halls beyond the world: a great mead hall in the cosmos. At night, they drink and they fuck and their horns never go empty and their dicks never go soft. In day, they ride out to hunt and to fight their enemies and to die again, and at night they return to the hall to do it all again."

Nauveena did not know how to respond.

"Your teacher was not a warrior. But he was brave. He was a scholar. So I hope there is a place for scholars, as there is for warriors. A library where he can go and read and write forever. A library where the books do not run out."

"And where the books are always organized?" Nauveena suggested, warming to the idea. "Categorized correctly and placed where they should be?"

"Yes, sure, if that would be nice for you?" Nauveena nodded. It would be. "Then it is there I hope your teacher goes." The queen wrapped Nauveena in another large hug, lifting her off the ground again, though not as high as before.

When she released Nauveena, the sorceress sat down, feeling empty, as if the queen had squeezed everything out of her with her hug. She liked to think of a *Library Beyond the World*, but she doubted its existence.

The queen looked up. Nauveena followed her eyes. At the gates of the hall, King Caron waited. He and the queen exchanged glances. Queen Breve placed her hand on Nauveena's shoulder and pumped it softly. "If you need anything at all, know I am here. Many fall in the north, and we have many ways to remember them."

Before Nauveena could say anything, the queen left. Nauveena watched her go. Caron slipped out first, with Queen Breve right behind.

In her grief, Nauveena did not look back at the drinking game. There, a young page tapped the King of Yülk on the shoulder and motioned to the door. King Ümlaut watched as first King Caron left the banquet hall, and then his wife.

Nauveena was not hungry. She saw Venefica gathering food for her on a tray — roasted lamb and bread and a stein of Clovis ale — but she did not want any of it. She did not feel she should be in the room, where the jokes and the merriment had already begun again.

She got up and left.

Nauveena found Snorri's room as it had always been: cluttered and messy. Cups half full of water and mugs half full of cold tea. Books open on his sofa.

Their chess game from months before remained unfinished. Nauveena studied it now and it became clear: Snorri was only a move away from check. She had not noticed, but neither had he — too distracted by the council.

On the windowsill, the parrots squawked. Someone would have to feed them. And water the plants.

On the nightstand next to Snorri's chair lay *Philosophies of Magic* with a quill stuck in as a bookmark. He had been reading it only the other night.

Nauveena took the book and clutched it tightly against her chest. She sobbed.

She could not be in the room any longer. It reminded her too much of her mentor. It had been a mistake to come here.

She brought the book with her and went outside. She strolled along the path, trying to control herself. But everywhere reminded her of Snorri. He had brought her to Athyzia and given her a tour of all the grounds. She remembered him leading her along the path as a child.

She paused on a balcony overlooking the lake. She still clutched *Philosophies of Magic*, but she did not cry as heavily now. Only a few tears rolled down her cheeks.

"There you are."

Nauveena turned around.

"Dry your eyes," Venefica said. Her consoling tone from the last few days had vanished. "The time for tears is over. You have wept enough."

"It is not just that he is gone," Nauveena said. "All his work is gone too. The council cannot continue."

"But it must continue."

"Who will lead it?"

Venefica looked at Nauveena.

"Me?"

"Who else?" Venefica asked. "Do not doubt yourself. We all know what you did. You held Athyzia when the Osseomancer bent his whole will against you. You must lead us now."

Chapter Two
The Bear, the Wolf, and the Owl

"What is it about the northern latitudes that brings out the beast lurking within man?"

~Navigations and Currents
Captain Kru
51 BU

"Why should we even have this council?" Nauveena asked. "What if Fallou gains the votes he needs? It is too great a risk."

"No, the council is needed," Venefica said. "Snorri was right. Each realm cannot turn away from each other and return to how things were before. We must remain united as we were against the Osseomancer."

"Snorri wanted to end it. He would not allow a vote on the matter of blood magic."

"I understand his thought, but he panicked after submitting to Fallou early in the council. I would have told Snorri to remain strong. We cannot leave the kingdoms of the east to their own devices. The common folk are scared. In their fear, they will turn to the Magic of Order."

"*Let them,*" Nauveena said.

Venefica looked aghast. "Do you hear yourself? 'Let them?' They will destroy the magic users in their kingdoms. Witches. Folk mages. Elves. The fears of the common folk will be stoked and ignited into a bloodlust. They will blame these mages for the war with the Osseomancer and take out their vengeance upon them."

"It is just..." Nauveena still doubted herself. She did not finish her thought.

A scream. A man's. The words came guttural and unintelligible, but they carried terrible anger and wrath and — Nauveena thought — sadness. Hurt.

It bellowed across Athyzia, ringing across the stone buildings — echoing and not subsiding, so they could not tell from where it came.

"What was that?" Venefica asked.

After the other night, Nauveena felt sheer terror. She could not experience danger so quickly again. She clutched *Philosophies of Magic* to her chest as if it were a shield protecting her. She thought of Snorri's fall from the tower. He had not screamed then. He had fallen silently, accepting his fate.

More screaming. Shouts. Another man. So loud that all of Athyzia could hear the course language.

"It sounds like it is coming from the direction of the northerners," Venefica said.

It was.

The screams transformed. They became the roars of a creature. A giant beast. Nauveena and Venefica could only watch as it bounded through Athyzia, revealing itself as it weaved between buildings: gray and silver and hulking.

They remained on the balcony, transfixed. The creature closed in, gaining shape.

Now, Nauveena knew what it was.

The wolf rushed in, snapping and snarling. Both women leapt back in surprise. The beast was massive. It whipped through the balcony, almost bowling them over with its hindquarters.

It could not control itself. It had been sent in flight. Panic. It thrashed about, flailing. Terrified. Afraid.

Nauveena and Venefica gripped each other tightly. They shrank against the balustrade. They cowered as the wolf whipped around, looking for an exit.

"What is it?" Venefica gasped. "Where did it come from?"

Nauveena knew.

The beast had raced into their midst as if it were being chased. She saw emotions etched into the wolf's face: panic, shame, fear.

But she also saw its eyes. And she recognized them.

King Caron.

The wolf whipped back its head and howled. The sound thudded into Nauveena's chest, pushing her back further.

As quickly as it had appeared, the wolf raced away into the labyrinth of Athyzia.

"What was that?" Venefica asked.

"We need to go," Nauveena said.

"Why? What was that? Where did it come from?"

But already, Nauveena heard what had been chasing the creature.

The black bear was monstrous. Larger than any animal Nauveena had ever seen before. It ran just as fast as the wolf, but Athyzia had not been built for such a hulking creature. Its shoulders collided with columns, smashing the marble and knocking busts from their pedestals.

"What is this?" Venefica had not yet understood the first creature. She didn't comprehend the danger coming.

"King Ümlaut," Nauveena said.

"What?" Then Venefica's eyes grew with understanding. They had seen the warriors of the north transform. The lineage of berserkers ran strong within them. But none achieved the might of their kings' animalistic transformations. Even in her panic, Nauveena noticed how the bear's black coat was speckled gray like King Ümlaut's beard.

Nauveena and Venefica had nowhere to go. They found themselves stranded on the balcony. Caron had just left, and they did not have time before King Ümlaut was upon them.

The bear reared up on its hind legs, arching its back and colliding with the top of a pergola. It yanked the structure from its foundation, splintering it and sending a cascade of fragments down onto the women. Colliding with the structure sent the bear into a deeper rage. The anger spurred the animal on, growing further in size. It cast about, looking for the direction the wolf had gone. As it did, it continued to roar and swing its massive paws.

As it swung, it came closer and closer to Nauveena and Venefica. When it saw them, the animal fell back onto all four legs and roared at them — unhinging its jaws to reveal teeth, each as large as Nauveena's hand. It closed the short gap between them. In its rage, the bear — King

Ümlaut — sought to destroy all in its path. Venefica pressed her body in front of Nauveena.

The bear swiped. Its claws slashed across Venefica's waist. The force lifted her off her feet and sent her spiraling towards the other end of the balcony. She landed lifelessly in a pile.

"Venefica!"

Nauveena stood alone before the beast. It snarled. Hot breath flared from its nostrils. It once again opened its jaw. Nauveena's head could have fit inside. The beast reared, prepared to strike.

Nauveena reacted the only way she knew how — the same way she had protected Athyzia through all those years.

The magic coursed out of her. From her chest, down her arms, and out through her fingertips. The vibrations of an electrical buzz filled the balcony. The power came out in purple tendrils, emitting from her fingers, flaring out and protecting her.

The aura surrounded her. A throbbing, pulsating bubble, limning Nauveena in amethyst light, her protections for Athyzia in miniature.

The bear pounded against the aura, but it would not break. Its force caused radiating patterns along the outer rim, but nothing more. The protections only enraged the bear further. It stood on it hind legs and roared once more. Then it pivoted away from Nauveena, towards Venefica.

The witch had not moved since she had been tossed so violently. King Ümlaut, in his altered form, had not even recognized her. He had only lashed out in anger, unable to find his true foe. Now, it rounded on Venefica again. She only lay there, helpless and immobile.

"Venefica!" Nauveena screamed. The sound remained trapped within her aura. The witch could not hear her, anyways.

Nauveena's body shuddered when she stopped producing the magical power. She slumped down momentarily, sapped from the energy the force had taken. She fell to her knees. And drew in a deep breath.

The bear had turned completely and now stood above Venefica.

Nauveena picked herself up. She could not get around the bear. The balcony was too small, and the bear too large. It rose again to its hind legs. It meant to come down on the witch with all its weight.

Nauveena knew now what had happened. King Ümlaut's queen. The secret everyone else had known but him. Its discovery had sent him into a rage. He could not control himself. The power made him formidable on the battlefield, but now, it threatened Venefica.

Nauveena made the only move available to her. She rushed forward and slid between the bear's legs. She skidded across the ground, landing beside Venefica. Just as the bear was coming down with its full weight to strike the witch, Nauveena let the magic radiate out of her. She held up one hand. The other she used to cover the witch.

The power from the one hand was enough. A shield. Tender magic. After having protected all of Athyzia, the small bit needed to stop the bear was not much at all. King Ümlaut bounced back, shocked by the immovable bit of magic. Waves of force ripped across the aura, but it did not bend. The Osseomancer had sent much worse.

Thwarted by the spell, the bear fell backwards. It sat and looked around, dazed. Nauveena watched from beneath her spell. Above the bear, in the space where the pergola had once been, came an owl — a beautiful snow owl, the size of which Nauveena had never seen before.

The owl flew down and landed on top of Nauveena's aura. It became Queen Breve rather quickly. Nauveena had wondered what animal the queen transformed into.

The northern queen came forward and placed a hand upon the bear. "Please, no. Not here."

The bear only looked at her in shock.

"I am sorry you found out this way. I truly am. I never wanted to hurt you."

Nauveena could see King Ümlaut's large features hidden within the bear's snout. He looked wounded, and not from colliding with Nauveena's aura.

"Did you ever love me?" The bear's mouth yawned wide to speak, growling the words.

"I did, and I still do. But I love another more. And you have done nothing to lose me except love me enough to be free." Queen Breve stroked the bear's paw gently. She had long ago learned how to soothe the king in such a state.

"I will kill him," King Ümlaut growled.

"Please do not," Queen Breve said. "He knows he has wronged you. Let that be enough."

"No, no. He will pay." As the queen calmed the king, the bear's features softened and gradually looked more and more like Ümlaut's. "I will fight for you."

"You will fight for me, or for your pride?" Queen Breve asked.

The bear's features returned. King Ümlaut roared, and the queen stepped back. "We could have peace. Do not throw the northern kingdoms into war over this."

The bear grew again. Queen Breve wisely retreated further. Nauveena strengthened her aura.

"Please. Let there be peace," Breve asked again before transforming back into the owl. She flapped her wings to fly above the bear. Her wingspan was the length of a grown man. "Know that I loved you."

The bear roared in response. Queen Breve flew higher, but low enough that the bear could see her and follow her from Athyzia.

When the bear had left, Nauveena let her aura disintegrate again. She shook Venefica. The witch still breathed, but the slashes across her waist were very deep. A pool of blood covered the cobblestones around her. Many of her braids had come undone, and her hair twisted out in frizzing curls.

Malachite rushed over. Nauveena looked up to see many had come from the funeral feast. The druid threw his cloak over Venefica, pressing against her cuts to stop the bleeding. "What happened?" he asked.

The scene spoke for itself. Nauveena could not find the words to describe it. Instead, only a single lingering thought prodded at her: *We just lost two votes.*

Chapter Three
Councils of War

> "When witches use body parts in their potions or utilize ancient curses, it is witchcraft and thought of as dangerous. When sorcerers perform such spells, it is called 'research.'"
>
> ~*Magic and Hypocrisy*
> Comus
> 157 BU

Venefica's body was brought to the infirmary adjacent to the Library of Maladies, where the Medicinal Mage, Caduceus, could see to her. She had not just suffered the cuts from the bear's paws, but in her collision, had slammed her head against the hard ground. Nauveena found a rather large bump on the back of her head. Her skull might have fractured from the impact. The concussion had knocked her unconscious.

Malachite requested the aid of the forest. He left Athyzia and spread word to the animals to gather what remedies they could. A stag gathered newt moss from the foot of the mountains. Several squirrels retrieved laurel, while a pack of foxes brought anemone.

The forests around Athyzia had many magical properties. The Botanical Mage supplied many soothing herbs. All these were mashed into a compound by Caduceus and pressed against the cuts to absorb the blood and close the skin.

Nauveena wondered what remedies Venefica might have used. She likely would have made a broth from something strange, though Nauveena did not know what — the blood of a castrated dog, perhaps — to fortify herself and gain strength. She would have sealed her wounds with a mushroom that only grew downstream of certain sheep pastures.

Such witchcraft and folk magic had been dismissed by most sorcerers. Others considered them taboo for tapping into darker magics. Only some paid them a mild curiosity. Nauveena was uncertain how effective such methods would be, but she had recently learned how powerful Venefica's own spells had been.

As far as the Medicinal Mage was concerned, the best remedy was leaving the witch alone. Nauveena was allowed to remain, but many other well-wishers were turned away, except for the king of Druissia, who could not be kept from the witch.

King Bane sat by Venefica's bed for many hours. He bent his head, as if praying. Nauveena paced behind him, uncertain what to do. She had sat on the terrace besides the king for many sessions. She had even spoken to him directly. But now she did not know what to say.

After some time, however, the king spoke instead. He did not turn his head to look at Nauveena, so she was not certain if he was speaking to her or to the air, making grandiose and poetic statements to ease his own mind. "The worst thing a king can see is his people suffering," he said. "A king is not a king if he cannot protect his people. I owe the witch my kingdom, but also my life. In trying to beat back the siege, I suffered a mortal wound. Surely, I would have died, but she produced the cure. I wish I could return the favor, but my own magic is clumsy, and only good for fighting."

Now, King Bane looked at Nauveena. His eyes were moist from holding back tears. "Will you watch over her?" he asked. "I would feel better if she had a friend beside her."

Friend. Nauveena was not surprised to be called such. She knew her closeness to the witch had not gone unnoticed.

"You must leave?" she asked.

"The war in the north demands my attention," King Bane said simply.

After colliding with Nauveena and Venefica, Caron had slipped from Athyzia and continued in flight through the forests and passes beyond the mountains. His soldiers heard his howl. He conveyed much in his wail. They abandoned their drinking games. They transformed into wolves.

They had been standing beside the men of Yülk, laughing with them, drinking with them, treating them like brothers. But with that howl, they knew they were now at war. They transformed and followed Caron from Athyzia.

When the men of Yülk learned what had happened, they transformed too. They raced to find their forlorn king. They would console him the only way they knew how.

Only six months after Pravulum fell, the peace had shattered.

"What does their war have to do with Druissia?" Nauveena asked.

"Any war in Jenor concerns the king of Druissia. My viziers wish to know how to respond. But it is not just the war in the north that concerns me. My viziers have come to me with disturbing reports from our borders. I will return when I can. Send for me if anything happens."

"Of course."

After King Bane had left, Nauveena leaned over the bed. She had spent so many nights with the witch, debriefing about the events of the day. She had gotten so used to those talks. Now, she could only think of what she would say to Venefica if she were awake.

She had come to rely on the witch for advice. She longed for such advice now. Should she continue the council? What should be done about the votes of the northern kings? She had come to rely on Venefica almost as much as Snorri for counsel. Now, she had neither.

Venefica was something other than Snorri, too. Nauveena loved Snorri, and missed him, but he had always been her mentor — the single authority in her life. King Bane had said it: Venefica was her *friend*, strange though it was. Nauveena had been alone in Athyzia so long, she could not remember the last time she'd had one.

Venefica had been hurt defending her. She should have acted sooner.

Her mind wandered. She still held Snorri's *Philosophies of Magic*. She tried reading, but she could not keep her concentration. Her eyes drooped, but she could not sleep.

Late at night, Queen Em' Iriild arrived. She placed her hand on the witch and listened to her labored breathing. Nauveena watched as the queen closed her eyes and absorbed Venefica's trauma.

"She will be alright," the queen said eventually. "She just needs time to rest and to heal."

With the Elf Queen's reassurances, Nauveena finally relaxed. She still would not leave Venefica's side, but she could sleep. She went to another infirmary bed and pulled the sheets over herself.

◆

For the first time in five nights — the first time since Snorri fell — Nauveena dreamed.

She wished she did not. When she dreamed, her sleeping became interrupted, agitated. She tossed and turned, trying to escape.

She continued to wander in this dream. But the dark, twisting corridors were gone. They had been replaced with the inside of a tower. She climbed the stairs within and continued to climb higher and higher. She did not know how far the tower continued.

When she found a window and looked out, all she could see was fog. Above, the top of the tower disappeared into clouds. She could only continue to climb.

The inside of the tower reminded her of that night. That dreaded night. Nauveena could not escape her memories. They now trespassed into her dreams. Those spiral stairs had also felt like they wound forever upward and would not end.

She could not escape something else, too. Below her, on the stairs, she could hear the faint sound of footsteps. The spy, the interloper, had returned.

Her memories did not trespass into her dreams alone. For the stranger did not belong either.

While the tower's stone and architecture had realistic qualities, these ended. The tower was composed of the ethereal quality of dreams. It did not exist anywhere.

The stranger, however, was real, physical, actual. He was not a dream, but had crossed into hers from somewhere else. He had first chased her in her earlier nightly dreams, and he had now followed her here.

Nauveena quickened her pace. She climbed the stairs as quickly as she could, trying to put distance between herself and the stranger.

She climbed, threw open doors, pushed through trap doors, only to find more stairs, more ladders. One chamber opened to another. The tower only continued.

And the stranger continued to follow.

In the morning, the new head of the Academy of Mages came to speak with Nauveena at the infirmary. Upon Snorri's death, leadership of the Academy had passed to the next most tenured mage: the Imaginary Mage, Pinerva.

Pinerva had devoted her studies to the subject of imagination, a field not all considered magic. She had published many books on the matter, and under her the Library of Imagination had grown. However, that had been many years ago. Now, she hunched her back and her hair had turned white. Nauveena wondered how wise it was to use seniority to select the Head of the Academy.

"I am terribly sorry about Snorri," the Imaginary Mage said to Nauveena.

Despite her being the new Head of the Academy, the Medicinal Mage had still shooed Pinerva from the infirmary so that Venefica's rest would not be disturbed. Now, she and Nauveena spoke outside. The morning was bright, and Nauveena was happy to be out in the sunshine and away from her dreams.

"He was a great mage," Pinerva said. "An example for us all. I know how close you were."

"Thank you." Nauveena bowed her head.

"I admired him as a colleague. He taught me many things. I want you to know, if you need anything at all, please do not hesitate to ask."

"Thank you," Nauveena said again. In the days since Snorri's death, many mages had shared similar sentiments:

"He was a pleasure to work with."

"He will be so missed."

"Let me know if there is anything you need."

Nauveena did not doubt Pinerva's sincerity; she had only run out of responses.

"And now, there is the matter of the witch. How is she recovering?"

"She will make it."

"What an ordeal. The shapeshifting ability can transform the mind as well as the body. The king of Yülk was not himself; he was the bear, driven mad with rage."

Nauveena nodded. She thought of King Ümlaut on the battlefields of the north. Likely, he was still pursuing King Caron there. When they arrived in the north, Caron would make his stand, and the two kingdoms that had stood beside each other the longest would clash.

"I have come to you to speak on the matter of the council," Pinerva said.

"Yes?"

"Snorri led the council in his capacity as Head of the Academy of Mages. Now, that role has fallen to me. But I have attended few sessions. Not many topics pertain to my specialties. And I will be quite busy transitioning to this new role. I wondered — this is the first council of its kind — there is no reason why it *must* be led by the Head of the Academy."

Nauveena remembered her conversation with Venefica right before the attack. She remembered the witch's confidence in her. "No, I suppose you are right."

"You know Snorri's mind more than anyone. You helped him plan the council. You attended all the meetings. Could you not lead it?"

"Yes, I think I will," Nauveena said. She could see a weight lift from Pinerva. The mage had been nervous about the prospect of leading a council she was unfamiliar with. "You are not the first to make the suggestion. But I do not know how well I will do."

"You will do fine."

"And I do not even know if the council will continue."

"Why would it not?"

"Well." Nauveena laughed to herself when she thought of all the events stacked on top of themselves, one after the other. "Snorri is gone, and it was his idea. And now, two members have left and are at war with each other. The council committed itself to maintaining peace in Jenor. Already, we have failed."

Pinerva stepped back, uncertain what to say. If anything, she only looked more relieved not to have to lead the council herself.

"If it does continue, I am certain you will do an excellent job." She smiled. "It is a remarkable idea — all the realms united together. You know, what I admired most about Snorri was his imagination."

◈

Nauveena returned to Venefica. The witch still slept. Nauveena listened to her ragged breathing. She shook. Already, the balm created by Malachite and Queen Em' Iriild's healing energy had helped. The Medicinal Mage had cleaned the dressings while she was away, and the bleeding had stopped. While Venefica's breath was still jagged, it now sounded like a heavy sleep with bothersome dreams more than anything else.

Still, she looked uncomfortable in her rest. She still wore her elegant crimson gown and the rat skull pendant as a necklace. The weight of it couldn't have been comfortable. Nauveena reached down to remove it, but, when her hands neared the clasp, she thought better of it. It would remain, even if it might not be the most comfortable to sleep with.

The Medicinal Mage entered the room. "You have visitors," she told Nauveena.

"More?"

"I asked them to wait in the library. I do not want too many bothering her," Caduceus said.

An enclosed skybridge connected the upper floors of the infirmary to the Library of Maladies. While Nauveena found the contents of the library useful, she did her best to avoid it. If she needed one of its books, she would check it out, rather than read it in the library itself.

The mage who designed the library had wanted to capture its purpose. Since the library collected accounts of all the terrible things that could happen to the human body, the mage commissioned several murals depicting those very things on the library's ceilings. The library consisted of tall walls ringed by balconies opening to the floor below. From every point, it was impossible to escape the paintings above.

To make the paintings more disconcerting, the mage had hired the famous artist Portyr to paint the ceilings. Portyr had a personal vendetta against Hermes of Qadma, one of the other mages of the Academy, supposedly for cuckolding him. He, therefore, chose to depict Hermes in all the paintings, which then cathartically showed Hermes suffering terrible harm and, more often than not, death.

While talented in many ways, Portyr had difficulty capturing human emotion. Each painting showed Hermes either smiling or only mildly inconvenienced by his predicament. He smiled while being burned at the stake. Again as the executioner readied his axe. He did look rather annoyed with his neck in a noose, and more annoyed at suffering from bubonic plague. However, these paled in comparison to what he probably should have been feeling.

Nauveena made a habit of avoiding the library as much as possible. She found Malachite, King Bane, Prince Javee, and Kìtrinos waiting on the main floor below.

"How is she?" Malachite asked when Nauveena finished descending the spiral staircase.

"Has there been any progress since yesterday?" King Bane asked.

"She will make a full recovery," Nauveena said. "I just saw her, and she is resting now. She will need much rest."

"I have half a mind to take my armies north," King Bane said. His introspection had turned to anger over the night. "Join Künner. Make King Ümlaut pay for what he has done."

"Please do not," Nauveena said. "Venefica would not want that."

King Bane looked as if he agreed. His viziers had also advised him against such action. But he needed his anger to go somewhere, and war was the only outlet he knew.

"Yes, please. We do not need the war to escalate," Prince Javee said. "There might be plenty of war to come. Only the other night, Kìtrinos foretold coming conflict, but I did not think it referred to this. What did you say exactly?"

"'With the coming of the long days,'" Kìtrinos said in her half-asleep lilt, "'two friends will become enemies and clash over love.'"

That would have been helpful to have heard sooner, Nauveena thought. Maybe she could have pieced it together. Then she thought of her own dreams. What did the new one mean? She had not been able to interpret her previous dreams beforehand either.

"My only question," Prince Javee said, "is who tipped off Ümlaut."

"What do you mean?"

"Well, Caron and Breve have been flaunting their affair under his nose for years. Everyone knew but him. Now, all of a sudden, he gets a clue and catches them."

"Who might have told him?"

"Anyone — everyone knew, right?"

Nauveena had a few guesses. But she did not voice these. Already, Prince Javee had turned to other matters.

"Will you be overseeing the council now?" he asked.

"I suppose I will be," Nauveena said. "As everyone expects it will be me anyways."

King Bane grunted. "No one else would be qualified to take over."

"Pinerva seems to think so too," Nauveena said. "She's just been to see me. As Head of the Academy, I suppose she makes it official. I will be leading the council going forward."

She felt a sharp ping of guilt. It should have been Snorri. The council had been Snorri's vision. He should have been able to see it through. She did not think she would do half as good a job.

"Of course, Snorri did want to *end* the council." Nauveena's revelation sparked looks of surprise on her guests' faces.

"Whatever for?" Malachite asked.

"Fallou's proposal. Banning blood magic. It was what Snorri and I were speaking about right before he..." Nauveena couldn't finish.

"Doesn't that make the council even more important?" Prince Javee asked.

"The council can condemn such thoughts," Malachite said.

"It can also validate them." Nauveena found herself repeating Snorri's last words. She had disagreed with him, but now, she wasn't so sure. "Just having a vote on the issue sends the message that it is worth discussing. And Fallou has a solid eight votes at a minimum. Even if we vote down such a ban, those votes will send a clear message on what the kingdoms of the east feel."

"They are making those beliefs known even without the council," King Bane said. "Druissia's borders have seen refugees since the war, but those numbers have increased in the last few days. Now, they speak of witch burnings and trials. Confessions given under torture. Confessions to things that are not even crimes. Fallou is using the reports he shared the other night to whip the common folk into a frenzy."

"He'll try to impose his will across all of Jenor," Nauveena said.

"Which is why the council must vote to stop him," Prince Javee said.

"And what if he gains the votes to force a ban through the council?" Nauveena asked.

"We can't let that happen," Prince Javee said.

"Even if the council votes against a ban, Fallou and the east would be free to do what they want in their kingdoms," Nauveena said.

"If they do, we are prepared to resist them," King Bane said.

"'Resist them?'" Nauveena didn't like the tone of that.

"Yes," King Bane said. "If the council votes against such a ban, but the east installs a ban anyways, we would be prepared to…"

"To what?" Nauveena asked, though already, she could guess it easily enough.

"Go to war," Prince Javee finished.

"War?" Nauveena couldn't believe it. "We have only known peace for six months." *And already that has ended in the north.*

"If it comes to it," King Bane said, "we must be prepared to enforce the edicts of the council. For the most extreme measures, we would go to war to uphold the council."

"The council is meant to prevent war, not cause it." Nauveena felt exasperated. How could she lead? She would not be able to keep the council from descending into war. She needed Snorri.

"Of course, we can only do it if the council votes against these bans," Prince Javee said. "Both our kingdoms are war-weary, and it will be hard to justify another war with Faulsk. But if the council condemns these bans, and Faulsk enacts them anyways, then we will have no choice."

"As much as Druissia wishes to absorb these refugees from the east," King Bane said, "if they increase, it will become untenable. We are still recovering from the blight. We will not be able to feed everyone. These people are entitled to live freely in their own lands."

"Of course they are entitled to that," Nauveena said. "The people of Jenor are also entitled to a world without war."

"But would the war not be justified?" Prince Javee asked. "If the kingdoms of the east are doing much worse to their own people?"

"If it comes to it," King Bane said, "we cannot go to war alone. We must have the backing of the Academy."

Ah, Nauveena thought, *here is the crux of it.* "The Academy has always abstained from the wars of man," she said. "The War with the Osseomancer was the exception."

"Yes, but if the council votes against these restrictions, then won't the Academy be forced to defend them?" King Bane asked.

"Is this not just a pretense to go to war with Faulsk?" Nauveena asked. Even if the council went exactly as she wished, she could not see a scenario where Faulsk willingly followed every edict they passed. What would happen then? Would Qadantium and Druissia go to war to defend the council? Did she even want that? Was it better than letting Faulsk continue their persecutions?

"I will not pretend their recent expansion is not troubling," King Bane said. "Jenor has never known peace when Faulsk has gained too much influence. Now, it has dominion over the middle kingdoms through the Magic of Order and strong alliances with Rheum and Lyrmica. If they are allowed to continue gaining strength, we soon might not be able to stand against them."

"They are always looking outward," Prince Javee said. "And this Magic of Order they have adopted only increases that drive. Their power increases with each additional common folk under their yoke. After Faulsk solidifies power in the east, they will look to Druissia next, and then to Qadantium."

"I cannot speak for the Academy," Nauveena said. She thought of Pinerva, the Imaginary Mage. She was much more occupied with academic pursuits than the arguments between men. She had not attended many sessions of the council. She would be quite shocked if she were required to go to war.

"But we must enforce the council rulings somehow," King Bane said.

"Snorri had hoped there would be no need," Nauveena said. "He hoped the council would come together in agreement. That through discussion, everyone could come to some sort of understanding. He had not anticipated how entrenched the Magic of Order would be."

"What would you suggest we do?" Prince Javee asked.

Nauveena had no idea. She couldn't believe anyone would expect her to. But of course they would, especially if she led the council. "I am still thinking of that," she said. "Part of me now understands Snorri's thoughts. Why have a council at all? And if we are to continue, we can't do much without the votes of the northern kings."

"What do you mean?"

"When King Ümlaut and King Caron left to go to war with each other, they brought their votes with them. Now only twenty-four will vote. But the northern votes would have very likely been with us. They would have been reliable numbers. Now, Fallou only needs thirteen for a majority. He is much closer to his goal."

"They can't make that big a difference," King Bane said.

"Two reliable votes makes all the difference in the world." Nauveena had studied the numbers so closely, she was surprised others were not as familiar. "Fallou has eight. Before, he needed fourteen for a majority; now, he needs thirteen. He is one vote closer. The southern merchants do not understand magic; who knows how they will side? They have three votes alone. Aryde only wants to protect themselves. The dwarves could be bribed with the Last Mountains. Our numbers are tenuous. It is one thing if this council votes against the ban, but *what if they vote for it*?"

"The only option is to speak with the northern kings," Malachite said. "They may not be persuaded to end their war and return, but they might see the sense in sending a proxy. They have an interest in many of the council's issues."

"A proxy? Is that possible?" Prince Javee looked at Nauveena.

"We never said it wasn't." On this, Nauveena felt confident providing a verdict. She and Snorri had discussed it at length. "Malachite is the proxy for the centaurs and animals, after all. Someone could act as a proxy for one or both of the northern kings." But there was a catch. "But the northern kings must grant their proxy."

King Bane sighed, understanding the issue. "And, of course, they are hundreds of miles away in the north."

"Someone must go to them," Malachite said.

"Can we not use speaking stones?" Prince Javee asked. "It is how I have been speaking with Qadma."

"The north does not hold any," Malachite said. "Someone must travel there to speak with them the old-fashioned way."

"Who would go?" King Bane asked.

"I have not been in the north in many years, but I still remember the way," Malachite said.

Nauveena felt heartbroken. "I will lose you too, then?"

"Only for a time," the druid said. "I will return as soon as I can. With a fast horse, I could reach the north in a few days. The difficulty will be finding them at battle and speaking to both sides."

"Take one of my steeds," King Bane said.

"Thank you," Malachite said. "I will leave now, so there is no more delay. With all this speech about proxies, I suppose there is the matter of my vote. I do not want us to be down another number. King Bane, now, in front of witnesses, I am entrusting you with my vote until my return."

King Bane bowed deeply towards the druid. Becoming his proxy was quite the honor. He was not only Malachite's proxy, but by extension, the voice of all the birds and beasts and centaurs — a great honor indeed. He looked truly touched to have been selected.

"However, I would advise you not to vote until I return," Malachite said. "Nauveena is right. It is dangerous without the certainty of the northerners' two votes. Do whatever you can to delay. I will be as quick as I can."

Without another word, Malachite turned from the group and rushed out of the library.

Chapter Four
Definitions of Magic

> "It speaks to the sorcerer's own entitlement that we have claimed the term 'mage' for ourselves. We call ourselves 'mage' so frequently — and to the exclusion of all others — that the term is practically synonymous with sorcerer, despite its original intent."
>
> ~*Notes on Magic*
> Snorri the Esoteric
> 57 BU

As King Bane and Prince Javee gathered their things to leave, Nauveena glanced at Kìtrinos. "Do you have a moment? There is something I wanted to ask you."

Kìtrinos looked at her, puzzled.

"We can stay," Prince Javee said.

"I think I would rather — I would rather it be private," Nauveena said.

Now, it was Javee's turn to look confused.

"I can meet you later," Kìtrinos said to him.

"Nauveena, as always, it was great speaking with you." King Bane bowed. "I will go now to look after Venefica. I cannot stay long, I am afraid."

"I will come as well if that Medicinal Mage will let me," Prince Javee said. "I do hope for a speedy recovery." Both said goodbye and then left down the wide aisle of the Library of Maladies.

When they had left, Nauveena turned back to Kìtrinos. "I wanted to talk to you about something."

"The vision you had with me the other day?" she asked.

Nauveena reeled back, startled. "Yes, how did you — "

"You've had it again?"

"I was having it frequently."

"The dark tunnel. The maze. I remember. Very vivid. You must be touched. You should have gone to Xanthous, and not Athyzia."

Nauveena was unsure how she felt about that. The oracles lived a life of leisure, with all the grapes they could eat and all the wine they could drink. They spent their days sunning themselves and napping. But she preferred Athyzia's books.

"For several weeks, I had the vision every time I slept," she said. "I carried a lantern to light the dark halls. But each night, the lantern would go out."

"I see — very foreboding."

"But I stopped having them."

"When?"

"The night Snorri fell from the tower."

"I see."

"I know what it means now — in retrospect. I only wish I could have interpreted it sooner."

"The true art in prophecy is finding meaning," Kitrinos said.

"Now, there is a new dream."

Kitrinos nodded as if she expected as much.

"I've only had it once," Nauveena continued. "Last night. I was no longer in a hallway, but a tower. It stretched up forever. I could see perfectly fine. It was not dark. But when I looked out the windows, I could not see the top or the bottom. The tower existed in fog."

"And you want to know what it means?"

"I do. But that is not my question."

"Oh." Kitrinos pursed her lips in anticipation.

"In the dream — in both dreams — there is *someone else*."

"It is common to see others in dreams."

"Yes, but I do not think he is supposed to be there. In the first one, I could hear his footsteps following me. Every time I turned to find him, the lamp would go out. Now, he is following me in the tower. I am climbing the stairs faster to get away from him."

"And you are certain he is not part of the dream?"

"Very much so," Nauveena said. "I have become quite conscious during the dream. And while everything looks real and is quite vivid, it is ethereal in quality. *Dreamlike,* for lack of any better word. But these footsteps, they do not belong. It is like the person has crossed over from another dream."

"How peculiar."

"Is that possible?"

"Is what possible?"

"For someone else to be in my dreams?" Nauveena asked.

Kìtrinos thought for a moment. "I am afraid so. Although it can only be done with very powerful magic."

"When you shared my vision, you did not enter it with me."

"I did not. This is an entirely different type of magic. Quite ancient. And dangerous. One should not travel through dreams. It is easy to get lost there."

"But who are they? Why do they want to be in my dreams?"

"It is likely whoever it was that followed you that night," Kìtrinos said. "And threw Snorri from the tower."

"How can you be sure?" Nauveena asked, although she had suspected as much.

"That is how the magic works. Your intruder could not have entered your dreams unless you dreamed about them *first.*"

"But when did I dream about them?"

"You dreamed about them when your vision prophesied being followed that night. That allowed the opening. Your intruder assumed their place in your dreams, and has been in them ever since."

Nauveena's mind spun at the revelation. It felt so utterly *circular.* Her dreams had been prophetic, and showed a future where her and Snorri were followed that night, but by dreaming of her stalker, she had allowed them entry into her dreams. She wondered if such entry to her dreams did not allow the intruder into Athyzia. But then, what came first? The intruder or the prophecy of him? She wanted to read more on such magics, but the literature was lacking. Anytime anyone tried to put it to words, it became confused.

"Is there not some way to find out who it was?" Nauveena asked. This was more important than the logic of dreams. She had her suspicions, but no proof. "Can we not use the prophecy and the dreams to reveal who it was? Who killed Snorri?"

"The prophecy will only reveal what it will reveal," Kìtrinos said. "Nothing more and nothing less."

"Well, what good is that?" Nauveena asked. "What good are any of these prophecies? Sure, I had a vision, but I did not know what it meant until it was too late."

"That happens often with prophecies."

"But how helpful is it, then?" Nauveena asked.

"Who said prophecies had to be helpful? We are given visions of the future which only become illuminated when we look back on them in the past."

"But if I had been able to understand the symbolism of those hallways, I could have..." Nauveena paused. She did not want to say it. "I could have *saved* him."

"Prophecies are not about changing the future," Kìtrinos said. "They are a result of our place in the cosmos. The past, present, and future do not extend in a straight line. They crisscross each other. And those who open themselves to those crisscrossing paths may have glimpses of them — but not more. Only through many years of practice can we ascribe meaning to our visions. The future cannot be read like you would read a book."

Nauveena groaned. "But do you see how frustrating that is?"

"It is frustrating because these prophecies are not what you want them to be."

"What good is seeing the future if I cannot change it?"

"That is something you must come to learn."

"If I knew my prophecy spoke of Snorri's death, I could have prevented it. But instead, I had a symbolic lantern being extinguished. What was I supposed to do with that? How is that useful?"

"You want a useful prophecy?"

"Yes," Nauveena said.

"You will have an unexpected visitor."

"What? Is that a real prophecy?"

Kìtrinos nodded. "Now, I must be going. I do not blame you for becoming frustrated. Many do when they first experience visions. If you continue to have them and would like to discuss, please come find me. I can teach you much about my art."

Nauveena watched as the High Priestess followed the path of Prince Javee and King Bane out of the library. She shook her head. She felt more confused than before. She had hoped Kìtrinos might dissuade her of the notion that someone else was in her dream, but the oracle had only confirmed it.

No sooner had Kìtrinos left the library than a shadow came to darken the doorway. The figure stepped forward, revealing itself as Fallou, the First Protector of Leem — an *unexpected* visitor indeed.

"What do you want?" Nauveena could have been more polite, but Fallou's sudden appearance had surprised her, and it was all she could think to say.

Fallou made his way down the library's central aisle. He looked up at the murals of the mage Hermes dying in every conceivable way. "How pleasant," he said.

"Can I help you?" Nauveena asked in what she imagined was a politer tone.

"How is she?" Fallou asked.

"Venefica?"

"The witch, yes. We have all been quite concerned. Such a tragedy. I am not surprised the king of Yülk lost control. Shapeshifting can often have adverse effects."

"Would you like to ban that too?"

"Wouldn't you?" Fallou asked calmly, as if his comment were not imbued with malice.

"Why are you here?"

"You have private councils with everyone else," he said. "Why not me? Certainly, there are issues we could discuss."

The First Protector of Leem pulled back a chair and sat down. He crossed his legs beneath his gray robe, an act that should have made him more comfortable, but the opposite effect played out in his mannerisms. The act made Nauveena uncomfortable too. Up until now, she had not thought about the fact that Fallou had legs beneath his robes. She didn't like thinking about the fact he possessed a body at all.

"You speak with the elves, the dwarves, Druissia, Qadantium. The list goes on and on," Fallou said. "But the Magic of Order is excluded from these private talks. Why? How does that help the unity of Jenor?"

"I see little reason for us to talk outside of council." Nauveena continued to stand. "When you make your thoughts so very clear. And speaking of unity in Jenor, how unifying is it to persecute your own citizens? King Bane speaks of refugees amassing at his border."

"Those accounts are overblown," Fallou said dismissively. "The towns on Druissia's borders are not always welcoming. Many were displaced by the war and are seeking refuge wherever they can find it. Faulsk has been quite welcoming. I only wish Druissia were too."

"This is not the account I have heard," Nauveena said. "Those refugees speak of unfair trials accusing them of crimes that other places might not consider crimes."

"I thought that was the purpose of this council," Fallou said. "To determine what is and what is not a crime so we can cease disagreements between kingdoms. Certainly, magic that might reawaken the Osseomancer should be deemed a crime. We have moved forward in rooting it out. The council should do the same. How can we not stand against the Osseomancer?"

"Of course the council stands against the Osseomancer." Nauveena finally sat, tired of the nuanced arguing. Everything with Fallou was couched, true meanings and intentions hidden behind vagueness. "But some of the activities you wish to ban have nothing to do with the Osseomancer."

"The Osseomancer was a well-known practitioner of blood magic. Those who continue the art wish to revive him."

"Why are you here?" Nauveena asked.

"I want to understand the state of the council," Fallou said. "The other Protectors and Keepers come to me asking when we will continue again. But I am in the dark. I have not been invited to these private conversations. No one has informed me when the next session will begin."

"Snorri just died."

"Almost a week ago. I imagine he would want us to continue as soon as possible."

A week? It had been five days, but for Nauveena it still felt so fresh. How could they even think of resuming?

"Also, if you did not notice," she said, "two of our council members went to war with each other and badly injured another council member in the process."

"I did not know the witch was an official council member."

"She advises King Bane."

"But it is still *his* vote?"

"Of course, but she is on the council. The matter stands that the council has been delayed for numerous reasons."

"I do not see how the squabbling of two barbarous kingdoms should delay the council."

"They transformed into a bear and a wolf and fought each other in Athyzia. Less than twenty-four hours ago. You will forgive me if I do not return immediately to council."

"I understand the council not beginning today. And I understand suspending the council to afford time for the Esoteric Mage's funeral. But I trust we will begin again tomorrow."

"No, we will not."

"No?"

"No. Malachite has gone north. He will try to persuade the two kings to make peace and return. And if they will not agree to that, he will ask them to give their proxy to someone who can attend the council."

"That could take a long time."

"And we will suspend the council until he returns."

"That could be weeks."

"Then we will wait weeks."

"That will not do," Fallou said. "As we have discussed, we all have pressing matters at home. The Osseomancer may have survived Pravulum. His followers seek to return him to power. We must remove this menace. And we cannot do so from Athyzia. We cannot afford to sit around, waiting for the druid to play peacekeeper."

"Malachite understands the need for haste. I do not believe it will take very long."

"My suggestion would be to continue the council in their absence," Fallou said.

"I will take that into consideration," Nauveena said, even though she would not.

"The northern kings sacrificed their votes when they went to war with each other. They could not control themselves; we should not be forced to delay the council on their behalf."

"I heard you the first time."

"Jenor stands on a knife's edge," Fallou said. "The Osseomancer was defeated, but for how long? As we sit discussing theories and politics in this council, his followers are gathering and devising ways to return him. We must move quickly to discuss those issues, to ensure he does not return."

"We will not ban blood magic," Nauveena said definitively.

"Let us vote. It is only right. Let us have the discussion. And then let the council make a decision. We have spent weeks debating the proper calendar and the sharing of books, but then you will not allow for the council to vote on these critical matters — at this, the most critical time."

"Blood magic and these other magics you find dark are not practiced by the followers of the Osseomancer alone," Nauveena said. "The source of magic is not what makes it good or bad. Only the mage producing the magic can determine that."

"I disagree with that wholeheartedly," Fallou said. Nauveena began to argue, but before she could he said, "Let me ask you a question: What is magic?"

"'What is magic?' What kind of a question is that?"

"What is the definition you would use?"

Nauveena felt suddenly stumped. Despite all the books she had read, she had never seen an actual definition of magic. Magic could be so many things. It avoided a single definition.

"Magic is magic," she said, feeling foolish. "It is moving objects with the mind, it is understanding where the stars will be tomorrow, it is curing fevers with ingredients from the forest, it is transforming into a bear, or a wolf, or an owl."

"But why is *that* magic?"

"It is magic because it is extraordinary," Nauveena said, feeling more foolish still.

"I will tell you how I think of magic," Fallou said. "There are some things that many people — if not all — can do. That follow the laws of nature: boiling water, churning milk into cheese, running, jumping. And then there are acts that only some can do, but not others: transformations, summoning, making potions. What is special about those second sets of things? Anyone can follow the guide to a potion, add the ingredients together, and mix them. But the concoction will only yield the desired effect if a magic user has done the mixing. If a common folk does, the potion falls apart.

"If everyone could follow the recipe and the potion worked, then it would not be magical. It would be bread rising in the oven, beer fermenting, or making any simple dinner. So what makes it magic is that only some can do it and not all. The common folk are then necessary — no, *required* — for magic. Their inability defines what is magic and what is just a simple task. Magic is achieving an effect that not all could achieve. And if everyone could achieve it, it would not be magic."

"What's your point?"

"My point is that most mages completely overlook the common folk, when if they did not exist, the mage would not be special in any way. The common folk make the mage and sorcerer extraordinary through comparison. So now let me ask you a second question: Why can some do magic while others cannot?"

Nauveena had studied this question quite thoroughly, but in front of Fallou, she could not articulate the answer. She only knew many theories, and she worried about voicing them. She was certain he would have some counterargument proving her wrong and once again making her feel silly.

Fallou did not wait for Nauveena to respond. "Magic itself has created a hierarchy," he said. "To some, it has given extraordinary abilities. To others, it has not. But those others were not simply forgotten. They were not given abilities in order to define those who were. To set them apart. To lift them up. And this hierarchy must be respected for magic to function properly."

"Does it say all this in your book?" Nauveena asked.

"*The Book of Order* contains many such wisdoms and more, yes," Fallou said. "Of course, it is not just a matter of magic functioning correctly. It is also a matter of magic functioning justly and fairly and well. Magic has been given to some so that its gifts can be shared with the world. Magic is meant to benefit all because it is defined by all — by both those with it and those without it."

"And let me guess: The peasants must remain poor and feeble for magic to truly work?"

Fallou looked genuinely hurt. "'Poor?' 'Feeble?' I would never describe the peasants in such a way. They are rich beyond compare. Because they are a part of the definition. Magic is not magic without the common folk. And so the common folk are immeasurably important. Magic would not exist without them."

"And why are you telling me all this?"

"So you understand what I seek from this council," Fallou said. "The Osseomancer abused magic. He wanted it to exist without the common folk, and he plunged Jenor into war. The Magic of Order is the only way forward. Let the council adopt it and finally achieve unity throughout Jenor — unity between mages, sorcerers, and common folk."

"And elves and witches?"

"They too are defined by the common folk. They should come to respect them. And see that they serve the common folk, not the other way around."

"Let's cut the charade." Nauveena felt her patience growing thin. "You might have some explanations for your rationale, but at the end of the day, you have one type of magic you want to make superior over all others. This, the council will not stand for."

"Who are you to say what the council will and will not stand for?"

"Because I am now leading the council, and I say why we have come together. Let us have peace and unity, but not at the exclusion of others."

"You intend to lead us? On what authority?"

"The authority of the Academy of Mages that originally called this council. That will be good enough for you." Nauveena remembered how Fallou had seemed to buckle when Snorri stood up to him. She could not allow herself to be spun in circles by his strange logic. She needed to be direct.

She had always had difficulty reading others; they were not books. Fallou especially concealed his thoughts, but she thought she saw a hint of a grimace there. He did not want her to take over, and for some reason, that emboldened her.

Chapter Five
Animals of Starlight and Memory

> "The summer months last much longer than they reasonably should. And when winter comes, it is mild and balmy and short. I believe the only reason the elves allow it at all is because their forest looks so pristine and beautiful beneath a light dusting of snow."
>
> ~*Seven Years in Saphalon*
> Pitrinois
> 274 BU

Nauveena did not know how long she could stall. She had already given Fallou a number of excuses to delay the council: Snorri's death, the northern king's fight, Venefica's injury, Malachite's absence. But he did not find any of these worthy of delaying the council.

Finally, she explained that she would need time to review Snorri's notes. The mage had kept accounts of the council. While these were detailed, they were also disorganized, and she had not had time to review and make sense of them. She did not even know how to do the bit of magic Snorri used to tally votes.

For some reason, Fallou accepted this excuse over the others, but likely because it would only delay the council a day. And Nauveena did need to review her mentor's notes before she could comfortably preside over the council.

Fallou left the Library of Maladies to give her time to prepare.

Nauveena proceeded to Snorri's apartment. She felt less saddened than she had the previous day. She now had a task at hand. She gathered his notes and brought them back to the infirmary. She would make sense of them while attending to Venefica.

Since then, Nauveena had pushed from one day to two, and from two days to three. Fallou came at the beginning of each, and she explained that Snorri had been very disorganized — which was quite true — and it would take her longer to prepare.

Each day, Fallou became that much less accommodating, and he had not been very accommodating to begin with. "I have received more troubling reports from the Ultimate Defender." He bowed in reverence to the leader of the Magic of Order. "More and more accounts are made of the Osseomancer's supporters gathering strength. In Upper Tuvisia, a conspiracy was uncovered to storm our defenses around Pravulum in hopes of resurrecting the Osseomancer."

"Well, if you are uncovering these conspiracies," Nauveena said, "it seems they are being dealt with well enough."

"It is only a matter of time before we miss one," Fallou said. "It only takes one. We must begin the council as soon as possible so we can come to agreement on how best to handle this threat."

Nauveena agreed respectfully, while seeing the underlying ploy. Fallou had also done the math. He knew the advantage he had been given with the northerners' absence.

Malachite corresponded regularly. He kept a relay of hawks flying to Athyzia with constant communication. He tied small notes to each hawk to bring his correspondence to Nauveena, while the hawks themselves could communicate with him directly.

Caduceus kept the infirmary windows open for fresh air. The summer was now in full swing. The solstice had passed, and the fresh air was welcomed inside the stuffy hospital. Every few hours, a hawk would land at the open window beside Venefica's bed. Nauveena would get up from her studies and untie the small note from the bird's leg and read the druid's rough handwriting.

Malachite had crossed the Yülk and found signs of the northerners' war everywhere. Their trail was easy to follow. He could follow the cloud of carrion birds circling above both armies.

As easy as they were to find, both armies kept moving. King Caron continued his retreat. He could not remain in Yülk and had fled for the safety of Künner. Caron and his armies crossed the Hiel. King Ümlaut followed that night. And Malachite the next day.

Once in Künner, Caron had sent his wolves far and wide. They howled loudly, recruiting warriors from all across Künner. He had begun to amass a formidable force.

Not to be outdone, King Ümlaut had recruited as he journeyed through Yülk. Malachite saw signs of Ümlaut's army swelling in size as he pursued.

Eight days after King Ümlaut had caught King Caron with his wife, both kings clashed in battle. Malachite watched from a hill several miles away. His hawks brought more detailed accounts of the battle back to him, but he could see the broad strokes from his position.

Despite rallying many to his side, King Caron was still outnumbered. The berserkers of Yülk had been filled with the same rage as their king. They mauled Künner's advancing forces, tossing men and wolves aside as if they were nothing.

Malachite watched as King Caron and Künner were routed. Künner's forces were turned from the battlefield and fled south, towards the city of Gülk, where they hoped to make their stand. Malachite hadn't taken long to find the two armies, but he could not approach them in the heat of battle. He hoped to reach King Ümlaut before he regrouped and chased his retreating foe. After that, he would need to cross the siege lines to speak with King Caron.

As word came from Malachite, Venefica continued to recover. The animals the druid had spoken to continued to gather the necessary ingredients from the forest. Many also came to Nauveena through the infirmary's open window, except the stag, who left fresh moss on the steps each morning.

Caduceus took the ingredients and continued to produce the balm and treat Venefica's wounds with it regularly. When the Medicinal Mage allowed Nauveena to look, she could see that the cuts had already healed well. They would not leave terrible scarring. The ingredients from the forest had healed them naturally.

However, Venefica remained unconscious. The throw had been the larger injury. The force had given her a terrible concussion. Nauveena worried that even when the witch recovered, she might be dizzy and confused for some time.

Queen Em' Iriild continued to visit regularly, usually in the deepest portion of the night, when she said her healing energy was the greatest. Caduceus did not turn the Elf Queen away. She knew how valuable the queen's healing abilities would be for Venefica.

King Bane came as often as he could, but Druissia's borders continued to demand his attention. Nauveena remained by Venefica's side throughout. She brought Snorri's notes to the infirmary and spent her days organizing them and coming up with excuses to delay Fallou.

She felt responsible for Venefica's condition. If she had reacted a moment sooner, she could have unleashed her aura and saved them both. But the bear had set upon them so quickly that she had not had time to react.

She had not reacted fast enough the night Snorri had been thrown from the tower, either. If she had lashed out with her magic, maybe she could have stopped the spy.

She replayed both moments over and over in her head. Next time, she would not hesitate.

Nauveena often spoke to Venefica as the witch slept. She thought this might be comforting. She read Snorri's notes. And she read the messages from the druid — although she was not sure how comforting messages describing war and death might be.

When she grew tired, she went to lay down in an infirmary bed across from Venefica. She wouldn't fall asleep immediately, but would twist and turn. When she did sleep, she continued to dream vividly.

◆

The tower stretched forever upward. Nauveena went to a window and looked out. Above, the night sky was concealed with clouds. The top of the tower disappeared into mist and moonlight. Below, she could see the earth vaguely through the fog — a hundred miles below.

The tower swayed in the wind. It was not structurally sound. No tower should stretch to such heights. It bent and contorted as it rose, unstable and elastic.

Nauveena had no other choice but to find the top. It might be her only escape. She had tried to find the exit of her maze before, only to learn later that that had never been the point. Now, she eagerly climbed each set of stairs, hoping the next might bring her to the top and out of the tower.

She was spurred on by something else, too. The only sound now was the stranger, the other, the spy, the intruder. He did not belong, and he chased her. She could only hike up her dress and climb the stairs as quickly as she could.

She looked down the twisting stairs and could see his shadow only a few steps below her. She did not hear a voice, but she knew he was telling her to wait. When she sped up, his footsteps quickened. His shadow stretched out long and thin, although there was little light to produce it.

She sprinted the final length of stairs and threw herself through a doorway. She thrust the heavy wooden door shut and bolted the lock. She felt a force collide with the door on the other side. He pushed against it, stronger than she could imagine. He did not use physical strength to move the door, but something else.

Nauveena could hear the lock groan. The door hinges heaved. She pushed her own weight against the door. She breathed a spell to seal it shut. She did not hear his voice, but she knew what he said: *So strong you are.*

No. It was all she could think. He should not be here in her dream.

Do you not want to meet? Do you not want your questions answered?

No, she thought again. She breathed it, mouthing the word over and over as if it were a spell too. *No.*

"Yes." And now, she heard him. The voice drew all the air from her. She could not speak. She pressed tightly against the door, but a part of her wanted to open it and let him through. "Yes, let me through. Let me help you."

◆

Fallou came that morning, as he came every morning. Nauveena chose to meet him outside the infirmary. She did not bother to let him in. She did not plan to speak with him long.

"I believe this has gone on long enough," he began. As he had every morning, he brought three Keepers with him. Today, he had brought three of the more sheepish-looking Keepers. As they all looked a bit sheepish, this was saying a lot.

"Good morning," Nauveena sighed. "What has gone on long enough, oh, First Protector of Leem?"

"We all know Snorri was not the most disciplined mage, but even he could not have been *this* disorganized. You have had more than a week. How can you still be going through his notes? If you cannot figure out his trick for voting, we can do something else. I thought his showmanship was a bit much, anyways."

"No, I have figured that much of it out." The fire and scales were a clever bit of transfiguration to be sure, but Nauveena could manage it. She was just the more impressed with Snorri's ingenuity.

"Then what is the delay?"

Nauveena bit her lip in frustration. Of course, there was no reason to delay. At least as far as Fallou was concerned. He did not want to wait for the proxy of the northern kings. She had begun to run out of excuses.

"Snorri outlined several exceptions for alchemy where he referenced passages from rare books. His citation method isn't as robust as I would like — he likely didn't think anyone would be reading his notes but him. But if I am to present these to the council, I would like to locate the original source so I know the full context."

"This hardly seems a reason to delay the entire council," Fallou said. The Keepers nodded in agreement. "Present the quotes as-is to the council, and we can decide if we need more context. We cannot have further delay. We must finish the discussion on alchemy quickly so we can turn to more pressing matters."

"I just need one more day," Nauveena said in her most demure tone.

"'*One more?*' You said 'one more day' nine days ago. The summer will soon be over. If you are not ready to begin the council tomorrow, then the Magic of Order can wait no longer. We will return home, and you can have the council without us."

Of course, if Fallou were to leave, that would solve everything. But then, they wouldn't truly have a council. Each realm would return home to continue their affairs alone. Now, Nauveena knew how the kingdoms of the east were conducting their affairs. They could not be left to their own devices.

That night, she did not try to track down Snorri's citations. Instead she only tried to think of another excuse to delay. She could think of nothing, and drifted off to the same, troubled sleep she had every night.

Once again, she was pursued and once again, she woke up breathless and paranoid. She was beginning to lose sleep.

Caduceus woke her early the next morning. "You have a visitor outside."

The summer sun streamed in. It seemed early. Early even for Fallou. Why had he come already? And Nauveena had not thought of any excuses.

Reluctantly, she dressed and went outside to meet with the First Protector. She would have to begin the council. She could not see any other way to delay.

However, instead of finding Fallou outside, she was greeted by a much more pleasant sight: Csandril Em' Dale.

"Good morning." The poet bowed enthusiastically. "I hope it is not too early. I was only on a walk. I have had much on my mind of late, and I wanted to know if I could speak with you."

"No, it is not too early. It is good to see you," Nauveena said genuinely. Since she had been expecting Fallou, Csandril was a most welcome surprise.

"I hate to bother you with this," Csandril said. "I know you have much going on. With taking over the council and everything. But once we do begin, the issue of the Elf Laws will be discussed soon, according to the agenda. How do we stand on the issue?"

"We will feel much better once we get a proxy for the northern kings," Nauveena said frankly. "That is my main concern and why I have been trying to delay the council. Without them, the vote is more tenuous."

"I see, I see." Csandril looked relieved that Nauveena had at least been thinking of the issue.

"I have done everything I can to delay the council, but Fallou wants to begin as soon as possible," Nauveena whispered. Fallou always managed to be right around the corner when she happened to be talking about him.

"Of course he does," Csandril said.

And then, as if on cue, and because Fallou did have a knack for appearing when it benefited him, Fallou and three Keepers of Order — different from yesterday — rounded the corner and walked towards the infirmary.

"Csandril Em' Dale," Fallou said. "You are a welcome sight."

"I am?" Csandril could not believe it. Nauveena neither. Mainly because it was not true.

"Yes. I assume your presence means we are set to resume the council? A momentous day to be sure. No doubt, the late Snorri will be very proud that — after much delay — his protege is prepared to begin his council once more."

"Well, you see…" Nauveena still had not thought of an excuse.

"Yes?" Fallou asked.

"The council must be delayed one more day," she blurted out.

"'One more?' How is that possible? Have you not made sense of those citations? I do not believe that is worth delaying the council."

"No, it is not that; it is just…" Nauveena had nothing. Ten days of excuses had caused her to run dry.

"I must say, this is getting outrageous. If I did not know any better, I would say you *want* to delay this council."

"No, of course not."

"The time of the Magic of Order is most valuable. We cannot sit around idly. If the council is not prepared to begin again, then I am afraid we must depart."

"No, let's not do that." Csandril Em' Dale held up his hands to steady everyone. The Keepers of Order looked at him curiously. Nauveena even more so.

"Why not?" Fallou asked.

"The council cannot begin today because…"

"Because?"

"…because the elves are throwing a feast for Midsummer's Eve."

"*You are?*" Fallou, Nauveena, and the three Keepers all asked at once.

"Of course," Csandril said. "That is why I have come to Nauveena so early this morning. And why she told you the council must be delayed once more."

"Correct me if I am wrong, but was Midsummer not almost *two weeks ago?*" Fallou asked.

"Yes, but due to our recent tragic events, Midsummer went uncelebrated. As you know, this is the highest of high holidays in Elvendom. We must celebrate, even if it is delayed."

"I see." Fallou looked suspiciously from Csandril Em' Dale to Nauveena. "I see."

"So, we cannot possibly begin the council today," Csandril continued. "We are preparing lavish celebrations, and all are invited."

"I look forward to attending. I have heard much of the elves' celebrations of Midsummer. I have very high expectations."

"As you should. The elves do Midsummer right: flowers, wine, mead, more food than you could possibly eat. If I were you, I would start preparing now."

"As we have every day, we will use this additional delay to meditate on Order. But please send for us when the celebrations begin. We can attend for a brief time. However, let me say this to you now Nauveena, as the new leader of the council: I do not believe you are doing the council any service by delaying it. If the council does not begin tomorrow, the Magic of Order will have no choice but to leave."

With this, Fallou turned and left, followed by his three Keepers of Order.

When he had turned the corner and gotten out of earshot, Nauveena turned to Csandril Em' Dale. "I didn't know you were celebrating Midsummer's Eve."

"Neither did I."

◆

Csandril Em' Dale and Nauveena went to speak with Queen Em' Iriild to ask her to have the Midsummer celebration. She considered the idea of the feast. "Midsummer has passed," she said, "but the worlds remain in eclipse still. Elves have not been in these forests in many ages. You are right to celebrate."

The other elves needed little convincing. With the council delayed, they too had sat around restlessly. And they had missed celebrating Midsummer as well.

While Nauveena had read about the elves' celebrations and their communion with nature, she had never expected to see such text come to life. She could hardly contain her excitement.

The elves opened long, thin chests that held delicate woodwind instruments. Csandril played a few notes, but they made no sound that Nauveena could hear.

"We will be back later tonight."

"'Later tonight?'" Nauveena asked. "Can I not come? I wish to see."

"You will see plenty, I assure you. But the animals are skittish and easily frightened."

The other elven minstrels took the wooden flutes as well. They followed Csandril through Athyzia's northern gate, playing the instruments, but making no sound. Nauveena went with them to the gate and watched them slip into the forest.

She returned to Athyzia and helped the remaining elves in their preparation. Queen Em' Iriild's maids-in-waiting began constructing flower arrangements: long garlands that continued on forever, wreaths, bouquets flowing and spilling from their vases. Peonies, roses, violets, lilies, certain flowers Nauveena had never seen before. Soon the banquet hall and courtyards of Athyzia were covered. She could not determine how the elves had produced the flowers, and so quickly.

The elves took over Athyzia's kitchens, sinks, and ovens. Nauveena came here to help in what ways she could. She was soon given the task of chopping carrots and dicing summer onions. The elves brought many spices and herbs from their forested gardens. She had never smelt such garlic before. The elven chefs prepared a great and fragrant feast: elaborate pastas of stewing vegetables, acorn pesto, balsamic glazes, and many flavorful pies, apple and blueberry, each drizzled with honey. The elves brought out their own special meads of the forest, which had been fermenting throughout the year in preparation for the Midsummer feast.

Csandril Em' Dale and the elven minstrels returned at the turn of evening. All the elves went out to greet them at Athyzia's northern gate. Others came as well: the dwarves, Prince Javee, King Bane, and the oracles. All waited in silence, with held breaths.

At first, Nauveena thought the elves returned alone. Then, as evening darkened, she could see they were trailed by movements of shimmering light. The light was like that which formed halos around the stars in the night sky, swirling and dazzling and transparent. As one cluster of lights neared her, Nauveena saw that it gathered into shapes: sinew and strong legs, a head and enormous antlers.

As the stag approached, towering above her, Nauveena stepped back. Then Csandril Em' Dale appeared beside her. He took her hand and guided it towards the stag's withers. Her hand brushed the starlight, and she found it thick and bristling, clumping between her fingers.

A herd of deer followed behind. More animals came as well: foxes and lynx, boars, raccoons, skunks, and a giant, prowling panther. Many birds descended from above: cranes, owls, swans, and condors. Golden eagles from another age perched on Athyzia's highest turrets. Each was composed of another light, ethereal and revealed only by the gathering night.

And there was the song, which Nauveena could now hear. The old instruments that had not made any sound earlier in the day now made a soft whistling. Each note rose a step higher than the last, before sliding down in a long refrain. She had expected that the music would be melancholy and sad, but now that she heard it, it could only be described as joyful.

The elves led the parade from the northern gate to the banquet hall. They gathered in the courtyard beneath the many flowers and the paper lanterns which had been lit for the occasion. Some of the elven minstrels exchanged their flutes for more modern instruments, and they began making music that everyone danced to.

The spirits floated along in an unseen current and came to glide through the celebrants as they danced. Several rabbits spun around Nauveena in a whirlwind. One brushed against her face, tickling her nose with its whiskers.

The dancing continued. And the drinking. Towards the middle of dinner, the Protectors and Keepers of Order and their Obeyers came to the banquet hall to eat. Nauveena had not expected them to attend. She watched as they looked about disapprovingly. She knew Fallou saw through Csandril's ruse, but he could not protest. He could only look on critically as Athyzia celebrated and partied and the council was delayed another day.

Another day.

Only one more day.

Nauveena wished she could have bought more time. She sat now, tired of dancing. Her feet hurt despite the enchantment of the elven music. One of the rabbits came and nuzzled against her. But she could only worry.

The elves had staged an elaborate celebration. The largest in their culture. To celebrate an event that had happened twelve days before. They had gathered the spirits of the forest. They had spent the morning arranging flowers, decorating, and cooking.

And they had only bought a day.

Tomorrow, Fallou would return, and Nauveena would need to think of something else to buy another in the hopes that Malachite could return with the two votes.

She wondered where he was. Certainly, he would have loved to be at the celebration. Even in the middle of summer, the north could be inhospitable. She hoped he kept safe as the mighty armies of the north clashed.

"No, no, what is this?" Csandril Em' Dale sat next to Nauveena. He carried with him a bottle of Yros — a green liqueur distilled from the sap of Saphalon and Free Oak's pines. "You are not supposed to look so upset on Midsummer's Eve."

"I understand, and this is all great, but it has only bought us one more day. Who knows how long Malachite will be?"

"That is tomorrow's problem," Csandril said as he produced two crystal chalices and poured the green Yros from its narrow bottle. He slid one glass to Nauveena. The elven liqueur had a stronger reputation than even their mead. It was brought out only on special occasions.

"I really should get back and check on Venefica."

"She isn't going anywhere. Come on. It is Midsummer's Eve, after all."

He pushed the small glass a slight bit closer. Nauveena took a sip cautiously. The first sip caused her mind to focus. The elves' music became more rhythmic. Csandril's features became fairer and more wonderful. The rabbit grew warmer, as if it were alive. The elf poured another. And another.

The night became a blur. She remembered the glass being refilled. She remembered the elven music. She remembered spinning back and forth as she danced, and the animals spinning around her. At one point, she became a part of the elves' traditional dance, and was lifted upon strong shoulders and carried around the room.

They left the banquet hall in a raucous parade that trailed through Athyzia before returning to the elves' chambers. There, the celebration continued. The music became more exuberant. The elves brought out a hookah and burned a pungent incense.

Nauveena spoke for some time with Prince Javee and Kitrinos, but about what, she could not remember. But she did not think of the council, or her need to delay, or Malachite alone in the cold north with a terrible war swelling around him. For the first time, she did not worry about Venefica's condition. And she did not think about the night Snorri fell from the tower.

For the first time in months, she was not at the council. She was simply Nauveena, and she had no responsibilities or worries.

She spent the night in the elves' chambers. The night became very late, and her exhaustion hit her in one single instant. She saw no reason to return to the infirmary. Not now. Not when the elves' cushions and sofas were so comfortable. Much more comfortable than the single bed in the infirmary. She wanted to remain with the spirits as long as she could. The rabbit came and lay on top of her blanket, while others floated around the ceiling.

When she did eventually fall asleep, she did not dream of the endless maze or the too-tall tower. She dreamed she was in a well-lit library with many stacks of books and a well-organized categorization system. She found books easily, and they had every one she could ever want.

◈

Csandril Em' Dale shook Nauveena awake. She opened her eyes slowly, one eyelid at a time. Her vision was foggy, blurred. She saw stars in her peripherals. Her head throbbed.

"Will you wake up?" he asked.

"Huh?"

Nauveena looked around. On either side of her slept an elven warrior. Her dress was wrinkled and twisted. Her corset untied. Her hair had been matted in one direction, and she found flower petals stuck inside the curls. The starlight animals had all evaporated, but she could still see the indentation where the rabbit had slept beside her.

"Looks like someone enjoyed Midsummer's Eve."

"Where am I?"

"You slept over."

"Oh." Nauveena began to remember snatches of the night before. She didn't want to ask Csandril to fill in the missing details.

"Don't you need to meet with Fallou?" Csandril asked. "It was around this time yesterday he showed up at the infirmary. I imagine he will be there today too."

"Oh, no." Nauveena's responsibilities came surging back at once, hitting her harder than all the Yros and mead from the night before. "I need to go."

Csandril had to help her up. She stood gingerly. If she moved too quickly, the entire room spun.

"Easy does it."

As Nauveena hurried through Athyzia, she thought of how poorly everything had gone since she lost Snorri. The northern kings were at war. Malachite had left. Venefica lay injured. And she had chosen to spend the night drinking with the elves.

Fallou would take one look at her current state and leave the council immediately. She would have no authority to stop him. She'd never had any such authority. She felt completely inept. Why had she thought she could stand before him and stop him from asserting his will? He had even bested Snorri early in the council.

Nauveena rounded the corner and saw Fallou with three Keepers of Order waiting in front of the infirmary. She paused to smooth her dress and pick the last few petals from her hair. She was certain she looked a sight. He likely disapproved of her spending any time with the elves, let alone sleeping in their quarters.

"I think it is very appropriate to begin the council today," Fallou said in lieu of a greeting. "I could not think of a better beginning. Our two-week hiatus ended with a celebration. While unsophisticated, the celebration was nonetheless representative of the many cultures at the council. And with that taken care of, we can begin."

"Good morning." Nauveena continued to smooth her dress as she thought of what to say. She could feel the eyes of all four men on her as she did so.

"Did you enjoy Midsummer?" Fallou asked.

Nauveena did not answer him. She needed another excuse. Anything to delay the council further. Buy Malachite one more day. But she knew even something legitimate would fall short. Fallou would only threaten for so long.

"What is it?" Fallou asked. He could see Nauveena thinking. His question pressured her. She could not think fast enough. Her head throbbed.

"We just…" She needed something.

"I hope you are not about to say that the council must wait one more day to start. If you did not review your teacher's notes yesterday because of the Midsummer's feast, that is a lack of discipline on your part. You cannot waste any more of our time. Either the council begins today, or we will leave."

Nauveena felt like she might vomit. She swayed while standing. The world began to blur again.

"Well, what is it? Will the council begin? Let us wrap up the alchemical issues and begin with the more pressing matters."

The Medicinal Mage rushed out of the infirmary. "Nauveena, there you are," she said. "I have been looking for you everywhere."

"Yes?"

"The witch, Venefica has just woken up."

Chapter Six
A Spell of Binding

> "In the eras before kings, magic was often used as an arbitrator. Even as bureaucracies developed and began to fill many of these legal functions, magic would still be turned to. However, this eventually fell out of practice due to the inflexibility of the magic involved. Most mages came to accept that even the most despotic of kings could be reasoned with. Magic could not."
>
> ~*Magica Obscura Volume XV*
> 172 BU

Caduceus had positioned several pillows behind Venefica so she could sit up. The witch looked around, blinking, a bit confused, when Nauveena entered.

"I've never been happier to see you," Nauveena said. And she truly meant it. Before the council, when she had only known of Venefica through rumors, she would not have imagined how worried she would be at the witch's injury — and how troubled she would be at her absence. Now, she rushed to her, and they embraced.

When they had finished, Nauveena took a step back, and Venefica studied her. The witch's eyes looked glassy, glazed, but still awake and alert. "What happened to you?" she asked. "You look worse than I do."

Nauveena had forgotten her unkempt appearance. She removed another petal from her hair. "I was with the elves last night. Celebrating Midsummer's Eve."

"Midsummer's Eve? How long have I been out? A full year? We were just past Midsummer when that bear came."

"No, no." Nauveena threw up her hands. "You have been out for eleven days. There's so much to catch you up on."

Nauveena pulled a chair over to Venefica's bedside and sat. She began with the rest of the bear attack: How she had shielded them both from more aggression. How Queen Breve had come in the form of an owl. How the queen had lead King Ümlaut away. How both kings had pursued each other north and to war. And how the resulting war had taken them — and their votes — from the council.

Venefica voiced a suspicion similar to Prince Javee's. "How convenient that King Ümlaut would suddenly pay attention to his wife's whereabouts."

They had both come to the same conclusion, but had no proof.

"We need those votes," Nauveena said. "We cannot do much without them. Malachite has gone north. To ask the kings to make peace — at least until the council is over — and to return."

"I can't imagine peace will come that easy," Venefica said.

"No. Ultimately, Malachite plans to ask each king to give their vote to someone else — either him or another — to vote in their stead."

"They may be more amenable to that."

"In the meantime, I do not want to begin the council until the northerners return or send a delegate. I have done everything I can to delay the proceedings, but Fallou insists we begin again. Csandril Em' Dale rescued me yesterday with the fabricated celebration of Midsummer's Eve."

"That was very clever of him."

"Now, you waking has delayed us one more day. But after this, I am out of tactics. Each day, I become more desperate to invent ways to delay the council. The only thing I have done as the leader of the council is stall. And I do not know how much longer I can even do this."

"He wants to press his advantage while we are without the northerners' votes."

The situation had not changed, but Nauveena felt a heavy burden lift. She once again had Venefica to discuss strategy with. She had come to rely on the witch over the last few months. In a short span, she had lost Snorri, Venefica, and Malachite. She had felt alone, isolated, lost. Even if they could not arrive at a solution, at least she was no longer alone.

"Where did the council leave off?" Venefica asked.

"Alchemy."

Venefica's memory was likely hazy, but the council had been suspended for half a month. The tumultuous events since had overshadowed the debates around alchemy.

"Yes, that's right. How far along were we? Couldn't we stretch that out?"

"We only had a few issues left to discuss. We got derailed by the report from Pravulum and then Snorri..." Nauveena paused, remembering her fallen mentor.

"But certainly, we could stretch the discussion if we needed to. You could begin with a recap — *a very long recap* — of discussions until that point. Each day, we could elaborate for long periods."

"You want to begin the council again?"

"Why not? You are the leader. You can control the pacing. We are now only working on the particulars of alchemical regulations. We can afford a vote without the northerners."

"Then Fallou cannot complain that the council has been delayed." It seemed simple enough.

"We should be able to delay a vote on other matters until Malachite returns. This tactic buys us time, at least."

"I suppose we could." Nauveena already felt relieved to have Venefica's guidance. The witch was right. Alchemy was relatively settled. Still, they could discuss it and give Malachite time to return. More important matters, ones that they would need every vote on — such as the Elf Laws — lay ahead.

"How far away is the druid?" Venefica asked.

"He had just watched the first battle between the northern kings," Nauveena said. "He planned to approach King Ümlaut the next day. But..." She paused. Her head still ached from the night before. *When had she last heard from Malachite?* "I did not receive a message yesterday. I was with the elves all day. I must have missed it."

Nauveena stood and went to the window. No hawk waited on the windowsill. The whole time she had spoken to Venefica, none had come. Usually, within that time frame, at least one would have come with a message.

She left the room, looking for Caduceus. She found the Medicinal Mage in the back room, cleaning sheets. "Hello," she said. "Have any hawks come through the window next to Venefica's bed?"

"Hawks?" Caduceus asked, confused. "I haven't seen a hawk or any other bird come through that window. I'd have shooed them away if they had. The sick don't need such disturbances."

"If they do come, don't shoo them away," Nauveena said. "They have a message for me."

Nauveena returned to her seat at Venefica's bedside.

"What's wrong?" Venefica asked.

"Malachite had been sending correspondences a few times a day. I missed his message yesterday, and I have not seen any yet today."

"That is nothing to fret about. Especially if he is in a war zone, as you say. I am sure he will send an update as soon as he can. Now, come, help me up. It would be nice to walk around."

Nauveena felt very strange, out of place. She had become leader of the council several days before, but it had not seemed real until she sat in the place once occupied by her former mentor. Now, the reality could not be denied. Snorri was gone, and she was leading the council instead.

The other obvious absence was that of the northerners. They had all been such large figures — in a very literal sense. Their two kings took up significant room in the center tables on their own. But the contingent behind them had been quite large and unique. Their armor and jewelry had stood in sharp contrast to the dull robes of those from the Magic of Order. Without them, the council felt significantly less crowded.

Nauveena might have felt stranger still in her new role if she did not have a task ahead of her. She would begin the sessions once again, but she did not plan to cede the floor to anyone else. She did not plan to let anyone else speak but her, at least for today. They would begin their session on the topic of alchemy, but — if everything went according to plan — alchemy would not be discussed.

In this manner, she hoped to waste the first day. As she waited — a bit longer than might be needed — for each member to settle in, she looked to the sky. No hawks in sight. Where was the druid?

Nauveena began that first day with a long-winded summary of the entire council up until that point. And by entire council, she truly discussed the entire council. She began with the fall of Pravulum and then

Snorri's first articulation of the need for a council. She recalled when he returned from the long war. She had expected her mentor to retire to a library and retreat once more from the world. But instead, he'd had another idea. Now was not the time to retreat. Now was the time for further work.

Describing Snorri organizing the council came easily enough. Nauveena remembered the details vividly. They had spent many long nights crafting the invitations. Snorri debated whether to begin with *Dear* or *Sincerely*, or simply *Hello*.

Those details came easily. And Nauveena did not need to push herself to lengthen her speech. In fact, she found these retellings therapeutic in a way. So much had happened since Snorri had fallen. She had not gotten a chance to recount to others her image of him — how she remembered him.

Her retelling did more than fill hours. She hoped to impart something else: how important the council had been to Snorri. How he envisioned the realms of Jenor gathering together to solve disputes amiably and civilly and without bloodshed. Already, the council members were at war with each other, and his dreams dissolved. But the council meant to begin again, and maybe hope still remained.

Nauveena did not want to shift from these first retellings. She wanted to keep speaking of Snorri in those simpler times, when the council had potential, and existed in their imaginations, away from reality. She did not want to relinquish him, because as she spoke of him from her memories, he came to life again. By shifting to other matters, she would lose him once more.

Eventually, she did speak about the rest of the council. She spoke of how each council member arrived. She spoke of how the votes had been determined. She spoke of the first days setting the agenda. And then each topic that had been discussed so far: Pravulum, taxonomies of magic, a universal calendar, the sharing of knowledge, and now, alchemy.

In the end, the summary had been necessary. The council had been suspended for more than fifteen days. And each council member needed a refresher. But it had been necessary for other reasons: for Nauveena to finally remember Snorri as she wanted him remembered.

While she had been speaking in long, grandiose language to stall and delay, it became something more. It became her eulogy to her fallen mentor.

But at the end of the day, the session ended, and she had lost one more tactic of delay. No hawks had arrived that day. While she spoke, she looked to the sky. Few birds came from the north. No messages from the druid. And now, they were one day closer to finishing the topic of alchemy.

◆

Csandril Em' Dale proved most capable of speaking for long times without anyone noticing how long he had spoken for. His prose made an hour feel like only a few moments. He enunciated. He paused at appropriate times. He stressed certain words over others to give his speech a staccato that was musical and engrossing.

Nauveena and Venefica quickly recruited him to their strategy. The night before a session, Nauveena would bring the elven poet several books on alchemical theories. Most of these, she had difficulty reading without falling asleep. But when Csandril repeated their passages, she found herself on the edge of her seat, learning many things she had not known.

In this way, they extended many sessions. When Csandril's spell had worn off, Nauveena could see annoyance on the faces of the Protectors and Keepers of Order. Often, they became enraptured by him and only afterwards realized an hour had been wasted.

She and Venefica recruited others to the cause. Soon, Prince Javee, Kitrinos, and King Bane joined the effort to extend the session. They added counterarguments and generally derailed the conversation in whatever ways they could.

Most importantly, they did *not* interrupt Csandril.

Not everyone excelled at stalling as well as Csandril Em' Dale, though. Others could speak for long periods of time, of course. But whereas Csandril could speak forever and say nothing, others attempting the same inevitably had to say something — and therein lay the problem.

King Bane always looked regal when he addressed the council. He wore a thin coat, embroidered with Druissia's bull ensign. His beard appeared lush and full. He addressed the issue of counterfeiting by means of alchemy. In his mind, he hoped to fill time by departing on a tangent.

"I worry much about the matter of unsanctioned alchemy," he said, looking properly noble as he did so. "This council has now shown solidarity around the issue of alchemy, but how do we enforce it? Each kingdom will not endorse the gold produced through such processes. We will not coin these imposter metals. But many alchemists are quite skilled in other crafts and might mint coinage resembling the official fiat of the realm. What should be done then? How can we stop such counterfeiting?"

The issue had been brought up several times, each without a satisfactory resolution. King Bane had correctly guessed that resurrecting the issue might derail conversations for the rest of the day and result in the session ending once again without a vote.

The council did, in fact, dissolve into murmurs and dissent and several side conversations. Nauveena did nothing to help it refocus. She might be blamed for not controlling the council, but for the moment, it suited her. She could let the arguments and the counterarguments and the counter counterarguments run their course. If they took the rest of the day, all the better.

Snorri would have refocused everyone. She could hear him now. "The council is meant to offer guidelines on the proper uses of magic. Let us do that. Other mages will see the wisdom of our decisions and follow accordingly."

Now, each side conversation bought Nauveena time, and she did not mind if it went against Snorri's initial intentions. He had not anticipated the northern kings going to war with each other, after all.

As the council circled around arguments, she saw Fallou ready himself to stand. He had not addressed the council in some time. Everyone quieted when he stood.

"The king of Druissia describes a valid criticism of the council," Fallou said. "Once again, a flaw in the very nature of our purpose is exposed. Twenty-six — now twenty-four — have come together to discuss these matters and settle them. Us twenty-four can walk away in agreement and follow these edicts. And we can implore our subjects to follow them. But we all know this is often not reality.

"I say this as the First Protector of Order in Leem. Subjects do not follow every decree. They often — as hard as we might try — have minds and actions of their own. Our king of Druissia here might outlaw alchemical gold production in his kingdom. And he might punish anyone who commits such felonies. But Druissia is a wide kingdom. As effective a ruler as he is, he cannot enforce the law in every corner."

"Thank you." King Bane nodded with approval. And that was when Nauveena realized something had gone wrong: King Bane had asked a question he did not know the answer to.

But Fallou did.

"One method remains to enforce any edict agreed upon by the council. One method that is simple and straightforward and binding."

"No." Nauveena now worked to refocus the council. "We have discussed this," she said, echoing Snorri's words. "Let us set guidance on these issues, but we will not enforce them in such a manner."

"I only recommend an option for us to consider," Fallou said. "Why should we reject the option so readily?"

"A binding spell can be very dangerous," Nauveena said. "The magic is not well-understood."

"But look who is gathered here," Fallou said. "And where. In Athyzia. The greatest center for learning in all of Jenor. And we have gathered with us the greatest and wisest minds in the land. Certainly, we could perform the spell without any adverse effects."

"Snorri warned against it. I do not take his warnings lightly."

"Do not dismiss the matter so readily. Think on it. Let us not make decisions in haste."

"My decision is not made in haste."

"We must be more diligent in our enforcement within our own kingdoms," King Bane now said, trying to correct the angle he had provided Fallou. "That must be the answer. We each must be able to control our realms adequately and enforce the council's decisions that way."

But it was too late. Nauveena could already see the idea gaining traction in the minds of others: the other Protectors, certainly, but also the merchants, the representative of Aryde, and the Burgomaster of the Bogwaah.

THE COUNCIL OF ATHYZIA

Even Csandril Em' Dale could not extend the session indefinitely. The topic of alchemy had to come to an end eventually. Its resolution had felt inevitable ever since Nauveena allowed the council to reconvene.

With the result preordained, she barely paid attention during the closing day. She and her fellow conspirators had no other arguments or theories with which to delay the conversation.

The issues had resolved themselves. Few could argue over them any longer. The only thing remaining was to vote.

In the end, Nauveena did not even know what had been resolved. The uses of alchemy had been limited. The discipline was wide-ranging, but its more controversial endeavors had been restricted or prohibited. Chief among them the transformation of base metals into gold and silver.

On this, each council member remained in agreement. And the vote reflected this. Each cast their vote into the fire, and the smoke followed its path over to the scales.

Nauveena could neither remember the final vote nor if anyone had voted against the measure.

They had extended the council by another seven days. Seven days during which she had heard nothing from the druid. Now, they would move to more pressing matters, and she did not know when — or if — Malachite would return.

"We have not heard anything from him." Nauveena and Venefica walked together after the final session on alchemy. "No news comes from the north. Only that they remain at war."

"The druid may not send messages for many reasons," Venefica said, trying to comfort her. "The roads might be tough, but he is more than capable. He cannot be much longer."

Riders had been sent north to find any sign of the druid. King Bane had commanded many of his men to go in search of Malachite. Each had returned without information. No animals or birds had come with word from him.

"What if he does not get agreement from the northern kings? We cannot continue without those two votes."

"We will deal with it when we get there," Venefica said. "Tomorrow, we are not in session. Another day."

"We have taken another day and another day and another, and nothing."

"Have faith in him. All we can do is take another."

Ahead of them, a robed figure stepped out of the shadows. Nauveena recognized the long body of the First Protector of Leem.

Fallou approached them both. "Have you considered my suggestion any further?"

"'Suggestion?'" Nauveena asked. "What suggestion?"

"The option to enforce the decisions of the council, of course. I understood you would contemplate the issue further."

"No, I never agreed to contemplate it further." Nauveena heard herself raising her voice. Fallou often managed to cause her to lose composure. "I said the council would *not* forge a spell of binding."

Fallou stepped back and put his hands together defensively, as if Nauveena's statement had been an insult aimed directly at him.

"My intentions are only to uphold the edicts of this council. I do not understand why they are met with such hostility. I understand the gravity of such a spell, which is why I have asked the leader of the council — first Snorri and now yourself — to endorse the idea. However, if the notion is nominated, then it would only need seven votes, like anything else."

"There are some issues I could override," Nauveena said. "If I deem them unwise, as I do with this matter."

"That interference seems out of the spirit of the council."

"It is very much in the spirit of the council not to make dangerous pacts. In this, Snorri was also quite clear. I am following his lead."

"I know you admired your mentor very much, but in this issue, I wish you would contemplate it independently."

"I am aligned with Snorri on the issue. Thank you very much. We can have no more discussion on it."

Fallou mercifully left. Nauveena and Venefica waited for him to turn the corner, then, they proceeded to Nauveena's chambers in the Tower of Yalde. They preferred to speak there, in private. They should not have been speaking so openly. Anyone could have come across them, as Fallou had. They both still feared the possibility of a spy eavesdropping on their conversations.

"You were quiet," Nauveena said once they were both safely inside her tower.

"What? Quiet about what?"

"Fallou," Nauveena said. Normally, Venefica did not miss an opportunity to argue with the First Protector. "Why didn't you say anything?"

Venefica did not respond right away. She appeared lost in thought. Nauveena could see something was on her mind.

Finally, the witch asked, "Is a binding spell really that bad?"

Venefica slumped down onto the sofa. Nauveena followed her and sat on the other end. "What kind of question is that?" she asked.

"Why be so fearful of the magic?"

"You are asking the magic to punish those who do not adhere to the pledge. Who knows how the magic might interpret that?"

"I know Snorri was against it, but the circumstances have changed. As I see it, we have three options before us. Tomorrow will be a recess. The next day, a new session will begin on a new topic. We either begin that topic. Suspend the council. Or..."

"Or?"

"Or have a different session on a binding spell."

"Why give in to Fallou?" Nauveena asked.

"What is the next topic?" Venefica asked in reply.

The witch knew perfectly well. Everyone did. The agenda was quite public. The council had been steering toward the topic for weeks. Now, it loomed in front of them.

"The Elf Laws," Nauveena said.

"Exactly. If we begin a session on the Elf Laws and go to a vote without the northerners, we are very likely to lose."

"And if we hold a session on a binding spell, it could go to a vote, and we are also likely to lose," Nauveena said.

"Out of the two options, the binding spell must be the lesser evil," Venefica said.

"I prefer no evil at all."

"Fallou will continue to push for the spell. He can add it to the agenda easily. He has the seven votes needed to add a topic. Then, even with the northerners' votes, he might manage to pass it. Why not get it over with, and give Malachite more time to return?"

"Snorri wrote much about binding spells in his notes," Nauveena said. "He cited examples of the spells being used in the past. One, he knew firsthand, as it happened early in his time at Athyzia. Two mages agreed to use a binding spell. The first mage loaned many volumes on transfiguration to the second mage. But he knew the second mage was forgetful and might never return the books. They performed the spell as something of a joke, thinking the matter was quite trivial.

"They set a time by which the second mage would return the books, and then bound the contract with magic, asking the magic to punish the second mage if he did not deliver the books on time. When the time came to return the texts, the second mage naturally forgot. He did return them several days later, however, always intending to honor the agreement.

"As the second mage had returned the books — albeit late — both mages assumed the spell would not be enacted. For many years, it was not. However, when the second mage had a child" — Nauveena paused to give dramatic effect and said the ending as if it were the climax of a ghost story — "the child was born with *chela* for hands."

"Chela?"

"Yes, pincers, like crab claws." Nauveena snapped her fingers together, mimicking a crab.

"And it was the binding spell?"

"What else could it be?" Nauveena asked.

"All because the mage returned the books a few days late?"

"The magic takes the spell very literally. It is dangerous to personify magic in any way and give it agency, which such a spell is doing. It is empowering the magic to interpret the bounds of the contract and punish as it sees fit. It cannot be controlled. Snorri gave many other examples: mages slipping on ice, falling off towers, losing hair. Once, all the descendants of a mage suffered terrible boils for seven generations. And it is not just individuals. It can apply to entire towns if the magic interprets the spell in such a way. The magic will treat any council decision as an oath and punish whoever breaks the oath."

"You say that like it is a bad thing."

"Isn't it?" Nauveena felt exasperated. She had been so relieved to have Venefica back, but now, she could not understand her new strategy.

"There might be another reason to do a binding spell." Venefica poured herself a glass of wine. "You say the spell would enforce whatever is agreed to in the council?"

Nauveena hesitated, then said, "Yes. I've said as much, haven't I?"

"If the council votes to remove the Elf Laws, the binding spell would enforce such a vote?"

Nauveena hesitated again, but then said, "Yes."

"If the council votes to make all sources of magic unrestricted, the spell would enforce such a vote?"

"Yes."

"If the council votes for the free sharing of all books — as it has — the spell would enforce such a vote?"

"Yes?"

Nauveena now worried she understood Venefica's thoughts.

"Then why fear such a spell?"

Nauveena did not have a response beyond repeating what she had already said.

"If we pass all the measures we wish to," Venefica said, "those from the Magic of Order could still choose to return home and ignore them. Nothing is forcing them to uphold the rulings of the council. Only their own good will and honor. And I doubt we can rely on that. The vote could say one thing, but the Magic of Order could easily go and do another."

Nauveena paused, thinking of another way to argue with the witch, but then she had another thought. "Both King Bane and Prince Javee are prepared to go to war if the edicts of the council are not followed. With a binding spell in place, there would be no need."

Venefica smiled smugly, pleased to see the sorceress had come around to her way of thinking.

"Of course, it requires getting the votes to pass such measures," Nauveena said.

"We will get the votes," Venefica said confidently. "Yes, Malachite is delayed, but he will return. And we will have a proxy from the northerners. Then we can pass each of those measures. Currently, Fallou thinks he has the advantage. Thus his haste. He wants to push through the binding spell, the Elf Laws, everything, while Malachite is away.

"Let him push through the binding spell. Then, when Malachite returns, let us hang Fallou on his own spell. We will pass each measure, and he will have no choice but to adopt them. Let us pass the binding spell. Then, let us prohibit the Elf Laws. Then, let us put in protections for all magic. Let us make Jenor free once and for all."

Nauveena could not reverse her position on the binding spell too quickly. A sudden change in her stance might rouse Fallou's suspicion. Instead, she and Venefica waited for him to raise the issue again.

They did not need to wait long. After the recess, Fallou began the next session by suggesting the binding spell once more.

Nauveena was ready for him. "I have warned against these types of spells," she said in response. "But my role as leader of the council is to advise, not force. If the will of the council is to place a binding spell on what we agree to, then I will not stand in its way."

"Your deference on the matter shows immense wisdom," Fallou said. "Indeed, it shows great restraint on your part to not interfere in the council."

"I only ask one thing," Nauveena said. "If the council wishes to impose a binding spell on the proceedings, I believe we should do so before proceeding further. A binding spell changes the nature of our discussions. The result of a vote is now bound by magic. If a binding spell is to be made, let it be made before we discuss other issues, so we can discuss those issues with the full knowledge of such a spell."

Fallou bowed. In this, he likely saw the sense of Nauveena's proposal. They went to the vote next and found an easy eight — the Protectors and Keepers of Order, General Dolcius, and Balzhamy — to add the item to the agenda.

Nauveena saw no reason why she should not get an extra day out of her concession. "We should move to add the item to the agenda immediately. However, since not everyone is fully prepared for discussions on the matter, let us suspend sessions for today and resume tomorrow."

She could see Fallou preparing to protest, but he withheld at the last moment. He had scored a victory, as far as he was concerned; he could concede the day.

As the council dispersed for the day, Nauveena looked to the sky. Not a single bird. She worried about the druid. Not about *when* he would return, but *if* he would return. Could something have happened to him?

The debate on the new proposal bought one more day. Nauveena requested the Arcane Mage come speak on the matter, as he was the current authority on such spells. She expected the Arcane Mage to stress the dangers of binding spells, but like most of Athyzia's sorcerers, he retained an academic fascination with the topic he had come to study. He spoke of the terrible harm the magic had chosen to enact on those who broke such spells, but he did so in such a manner that no one paid much mind.

Snorri would have stressed the disasters that could have resulted from similar spells. Again, Nauveena thought of her mentor's notes. Terrible calamities had been visited upon those kingdoms that broke such spells: famine, plagues, floods, earthquakes, locusts, frogs falling from the skies. One account spoke of orc bandits raiding a village on the Vurve after it broke a binding spell. Entire kingdoms had the earth give way beneath them, and been swallowed whole. A mage's wife had woken with no bones in her body the morning after breaking a binding spell. Some of these had happened centuries ago, and might have been exaggerated legends, but there must have been some truth hidden deep within.

The Arcane Mage spoke in such a way as to present them as a history, either to be bored or fascinated with, not as the warnings they surely should have been. At the end, Nauveena felt the need to add her own warning, first to continue to show Fallou she was against the measure, but also in the vain hope she could still prevent it.

While Venefica might have wished for the measure to pass, Nauveena still harbored a secret hope that it might fail, especially the more she read on the subject. The punishments for breaking the binding spell had begun to look like the murals on the ceiling of the Library of Maladies. She could see the witch's logic, but she worried about the risk. They would be bound by whatever was decided by the council. And Malachite was still nowhere in sight.

In the end, each member felt educated enough to vote. While the vote was anonymous, Nauveena could guess how it went. Very few voted against the measure. All six from the Magic of Order voted to hold the binding spell. General Dolcius certainly did. As did the mage, Balzhamy, who should have known better.

Based on the final tally, the Bogwaah, the southern merchants, and Aryde must have voted for the measure. Nauveena worried what it meant that they had all sided with Fallou on something so consequential.

Those thirteen would have been a majority, but another two, Druissia and Dunisk, were delivered by Venefica. When the extra two came, Fallou himself looked surprised. He had counted on his thirteen to deliver the day. The extra two — inconsequential in the outcome — could only rouse suspicion.

One more day. Nauveena bought herself one more day.

They would spend the next day crafting the spell itself. Each spell was customized to the particular situation. While the council had voted to proceed, Nauveena warned again about the dangers of such a spell. They could not proceed lightly. They could not recite any odd words. They needed to be deliberate and careful in the actual phrasing of the oath.

The next day began with blue skies. However, far on the horizon, in the west, dark storm clouds gathered. The council began crafting the binding spell while the clouds rolled in, threatening a summer storm. Such storms often came from the west and became trapped against the mountains. It would begin raining soon.

Snorri had placed a charm over the council's seats on the terrace, an invisible umbrella to deflect rain. Nauveena hoped the charm still remained. The clouds thickened. Dark waves rolled in and against each other. They had begun gray when stretched out over the fields of Druissia, but now, as they collided with the high mountain peaks, they pressed together, thickening and darkening.

Nauveena watched the proceeding with a feeling of foreboding. She could not get Snorri's words from her mind: "It is a fickle magic. And volatile. The spell must be specific. Even the wisest mages can make mistakes. Maybe it can be done over a simple contract — a negotiation between neighbors. But something like this, with twenty-six members. No. Too dangerous."

The council did not proceed recklessly. The Arcane Mage returned again. His expertise in the magic of utterances was needed. Together, the council crafted the language of the spell, fiddling over every detail, every word.

In the end, the actual ritual was simple. The council needed only recite the same words together. The magic relied on their collected powers and their wills and their promise.

The Arcane Mage led them in reciting the spell. Each council member had been instructed to hold hands — symbolic of the bond that would form between them. Each member closed their eyes and repeated the lines together. Nauveena joined in reluctantly, her voice barely a whisper as she recited the words. The Academy of Mages might not be a full voting member of the council, but Nauveena felt it was important that she and it were bound by the spell, the same as all the council members. She could not ask others to bind themselves to the outcome of the council, but not herself.

Still, a deep feeling of regret swelled within her. Should she have held strong? Venefica had seen the spell as the best path forward, but was it?

But now it was too late, already the council had begun to recite the words.

The Protectors of Order recited in unison with each other, well-practiced in group chants. The others remained more scattered. They recited at different paces. Csandril Em' Dale's voice registered over the others, reciting the words in an eloquent fashion.

Gathered in Athyzia
Are those who wish to agree
Matters that once divided
Must be met with unity

Let each member speak
Let each have their day
Provide their wisdom now
And give their final say

Listen to each other
And hear every word
Solve conflict through speech
Rather than the sword

But when the council ends

And a ruling is found
Whatever the edict
Let all gathered be bound

Lock each and all
With the force of magic
And let any who waver
Meet an ending tragic

The first crack of thunder sounded with the final word. A streak of lightning followed. Then the rain fell. It came down in a heavy sheet, not bothering with an initial drizzle. The rain collided with the invisible aura hovering above the terrace. Snorri's charm still remained.

With the second crack of thunder, Nauveena looked to the sky. Through the rain, a large bird flew, unbothered by the downpour.

The hawk landed in a tree some way from the terrace.

Nauveena stood from the council and rushed to the tree. The hawk swooped down and landed on her outstretched arm. A small parchment had been tied to the bird's leg. She untied it as Venefica rushed over and read the note over her shoulder.

Csandril Em' Dale rushed over as well. "What does it say? Is it from Malachite?"

"It is," Nauveena said breathlessly. "He is only — "

Bells began tolling. *Dong. Dong.* The warning bells of the lookout tower. They sounded alone through the steady tumult of rain. *Dong. Dong.*

Someone was approaching Athyzia.

Nauveena rushed from the terrace and into the rain. The downpour came so completely that she was instantly soaked. She did not care. She rushed to Athyzia's central courtyard. Others followed not far behind.

They gathered in the courtyard as the main gates opened. Nauveena could hear Venefica by her side now. She panted in the rain. The rain was cold, but she did not care. The water ran under her dress.

A figure on horseback rode slowly through the gates. He slumped in his seat. Nauveena rushed to him. His cloak covered his entire face, already drenched by the summer storm.

Nauveena peered beneath it. The druid's tired eyes stared back.

"It is you. The hawk just came."

Malachite slumped from his horse, and Nauveena threw her arms around him.

"Do you..."

"Yes, I have it. Is the council still in session?"

"We just — we can be."

Nauveena turned from Malachite and led him back towards the terrace. Others came to crowd around them. Everyone knew where he had been. Many had wondered when he might return. They asked for news from the north.

"How is the war going?"

"Have the northern kings killed each other yet?"

"Why have you been delayed?"

Malachite answered none of these questions. He had clearly been riding for days. His beard had become unruly and unkempt. He looked thin and tired.

Venefica came close. She too hugged the druid. She had her own question, which she asked out of earshot. "Who have they given their votes to?"

"It is good to see you have recovered," Malachite said.

"Who is their proxy?" Venefica asked again.

"We will find out together."

The council returned to the protection of the terrace. The rain parted below the charm Snorri had placed over the council's meeting space. However, Nauveena and everyone who had rushed to Malachite remained drenched. None seemed to care. They all looked eagerly to the druid.

Only the Magic of Order had remained on the terrace. Each appeared perfectly dry. They watched the druid with little apparent interest. Malachite pushed back his hood and shook his hair, sending a spray of rainwater around. He ran his fingers through his hair to remove it from his face, then looked at each council member as if trying to remember them.

"What news do you have from the north?" Lord Ferrum asked. All the dwarves had raced excitedly to the courtyard to greet the druid. They remained great friends with the northerners, and had been quite concerned about the war.

"The northerners remain at war." Malachite spoke softly. Nauveena could see he was on the precipice of exhaustion. "They have inflicted much damage upon each other. Both feel betrayed and fight with the intensity of one who has been wronged. The war will be long and bloody, I am afraid to report."

A pall, in tune with the steady rain above, fell upon the council. Reports of such a violent war brought great sorrow to all.

"I met with both kings. And I urged them to put their arms aside. Neither would without assurances from the other. Several times, I relayed messages between camps, working towards an agreement. But none could be possible. Eventually, I was forced to abandon the idea of peace."

"This is very troubling to hear," Lord Ferrum said.

Malachite nodded in agreement. "I reminded both kings of the council here. They had an obligation, I explained. Leaving the council without their representation would be a dereliction of duty. On this, they both agreed. But, with the war, neither king could return themselves. To this, I recommended a compromise. If they could not return, then they should delegate another to speak for them and represent them at this council. Both have nominated such a proxy and sent me to give their nominations to the council."

General Dolcius stood to protest. Nauveena noted he was as equally dry as the protectors, not having come off the terrace at Malachite's arrival. "A proxy is all very well and good, but how do we know the druid truly conveys the wishes of the kings of the north?"

"Because I have proof of their intentions," Malachite said, silencing Dolcius. "Both kings have sent their proxies through crystals. An ancient magic, but well-protected and verifiable that the message came from them."

Malachite approached the central table where Nauveena sat. On this, he placed first one and then another crystal. The first was a rough, chipped ruby that sparkled in some places. The second was completely round — a black stone the likes of which Nauveena had not seen before.

"Separately, both kings recorded messages and ensnared them in the crystals. Together, we can hear their messages once. Let us listen together and take their wishes as final."

The council nodded in agreement. Even Dolcius and Fallou did not object. They could not argue with messages transported through crystals.

Malachite stepped away from the table. Nauveena now stood and approached the two stones. She looked at the council. Each looked to her eagerly. To the first, the ruby, she came forward and placed her hand upon it. Not much was needed to activate the spell. A soft purr of magic spread from her fingers and collided with the stone.

Nauveena stepped back. The crystal remained still for a moment, and then shook on the table. Finally, it lit a dull red. The light emitted from it, spreading upwards to illuminate a long space above.

Into this space, the image of King Caron appeared. His normal allure had retreated. Instead, he looked weary and afraid. He glanced around the council.

Then he spoke.

"To the council, please excuse my absence. It was unplanned. And I regret to abandon a conference with such lofty goals. I do not wish for the council to be disbanded on my account, so let another speak for me. In my place, I will nominate a delegate to vote on my behalf. Dear council, please accept Lord Ferrum Rüknuckles of Gemhaven to vote for the kingdom of Künner until I can return."

Everyone on the terrace turned to look at the Dwarf Lord, who looked equally surprised.

"He's to have two votes?" General Dolcius asked. "How can that be?"

"You heard the king of Künner," King Bane said. "In Malachite's absence, I acted as his proxy. Lord Ferrum will act as King Caron's."

The dwarves — especially the northern dwarves — had always been close friends to the northerners. Nauveena was not surprised Caron had selected Lord Ferrum.

"What about King Ümlaut?" Prince Javee asked. King Ümlaut's message resided in the black stone.

"Should he still get a vote?" Balzhamy of Lyrmica asked. "Considering what he did to the witch."

"Thank you for caring *so* deeply about my well-being," Venefica said.

"Yes, he still gets a vote." Nauveena stepped towards the dark stone. She again placed her hand on the crystal and activated it with her magic.

She stepped back as a purplish light illuminated the stone. Again, the light contorted into an image: this time that of King Ümlaut. He did not speak right away, needing a moment to compose himself before recording his message. Then he began.

"My sincerest apologies to all of Athyzia. Please know I was not myself. To the witch Venefica, I hope you can forgive me. If there is anything I can do to repay what I have done to you, please let me know. The people of Yülk are not as savage as my actions have demonstrated."

General Dolcius scoffed. The rest of the council continued to watch the image of Ümlaut.

"It is my belief that this council is the utmost good. And it is my deepest regret that I can no longer attend. I appreciate still being able to participate in some fashion, even if it be with a proxy. For my representative, I elect an old friend, one trustworthy and honest. My proxy will be Lord Ferrum, the dwarf."

If anyone had not looked at Lord Ferrum before, they did now.

"Did each king know they were giving their proxy to the same person?" Csandril Em' Dale asked.

Malachite shook his head. He too looked surprised. "Not at all. I don't think they would have done so if they had."

"What does this mean?" Lord Ferrum looked the most confused of all.

Nauveena alone addressed the Dwarf Lord. "It means you have three votes."

Chapter Seven
A Long Night

> "As the honest count the hill's many grains of sand, the wicked will ascend it and make themselves king."
> ~*Collected Wisdoms of Before*
> 941 BU

More objections continued from the Protectors of Order. "How can one member control three votes?" General Dolcius asked.

Fallou controls eight votes, Nauveena thought.

Lord Ferrum himself answered. If King Bane had appeared honored when Malachite made him proxy, the Dwarf Lord beamed by comparison. "It is a great honor, and I will treat it as such. I will not consider them my votes, but will instead vote as I imagine King Ümlaut and King Caron would vote."

The storm had grown more intense. Now, the rain came at a sideways angle. It curved around Snorri's protective charms. Despite already being soaked through, Nauveena and the other council members who had gone to greet Malachite did not appreciate the additional spray.

Between the binding spell and Malachite's return, the day had been busy enough. Nauveena dismissed the council, and each member retreated through the rain with their heads bowed.

Without having to speak, Nauveena, Venefica, and Malachite made their way to Nauveena's tower. Once inside, each found some private room to change and dry themselves. Malachite had fresh clothes brought for him, while Venefica slipped into something belonging to the sorceress.

They dressed quickly. The two women waited anxiously to speak with the druid. They came into Nauveena's solar still drying their hair, eager to speak with Malachite.

"Can I get you anything?" Nauveena asked.

"Coffee. If you have it." It had been a long trip.

Nauveena made a pot of coffee while Malachite began his story.

"I apologize for my delay," he began. "I wanted to send word ahead of me, but I feared it was too dangerous. Only when I could see Athyzia's towers did I send a hawk ahead."

"'Too dangerous?'" Venefica asked.

"Yes. I must start from the beginning." Malachite folded into the sofa, looking drained. His haggard appearance explained enough. He must have done everything possible to return. Nauveena hurried with the coffee. She could hear him from her place at the stove.

"I left our meeting in the Library of Maladies and set out at once. I took the swiftest horse from Athyzia's stables, one of King Bane's mares. It rode swiftly, and I made good time. I expected the land to be deserted, devoured still by the blight. But the road north was crowded with refugees flooding out of the middle kingdoms. I had not expected such numbers. Even though I rode with urgency, I stopped several and asked if they had been displaced by the War with the Osseomancer. They shook their heads. No. They had been forced from their homes for other reasons.

"The Magic of Order has outlawed much magic in their lands. They have gone from home to home, looking for evidence of any magic practiced by those other than the Magic of Order — folk mages, elves, witches. Neighbors now tell on each other. All it takes is one anonymous tip, and Keepers of Order arrive at your home to arrest you.

"The raids have intensified these last few weeks, since the report came from Pravulum. The threat of the Osseomancer's resurrection has heightened everyone's fears, and the Magic of Order has responded by arresting any who might follow him — even though few do, or ever did. Many have been forced to flee.

"Even with these crowds, I made good time and arrived on the banks of the Yülk by the end of the fourth day. I crossed over that night. I sent word back with Gwalk, a hawk companion of mine. He and his brothers made themselves of use to me. I wanted to keep you updated on my progress."

Nauveena brought a cup of coffee to the druid, who took it gratefully. "And I was pleased to be updated on your progress. But the hawks stopped coming. What happened?"

"I will get to it. I crossed the Yülk and immediately saw the signs of war when I entered the northern countries. Towns burned. Small skirmishes had left the dead everywhere. War is not pleasant, but I followed its signs to the northern kings. Their trail was easy to follow. After three days in that country, I crossed into Künner.

"I came closer to the armies. I watched them clash from a position on top of a hill a few miles from the battle. Gwalk and his family flew above the battle and brought word back on the progress. I knew I could not approach either king during war. I could only wait."

"That is the last message I heard from you," Nauveena said. "That you had witnessed the first battle."

"Yes, it was the last one I sent. After I sent Gwalk away with that final message, I turned to watch the battle again. Then a troop of horsemen approached me. Few warriors in the north ride horses. They prefer to transform into animals themselves, and have no need. I found their approach strange. I remained apprehensive, but let them come. Until it became too late.

"As they came close, I offered greeting and asked the riders what they sought. They did not respond, but drew arrows and fired upon me. I know few magics for combat, but composed a simple spell to repel the arrows. I then gave flight, and they chased me. I only escaped by riding into King Ümlaut's camp and requesting sanctuary."

"Who were they?" Venefica asked.

"I still do not know. And neither did King Ümlaut when I met with him after the battle. He had many things on his mind, but he found the appearance of strange riders in the north disturbing. I met with him and asked him to make peace. He would not, but asked me to approach King Caron with the same request. If King Caron would surrender himself and allow Ümlaut to fight him in single combat, then Ümlaut would end the war.

"Because of the riders, Ümlaut sent me with a detail of Yülkan warriors as escort. After losing the battle, King Caron had retreated to Gülk. They escorted me there, and I called upon King Caron. I urged him to fight in single combat with Ümlaut and end the conflict. The fight was between them; why should so many others die?"

"And he said no?" Nauveena asked.

Malachite nodded.

"*Coward.*" Venefica continued to dry her long black hair with a towel. She had poured herself a glass of wine.

"Where was Queen Breve?" Nauveena asked.

"She was with Caron," Malachite said. "And she begged him to fight in single combat. His position appeared hopeless. He was besieged in the city. No hope would come. He should have fought in single combat. I think Queen Breve saw him as a coward then. I think she had come to regret her choice. But she could not unmake it.

"I asked, if he would not make peace, then to give a proxy for the council. At first King Caron refused, but Breve demanded this of him. He could not delay the council. Or not be represented. Finally, he relented and agreed. He privately transcribed his message in the ruby and provided this to me. As is the way with crystals, the message can only be heard once, so I could not listen to learn who he had chosen.

"I then returned to King Ümlaut. I did not have an escort, so I traveled quickly through the night. I feared the riders found me by following the hawks. I asked Gwalk not to come to me any longer, so as not to expose myself. I could not deliver any other messages or risk the riders finding me again.

"I returned to King Ümlaut's camp once more and delivered King Caron's message. I said, even if King Caron will not fight in single combat, make peace anyways. Everyone will now see Caron for the coward he is. Your honor will remain intact. You have nothing to gain from this battle.

"But King Ümlaut would not listen. He turned his back on me. He would not make peace. He would wage war until he had killed King Caron. With peace no longer an option, I asked for Ümlaut's proxy. The king initially would not give it. But then I told him that King Caron had also refused. This lie did the trick, and King Ümlaut recorded his message. This, I could not hear either. At the time, I had no idea that *both* had made Lord Ferrum their proxy. I never would have guessed. A part of me had hoped they might make me their proxy, and then their votes would be more protected."

"The northerners have always been close friends with the dwarves." Nauveena thought of how frequently the dwarves had been drinking with the northerners when she went to visit.

"It does not sound like it took you long to get the kings' proxy," Venefica said. "Why, then, were you so delayed?"

"You are right," Malachite said. "I had the kings' proxy eleven days ago. It took me those eleven days to return. I left Ümlaut's camp the next day and set out south. I wished to send Gwalk with another message, but I feared alerting the riders to my whereabouts. I crossed the Hiel that day and continued through Yülk. The common folk of that land were quite fearful of the war. They would not receive me. The Osseomancer never crossed into their lands, and it had been long since they saw war directly.

"I came to the banks of the Yülk and prepared to cross. As I approached the ford, an otter came out of the river's reeds with an urgent message: On the opposite bank, a patrol of strange riders waited. The animal did not know what they wanted, but feared he should warn me. I asked other animals — geese and ducks and two very articulate salmon — for reports of the opposite banks, and soon confirmed the ambush waiting for me on that side.

"I could not cross the Yülk at that point, so I traveled upriver, towards the First Mountains. I knew of many places towards the mountains where I could cross and slip south. Now, however, as I headed south, my course would take me through Pravulum.

"While I did not know the identity of these riders, I had my suspicions of who had sent them. If they were connected to the Magic of Order, it would not be wise to cross Pravulum on the eastern side, where the Magic of Order guards the dark citadel. I then decided to stay to the west, and pass Pravulum on the western edge.

"The western edge is guarded by a contingent of elves from the Wild, led by a cousin of Zufaren. While I tried to give Pravulum a wide berth, so as not to be delayed, the elves' patrol found me riding through the mountain passes there. They asked me my business. When I explained who I was and that I knew Zufaren, they offered me rest and nourishment.

"At this point, I had been traveling for many days, and was indeed weary. I went to their guard towers on the western edge and rested for the night. While in their company, I spoke of the events of the world. For some time, I too had been curious about the reports of the Osseomancer's sighting at Pravulum. I asked the elves if they had seen him."

"Had they?" Nauveena asked.

"They shared an interesting piece of information," Malachite said. "They had seen a man wandering the fields around Pravulum. But when they approached the man, he did not attempt to blind them and flee. He sat with them and spoke with them at length. The man did not know who he was. But the elves think they know his identity."

"The Osseomancer?"

"No — Caeruleom."

"The Blue Wizard?"

"Indeed. The man was much older than the Osseomancer had been, and had an appearance more similar to the Blue Wizard. He spoke pleasantly and did not try any tricks or charms. The elves did not fear him and allowed him on his way. They planned to send a message to their queen explaining this. I told them I was headed to Athyzia and would deliver the message myself. And I asked them to keep the information secret for now."

"Secret? Why?"

"If it is indeed the Blue Wizard, he is in a weakened state after his battle with the Osseomancer. There are many who do not wish him to return. Of course, it is likely that Fallou and the Magic of Order have already surmised this is who their sentries encountered, and are hunting him themselves. But I did not want Fallou to know that we know. They have used the report to create hysteria. We must be cunning in what we do with this information."

"We must find him," Venefica said. "He would prove an immense help to the council."

"I agree. And a part of me wanted to go in search of him. But I knew I could not delay my arrival with the northern kings' proxy. After resting with the elves, I set out once again. The elves took me as far south as their watch extended.

"No sooner had I left the elves than I saw the riders coming for me. How they found me, I do not know. All around Pravulum is devastation.

It is easy to see for many miles on those desolate plains. No doubt, they waited for me. And fortunately, I could see them coming.

"They knew my destination and planned to cut me off from reaching Athyzia. I had no other choice but to swing out west, in a wide arch through Druissia. I traveled almost as far south as Saphalon Forest. Once within the forests, I could easily escape them. And in this way, I journeyed the rest of the way back."

"The most critical matter now is the dwarves," Malachite said after he finished his coffee. "I had not anticipated the northern kings both giving their proxy to Lord Ferrum. He might now be the most powerful member of the council, with three votes and a strong ally in Galena and the southern dwarves. Combined, the dwarves have a total of four votes."

"Lord Ferrum would vote against the Elf Laws, no doubt," Nauveena said.

"How can we be certain?" Venefica asked. "Will Lyrmica offer the Last Mountains again? And at a lower price? Wouldn't the dwarves' additional votes change the calculus?"

A knocking echoed through the tower, coming from the door below. Nauveena rushed to the window and looked out.

Since they had gathered in the tower, night had come. With the rain, the darkness was complete. Through sheets of rain, Nauveena saw a small group gathered below: the Elf Queen surrounded by four elven escorts. While they carried no lights, they were still illuminated in the dark night, so she could see them clearly.

Nauveena descended to the base of the tower and let them in. Queen Em' Iriild wore a hooded cloak of the finest silver silk. Despite the rain, she did not have a drop on her. Neither did her elven guards.

Nauveena welcomed the Elf Queen and brought her upstairs. The elven guards remained below.

"I expected to find you here," Queen Em' Iriild said. "Druid, I am pleased to see you have returned safely. I am curious why you were delayed, but tonight, I have another question. If I am not mistaken, the next topic for discussion is the Elf Laws. We have delayed long enough. Do we have the votes to overturn them?"

"Our primary concern now is the dwarves," Nauveena said.

"The dwarves? Why would they be your concern? It is the vote on the Elf Laws coming next."

"Tonight, the dwarves gained control of four votes," Malachite said. "I have been away, but I would imagine those would be pivotal in overturning the Elf Laws. Am I wrong?" he asked Nauveena and Venefica. "How does the vote currently stand?"

While Nauveena's primary focus had been delaying the council until Malachite's return, she had still been actively meeting with the council members. "The dwarves' votes are indeed important, especially now that they hold two more," she said. "We can count on Druissia and Dunisk?" she asked Venefica.

The witch nodded.

"That is two," Nauveena said. "Malachite is three. Prince Javee and the oracles make another two, for five. Then the elves themselves provide three more votes, getting us to eight."

"We only have eight?" Queen Em' Iriild asked in disbelief.

"Those eight are firm and dependable," Venefica said.

"I thought the northerners would have been firmly in that category," Nauveena said. "And with the dwarves, they still might be. The dwarves now have four. Once we confirm their allegiance, we can count on twelve."

"We must have thirteen, at least," Venefica said. "To force the tie, with you acting as the tie breaker."

"Yes, we must have thirteen," Nauveena said. "Eight we have. Four are with the dwarves. Another eight are strongly with the Magic of Order. We are unlikely to gain any from this number. Six remain unaccounted for: three for the southern merchants, then Aryde, the Bogwaah, and Skiel."

"Skiel?" Malachite asked. "I thought we could count Skiel to our side?"

"Every time we have spoken to them, they have requested we make exceptions in the vote against necromancy," Venefica said. "Carve something out so they can continue to practice it. The northerners also had an issue on this, but I imagine they would have come along. Skiel remains more dependent on the magic. If they learn they might be a swing vote, they might use it as leverage."

"*Necromancy?*" the Elf Queen hissed. "We can never allow such a practice. It is the stain that separates elves from men. We could not vote for it in any way."

"It is not like the Magic of Order will grant such exceptions," Malachite said. "They will have nowhere else to turn but us."

"We must win the vote now," Nauveena said. "If we can reject the Elf Laws, the eastern kingdoms will be forced to dismantle them; they are now bound by the oath spell they recited today."

"A binding spell?" Malachite asked, looking surprised. Nauveena had yet to share with him all that had happened while he had been away.

"Yes, a binding spell," she explained. "We finished reciting the oath shortly before you arrived. We are now locked to whatever the council decides. Any who deviate from the edicts will be punished by the magic of the vow."

"I thought we wished to avoid such a spell?" Malachite asked.

"Once, we might have, but think what we can now achieve," Venefica said. "Before, if we had achieved a vote to end the Elf Laws, the eastern kingdoms could have returned home and ignored the council's edicts. Now, if we pass such a measure, they will be bound to it through magic. We may actually improve the lives of those in the east."

"But we must have the vote," Queen Em' Iriild said.

"We will," Venefica said. "The dwarves' votes remain most important because of their number. If we lose them, it will not matter where the other undecided realms stand. We must go to the dwarves now."

"I imagine they will still be awake," Malachite said. "It is dark, but not very late. The storm makes it seem later than it is."

"And the dwarves hardly sleep, anyways," Nauveena said, thinking of the dwarves' love of coffee. "But we also must have one of the others. Should we not begin speaking with them as well?"

"That is wise," Malachite said. "I can speak with the southern merchants. They have three votes, so should be the second priority."

"And I can meet with Skiel if you go see the dwarves," Venefica said to Nauveena.

"How can the elves assist?" Queen Em' Iriild asked. "The vote is most important to us, after all."

Nauveena remembered how harshly the queen often spoke. She worried how the queen might react if the other realms said something she did not want to hear.

"We should approach the other realms first," Nauveena said. "With us, they might speak more freely. If we need aid, I imagine Csandril Em' Dale would be most useful. He can be quite persuasive."

"We can meet with the Bogwaah and Aryde after," Malachite said.

"The elves thank you all for your service," Queen Em' Iriild said. "For so long, we have been forced to live as strangers on our own land. We look forward to the day when we can be treated as equals."

Nauveena alone went to the Library of Erudition. As expected, she found the dwarves still awake. They no longer read through the library's vast collection, but instead talked excitedly with each other about the day's events. None could believe Lord Ferrum had been entrusted with both of the northern kings' votes.

The library's books remained in tall piles, forming a veritable maze Nauveena needed to pick through. The dwarves appeared in no shape to put them back, especially not tonight. They oscillated between cups of coffee and Clovis ale, sometimes mixing both together and becoming quite frenzied as a result.

Nauveena could not imagine that the mixture tasted good. She remembered Grufton Mann speaking of a coffee-flavored rum from the Distant Lands. How had the merchants not tried selling this to the dwarves? She could only imagine the state of the library if the dwarves were to get their hands on such a drink. She didn't know when or how the books would return to their shelves as it were.

She found Lord Ferrum and Galena seated at their center table. They each drank from a cup of coffee, still warm, with trails of steam rising above them.

Nauveena looked around the stacks of books separating them. For a moment, she paused, considering how to begin. *Should she be direct?* They must both know why she had come. Being too coy might be insulting to them. She did not know dwarven etiquette very well.

"Quite the day," she said instead. She would see how they responded.

"You can say that again," Lord Ferrum said in a fast sputter. He likely wasn't on his first cup of coffee. His eyes were wide with the effects of caffeine.

"I know you were close with the northerners," Nauveena said, "but I cannot imagine you expected them to make you their proxy."

"Not at all. Quite surprised, I was, young sorceress. If only the northerners could return themselves. I wish the druid had more luck convincing them to try peace."

"The Künner king is a coward," Galena said. "The conflict is between the two kings. No one else. Let single combat settle it. Caron is many years Ümlaut's junior; he should not fear him in battle. And if he does, he should have thought of that before sleeping with Ümlaut's queen."

Nauveena remembered how large Ümlaut had been when transformed into a bear. King Caron had been enormous as well, but nowhere near the bear's size. She understood why Caron might refuse single combat. But Galena had a point. How many would die in a fight that only involved two men?

"I wanted to get your thoughts on all these matters," Nauveena said. "And I am also curious if, now that you are the northerners' proxy, has Lyrmica approached you once more on the matter of the Last Mountains?"

"The Last Mountains?" Lord Ferrum took a sip of coffee. "No, no, I have not seen Balzhamy since today's session. They have not mentioned anything on the Last Mountains. Why do you think they would?"

His eyes became — if it were possible — somehow wider as he understood Nauveena's point. "Ah. You reckon their tune might change now that I control two more votes? Is that it?"

"Yes, I imagine it might change the calculus for them," Nauveena said.

"I had not considered *that*." Lord Ferrum drank his coffee, thinking. "I had not considered that. But no, no," he said more to himself than anyone else. "No, even if they were to come down, I don't think it fair. I have been entrusted with Ümlaut and Caron's votes. I cannot sell them to the highest bidder."

Nauveena took a deep sigh of relief. She knew dwarves prized honor quite highly. She just didn't know if they prized it more than gold and silver and gems. But Ferrum's quick reaction reassured her that she need not worry.

"Let us wait a moment now." Galena placed a hand on Lord Ferrum's shoulder. "Of course we should honor the northerners' interests in those issues that might impact them. But many issues might not. In those regards, we should be able to do as we see fit with the votes."

Nauveena's heart skipped a beat.

"Well, I had not considered that," Lord Ferrum said.

"But I am certain that the northerners have an interest in most of the topics put before the council," Nauveena said. "They would want one outcome over another, at least. That should be respected."

"Look, the dwarves have suddenly found themselves with much power," Galena said. "When was the last time the dwarves were in such a position to influence all of Jenor? We must use our position wisely."

"As long as we don't do anything that would negatively impact the northerners," Lord Ferrum said.

"Of course," Galena said. "But us gaining control of the Last Mountains would not negatively impact them."

"Yes, but what you might have to vote for could," Nauveena said. "Balzhamy won't give the Last Mountains freely."

"We should at least hear his offer, if he plans to make one," Galena said.

"Oh, yes, there's nothing wrong with that," Lord Ferrum said.

"If they make an offer, please come find me or Venefica or Malachite right away," Nauveena urged. "Let us know the terms of the deal — what they are offering and what they want in return. Let us see if we can counter them."

"Yes, yes, we can do that," Lord Ferrum said.

"Counter?" Galena asked. "What can you offer better than the Last Mountains?"

Nauveena left the dwarves. If Lyrmica had not made a new offer, there was little for her to do at the Library of Erudition. Just learning that Lyrmica had not made a new offer was enough.

And maybe they wouldn't? They had already given a low offer on the Last Mountains in exchange for the dwarves' support. Nauveena could not remember the details on the different tax rates. All she knew was that it was not enough for the dwarves.

Maybe Lyrmica would not go lower? Maybe the Elf Laws were not important enough to exchange the Last Mountains over? Fewer and fewer elves remained in the east. How important was enforcing the unfair laws, anyways? Was it worth losing the riches of the Last Mountains?

Nauveena had never been motived by such things, so she could only guess. For now, it seemed Lord Ferrum's additional votes had not changed Lyrmica's position.

When Nauveena reached the tower again, Venefica had already returned, while Malachite remained with the southern merchants. After the dwarves, their votes might be most important of all, since they controlled three in total.

The witch waited on the sofa with a glass of wine. She poured one for Nauveena as the sorceress explained what had happened with the dwarves.

"I was certain this would change things," Venefica said. "I cannot imagine Fallou will stand back and let us overturn the Elf Laws. Especially if they are now bound to the council's decision."

"Maybe they see how unfair the laws are," Nauveena said. "And want to overturn them."

"I doubt that very much."

"But who do these laws even benefit? Why continue them?"

Venefica poured more wine for herself. "Many benefit from the Elf Laws. Same with these newer restrictions against witches. The ruling classes in the east have long distracted those below them by turning their hatred towards other groups rather than the ruling classes themselves — the ones oppressing them and making their lives worse. Now, they are using the fear built up during the war to escalate the tension and, while the masses are distracted, exploit them further."

"But the fear is real," Nauveena said. "Those kingdoms suffered like everyone else during the war. The people of Wabia saw their Library of Ülme burned down, after all. The fear is not manufactured."

"The fear is real, of course. But where the fear is directed has been misplaced — manipulated. Some witches might have supported the Osseomancer initially. But like me, they eventually turned from him. He has very few supporters remaining. Many fewer than Fallou would like you to believe.

"And say what you will about the Osseomancer, but I do not believe he would burn down a library like the one at Ülme. He sought knowledge. Maybe so he could hoard it and enrich himself, but he certainly did not want it *destroyed*. Why did he long to enter Athyzia? Not to burn her books, but to read them. I can't imagine he would set fire to Ülme."

Nauveena thought for a moment. She found it hard to shake the images from the war — the Osseomancer marching on the city and setting fire to everything. Maybe his armies had grown overzealous and acted against his wishes?

But he commanded those armies through magic. They could not act without his say. And he had begun the war to capture all the magical knowledge available to him. Why would he destroy Ülme? Especially when he had captured the city and had the library at his disposal.

"How was Skiel?" Nauveena asked.

Venefica rolled her eyes. "Guess what they wanted to talk about."

"Necromancy?" That was always the topic with Skiel.

"Of course," Venefica said. "This was the most explicit Veeslau has been. Skiel needs necromancy so they can continue to avoid the dragon. They will not oppose a ban on necromancy's general use in warfare or other nefarious ways, but they need it to remain open for commercial uses.

"But Veeslau the Unbound has become bolder still. Not only does he want an exception, he does not want the council to know it came from Skiel. Necromancy has gained a bad association since the war, and Veeslau does not want Skiel associated with it as well."

"'A bad association?' Is that what he calls it?" Nauveena thought of the hordes of undead creeping through the mountains towards Athyzia, decaying flesh still clinging to their bones. "How will he get his exception then?"

"He asks us to propose it and find a reason for it that does not expose Skiel's practices."

"Then forget Skiel," Nauveena said. "It is their fault for staking their entire kingdom on such an awful magic. We are working to prevent the Magic of Order from becoming too strict, from banning other magics — not necromancy. We are trying to overturn the Elf Laws. We do not need to extend ourselves for necromancy. It should be banned. The dead are commanded against their wills and their bodies threatened."

"But we need Skiel. They too have done the math. Even if we secure the dwarves' four votes, we need either the three southern cities, or at least one of Skiel, Aryde, or the Bogwaah. Veeslau knows this. He will use his vote as leverage to gain the exceptions he wants."

Nauveena sighed with frustration. How had it come to this? They would barter votes on one issue for votes on another. Snorri had not begun the council for it to turn into this. But she needed to weigh the two issues. Yes, the use of necromancy was abhorrent, but so were the Elf Laws. And the Elf Laws negatively impacted the living; certainly, they should take priority.

"Veeslau will only vote down the Elf Laws if we grant his exception?" Nauveena asked.

Venefica nodded. "Skiel cares little about the Elf Laws. Few elves reside in Skiel. They have Elf Laws, but these are a holdover from the First Faulsk Empire. They are barely enforced. Skiel does not care one way or another about them. Why not use their position to gain an exception on necromancy?"

Nauveena sighed. "Well, if it comes to it, we can convince the elves to vote for the exception then."

"I am not sure we can."

"Not even to remove the Elf Laws?"

"You heard Queen Em' Iriild," Venefica said. "I fear she will take a hard line on necromancy."

"But why? Human mages cannot even perform necromancy on elves. Why should they care what magic is practiced in a kingdom so far from their own? It's been going on for ages. What harm is there to the elves in letting it continue?"

"At the beginning of the world, the elves' creators gifted them with extraordinarily long lives," Venefica said. "Elves live longer than even the oldest mages. But with these long lives came an understanding. Their lives would be long as long as they did not ever try to extend them. They view death as a duty they must accept for the gift of life. They will not alter death, either for themselves or any other creature, including man."

"But Skiel can't get an exception from the Magic of Order," Nauveena said. "They are just as strict as the elves on this topic. Don't they view necromancy as a dark magic? Akin to blood magic?"

Just then, the door slammed open, and Malachite rushed in, shaking the rain from his hair. He had looked exhausted before he left, but now, he looked on the verge of collapse.

"The southern merchants are lost."

Malachite collapsed into a chair as Nauveena tossed him a towel. He dried his hair. Outside, the rain continued to stream down violently.

"Lost?" Venefica asked.

He nodded. "Fallou has bought them."

"All three?"

"Yes." Malachite sighed. "They will all vote to uphold the Elf Laws."

"Bought their vote? How?" *Certainly, that shouldn't be allowed by the council*, Nauveena thought. Couldn't she intervene?

"Not with actual coin," the druid explained. "But they have, more or less. Each values their status as an independent city more than anything else. They each gained their charters long before the First Faulsk Empire. They will do anything to maintain them. They care little about the Elf Laws. It is a small price to pay to maintain their independence."

"But how would they lose their independence?" Nauveena asked. "Those charters can't be revoked now."

"The Second Faulsk Empire and its allies have enough military might to do what they like," Malachite said. "Charters be damned."

"They will invade those cities if they don't vote with them?"

Malachite nodded.

"That's extortion, then. We should put a stop to it."

"Fallou will certainly deny it. They haven't explicitly threatened them. But they have stressed how important upholding the Elf Laws is to Valinka and Phryza and Olmtpur. They've essentially said that each kingdom should be allowed to operate as they always have. The insinuation is clear: if the Elf Laws are overturned, they will revoke each city's charter."

If the three merchant cities planned to vote to uphold the Elf Laws, it only made the remaining three — Skiel, Aryde, and the Bogwaah — more important. Skiel's leverage had increased.

"So, they are out." Venefica refilled her glass. "We must have one of the remaining three, assuming we don't lose the dwarves. I am worried about Skiel. We must turn our focus to Aryde and the Bogwaah."

"Aryde also values their independence," Nauveena said. "It is likely Fallou has made similar insinuations to them. I can go speak with them."

"And the Bogwaah?" Venefica asked.

The Bogwaah. Nauveena had not considered them. They could not be threatened by Faulsk and the middle kingdoms militarily, at least not easily. They lay on the other side of Jenor. They were neighbors to the elves of the Wilds. Without Zufaren and his warriors, the Bogwaah would have been overrun by orcs long ago.

They needed to talk to the Burgomaster.

"I think that should be me," Malachite said. He looked like he might fall asleep, but they all knew Venefica's reputation. The other realms were less likely to trust her. "I have traveled through the Bogwaah frequently. Hopefully, they still consider me a friend."

Nauveena hoped the foreign minister of Aryde, Fichael Porteau was still awake. It was now almost midnight, and with the constant rain, felt somehow later still. She knocked on his door, a hood pulled over her head to protect her from the rain. She heard her knock echoing inside Porteau's apartment, then, a moment later, shuffling inside. Someone approached the door. It swung open to reveal the tired face of the foreign minister. If Malachite had looked exhausted, Fichael Porteau appeared to have not slept in several days.

He peered into the dark. "Sorceress?"

"Can I come in?" Nauveena knew Fichael feared spies as much as she. They typically spoke in a tight alley near his apartment, but tonight, with the rain, she didn't think that was suitable.

As she expected, Fichael's eyes flickered wildly into the dark behind her before he said, "Yes." He couldn't see anything, and likely neither could a spy, but he could not be too careful.

Nauveena entered his chambers and immediately smelled the stale smoke of Fichael's smoke leaf. The scent hung all around the room. He preferred to smoke outside to avoid creating such an atmosphere, but had clearly been smoking so regularly, he had developed the habit of smoking inside now too.

One half-smoked cigarette remained in an ashtray. He picked this up and began smoking as Nauveena came further into the room.

"Do you know why I am here?" she asked.

"The elf vote is tomorrow," Fichael Porteau said. "I imagine you want to know where Aryde stands."

"I wish I were not that transparent."

"I have been working in parliaments for many years. Most do not come unexpectedly in the middle of the night for casual conversation."

"Then I must ask where you stand."

"I hate to disappoint you, but I imagine you can guess. Especially if you have spoken with the other council members. I imagine Valinka and Olmtpur have been given a similar, veiled ultimatum: continue to vote as a collective with Faulsk, or else."

"I was hoping I would not be too late."

"That has been the reality for a *long* time," Fichael said. "Faulsk has only become more aggressive in its insinuations. The business of the Osseomancer's supporters is of particular concern, and Faulsk claims we are not doing enough to stop them. They claim we are harboring these enemies."

"The whole thing is a lie. Witches and folk mages are not holding secret rituals to sacrifice children. They do not want the Osseomancer to return. They want to move on with their lives."

"I know that. I've been having lengthy correspondences with our Minister of Magical Affairs. We have been speaking daily, thanks to the speaking stones. He is adamant these charges are false. But Faulsk does not believe him or anyone else. They say if we do not apprehend these criminals, then they will have no choice but to come in and take matters into their own hands. They are claiming it is for the safety of all Jenor. Neither Faulsk nor Lyrmica have ever recognized Aryde's independence. As far as they are concerned, we are still in a rebellion. And now, we are harboring supporters of the Osseomancer. They are looking for any excuse to invade. Voting against them might be just the excuse they need."

Nauveena felt her heart sink. They might be able to secure the dwarves' vote, but it would not matter. The merchants and Aryde would be too scared to vote against Faulsk and Fallou. Skiel had their own issues. She was now counting on Malachite to convince the Bogwaah.

"We've been relaxing the Elf Laws in Aryde little by little." Fichael finished one cigarette and began another. "Democracy is a slow process. Most of the public is against the laws, but it still takes time dismantling them. Part of our rebellion began to protect magic. But if we are invaded, we won't be able to continue this. The Elf Laws will become stricter. Those accused of supporting the Osseomancer will be held without trials or rights. We could vote against Fallou in the council, but we cannot stand against him and Faulsk *militarily*."

"If Faulsk is looking for an excuse to invade," Nauveena said, "it is only a matter of time before they find one. If not your votes here, then they will make up some other pretext. Why not make a stand in the council? If we can strike down the laws, the other kingdoms will be forced to respect them because of the binding spell. You have power because of it."

"I have considered that," Fichael said. "But it is not my decision. I represent a parliament. And our leaders have written me demanding that I vote with Fallou. The Magic of Order has been communicating with our parliamentary leaders through backchannels."

"You will vote to uphold the Elf Laws, then?"

"My hands are tied."

Nauveena felt suddenly quite tired. The long day and now night had finally caught up with her. She appreciated Fichael Porteau's honesty, even if she did not like what he had to say or what it meant.

"I might have one piece of good news for you," he said. "Rising tension exists between Faulsk and Lyrmica."

"What? How do you know that?"

"As I said, I have been in these types of situations before. It is helpful to gather information however you can."

"Why is there tension?"

"Over the dwarves. Faulsk wants to lower the tax rate on the Last Mountains, assuming the dwarves give their — and now the northerners' votes — to them. But Lyrmica won't go any lower. Fallou and Balzhamy have been fighting over it all afternoon."

That explained why no one had approached the dwarves. *Yet.*

Nauveena appreciated the turn of good news. However, she couldn't see how — in an argument between Faulsk and Lyrmica — Faulsk would lose.

◆

Nauveena was exhausted, but she remained awake, waiting for Malachite to return. She hoped he would bring good news. Outside, the summer storm raged on. The tumult of rain was only interrupted by bright streaks of lightning and accompanying crashes of thunder.

Malachite remained away far into the night. Venefica finished her bottle of wine and began to doze. She and Nauveena both sat on the sofa, waiting for the druid, and in her sleep, the witch's head came to rest on the sorceress's lap. Nauveena let her rest there, and came to pet the tight braids of her hair absentmindedly as the witch slept.

Finally, as Nauveena almost succumbed to sleep herself, the doors to the tower burst open. Malachite came rushing up the stairs. Nauveena shook Venefica awake as he entered the room.

"I hope you have better news than I," Nauveena said.

"It has been a long night." Malachite collapsed into the chair across from them. He pushed his wet hair out of his face. "You can never be too direct with the Burgomaster. You must discuss all matters with him besides the one you are interested in first. And so, for many hours, I needed to entertain his idea that all magical ingredients should be produced exclusively in the Bogwaah."

"But you eventually discussed the vote?"

"Yes." A smile broke out on Malachite's face. "Yes, we eventually did. The Bogwaah owes their entire existence to the elves of the Wilds. Without them, they would have been overrun by the orcs long ago."

"So they will vote against the laws?"

Malachite nodded. After his long journey and the even longer night, it was all he could muster.

Nauveena rushed across the room to hug him. After so many hours, she could finally go to sleep.

Chapter Eight
The Last Mountains

> "Words may be grown as in an orchard. Organic, they cross-pollinate and ripen and swell. But numbers have always existed, before even the stars. Their glittering patterns are like diamonds buried deep within the hardest stone. They must be mined."
>
> ~*Phantom Knowledge*
> Tok the Dogface
> 729 BU

Despite her excitement, Nauveena fell asleep immediately. She slept soundlessly, uninterrupted by dreams. She was grateful not to dream that night. She did not have the energy, and her dreams had become too realistic. Even the dream she'd had recently — in the beautiful library — would have been too much. She only needed sleep.

She woke mid-morning. The rain continued, but had changed intensity. Thunder and lightning no longer accompanied it. Instead, a fierce wind whipped the rain sideways. The clouds remained, but mixed with daylight to create a dull gray light.

The weather had changed gradually throughout the night, and Nauveena felt like she had fallen asleep during a story and had now woken after missing critical plot points.

After dressing, she went to her solar to reconvene with Malachite and Venefica. Having rested, she now let herself feel the excitement. Throughout the night, they might have struck out on the votes of the merchants, Aryde, and maybe even Skiel. But they only needed one and they had it.

Nauveena had not even shared her one piece of good news. Fichael Porteau had reported that tensions were growing between Faulsk and

Lyrmica. While the Last Mountains bordered Faulsk, Rheum, and Aryde, Lyrmica controlled the majority of the dwarves' old mines. While Lyrmica might follow Faulsk in most matters, they disagreed on the mountains, and with that, Faulsk could not secure the dwarves' votes.

Nauveena entered her living room, excited to share this news, but instead found one more than she had expected.

Csandril Em' Dale.

The elf looked so well-rested, Nauveena became conscious of her own appearance. Despite sleeping for several hours, her hair was messy, and bags appeared under her eyes. She had never seen an elf look tired; they always looked as if they did not need sleep. She only worried for a moment, and then the excitement returned. Csandril had undoubtedly come on assignment from Queen Em' Iriild. Nauveena was pleased he could leave with good news.

"Good morning," Csandril said in the cheeriest voice possible. Typically, were Nauveena feeling as tired as she currently felt, she would not have considered it a good morning. But now, she could not help but agree.

"I trust you have heard the good news," she said.

"You three have become quite the political agents," Csandril said. "Perhaps there are jobs for you in Aryde's parliament when this is all over."

"I would much prefer to return to Athyzia's libraries, if I am given the choice."

"You can do whatever you like. The elves will even build you a new library, filled with all the volumes of our vast knowledge we are able to share. I am sure even Queen Em' Iriild could not say no to it — if we remove the Elf Laws."

"That won't be necessary." Nauveena felt herself blushing. And what had she ultimately done? Malachite had spoken with the Bogwaah, after all. Not her. And they likely had not needed much convincing. They had never practiced the Elf Laws in their territories. They neighbored the Wilds and owed their protection to Zufaren's warriors.

Nauveena had not finished blushing when they heard a knock. It seemed Csandril would not be the only visitor of the morning.

Nauveena went to her window and looked down. A strange dwarf looked up at her through the swirling rain. "If you wouldn't mind letting me up," he shouted against the gale. "I'm getting soaked through down here."

Nauveena went to the base of the tower. Once at eye-level — or at least not looking down at him from the tower's height — she recognized the dwarf as Hortrid, Lord Ferrum's nephew and squire. He was much younger than the other dwarves who had come to Athyzia, and as such, his beard only reached a portion of the way down his chest, and he seemed somehow shorter than even the other dwarves.

"Morning, morning." He bowled through Nauveena, trying to get inside. With the door open, she felt the spray of rain and understood why the dwarf moved so quickly to escape it.

Once inside, Hortrid squeezed the excess water from his beard, creating a puddle on the floor.

"Good morning," Nauveena said as sweetly as she could. Now that the shock of the dwarf's appearance had subsided, she realized what it meant: news from Lord Ferrum. She could only imagine what that might be. But of course, there was only one real possibility.

The morning's excitement dissipated quickly.

"My uncle sent me," Hortrid said. He sniffed the air. "Is that coffee? Is there any?"

"I can get you some, but what is it? Why has Lord Ferrum sent you?"

"He'd like to see you. He has news for you."

Nauveena shot up the tower as quickly as she could. Malachite and Venefica were still speaking with Csandril. She told them about Lord Ferrum's messenger, and they quickly readied themselves to come with her. They too guessed what the summons might mean. Had they gotten too far ahead of themselves?

As they were leaving, Nauveena managed to fill a mug with the remaining coffee and pushed it into Hortrid's outstretched hands. Despite it still being piping-hot, he drank it in a few seconds and then led them outside.

The group dashed across Athyzia. Nauveena pulled her hood down to protect from the driving rain. Despite it, the wind changed direction and sent sprays into her face.

They found a calmer scene in the Library of Erudition. Several dwarves read in a corner. The books were still stacked in a maze pattern, but Hortrid knew the route well and led them through quickly.

Lord Ferrum and Galena sat at their central table, talking to each other. They stopped speaking when the group approached.

"I brought them, as you told me to, uncle," Hortrid said.

"Hortrid, I have told you, when acting as my squire, you must refer to me as *Lord Ferrum*. That is the custom."

"Right, sorry. I forgot, uncle."

"Lord."

"Oh, right. Uncle — ah — Lord Ferrum. Anyways, here they are."

"You sent for us?" Nauveena asked.

"Yes, I wanted to see you," Lord Ferrum said. Nauveena felt her heart beating. She knew why he had called her, but she still held a secret hope that she might be wrong. He took a long time to speak; all the while, it felt like her chest might explode. "A messenger has come from the mage Balzhamy. It seems they have reconsidered the Last Mountains. They would allow the dwarves to reenter and pay only a twenty-percent tax rate on whatever is mined."

"*Twenty percent?*" Malachite said. Nauveena felt her heart sink. The dwarves would have to accept. "They were offering forty before."

"We know." Galena couldn't help smiling. She seemed unable to believe the low terms. "They only ask that we vote with them for the rest of the council."

"But not only with our votes, but with the northerners' votes too," Lord Ferrum hid a smile as well, but one not as wide as Galena's. He seemed much more conflicted.

"A twenty-percent tax rate is very low," Galena told Lord Ferrum.

"We have been entrusted with these votes. We cannot betray the northern kings in such a way." The messenger from Lyrmica must have come quite recently, as the news seemed fresh for Lord Ferrum and Galena as well.

"We can offer our votes, but not the northerners'," Galena said. "But I am not sure they would still offer twenty percent."

"Even twenty-five percent would be great." Lord Ferrum perked up at the idea. As long as he did not need to betray the northerners' votes, he was quite fond of the deal.

Only securing the dwarves' two votes will be enough, Nauveena thought. Especially knowing how the merchants and Aryde would vote. If Fallou could control the dwarves' votes, then he would have fourteen, and the Elf Laws would remain.

With the dwarf votes and the northerners' votes, Fallou could likely pass whatever he wanted. He could ban whatever magic he liked, and Nauveena could do nothing to stop him.

"Have you called us here to ask our opinions?" Malachite asked, interrupting the two dwarves as they debated each other.

"Something like that," Galena said. "When the sorceress came last night, she asked us to send for her right away if Lyrmica changed their offer on the Last Mountains, so you could counter. Well, Lyrmica has made a new offer. *What is your counter?*"

"Those cave-dwelling nincompoops. Those blind, scraggly-bearded earth munchers. Those greedy, crooked-toothed rock pushers." As soon as they left the Library of Erudition, Csandril Em' Dale released a steady stream of insults launched at the dwarves. He normally could control his speech to great effect, but now, it seemed to control him instead. "Those stumpy, hob-nosed, club-footed boulder lovers. Those — "

"*That's enough,*" Nauveena snapped. She had never heard such insults before. Elves and dwarves had a much longer history together and, evidently, elves had a long list of insults specifically tailored for the dwarves.

"They are auctioning their votes to the highest bidder," Csandril said. "Ümlaut and Caron's votes, too. Ferrum might think he isn't, but Galena will convince him eventually. He likes to think he's all high-minded, but he can't resist all those diamonds and rubies in the Last Mountains. And they're *just rocks.* That's all. Sure, they might help in some magic. But that's not why the dwarves want them. Not surprising that dwarves would be fascinated by shiny stones found in the ground. Oh. Those nearsighted, short-fingered troll humpers."

"Is there anything we can offer?" Malachite asked, ignoring Csandril.

"What's better than the Last Mountains?" Nauveena asked. Dwarves had mined deeply in all the other mountain ranges in Jenor. The Last Mountains remained untapped, filled with resources. The dwarves had only mined them for a short time before Lyrmica saw how rich they had become and wanted the mountains for themselves.

"Galena is right," Venefica said. "It is the first time the dwarves have had this much power. They are normally an afterthought. I don't blame them for using their leverage now that they have it."

"But the northerners' too?" Csandril asked. "They benefit from the riches extracted from the First Mountains in the north. If new mines are opened, the dwarves will shift their operations, and the northerners will lose out."

"Maybe Lyrmica will not offer the same tax rates if they are only getting the dwarves' votes," Nauveena said. "It was only the dwarves' votes originally, and Lyrmica only offered a tax rate of forty percent. The additional two votes dropped it all the way to twenty."

"The additional two votes and the binding spell," Venefica said. "There's more at stake now. Even if the dwarves withhold the northerners' votes, the tax rate might still come down."

"And they will offer the northerners' votes," Csandril said. "You don't know dwarves as well as I. They live most their lives underground. It messes with their heads. Oh. Those sweaty, heavy-footed, cowardly, pebble-brained halfwits. Of course they'd be the ones to doom the elves and continue the terrible laws."

Nauveena could feel Csandril's pain welling up inside him. She wanted nothing more than to offer a salve, but she did not know how.

"You know, Queen Em' Iriild is prepared to leave the council if the laws remain," Csandril continued. "She will not stay in a council that treats elves in such a way. I must say, I agree with her. The elves will walk if the Elf Laws are not overturned."

Walk? Nauveena could not believe it. *The elves would leave the council?*

"We cannot have that," Malachite said.

"You would doom all of Jenor," Venefica said.

"If the laws remain, then it is clear we are not a part of Jenor any longer," Csandril said bitterly. Nauveena could hear the hurt in his voice.

"The dwarves at least gave us the opportunity to counter," Nauveena said.

"Sure, counter, but with what?" Csandril asked. "What is better than the Last Mountains?"

"Nothing is better than the Last Mountains," Nauveena said. "But why couldn't we offer the Last Mountains ourselves?"

"How can we offer them?" Malachite asked.

"Lyrmica is not the only kingdom with entrances to the Last Mountains." Nauveena turned abruptly and began walking in the other direction.

Their small group had been discussing the matter while walking towards her tower. Now, she led them in the other direction. Towards Aryde.

"When the dwarves occupied the Last Mountains, they built many entrances to their mines," Nauveena said. "When they first brought up the mountains, I researched them. The Library of Maps has many charts of the mines. Most entrances fall into Lyrmica's territory. But some exit to Faulsk. Others to Rheum. But at least five exit into Aryde."

"It would have been Lyrmica when the dwarves were there," Malachite said.

"Yes, but now, that territory is firmly in the hands of Aryde. They have been mining it, or at least trying to, but like Lyrmica, no one can mine as well as the dwarves."

"So, you will... what?" Venefica asked. "Ask Aryde to grant the dwarves access to the Last Mountains?"

"It is worth a try." As the group approached Fichael Porteau's apartment, Nauveena turned around. "However, I might have better success if I try it alone. Such a large group might be overwhelming."

Each nodded, understanding. They turned and slipped through the rain.

Nauveena turned back to Porteau's apartment and approached. As she had the night before, she knocked on his door and heard it echo inside.

Fichael answered, looking just as tired as before. "You've returned?"

"I have news," Nauveena said.

"Yes, I heard. Lyrmica caved. A twenty-percent tax, is it?" Aryde's foreign minister was well-informed. Nauveena imagined that, as such a small nation it was critical to know as much as possible.

"I've just come from the dwarves," she said. "Can I come in?"

Fichael Porteau's eyes flickered behind Nauveena. At least in the cloudy daylight, he had reason to be apprehensive. He opened the door a bit more to allow her inside.

The same scent of stale smoke greeted Nauveena. She coughed. Fichael studied her, unsure why she had come. She was uncertain herself.

She coughed a bit longer, using the moment to gather the rest of her plan together.

"Lyrmica dropped their tax rate significantly in exchange for the dwarves' votes," Nauveena began. "Both their original two and their two proxy votes from the northerners."

"It was only a matter of time before Balzhamy gave in to Fallou," Fichael said. "Lyrmica is a puppet state at this point."

"The dwarves are, of course, considering the offer," Nauveena said.

"I thought they would have already accepted."

"Lord Ferrum is hesitant. He will not barter his proxy votes the way he would barter his own. But the dwarves' original two votes are as good as gone. Which means Fallou and the Magic of Order can pass almost anything they want on their agenda — beyond just the Elf Laws. They can ban other magics. They can restrict different sources. I know you are not a magical user, but these are serious infringements. The magic users in Aryde will not want these rulings."

"I agree with you on that much. On more important matters, Aryde might consider voting against Faulsk. But if Fallou secures all four of the dwarves' votes, it won't matter."

Nauveena smarted momentarily upon hearing Fichael Porteau refer to the Elf Laws as unimportant, but she remained focused. "Which is why we must secure the dwarves to our side."

"*Our* side?"

"We must ensure that the dwarves remain independent and not in Fallou's pocket."

"And how do we do that?"

"Aryde can offer the dwarves access to the Last Mountains. For a five-percent tax rate or *no tax rate at all*."

Fichael Porteau gagged so hard, he almost swallowed his cigarette. "Are you mad?" He gasped between coughs.

"Not at all."

"Last night, I told you I could not vote down the Elf Laws because Faulsk would view it as a provocation." Fichael found a glass of water and had a sip. He breathed, recovering from his earlier shock. "Now, you want us to offer the dwarves access to the Last Mountains? That would be as clear a provocation as anything we could do."

"But last night, you also said that Faulsk and Lyrmica will invade you eventually either way," Nauveena said. "They might use your vote at the council as an excuse. Or they might lie about you harboring agents of the Osseomancer. Or they might come up with something else entirely. Either way, they will come and divide Aryde between them."

"So we should just get it over with?"

"No, you should begin preparing your defenses. Even at a twenty-percent tax, Lyrmica will be greatly enriched by the dwarves. And, by extension Faulsk. If you offer the dwarves access, Lyrmica will be cut off, and you will be made rich instead.

"And what's more, you will then have an ally in the dwarves. You would not ask for anything else from them. Not their vote. Nothing. But they would smith the finest weapons for you. And they would have something at stake to continue your independence.

"The dwarves were driven from those mountains before. They will not be driven out again. They will fight with you and for you. If you think your enemies are prepared to invade, why not strike first? Remove their resources. Gain a strong ally. They will not expect it."

"We would almost immediately go to war," Fichael said. "The council would dissolve."

Not for the last time, Nauveena thought this might not be such a bad thing. "It is worth the risk," she said. "And it is better than the alternative: letting Fallou secure the dwarves' vote and then bending the entire council to his will."

"I must say, I was not expecting this," Fichael said. "All I can say is: I will consider it. I am not dismissing it right away. But I must speak to others. I cannot make such decisions on my own."

◆

Nauveena could not ask for much more from the foreign minister. She had entered his apartment with no expectations. She had formulated her plan on the way there, and so had no time to anticipate how he would react.

Of course he could not act alone. He would need approval from others in his government. Nauveena hoped it would not take too long.

Athyzia's mages had many ways to send messages quickly, and she would make sure these abilities were offered to Fichael as well.

She returned to the Tower of Yalde, where the others waited eagerly. She explained her conversation with Fichael Porteau. Each reacted in turn. Malachite and Venefica remained doubtful, while Csandril only continued to curse the dwarves.

After their reactions, little remained but to wait. Malachite napped in a guest room, still tired after his long journey. He would have preferred to return to his own chambers, but did not want to miss anything.

Venefica opened a bottle of wine. Csandril remained in the apartment. Nauveena suspected his queen had tasked him to remain with their group to keep abreast of their progress.

Nauveena could think of little else to do but read. She returned to one of her favorite grimoires, which not only provided spells, but their workings and origins and changes throughout the years.

The day crept towards evening. The storm wore itself out. The previous night's intensity dissipated. Even the strong winds from the morning had exhausted themselves. Now, only a light mist came from the sky. The clouds thinned in areas, allowing the final gasps of day to leak through.

Nauveena had almost finished her book when a knock came at the door.

Aryde?

She rushed to the window and looked out.

Below, a squat figure waited next to the door. He raised his hand to knock again. Even in the twilight, she recognized him. He was not the representative from Aryde, but Lord Ferrum's nephew Hortrid.

"Come on in." Nauveena remembered how little the dwarf had cared for the rain earlier that morning.

"No need for that. My uncle — ah — Lord Ferrum sent me. He wants to see you lot all again." He motioned back across the bridge in the general direction as the Library of Erudition.

Nauveena gathered the others, and they followed Hortrid to the library. They found Lord Ferrum and Galena at their central table. Galena smiled, while Lord Ferrum could not meet their eyes.

"I doubt you've changed your minds," Csandril said.

"I'm afraid we haven't." Lord Ferrum stared at a spot in the middle of the table.

"Then why have you called for us?" Nauveena had retained a small sliver of hope that they might reverse course. The dwarves had experienced discrimination similar to the elves. Maybe they would see the need for voting to remove the Elf Laws.

"We only thought it right to tell you in person," Galena said. "We've officially taken the deal with Fallou."

"You pebble-brained — " Venefica sharply elbowed Csandril before he could begin.

"You know, the council is not meant for such bartering." Nauveena attempted her best Snorri impression. "It threatens the council's whole integrity."

"We said as much." Lord Ferrum threw up his hands. "We told them we wouldn't take it."

"Then what happened?" Malachite asked.

"They lowered the rate."

"Ten percent," Galena said. "We will never get a better deal."

The original offer had been forty, then twenty, and now ten. Nauveena saw how hard it was to turn down.

"Ten percent in exchange for?" Nauveena asked.

"Our two votes and the two votes of the northern kingdoms," Galena said.

"We had no choice." Lord Ferrum turned his palms upwards to indicate his helplessness.

"'No choice?'" Csandril leaned over the table so his long, slender nose touched Ferrum's own bent one. "'No choice?' Of course you have a choice. There is always a choice. And like the dwarves have always done, rather than choosing others, they have chosen themselves. They have chosen gems and gold over their fellows' well-being."

"Don't put it like that," Lord Ferrum wailed.

"Now, you watch it." Galena waved a finger between Csandril and Lord Ferrum. "Don't pretend the elves have always shown generosity to the dwarves. Where were you when Lyrmica drove us from the Last Mountains? Where were you during the Eleven-and-a-Half-Year War? You did not come to the aid of the dwarves then."

For once, Csandril Em' Dale was at a loss for words.

"This offer is too good to not accept," Galena continued. "And we need it. Ten-percent tax rate or forty, we *need* to be in those mountains.

The dwarves are in a more desperate situation than we've let on. Our gems were needed against the Osseomancer, so we mined deeply for them. Even before the war, they were becoming scarce. We dug deeper than we ever had before. We pulled all the gems we could from our mountains. Both in the north and the south. There's none left. We need *new* mountains."

"And you should have them," Nauveena said.

"You said you would counter," Galena said.

"I am working on it. If a similar offer came from Aryde, but with no attachments as far as voting was concerned, would you take it?"

"Aryde?"

"Yes, Aryde. They have entrances to the Last Mountains too. And certainly, you could open more once inside their lands."

"And they are prepared to make such an offer?" Galena asked.

"I believe so."

"How certain are you that Aryde will offer the Last Mountains?" Malachite asked when they left.

Nauveena smiled nervously. "Porteau said he would need to check with his fellow ministers. It is not his decision to make alone."

"There's no way they'll do it," Csandril said. "These politicians are nothing but church mice. They know such a move would antagonize Faulsk and Lyrmica."

"He at least did not say *no* right away," Nauveena said.

"The sessions begin tomorrow," Venefica said. "It would be unwise for us to begin without knowing where Aryde stands. They may be our only hope of securing the dwarves' votes once more."

"Those potbellied, mushroom-licking, stalactite-riding, bat-fearing —"

"Is that helpful right now?" Venefica asked the elf. Then she said to Nauveena. "We must go to the foreign minister."

"Now?" Nauveena asked.

"Yes, now. And with haste. The matter cannot rest. Let us not begin session without the votes."

The entire retinue — because, at four, Nauveena felt like they were indeed something deserving of a word — marched swiftly across Athyzia to Fichael's apartment. The rain had completely let up at this point. Now, with night settled in, all they could hear was the leaves dripping in a soft echo of the storm that had raged since last night.

Fichael Porteau looked surprised when he found all four waiting on his doorstep.

"I apologize for the intrusion," Nauveena said defensively. His surprise validated her decision to come alone the night before. This type of maneuvering should be done with as few people as possible, but tonight, there was no time.

The foreign minister regained his composure, hid his shock, and welcomed the group inside. "Please come in." After they had entered, he glanced outside before shutting the door.

He motioned for the group to find a seat. The stale smoke stained the room. Nauveena could see Csandril sniffing furiously, confused by the fragrance. The plant smoked and cultivated by the elves smelled much sweeter than Fichael's smokeleaf. Despite the smell, the new plant seemed to be becoming more favored in the east.

"I've had a busy day," Fichael said when the group had sat. "I thought long about the idea you brought to me. Aryde lives in fear that Lyrmica and Faulsk will conspire against us. We won our independence after many long, hard years of fighting. And we fear losing it. You are right. Regardless of what I do here, Faulsk will find a reason to invade. It is right that we begin to prepare ourselves for that eventuality. We must find allies. And weapons. And weaken our coming enemies. Maybe we should take the first blow and use the element of surprise."

"Have you shared these thoughts with your countrymen?" Nauveena asked.

Fichael nodded. "After much contemplation, I used Athyzia's speaking stone to send messages to my fellow ministers: the Minister of War, the Minister of Magical Affairs, the Minister of Defense, and the Minister of Finance. I told them that it might be necessary to act now, while we still can. And I also implored them to think of what the vote would mean: not just for Aryde, but for all Jenor.

"Aryde fought for independence so we could live freely — so that all in our realm could live freely. The Elf Laws restrict that. And we must stand for freedom and equality. Not just in Aryde, but in all Jenor. We should not vote to continue these terrible laws. And we should not vote for others that would ban certain magics."

"And they agreed?" Nauveena asked. It didn't seem possible. It had been a shot in the dark. Now, for the briefest moment, she had her hope renewed.

But only for a moment.

"Only the Minister of Magical Affairs wished for me to vote against the Elf Laws. All the rest are too fearful of Faulsk. They implore me to stay with the original plan."

"And the Last Mountains?" Nauveena asked.

"The Minister of War raised valid concerns. The dwarves have never been known to fight. Yes, they were instrumental against the Osseomancer, but only for the gems they could produce. Very few of their warriors met the Osseomancer's army in battle.

"The Minister of Defense argued that while we could offer the dwarves the Last Mountains, they would have no way to get there. The dwarves would need to cross through Rheum or Faulsk to reach us. They could sail, but dwarves are not very fond of sailing.

"And the Minister of Finance said we could not possibly allow mining in the Last Mountains without *some* compensation. After all, such mining would interfere with Aryde's watersheds. We would need to collect a twenty-five percent tax at least to make it worthwhile."

Nauveena left Fichael Porteau's chamber heartbroken. Her plan had failed. But worse, Csandril Em' Dale had seen the plight of his elves dismissed so easily. Aryde — the one society in all Jenor founded on freedom and equality — cared more for itself than the fate of the elves. They cared little if the elves continued to be mistreated in Jenor's kingdoms.

For the second time that night, the elven poet had few words.

Over the last few weeks, messengers had brought back more word of mistreatment for the elves. Along with the witches and other folk mages, those kingdoms that followed the Magic of Order now saw elves as followers of the Osseomancer and blamed them for the war. More and more were being tossed from their homes and forced to wander, if they were not subjected to worse.

The dwarves too would be mistreated. Few men would remember the dwarves' sacrifices during the war. Now, many of their mountains had run dry, becoming barren of riches. Nauveena could not blame them for seeking a livelihood wherever they could get it. It was a shame she could not offer them the Last Mountains, as she had tried.

"We must suspend the council," Venefica said. "With the binding spell, the Elf Laws could become ingrained for a thousand years. Kingdoms might be unable to reverse them."

"Curse that spell," Nauveena hissed. "We should never have done it. I should have listened to Snorri. There is no way to know how the magic might behave."

"We cannot go forward with the vote," Malachite said. "That much is clear. Too much is at stake. Even if it means abandoning the council."

"We cannot hope to overturn the Elf Laws with all four of the dwarves' votes going to Fallou," Venefica said.

The group stumbled back in the dark. Normally, Nauveena might have cast some charm to light the way, but now, she did not bother. She only thought about what she might do next. Could she dissolve the council? Snorri had threatened it. But how could she do it? Especially now, with the binding spell.

Csandril cursed the dwarves under his breath once more. But Nauveena could not focus on him any longer.

She suddenly had an idea.

◆

All evidence of the summer storm had vanished by morning. The trees and grass had dried. No puddles appeared among the cobblestones on the terrace. The birds sang as if no storm had ever come or would ever come again. The bells tolled gracefully, summoning all to the council.

Nauveena waited for all to have a seat. She looked out at the council. It still felt strange without the northerners occupying one large section.

The council felt stranger still not to have Snorri. Nauveena still expected to glance over and find her mentor sitting beside her, perhaps looking for his glasses. Since his death, the council had proceeded in unusual ways. She wished that he could have been guiding the council through them, and not her.

At least Malachite had returned. Nauveena felt emboldened to have the druid at her side. She also glanced occasionally at Venefica, seated next to King Bane, at the table across from her.

As usual, the Protectors of Order arrived before everyone else. Nauveena made a special point to look Fallou directly in the eyes. His face remained blank, and she could not read it. Perhaps he wanted to gloat. In his mind, he had secured four votes to his side.

With the merchants' three votes and the four controlled by the dwarves, Fallou had enough votes to pass any measure he wanted, regardless of how anyone else voted. *If he's gloating, let him,* Nauveena thought as she waited for the rest of the council to take their seats. He would not be gloating soon enough.

The dwarves took their seats last, and Nauveena noticed that Lord Ferrum still could not make eye contact with most of the council. Galena, however, had found reason to smile.

"Before we begin, we have a few housekeeping issues." Nauveena stood to address the council. In all their weeks delaying the council, she had gotten more comfortable speaking in front of such a large group. "First, we should recap the events from two days ago.

"Going forward, the council is now bound by a magical oath, recited by all members of this council, except for Malachite. Remember this as you vote. The magic will hold each and every one of you and your realms to the decisions made here. The edicts of this council are now magically sealed. Vote accordingly.

"Next, we have the issue addressed at the very end of our last session," Nauveena continued. "The proxy vote for the two northern kingdoms: Yülk and Künner. As we all witnessed through the crystal messages, both northern kings entrusted their votes to the Dwarf Lord Ferrum."

"Lord Ferrum," Nauveena said to the Dwarf Lord, who shifted his gaze, trying to avoid the sorceress as she looked at him, "do you accept these votes?"

Lord Ferrum's head pressed into his shoulders as he tried to appear smaller.

"Do you accept the responsibility of acting as the northern kings' proxy?" Nauveena asked again. Her glare in the dwarf's direction intensified. "To vote in their best interest and represent their kingdoms as they would themselves?"

Lord Ferrum ducked down further still. Silence fell on the whole council until finally he released a slight squeak. "*Yes.*"

"Yes? You accept them?"

A squeak, softer still: "Yes."

"Yes, yes, he does." Galena stood and responded for Lord Ferrum.

"Very well, then," Nauveena said. She paused before continuing. "With these matters taken care of, we can turn to today's session. Today, we are scheduled to discuss the Elf Laws. These are all codes restricting the lives of elves. A very important issue indeed."

"Excuse me." Venefica stood across the terrace. "Before we begin the scheduled topic, is the time at the beginning of each session still reserved for other topics to be added to our schedule?"

"Yes, of course." Nauveena hoped her response did not come off as rehearsed. "We can hear other topics to be added to the agenda, if there are any."

Nauveena looked across the terrace, waiting to see if anyone would say anything. She caught Fallou's expression again, and thought he looked puzzled.

After waiting a moment, Nauveena heard Malachite stand beside her. "I have an issue I would like to propose to the council."

"Yes, please speak."

"It has come to my attention that many of the mines and quarries across Jenor were exhausted in our efforts against Pravulum. The gems mined in Jenor's mountains have many magical properties and were crucial in pushing the Osseomancer back. I fear — with recent reports that the Osseomancer might have returned — that Jenor might be in grave danger if we can no longer produce those gems."

"Is this true?" Nauveena glanced in Lord Ferrum's direction.

Once again, Lord Ferrum averted her gaze. Galena responded. "Gem production has slowed in some key mines."

"If the Osseomancer returns, we will be defenseless without gems," Malachite said.

"What can we do?" Csandril 'Em Dale asked, delivering the line so naturally Nauveena forgot she had told him to say it.

"I have heard that the Last Mountains have not been mined in many decades and might yield many valuable gems," Malachite said.

"Is that so?" Csandril asked.

"Where is this going?" Balzhamy of Lyrmica asked. The point of his oversized hat drooped into his face, forcing him to reposition it. "Lyrmica is mining those mountains; we can produce those gems."

"You are all conspiring on this," General Dolcius said.

Nauveena chanced a look at Fallou. He remained calm as the other Protectors spoke in anxious whispers with each other.

Malachite continued. "It is my fear that without the dwarves mining the Last Mountains, we will be completely without gems if the Osseomancer were to rise again. I propose to this council that the Last Mountains and — in fact — all mountains be made free development zones, open for mining to all members of the Great Alliance that fought against the Osseomancer, to the benefit of all Jenor."

"'All mountains?'" Queen Yellialah of Dunisk asked. The gray-haired queen's kingdom bordered a large section of the Oureas Mountains, and they likely taxed the dwarves as well.

"At the rate dwarves mine, all of Jenor will be enriched." Venefica shot Queen Yellialah a look. Nauveena had spoken to many members of the council of their plan, but they had not had time to speak to everyone.

"There are no better miners than the dwarves," Csandril sang in his elegant prose. "As soon as their pickaxes touch soil, gems spring from the earth like flowers. Their tunnels unearth great riches. Any who *trade* with our height-challenged brethren will be immediately enriched as well."

Csandril's words had been the most constructed. Nauveena looked at Grufton Mann, the leader of the merchants' guild of Valinka, for his reaction. Csandril's words had the necessary effect. She noticed Grufton exchange looks with his fellow merchant leaders. The merchants had been unable to trade with the dwarves throughout the long war, and were now remembering how valuable of trade partners they were. They would be more valuable still if they had all the riches of the Last Mountains.

"This matter seems most pressing," Malachite said. "We have only recently heard reports of the Osseomancer wandering near Pravulum.

We cannot wait on the matter. If we have seven to vote to add the matter to the agenda, then we should add it and discuss it *today*."

"Do we have seven?" Nauveena asked. Immediately, she saw the hands of the elves. That made three. Malachite. King Bane. Queen Yellialah. Six already.

Nauveena looked in the direction of the dwarves. Galena had driven Lyrmica down to a ten-percent tax rate. But now she was being offered *no tax rate* at all. And not only for the Last Mountains, but all the mountains of Jenor.

"You have the dwarves' votes." Another two. "And as proxy of the northern kings, we offer their votes as well." They had reached ten, and they only needed seven to add the item to the agenda.

Nauveena let the council discuss the matter for a short period before turning it over to a vote. They had the numbers easily enough. Not just the initial ten, but Prince Javee and Kitrinos as well.

The merchants had needed little other convincing than the trade opportunity that would come from wealthy dwarves.

The Bogwaah made fourteen.

Nauveena would not even need to act as a tie breaker.

As the votes came out of the fire and the scales tipped, Nauveena looked at Fallou. It was now her turn to gloat.

But the First Protector of Leem kept his emotions hidden. Nauveena could not read them at all. She could not tell what he was thinking — only that he was indeed thinking.

And that worried her.

Chapter Nine
Praqnechne's Grimoire

> "Jenor remains more than just what is shown on her map; each slice of her history is layered over her like the leaves of a manuscript."
>
> ~*Temporal Spells and Artifacts*
> 63 BU

The celebrations and merriment lasted long into the night. The elves invited all — *almost all* — back to their chambers. They uncorked bottles of their finest meads. They served Yros. Their minstrels played a fast tempo. Csandril 'Em Dale had already composed many words to the tune. He sang of Nauveena's cleverness and the dwarves' kindness and generosity and craftsmanship.

"I never doubted you." Csandril 'Em Dale squeezed Lord Ferrum tightly between verses.

The Dwarf Lord still looked shocked to have been granted rights to all the mountains of Jenor. Galena, however, had already sent word to Lord Saxum of the southern dwarves. She wished to dispatch a mining party to the Last Mountains right away.

Without any need to deal with Lyrmica and Faulsk, the dwarves were free to vote however they wished. And after the night's celebrations with the elves, Nauveena had little doubt how Lord Ferrum and Galena would vote in the days to come.

Lord Ferrum's nephew Hortrid slept in one corner. The Yros had been too strong for him. Lord Ferrum tried to wake him and bring him away.

The drink might have been too strong for Nauveena as well. She still remembered its effects from Midsummer's Eve. She felt herself growing tired. As much as she wished to continue dancing — and the music urged her on — it had been many long days. She needed sleep.

She returned to her tower and fell asleep in her dress without even untying her corset. The liquor had made her head spin, and she could think of nothing other than shutting her eyes and placing her head on her pillow.

She recognized the dream for its similarity to the others, when she had wandered the dark maze and climbed the swaying tower. A candle flickered in front of her, and she knew where she was. She sighed deeply, relieved. She had worried she might be somewhere else.

She had tried to escape those other dreams and felt both chased and captured at the same time.

Now, however, she did not want to leave.

She was in the library.

A golden chandelier lit one candle at a time. The room unfolded from shadows to a brilliant, wonderful light that Nauveena could easily read by.

She read the titles along each spine. *Two Hundred and Thirty Magical Aphorisms. A Treatise of Divination. Origins of Thaumaturgy. The Last Manticore.*

She ran her fingers along the covers. She knew the names of each. But each had been lost. Some recently, their only copies burned with the Library of Ülme. Others had been lost long before that. Some only existed as legends, referenced in other works.

She pulled one from the shelf: *Magic Inside Us*, said to have been lost in the great floods. Now, she held it in her hands. She opened it. She flipped through the pages. The pages were worn and aged, but she could read the text clearly.

She only wished Snorri could have seen the vast volumes available. Each held unspeakable knowledge. And she could hold each in her hands.

"*It can all be yours.*"

The voice came from nowhere and everywhere all at once.

"Hello?" Nauveena heard herself saying. Her voice too did not come from within her.

She waited, holding her breath for a response. None came. She looked around the library. The shelves stretched in every direction. She could see nothing but stacks of books — all those that had been lost. Was it possible? Had they all been found? Here?

"Hello?" she dared say again. Her heart clutched.

A moment. A doorway appeared at the other end of the library.

"I thought you might like this very much."

"I do. I do." Nauveena desperately wanted the voice to know she did. She did not want him to think she disapproved. She wanted to be allowed to stay as long as she wanted. She wanted to be allowed to return.

The doorway was lit by a light similar to the chandelier's, as if another library might lay beyond. Another filled with more books? Was that possible? More books? More knowledge?

The light from the doorway dimmed. A figure now stood there.

Nauveena could not see his features — only that he was very tall and that he was looking at her, studying her.

She noticed a table between herself and the doorway. On the table, a thick, leather-bound book sat on display. She approached the table as the figure watched her. She stood over the table and the book and looked down.

"This is..."

"Yes."

"I thought it had been destroyed."

"Nothing is ever destroyed."

Nauveena reached down. Her hands paused above the book. "Can I?"

"Of course. It is yours."

She lifted the book towards her. She opened it. The text was all there. *Praqnechne's Grimoire*.

"But how?" She looked at the figure. She knew the lighting meant she could be fully seen. But the figure was lit from behind, and she could not see him at all. He existed only as a shadow.

"Because of you. You have made this possible."

She leafed through the book. The first spells ever written in Jenor. The first magic ever practiced. The first understanding of the world. And she held it in her hands.

She began at the beginning, reading each line. She could not put the book down.

But she knew it was still a dream. She would have to wake. She would lose the valuable text.

The figure read her mind.

He knew her thoughts.

"This can be forever."

"How?"

"You can make it so."

"But how?"

"*You only need to let me in.*"

Nauveena woke to the dazzling light of morning. Athyzia's bells to summon everyone to council would not toll for some time. In the height of summer, the sun came well before the bells.

Nauveena gasped. She felt all over her body. She was wearing the same dress as the night before. She was in her bed in the same position in which she had fallen asleep. She had not moved. She had not gone anywhere.

But the library had been *real*. It existed somewhere, even if she did not know where. She wished to return to it. To find it and soak up all the knowledge that had been lost over the centuries.

She wanted to fall back asleep. She wanted to ask the stranger what he had meant. How could she make the library last forever? How could she bring all those texts back?

She lay back in her bed, unprepared for the council. How was it morning already? She felt that she had not been dreaming long.

She glanced at her window, at the early morning light.

On her bedside table, she noticed something that had not been there the night before: a large, leather-bound book.

She reached over and lifted it up. She remembered the weight. She opened it and leafed through it. She remembered the words.

Nauveena returned to the library the next night. And the night after that. Her dreams began to feel longer, so she had more time to linger in the library and to read. She began to understand how it had been organized, so she could find books with ease. As soon as she fell asleep, she found herself transported. She walked along the shelves, overwhelmed at times with the sheer number of choices, before eventually finding what she wanted to read.

The figure remained in the doorway, but did not speak often. He seemed content to watch her as she retrieved a book and found a large chair to read in.

When she woke, the book would appear beside her. Each night, she rescued one more volume from the Library of Dreams.

During the day, she could not wait to return. She spent her waking hours thinking of her dreams, wishing she could return to the library.

Never before had Nauveena prepared for sleep in such a way. She applied kohl before bed, when normally she would remove such cosmetics. She spritzed perfume onto the nape of her neck. She wore her finest dresses. She made her hair curl in a particular way.

She would consult the annuls of lost books that Athyzia had maintained, trying to determine which volumes she would look for and which she would pull from the dream.

After a recess, the council had begun the next session on the Elf Laws. After working for so long to gather the votes to overturn such laws, Nauveena now could hardly pay attention. Her mind remained on her dream. Each day, she wished to return to it, even as she oversaw the council.

She had become quite skilled at presiding over the council now. She began each day's session. She recapped the previous day's discussion. She facilitated and ended conflicts when tension rose.

Queen Em' Iriild spoke on the elves' history and their treatment since man had entered Jenor. After she spoke, Csandril 'Em Dale spoke for an equal length on his own experiences. His eloquence moved the whole council. Even some of the Protectors might have been convinced of the unfairness of the Elf Laws.

Nauveena was hardly aware of any of it. Her focus remained on the library. How many books remained there? It seemed such a slow process to rescue only one a night. She needed to retrieve more.

She paid little attention to the events of each day. She felt safe in the vote. Occasionally, she would glance at Fallou, wishing she could read his mind. But the First Protector of Leem remained as calm as before.

But she had won. She had won, and now she had been gifted an enormous treasure. She would build a new library in Athyzia, and place spells that would protect it forever, so the knowledge would never be lost again.

Certainly, Fallou must know how the vote would go. Thirteen would vote to remove the Elf Laws. And Nauveena would decide the tie.

The discussion and debate at this point was meaningless. The votes had been decided. It was only a matter of time.

Fallou never registered emotions, Nauveena told herself. Maybe he did not have any. He believed in Order. He acted without feelings, and when he had been beaten, he did not register the pain in the same way.

The council had extended into late summer. The sun remained quite hot. The humidity rose. Nauveena cast a charm to provide shade for those gathered on the terrace.

Despite the heat, she knew in a few weeks, the summer would turn. The first acorn would fall in the forest. Already, the days were growing shorter again. Fall would come. The leaves would drop.

The Elf Laws would be voted on. They would be removed. Relations between magic users and common folk would be voted on next. Then necromancy.

Fallou would not be able to ban the magics he wanted. The council would proceed in an orderly fashion. They would fix the problems that had ailed Jenor for generations.

Then, when fall came, they would leave, and the world would finally know peace.

"What is the dream?"

"The dream?" Nauveena did not understand the question. The council had just finished its sixth day discussing the Elf Laws when Kitrinos cornered her in one corner of the terrace as the others filtered out.

"I see you," Kitrinos said. "You sleepwalk through the council procession. You appear half-asleep. You would rather live in a dream than reality."

"I don't know what you mean."

"Yes, you do. We have discussed how vivid your dreams are. What is this one?"

Nauveena stepped further back from the oracle, but now, she was against the balustrade. Behind her was the lake. Still, she did not want others to hear. She had not told any one of her dreams, not even Venefica. She kept the books hidden beneath her bed.

"I dream of a library," she told the oracle.

"A library?"

"The books — they were thought to be lost forever — but they are all there: *A Treatise of Divination. The Godhead Fallacy. Praqnechne's Grimoire.*"

"Books?" Kitrinos looked confused. "This is not a vision of the future?"

"No. I do not think it is."

"Is anyone else there?" Kitrinos' eyes had grown wide with fear, and now Nauveena grew worried herself.

She nodded.

"Who?"

"I do not know."

"You should have come to me much sooner," Kitrinos said. "Someone has entered your dreams before. The same one who chased you the night Snorri fell."

Someone had followed Nauveena into her dream of the maze. And chased her through the crooked tower. Now, that same person watched her as she read in the library.

"There's more," Nauveena said, ready to confess. "The books — they are real."

"Real? You mean they seem real in your dream?"

"No. Whatever book I am reading, when I wake the next morning, it is beside me."

Another side conversation from across the terrace seized their attention.

"You said he would not return." Yellialah, the queen of Dunisk, had cornered Venefica and now raised her voice.

"Please, not here," Nauveena heard the witch say.

She could think of nothing but rushing to Venefica's rescue. She broke from the oracle and strode across the terrace. "What is happening here?" she asked. Up close, she could see the queen was not only thin and frail, but tired as well.

"He is, he is, he is." The queen was on the verge of tears. Nauveena remembered the story Malachite had told her. The queen's youth had been stolen by the Osseomancer. Nauveena could see the frightened child within. It had taken her many years to escape the Osseomancer's spells. Had the experience weakened her? Stained her hair this silver color?

"What is it?" Nauveena asked again.

Venefica was preparing herself to speak when Malachite rushed across the terrace.

"You both need to come quick."

※

"What could possibly be so urgent?" Nauveena asked when the three had found a private room within the Library of Esotericism.

Nauveena had wanted to return to the Tower of Yalde, where she could guarantee their privacy. However, Malachite insisted they talk even sooner, and the Library of Esotericism was closer to the terrace.

"I was in line at the banquet hall when I overheard news that could ruin everything."

"Everything?" Venefica asked.

"Fallou has gotten to the Bogwaah," Malachite said.

"The Bogwaah?"

"I heard the Burgomaster explaining that he plans to vote to uphold the Elf Laws. Once I heard that, I had to confront him. He tried to deny it, but then eventually relented."

"The Bogwaah will vote to uphold the Elf Laws?" Nauveena could not believe it.

"What could Faulsk possibly offer?" Venefica asked. "They cannot threaten to invade them like they can with Aryde. They have no claims to the Bogwaah's lands, and what's more, even if they gather a great army, they would need to march it through Druissia first."

"They have not gained the Bogwaah's vote with threats." Malachite sat. "Instead, they have offered the Burgomaster a *deal*."

"What kind of deal?" Nauveena asked.

"The Bogwaah will be the official supplier of all magical materials for the Second Faulsk Empire, the middle kingdoms, Rheum, and Lyrmica."

"They will have a monopoly on the trade?"

"It would appear that way. It is what the Burgomaster has been trying to secure since he arrived at the council. He wanted such a deal with all Jenor. Fallou can offer him half, and he will settle for it. It would appear that their *Book of Order* has much to say on where magical ingredients should come from. And that they must be produced in a specific way. And it just so happens that it is exactly how the Bogwaah produces their goods."

"The book actually says *that*?" Nauveena asked. Of everything, this seemed the most suspect.

"Of course it doesn't," Venefica said. "But who can refute it?"

"Magic practiced with any goods not purchased from the Bogwaah will be made illegal," Malachite said. "At least within the kingdoms of the east."

Chapter Ten
Dreams and Crystal Balls

> "He will come to offer you such treasures as you cannot imagine. He will offer life never ending. But to accept such gifts would be to bite into a peach and find it withered and decayed and filled with worms."
>
> ~Kitrinos, the High Priestess of Xanthous
> 27 BU

"We must speak to Skiel," Nauveena said.

"Veeslau will ask for the same thing as before," Venefica said. "An exception on any law prohibiting necromancy and the enchanting of the dead. They need the dead to pilot their ships around the dragon. Unless the elves allow necromancy to continue in some capacity — even limited — we will have no luck."

"Certainly, if this is the only way to remove the laws, the elves will relent," Nauveena said.

"You do not know the elves well," Malachite said. "I spent many years among them in my travels."

"The elves might not yield on this issue, but they can secure the vote in another way," Venefica said. "Our focus should not be Skiel — not yet. Let us first see if we can pressure the Bogwaah and their Burgomaster. Come. We need Zufaren."

Venefica led them from the Library of Esotericism to the elves' quarters. They found Csandril 'Em Dale and the warrior Zufaren in the gardens of the elves' courtyard. Since the elves had made the apartments their home, the gardens had burst forth with growth. Nauveena came often to marvel at their beauty.

Nauveena let Malachite explain the latest development. She did not want to be the one to deliver bad news.

"Those greedy, frog-loving — " Csandril said when Malachite had finished. "If it were not for Zufaren and the elves of the Wilds, they would have been pillaged by the orcs too many times to count."

"I thought our friendship with the Bogwaah was stronger than this," Zufaren said. "We have protected them for many years. Ever since they built their first outposts along the floodplains."

"The only reason they can even produce magical plants is because of the runoff from the Wilds," Malachite said. "The silt is magically infused. They should be much more grateful."

"You say you are the only thing protecting them from the orcs?" Venefica asked.

"The Bogwaah's towns are small and peaceful," Zufaren said. "They could not defend themselves from the orcs without us."

"Then why don't you stop?"

"*Stop?*"

"Yes, stop."

"The orcs would run rampant, destroying everything in their path."

"Protect the Wilds, of course," Venefica said, "but let the orcs through elsewhere. Let them overrun the Bogwaah. Your relationship with them should not be so one-sided. How many elven warriors have fallen keeping the Bogwaah safe? And what have you received in return? You do not benefit from their agriculture. You farm on your own. The least they could do is vote down the Elf Laws."

"No, we could never," Zufaren protested.

"They are taking advantage of your goodwill," Venefica said.

"Many innocent lives would be lost if we did not hold back the orcs."

"At least present it as a possibility," Venefica said. "I understand not wanting those deaths on your conscience. You are too noble for that. But the Bogwaah should learn that their protection does not come without cost. Let them know it can be withheld at any time."

Zufaren looked at Csandril, confused and unsure how to respond.

"It could work," Malachite said. "Ideally, the threat of orcs would outweigh their greed."

Nauveena had been following the conversation with bated breath. Could it work? Had Venefica been right to come to Zufaren? But the elven warrior was already shaking his head. "No. No. It is not possible."

"You wouldn't have to do it," Nauveena said. "Just *threaten* it."

"You do not understand. We have been charged with holding back the orcs. Even a suggestion of ending our vigil would be a dereliction of duty."

"The Bogwaah needs to understand what you do for them," Venefica said.

"We could suggest it to them," Nauveena said. "It need not come from you."

"No. This is the last I will hear of it." Zufaren stood now. "Our duty is to protect Jenor from the orcs. We do not do so for reward or recognition, but because we have no other choice. To make it political would endanger us all. We would be no better than the orcs themselves."

With that, Zufaren stormed from the garden. When he left, Csandril Em' Dale looked around. "A good idea. But I'm afraid he's not interested."

"He has spent too long with your queen," Venefica said. "I remember only recently his bitterness at having to defend the Bogwaah. It seems Queen Em' Iriild has poisoned his mind with ideas of *honor* and *valor*."

"We must think of something or the Elf Laws will be upheld," Nauveena said. "Could you convince him?"

Csandril was quite skilled in the art of persuasion, but he shook his head. "I am afraid I will have no effect. He is quite dug-in."

"We do not have many other options." Nauveena grew frustrated. Csandril still seemed cheerful. That was just his nature, she knew, but they were doing all this work for him. The Elf Laws impacted Csandril and his kind, not Nauveena. Yet she had been running from meeting to meeting securing the votes. Now, when they asked the elves to help them, they refused and made her feel corrupt for her suggestions.

"We must now turn our attention to Skiel," Malachite said. "Venefica, I know you think they will not turn, but we must plead with them once again."

"They know how important this vote is," Venefica said. "They want necromancy protected. They will withhold their vote until it is."

"Can we not kill the dragon?" Nauveena asked. "Promise them aid ridding the Dark Sea of the beast once the council is over. That would solve all their problems."

"That would solve *none* of their problems," Venefica said, incredulous. "Do you not understand? They want the dragon. With Borkha restricting passage, they are relied on to move goods through the Dark Sea. Only Veeslau the Unbound and his fellow mages have the ability to use necromancy in such a way. If the dragon is gone, the sea would be open, and Skiel would lose their position in the trade route."

"Not to mention how difficult it is to kill a dragon." Csandril smiled coyly.

"Well, then, you think of something," Nauveena snapped. She grabbed Csandril by his collar, lifted him up and shook him. He was quite light. "We bring you ideas, only for you to shut them down." She couldn't believe her own anger. Just that morning, she'd thought she had all the votes under control. "You need to help us."

"Easy, my apologies." Csandril held his hands up defensively. "Of course, your work has not gone unnoticed. Please, let me know what I can do."

"You need to allow necromancy to continue," Nauveena said, letting him go. "The elves must learn compromise. What is more important? Allowing Skiel to use corpses to sail their ships or freedom for all elves? You are not able to have both. If you wish to live in the world of men, you must learn to look the other way once in a while."

"Of course, of course." Csandril still held his hands up defensively. "You command my vote however you wish."

"We would need all three," Venefica said.

"Then I will see what I can do. I will try to speak as convincingly as our Nauveena just did."

◆

"I will go to Veeslau the Unbound at once," Venefica said as they left the elves' compound. "I will let him know we may have movement on the elves. How soon will we vote?"

"We do not have much left to discuss. Maybe another day," Nauveena said. "Tell him that he is unlikely to get a deal with Fallou and the Magic of Order either. They have taken as hard a line on the magic as the elves. If we don't grant their exception, no one will, so they might as well vote with us."

"I do not know how convincing that will be," Venefica said. "But I will try it."

"Also, there is another thought I have been having," Malachite said. "After I returned from the north, I sent hawks towards Pravulum to search for Caeruleom. If he has indeed survived, I would want him to attend the council. He proved pivotal in the Osseomancer's defeat. As a wizard, he represents an ancient order. Would he not be deserving of a vote?"

"Yes, of course, of course." Nauveena felt flush with excitement at the idea of another vote they could count on.

"I will go meet with Gwalk now and see if he has any news."

"Even with his vote, we will need Skiel," Venefica said. "Fallou will have fourteen with the Bogwaah and Skiel. We would have twelve. The Wizard would make it thirteen."

"Go anyways," Nauveena told Malachite. "And you go," she said to Venefica, "and convince Veeslau."

"We will meet you in your tower afterwards," Venefica said. Then she and Malachite set off in the direction of their assignments.

◆

Nauveena went to her tower to wait for whoever finished first. Night had begun to creep in, and she picked her way through Athyzia in the gathering dark. She knew the way well.

Once in her tower, she felt unsettled, impatient. She did not like waiting. She did not know how long she would need to wait, and her head spun with the day's events. Perhaps a book could calm her at least and help her focus?

She retrieved *Praqnechne's Grimoire* from where she had hidden it under her bed. Why had she hidden such a book? Why didn't she want anyone else to know? She shrugged off the questions. She had already read through the text several times, both in her dreams and at night as she waited to fall asleep again.

How long had she wished to attain such a text? She thought it had been lost forever. Now, she felt tired when she began to read. Normally, she could stay up very late reading, but tonight, her eyelids felt heavy. They kept sliding down. She felt herself nodding off.

The day had been draining of course. And hot, despite her charm to provide shade. She should stay awake. Malachite and Venefica could return at any moment. It would not do to fall asleep.

Nauveena fought the feeling. Outside the tower, the summer breeze stirred the lake to create a gentle lapping sound as waves flickered against the tower's island, rhythmic and soporific. The wind itself came through the window and brushed across her, a soothing lullaby.

She could rest her eyes while waiting. She saw nothing wrong with that. Once her friends returned, they might remain awake long into the night discussing the next course of action.

She should rest while she had the chance.

She shut her eyes, yielding to sleep.

The chandelier glittered. The candles reflected off the gold. Flickering light played with the shadows, but still cast enough illumination to make reading easy.

Once again, Nauveena wandered the library's many aisles. She ran one finger over the spine of each book she passed. She felt the rough leather. How much knowledge lay housed in each? How many secrets did each book keep? What would she discover tonight?

"*What will you read tonight?*"

Nauveena saw the figure in the doorway. He stepped forward, but remained cast in shadow.

She had felt tired before, but she also secretly knew she wanted to come to the library. Each night presented an opportunity to find a book that no one had read for many years.

"They say a monastery on the Alcyon coast kept records of the movements of all the comets and celestial bodies for three hundred years," Nauveena said. "It is the only account of the cosmos from that time period."

She twirled a curl of her hair around her finger. She approached the figure, but did not dare come too close. "But it was lost in the War of the Three Wizards," she said. "No one ever made a copy. Think what could be learned of the cosmos. Do the comets repeat themselves? Were they the same planets a thousand years ago?"

"*Braxtus's Nightly Observations?*"

"That would be it."

The figure now came fully into the light, so Nauveena could see him for the first time. He was indeed tall, with dark features and silver hair. A strong, pointed jaw. Young and handsome. The golden candlelight reflected in his eyes.

Nauveena followed him down the aisle as he led her to the book. He stood to the side as she pulled it from the shelf. The cover contained only the simplest imprint of a star. Inside, in fine, handwritten cursive, was the title. After that came pages of logs and observations.

How many monks had stayed up through the night to record the sky? Nauveena pictured their toil: each night alone beneath a blanket of stars, speaking to their brothers across generations. With each recording, they imparted a piece of themselves, a faint pulse that would stretch into the years.

Magic had been whispered into each letter. Lives had been dedicated to the project. Now, their efforts would not be lost. Their toil would not be in vain. Nauveena held them in her hands.

The man spoke in his calm, commanding voice. "A shame something so valuable could be lost for so long."

Nauveena nodded.

"All knowledge should be free. We should not try to capture it or hoard it. It should not be hidden away. It must be shared and cherished."

"Yes."

"Like magic."

"Yes."

"There are those who wish this were not so."

"I know."

"There are those who wish to control all magic and all knowledge."

"I know."

"We can stop them."

Nauveena felt a sudden power surge through her. For so long she had been afraid of Fallou and the Magic of Order. But what great power did they have? She had defended Athyzia during the war. She could wield powerful magic.

Why should Fallou control the vote?

She could stop him one way or the other. They need not plead to the Bogwaah or to Skiel. They need not make compromises. She knew how the world should be — safe and free and equal. She had the power to make it so.

Once she removed Fallou.

Could she?

She had the power. She had never seen Fallou do magic. She did not know if he even could.

But she knew she could. She had the ability to wield such terrible and powerful magic.

Fallou should fear her. Not the other way around.

"You want to stop him?"

"I must." Nauveena stepped towards the figure. "He wants to use the council for his own purposes, to control us all."

"They are fanatics, and they are fearful. They must not be allowed to win."

"I will not let them," Nauveena said. It would be a simple matter to reach up and touch the man's face.

"Let me help."

Nauveena looked into the figure's eyes. They now not only reflected the candlelight, but a universe of stars. A powerful ally. She alone could stop Fallou.

But why stop there? She should free all the kingdoms from the tyranny of the Magic of Order. She should defend those who could not defend themselves.

She looked further into the figure's eyes.

"I could only watch as they burned their own libraries," he said. "I came to protect their knowledge. But I arrived too late."

"No." Nauveena stepped back.

"Think what we can do together. We can finish what I started."

"I know who you are."

"Let us stop the restrictions of magic. Let there be no end to our power."

※

"Nauveena. Nauveena. Wake up."

Nauveena felt herself shaken awake.

"*Nauv?*"

Venefica stood in front of her, shaking her shoulders.

"Wake up."

Nauveena gripped Venefica's arms with her hands to steady herself.

"You were having a nightmare," the witch said. "You were screaming in your sleep."

"It's ... it's him."

"What?"

"We must send for the oracle right away."

Although it was not very late, Kitrinos had already gone to bed. A messenger went to wake the oracle and bring her to the Tower of Yalde.

As they waited, Nauveena explained what had happened as Venefica paced. "The books are real." She went to her bedroom and returned with an armful. She still had each of them. They were authentic. She had made sure of it. Regardless of how they had come to her, they were invaluable.

"How is that possible?" Venefica asked.

Kitrinos arrived with Prince Javee. "You sent for me?"

"Yes," Nauveena said. "You were right about the dreams. They were something else entirely. In the first dream, I thought the person following me did not belong. Then the dream proved prophetic. The night Snorri was thrown from the tower, we had been followed. The footsteps sounded the same.

"After Snorri's death, I began to have a different dream. Now, I was in a tall tower. But I was still pursued. Now, I could nearly see my stalker. He trailed behind me on the stairs. But his footsteps were the same. He wanted to catch me. And he called out to me, asking me to stop. But I did not dare.

"Then, I dreamed of the library. And it could not have been a more wonderful dream. When the figure appeared, even though I connected him to the other dreams, I accepted him. He had learned how to get me to stop running. He offered me something to make me stay and so I spoke with him."

"I believe your first dream was a prophecy," Kìtrinos said. "A premonition of the night when Snorri would be thrown from the tower. But as the dream reflected the footsteps from the future, it offered an opportunity — a way in. Whoever this is, they occupied the footsteps and entered your dreams."

"I know who it is now."

"You do?"

"It is the Osseomancer."

No one questioned Nauveena's assertion. They all knew it was true.

"How do we stop him?" Prince Javee asked.

"He is obviously very weakened," Kìtrinos said. "It might be possible to capture him in such a form. I am well-learned in the area of prophecy, especially those of dreams. But not dreams themselves. This is very clever magic, and I am not sure I am equipped for it."

"He wants to enter Athyzia," Nauveena said. "That has always been his aim. I prevented him during the war, and now he is trying a different way."

"We must send for the Head of the Academy," Kìtrinos said. "Pinerva studies the magic of imagination and will have some insight into dreams. Combined, we can determine what should be done."

"Let us do so immediately," Venefica said. "Let us deal with him once and for all, *tonight*."

Another messenger was sent to retrieve Pinerva, recently made head of the Academy of Mages. Now, the night was getting late. Nauveena worried the constant comings and goings to her tower would raise suspicions. Anyone watching would see the messengers leaving and returning with others.

But they had few options, as far as she could tell. If the Osseomancer had returned, they needed to deal with him right away.

Pinerva came quickly. She looked both frightened and confused as Nauveena recounted her story. She thought for a moment when Nauveena had finished.

"Legends speak of the ability to perform such magic," the Imaginary Mage said. "If true, the Osseomancer's skills are beyond compare."

"It is true," Nauveena said.

"I do not doubt you. But it is quite a feat for him to enter dreams, especially in his reduced form."

"Perhaps he is able to *because* of his reduced form," Venefica said. "He is shapeless. Without body. He exists in a shadowland. A half-life. He might already be in the world of dreams, and it is therefore easy for him to move from one to the next."

"But entering someone else's dream is something else entirely, and takes much wisdom and skill," Pinerva said.

"Well, can we stop him?" Prince Javee asked.

"We might have an opportunity," Pinerva said. "Ways exist to contain dreams. We utilize the method often in my field. If he enters a dream again, we could place the entire dream into a bowl of water or an amphora and seal it with the Osseomancer contained inside."

"There we go," Prince Javee said triumphantly. He retrieved one of Venefica's empty wine bottles and offered it to Pinerva. "Let's put him in there."

"We will need something a bit stronger than that," Pinerva said.

"I might have something," Kitrinos said and quickly left the room and tower.

"While she is away, could you produce a sleeping potion?" Pinerva asked Venefica.

"Of course. I know many recipes."

"One that produces strong dreams," Pinerva said.

"Why a sleeping potion?" Nauveena asked.

"To capture the Osseomancer, he must enter a dream again. Then, we can move the dream into another object."

"And someone needs to be asleep for that to happen?" Nauveena asked, although she already guessed the answer. Who would need to sleep? Whose dream would the Osseomancer enter? He had only entered her dreams before. They would need him to enter her dreams again.

"It would need to be you," Pinerva confirmed.

"No. I can be helpful in performing the spell."

"I can manage on my own."

"I would prefer to not be asleep during this."

"We need him to enter someone's dream," Pinerva said.

Nauveena looked to Venefica.

"Not me," said the witch, already in Nauveena's kitchen, looking through the cupboards. "He will not come into *my* dreams."

"No, not you," Nauveena responded. "Queen Yellialah."

◈

Queen Yellialah took some time to be woken from her sleep and brought to the Tower of Yalde. As they waited, Kìtrinos returned with something wrapped in a silk shawl. She placed the object on the central table and unwrapped it. In the center sat a crystal ball.

"That could work," Pinerva said, inspecting it. She recited a handful of verses over it.

Nauveena marveled at the orb's beauty. It contained such simplicity in its transparency. She might not have even known the orb rested on the table, except it contorted the light and gave a soft glimmer where it curved. A perfect sphere.

Venefica remained in the kitchen, adding ingredients to a pot on the stove. Chamomile. Celandine. Basilisk eggshell. "You are running low on moon clover."

The witch was about to say something else when she was interrupted.

"What is this about?" Queen Yellialah entered the tower, trailed by two knights of her queen's guard.

"We would prefer to speak with as few around as possible," Pinerva said.

"They will remain," the queen said.

"You may not want them to hear this," Venefica said.

"They have been assigned to protect me."

They didn't have time to argue. Nauveena approached Queen Yellialah. "You have seen him in your dreams?"

Queen Yellialah did not respond.

"He has come to you, hasn't he?" Nauveena asked again.

The queen looked to Venefica. "I told you he stalked me. I knew who he was. Each morning, he would be there. I became afraid to fall asleep. He reminded me of when I had been his servant. You dismissed me."

"I thought it was only a dream," Venefica said.

"What did he say to you in your dreams?" Nauveena asked.

"He wanted to see Athyzia. He was very curious. He could not believe I was here. He made me show him it."

"Show him Athyzia?" Nauveena asked. "How?"

"I do... I do not know." If anything, the queen looked embarrassed. "It is magic. It is beyond me. Isn't it for *you* to explain?"

"You would dream even while awake," Nauveena guessed, although it was more than a guess. She remembered the far-off look the queen often had during council sessions. Many sessions were long, and often other members would get glazed-over looks, but not like Yellialah.

The queen nodded. Her knights looked at her in confusion. Having the confession coaxed from her, the queen found it easier to continue. "It began as dreams. I often dreamed of Pravulum, long after I left. I remembered the way he..." This, she would not say. "The memories have always been with me. Especially in my dreams. And I would dream of him often. But recently — since coming here — those dreams were more than memories. He was speaking to me, but it wasn't my memory of him. It was *him*. We spent many nights together, but soon, we began to spend the days together too. Not the entire day. He would come in and out as his curiosity demanded."

"He only wanted to see what Athyzia looked like?" Pinerva asked.

"It was all so very strange," Queen Yellialah said.

"There is more." Nauveena thought the queen was withholding information still.

"You must tell us," Venefica said.

The queen looked at them bitterly. She did not appreciate being forced to confess. "At first, he was just with me, but then... it seemed he was in more control than I was. He would guide where we went, and I would just watch. And then..."

"Yes?" Nauveena would not let her stop now.

"On the night Snorri died. When I fainted. I dreamed. Or I thought I dreamed. A terrible, terrible dream. I stalked you both, but then Snorri found me, and I ran. But it was not me running. It was *him*. I have not had such stamina in many years. Or such speed. I could never have escaped you had it only been me. And..." She paused, unsure how to say it. "And I had magic."

Queen Yellialah looked as in disbelief at this revelation as the rest of them. "Great and terrible magic," she continued. "As soon as I wielded it, I no longer wanted it. I hated the way it coursed through me. I hated what was done with it. I hated the look on Snorri's face. When he saw it was me. When..."

Now, Yellialah had come too far. The rest was too difficult to speak of. Nauveena took pity on the queen, so frail and frightened.

"It was the Osseomancer that night, controlling you," Nauveena said. She remembered the hysteria. Fallou had only just read the message from Pravulum. She had not believed the Osseomancer had been responsible. But he had returned, and he had been in Athyzia. Or at least a part of him had, even if it had been Yellialah they were chasing.

The queen began sobbing. "It happened so quickly. I do not even remember how I escaped from the tower. I suddenly awoke in my own bed. I thought it was all a nightmare. I did not think it would come true. Then, when I woke, I heard the alarm. I learned the news that Snorri had fallen from the tower. Comus — the Osseomancer — he used me. I thought he came into my dreams to see me. But he only used me."

"You did not know," Kitrinos said, trying to comfort her. "You did not know it was real."

So much more went unsaid. They all hung their heads. It was a terrible revelation, but they did not have time to dwell on it.

"Now, we have a chance to get him." Venefica returned to the kitchen. Her potion simmered on the stove. She removed it and wafted the scent. For a brief moment, her eyes closed. "It is ready."

There was no point dwelling on the queen's revelation. There would be time for that later. Now, they needed to focus.

"What is ready?" Queen Yellialah asked.

"A sleeping potion," Kitrinos said.

The queen's knights took a step forward.

"We need you to take it," Venefica said while ladling the potion from its pot into a bowl. "We need you to fall asleep, so the Osseomancer can enter your dream."

"No. No. Absolutely not." Queen Yellialah shook her head.

"You must."

"You cannot make me."

"You will be perfectly safe." Kitrinos touched the queen's frail hand with her own. "We plan to capture only that which is in your dream. Nothing else. You do not need to be afraid."

"That is not what I am afraid of," Queen Yellialah shrieked. Her features became quite harsh, and she leapt back. Her knights stepped forward to protect her. "How can I see him after what I've just learned? I allowed him into Athyzia. If it had not been for me, Snorri would still be alive."

"It does not matter now," Kitrinos said in a soft, comforting voice. "You did not know. But now you do, and you can help."

Yellialah's knights took another step towards their queen.

"You wish for me to be *bait*?" Yellialah asked. "Cheese in a trap?"

"He will come to you in your dreams," Nauveena said. "This is our chance to capture him."

"But why must it be me?" Yellialah asked.

"There is no one else," Nauveena said, knowing it was not true. She too could be bait, but she wanted to remain on the outside, where she would have the most control. Why should she be used, when there was another? "You are the only other whose dream he would enter. We are needed to perform the spell."

Yellialah still did not look convinced.

"This is your chance to undo the damage he has caused," Venefica said. "He tricked you before. Now, turn the tables."

The knights placed their hands on the hilts of their swords.

Yellialah looked at them. "No," she said reluctantly. "The witch is right. I must."

Both knights stepped back as Venefica brought the bowl from the kitchen. The contents were something between broth and porridge, with several milk teeth suspended within.

Kitrinos laid Yellialah across the couch and then Venefica handed her the bowl. "The potion provides a very calm sleep, very prone to dreams."

"Perfect," said Pinerva.

Queen Yellialah tilted the bowl so she could drink its contents while laying down. She drank it easily and placed the bowl on the floor. She had barely finished when her eyes began to close.

Everyone else in the tower closed in around her, watching as the queen slowly drifted to sleep.

"You will not interfere," Venefica said to the knights. "Under no circumstances."

They both nodded nervously.

"When will we know that the Osseomancer is in her dream?" Nauveena asked.

As answer, Kìtrinos sat at the table with the crystal ball. She waved her hands over the orb, muttering poetry of her own language. Slowly, the transparent orb filled with a golden cloud, moisture suspended in the orb's void.

Everyone's eyes turned from the sleeping queen to the crystal ball.

Kìtrinos stood and lifted the ball in her hands. "You two," she said to the knights, "move this table closer to the couch."

The knights did as they were told. They brought the round table closer to the queen. When she was satisfied, Kìtrinos took a seat at the table, placing the crystal ball once again in the center. The mist inside continued to gather density, filling the orb. The knights brought the remaining chairs and placed them around the table.

Pinerva extinguished the candles lighting Nauveena's apartment. In their place, she lit six, which she positioned around the table at equal distance from each other. She instructed the knights to move other pieces of furniture out of the way. They rolled up the rug. They carried a papasan into the hall.

When the space had been cleared, Pinerva pulled a piece of chalk from her sleeve. She traced onto the floor, from one candle to the next in the shape of a hexagram.

In the room's new darkness, the golden cloud filling the crystal ball provided a soft illumination. When Pinerva had finished, she took a seat at the table beside Kìtrinos. Nauveena sat on the other side of Pinerva. Prince Javee came after, sitting on the other side of Kìtrinos. Last, Venefica sat next to Nauveena, between the sorceress and Queen Yellialah.

The knights, no longer useful, retreated, pressing themselves against the wall to make themselves as flat as possible. The crystal ball continued to fill with the golden substance. The others watched as Kìtrinos waved her hands above the orb. The cloud within contorted, slowly taking shape.

"Is that..." Prince Javee said.

Kìtrinos nodded. The queen had begun dreaming.

In the orb, the scene was cast in shades of gold. A room formed, ringed with thick carved columns. A fire burned in the center. A table ringed the fire. Two figures entered the room. One sat at the table.

Despite the excitement, Nauveena felt herself succumbing to sleep. Her eyes were impossibly heavy. She felt like she had drunk Venefica's potion as well. Her eyes strained to watch the strange scene painted all in gold. The light coming from the orb made her feel drowsy. She felt her eyelashes flicker.

◆

The room Nauveena had witnessed in the crystal ball was no longer golden. But it remained monochromatic. The columns, instead of the atmospheric gold, were a resolute black. Nothing could have existed in a more solid definition. The dark columns absorbed all colors. The floor too was the same color. The table and chairs were a deep onyx. Even the fire roared with dark flames.

He sat at the end of the table. He no longer wore the unassuming robe he had worn in the library. Now, he wore a cloak of black. Mirrored, it reflected the burning, dazzling fire.

At his side stood Queen Yellialah.

Only it was not the queen.

Not as Nauveena knew her.

She was a young maiden. No more than twenty. And no longer frail and withered. She wore a dress of sheer silver silk, with many slashes to reveal her dark skin underneath.

Now, Nauveena knew where she was.

Pravulum.

The awful tower.

The dark citadel that the Osseomancer had made his home and from which he had waged his forever war.

How could it be? How could it still exist?

The dream was Yellialah's. The Osseomancer's spell had never been fully broken, and a part of the queen yearned to return to those years when she had served him in his dark tower.

It's only a dream, Nauveena told herself.

But something else told her it wasn't.

"You were hard to appease." He held out a silver goblet, which Yellialah filled. She smiled. "But then I realized you were not much different than her." He motioned towards Yellialah. "I only needed to let you dream. And you would show me what you wanted."

◆

"Nauveena," Venefica gasped. She saw the sorceress sleeping beside her.

"She's asleep?" Prince Javee asked.

"Yes." Venefica shook Nauveena wildly to wake her.

"A spell of the Osseomancer," Kìtrinos said.

"Is she..." Venefica need not ask. They looked into the crystal ball. A third figure appeared in the golden scene.

"She is in the queen's dream," Pinerva said.

"If she remains there, she will be captured in the crystal too," Kìtrinos said.

"We must stop, then," Venefica said.

"We cannot," Pinerva said. "Not after the spell has begun. Not if we want to capture him."

◆

"Your dreams are admirable," the Osseomancer said. "And not so different from my own. How much knowledge is in the world? How much has been understood of our place and our meaning, only to be lost? How wrong are we to want to have a greater understanding of these mysteries?"

"Now that I know who you are, you cannot trick me," Nauveena said.

"'Trick?' What trick? I only wish to help you. We are not so different. We share a common enemy. These acolytes of order are afraid of the mysteries of the world. They make up lies, so they need not seek the truth."

Nauveena approached. She had not intended to, but her feet made the movement anyway. Yellialah looked on jealously.

Nauveena remembered her feelings from before. She was more powerful than Fallou. She knew it. She could cast him out. Destroy him.

And if she couldn't...

The Osseomancer could.

"You must stop," Venefica demanded.

The witch could only watch as her friend walked closer to the Osseomancer in the crystal ball. The goal had been to transport the entire dream to the ball, and everyone inside except the queen, whose dream it was. All the interlopers would remain inside the dream. But that had been before Nauveena had become such an interloper.

"Nauveena will become trapped with the Osseomancer forever?" Venefica asked.

Kìtrinos nodded. "We cannot stop now."

Venefica stood from the table.

"Where are you going?" Pinerva asked. "Do not break our concentration."

"I cannot let her be trapped."

A bit of the sleeping potion remained in the cauldron. Enough for a few minutes. The small amount would cause dreaming too.

"Be careful," Kìtrinos said. "We are close to transporting the dream. Then, you will not be able to escape."

"Why let these acolytes — fearful and cowardly — dictate how magic is practiced?" the Osseomancer asked. "Only the most powerful of mages and wizards and sorceresses should."

"Nauveena," a voice called from the other end of the hall.

Nauveena turned.

"Do not listen to him." Venefica approached. "Do not fall for his beauty. His deception."

"He speaks the truth," Nauveena said. "We cannot let Fallou control the council. He has won the Bogwaah. Skiel will not budge. If we do not stop him, he will turn magic into something base and simple and common."

"There are worse things than that," Venefica said.

"The witch too is fearful," the Osseomancer said. "She held great power once. But she was too afraid to wield it."

"Do not listen to him," Venefica urged. "He has great power in his words. He can persuade if left unchecked."

"But how else can we stop the Magic of Order?" Nauveena asked. "We have tried everything else. He is weakened. Let us use him to achieve our goals."

"Never," Venefica said. "You must wake up. They are beginning the spell."

"You cannot contain me," he said. "Even in this form, I am too much for your skills."

"Nauv, listen to me," Venefica said. "I once felt the way you do. His goals are different than yours. Do not let him deceive you. He will do worse than Fallou. He will make all the magics his and bend them to his will."

"Why did you turn from me?" he asked Venefica. "When you could have been a great and powerful queen."

"Magic should be free," Venefica said. "But it should be through the will of all, not just one."

Undeterred, he turned back to Nauveena. "Sorceress, you know what I say is true. Without me, the acolytes will diminish all magic but their own."

"You must wake up." Venefica reached out her hand. Nauveena looked at it. "They are beginning the spell. Come."

Nauveena glanced at Venefica's hand once more. She heard the Osseomancer speaking behind her. How could she turn from what he offered? So much power and knowledge and secrets.

Together, they would triumph over Fallou.

"They are both in the crystal." Prince Javee gasped at the appearance of Venefica within the orb. His own magic did not extend far beyond pyromancy.

Kitrinos nodded. "The dream is so powerful, it is all around us, streaming from Yellialah to the orb. Soon, it will be completely in the orb. As soon as one falls asleep, they will enter it, it is so powerful."

"But it is Yellialah's dream?" Javee asked.

"It is," Pinerva answered. "But the Osseomancer has most certainly shaped it, as he has for many of Yellialah's dreams. He contorted them, so she could not tell dreams from reality. He made her dream even while awake, and through such ways, moved through Athyzia, seeing all."

"And we can contain him?" Prince Javee asked.

"We can try," Pinerva said.

"But to do so, we will need to hold the whole dream and everyone within," said Kitrinos.

"Come with me."

Nauveena could not help but follow the Osseomancer's command. He walked across the room. The wall pressed back, revealing a large room beyond. She came to the opening and looked beyond.

"Nauveena. We must go," Venefica urged.

But the sorceress did not hear her. Before her stretched the library. She could not understand how it fit inside Pravulum. It seemed too large for any single building to hold. Rows and rows of books stretched in front of her, each so tall they needed ladders with many rungs to climb.

How many volumes had been lost through the years? The works of so many philosophers, mages, scholars. They had toiled. They had spilled their lives onto those pages, only to have floods and fires and time destroy them. How much knowledge lay beyond her grasp? How many secrets did she not know?

She followed him into the library. She did not know where to begin. She went to one shelf and began reading the titles. It was now all hers, she knew. He had given it to her.

"There are those who want to destroy all this."

"Nauveena, do not listen to him." Venefica swept into the library to stand between the Osseomancer and the sorceress.

"She does not need to listen to me," he said. "She already knows what I say is true."

"He is trying to tempt you."

"Together, let us rule over all. Make a free magic. Together, we can hold all the knowledge. Our reign will be one of intelligence and learning."

Venefica turned from Nauveena to face the Osseomancer. "You cannot have her."

"She is free to make her own choice."

Nauveena did not hear either of them. Instead, she pulled a book from the shelf: *Da'Hote's Codex*. She began reading the swirling handwriting and illustrations of the famed wizard's inventions.

"Nauveena. Please. Put it down." Venefica turned again to Nauveena. She took the book from her, snapped it closed and put it back on the shelf. "All these books come with a terrible price."

Nauveena's eyes were wide with wonder. Venefica now took her hands. She looked her in the eyes. "Please. You must listen to me. I once felt like you did. I was tempted by the power he offered. But to accept it means you are no longer your own."

"I think her choice has already been made." The Osseomancer laughed. "You had your chance."

Venefica released Nauveena and turned to the Osseomancer. "Take me."

"What?"

"Take me instead," Venefica said. "The same deal as before, but now, seal it with magic so I cannot run from you."

"Why must I only choose one of you?"

◆

"You must stop," Prince Javee said.

He had watched as Kitrinos and Pinerva recited their strange spells. The image in the crystal ball solidified. He understood what this meant — even if he did not understand how. More and more of the dream was being captured within. Soon, it would exist nowhere else.

"We must continue," Pinerva said. "We have him in our clutches. If we stop, all will be lost."

"But Nauveena. Venefica. They are in there. They will be captured in the dream as well."

"We are not holding them in the dream," Kitrinos said. "Us stopping will not wake them."

"I do not see any other choice," Pinerva said. "We cannot turn back."

"They would want us to continue," Kitrinos said. "There is no other way."

Prince Javee could only watch as the two women continued to recite their spell. The image became clearer and clearer. Nauveena and Venefica walked within.

"We must do something." Prince Javee reached over and began to shake Nauveena. "Wake up."

"That will do nothing," Pinerva said between her chants. "Only they can wake themselves."

◈

Nauveena reached for another book, but a portion of Venefica's voice broke through. The witch's desperation leaked out. "Release her. It is me you want. Ever since I abandoned you."

Nauveena opened the book, but now, the text wriggled and contorted. She could not read it.

"Think what we can accomplish together," he said. "All the world can be ours."

The Osseomancer stepped towards Venefica. He put a hand out. Long, twisted fingers stretched out, hovering above the witch's throat. His hand stopped. His fingers twitched. They did not come closer, as if some force stopped them. The ruby eyes of Venefica's rat skull pendant glowed.

Venefica turned to Nauveena. "Do you know why I spurned him?" she asked. "Why I abandoned him?"

Nauveena shook her head. She had long wondered why the witch, after serving the Osseomancer faithfully for so long, had left him and come to the aid of Druissia and the Great Alliance.

"I was there when he began his campaign against Jenor. For years, we watched as men put restrictions on their magic, bending to the fears of the common folk — so simple and stupid. A new cult rose in the east. One that promised to order magic."

"You saw then the ruin such acolytes would bring against the world," the Osseomancer said. "Do you think they are not still a threat?"

Venefica ignored him. "The power of magic is that it is untamed and wild and free. Man wishes to bind it with canon and dogma, to codify that which cannot be contained. They will define it and parcel it out until there is nothing left. We wished to prevent that. To protect magic. All magics, even the most unkempt and feral."

"Necromancy?" Nauveena asked.

"And many others. We became the master of them so they could continue. But what began as a mission to protect magic became something else entirely. We became lost in our fury."

"It is you who betrayed the magic," the Osseomancer said. "Not me."

Now, Venefica did address him. "You wished to hoard it like a dragon with golden coins. You would not rest until you had mastered magic in all its forms. But magic can have no master. Even the act of writing it down restricts it. Magic does not fit into written words. It is beyond that. And what you wished to do would have enslaved it."

"I would set it free."

"You would be its master. You are no better than Fallou."

"That is why you turned from him?" Nauveena asked.

"We had long argued over the cost of his campaign. Even when I wanted to protect magic from those strange cults of order, I did not relish the means. But I did not see any other way. Or at least, this is what I told myself. At other times, I thought, if I was there, maybe I could curb the worst of his impulses."

"My impulses?" The Osseomancer laughed. "I saw your face when I opened those tombs, as I raised *our* army, and the common folk, for so long dumb and ignorant, fled from us."

Venefica did not respond. Nauveena doubted the witch could deny such an accusation.

"It does not matter," she said, taking her friend's hands. "It is the past."

"Leave Nauveena. Go. He can have me."

Now, Nauveena saw the library for what it was. She saw the dark magic that had constructed it, and the Osseomancer as its architect. She felt Pinerva's spell tightening. Soon they would be trapped there forever. Was even all this knowledge worth it? Even if it was real?

She dropped the book and turned to the witch.

"No, he cannot hold us," Nauveena said. If she wanted to, she could escape the dream. She'd always had such power. She only needed to wake up.

"All of Jenor will belong to us." The Osseomancer's voice began to fade. "All knowledge will be ours. There is nothing we won't know."

Nauveena woke startled in the chair. The crystal orb remained on the table. Its golden light reflected off the faces of Pinerva and Kitrinos and Prince Javee.

Both Pinerva and Kitrinos muttered spells in different tongues. They waved their hands over the orb. The golden mist inside contorted, filling the orb with the scene Nauveena had just left. Prince Javee looked at her with relief.

She looked to her side to find Venefica waking as well. They did not speak. They turned to the orb to watch. The golden light dimmed. Each bead of moisture turned gray and then simmered and transformed to black. The light extinguished. Instead of casting light, the crystal now absorbed it, becoming darker and blacker.

The six candles positioned at the points of the hexagram blew out, casting the room into darkness. Nauveena saw the others as shadows around the table.

Only the orb could be seen clearly. While it drew in light, it remained clear within the darkness. The black cloud swirled. The scene of Pravulum vanished. The cloud twisted into a different shape.

Nauveena recognized the face she had tried to see for many nights in her dreams. As the face took shape, she saw subtle differences. The handsome features remained, but a fearsome shroud had been draped over all. The same face that she had found so beautiful was painfully distorted and made ugly.

A smile broke through, etching itself on the grim face. He began laughing.

"We cannot hold him," Nauveena said.

"We must," Venefica said.

Pinerva and Kitrinos increased their chanting. It would not be enough. Nauveena joined. She did not know their spells, so she added her own: one which would fortify theirs. She chanted in unison. Their voices melded together in an eerie song.

The cloud contained within the glass gained texture and definition. It contained no colors, but now, it showed a human face suspended in the crystal orb.

They chanted faster.

The wind howled. It whipped through the open window. The curtains blew in the dark. Outside, Nauveena heard the waves increasing in their might.

"We will have him," Venefica whispered.

Nauveena was unsure.

It was not possible.

The queen of Dunisk seized on the couch. She thrashed violently. Her knights stepped forward, but Venefica threw up her hands. "Do not come further."

The crystal ball vibrated on the table. It shook and quivered. The face within looked at each participant in turn, laughing.

Now, they could hear the laughter. It consumed the tower.

The wind thundered against the tower. The gust came so strong, Nauveena thought the tower might fall over from the force. Another gust. It continued in its intensity. One of the knights rushed to close the window, but the wind blew him backwards.

Nauveena found herself gripping the table to remain seated. She chanted louder still, strengthening Pinerva and Kitrinos' spells.

The tower now swayed viciously. The table shifted from the force. The wind had struck with such intensity, Nauveena was certain the tower would break. It heaved, shifted back, and was rocked again by another gust. The wind ripped the tapestries from the wall. They swirled around the room with loose papers and quills and anything else not heavy enough.

The crystal rocked wildly. It rolled in circles around the table. It could easily fall off, but Nauveena dared not touch it.

It quaked now with tremors. The face within contorted further with laughter. It would not hold.

The orb shattered.

Glass fragments spun into the air. One shard slashed Nauveena's cheek.

The ball released its dark smoke. The phantom burst forth in a giant cone, expanding out into the room. The roof exploded with the force of the cloud, launching bricks and stone and masonry into the air. The night sky appeared suddenly. The stars and moon seemed dazzlingly bright compared to the previous dark.

Another light came from across the table. Prince Javee stood. He held a small flame in each hand, prepared to hurl them upwards at the cloud.

With no roof and no walls, the wind became a spinning cyclone.

"Do not leave the table," Kitrinos yelled.

Nauveena had stacked her books in the corner. The ones she had kept under her bed and brought out to reveal to Venefica and the others as proof of her dream.

Now, the wall fell outward into the lake. The top half of the tower splintered. Fragments were flung into the air and caught in the wind. Larger pieces of the tower — battlements, beams, stairs — splashed into the lake below.

The wind twirled violently through the room, lifting everything that had not been nailed down. Nauveena saw the books. The wind gripped them and pulled them into its embrace.

Each book was lifted. The thrashing gusts opened them. In the melee, the open books looked like bats flying out of a belfry. They flew in a swarm, but slowly grew further and further from each other.

The books had been lost before. Nauveena could not lose them again. She understood their source, but she did not care.

She would never see that library again. Many other books would remain lost forever. But these, she had rescued.

She raced to them, leaping into the air to try to secure them and pull them from the cyclone.

She reacted too late.

The books had flown too high. She read their titles as they went.

A Treatise of Divination. Origins of Thaumaturgy. The Last Manticore.

Praqnechne's Grimoire.

Other books entered the swirl — the ones from Nauveena's own collection. The ones Snorri had given her: *Phantom Knowledge. Collected*

Wisdoms of Before. Seven Years in Saphalon. These were not rare; other copies existed, but not ones that Snorri had given her. They suddenly mattered more than the other books.

Snorri's notes became a mess of papers. They cartwheeled around each other. These could not be replaced. Then Snorri's copy of *Philosophies of Magic* flew into the air.

Nauveena leapt for it. Her fingers grazed the edge of a page, but then it flew off. Lost.

Venefica too rushed from the table. She tackled Nauveena by the waist, bring her to the ground. She pushed the sorceress into the corner and covered her with her body.

The smoke rose above the cracked tower, commanding the swirling wind. Stone and bricks and pieces of furniture were caught in the tumult. Debris came raining down on those exposed below.

Prince Javee launched one fire ball after another, knocking the rubble off-course before it could collide with those below.

The knights rushed to protect their queen. One lifted her from the couch and rushed downstairs, holding the queen aloft, while the other unsheathed his sword and threatened the oncoming projectiles as best he could.

An empty wine bottle careened out of the night sky. The knight swung his sword, shattering the bottle. A vase dived in his direction next. He ducked out of the way. As he regained his balance, a cauldron smashed into his shoulders, throwing him to the floor.

Pinerva and Kìtrinos abandoned the table and the now-shattered orb. The mission had been lost. They could only watch as the cloud filled the night sky, spurring the wind and elements into higher intensity, laughing all the while.

They stepped behind Javee. The prince continued to send his fire heavenward, small spurts of light that redirected the projectiles before they landed on those below.

The wind howled as it swept through the exposed tower. A broken column ripped though the night sky. Javee's fire missed, and the piece hurtled into his chest, sending him backwards. He was thrown to the floor. As he flailed, trying to stand, a sconce whipped down, pinning one arm to the floor.

Above, more of the wreckage was bundled together, herded by the wind. The cloud pulled the remains of the tower higher, poised to strike.

Nauveena pushed Venefica off her. The debris swirled above. She only hoped she was not too late.

The magic laced out of her fingers. Electric buzz. Purple tendrils expanding over the entire tower. It enveloped her now-exposed solar.

From far away, the scene would have been quite the sight. The tower had been splintered into a thousand pieces that littered the night sky. Now, Nauveena exerted a powerful aura that glowed amethyst in the night sky.

In the mountains, the first blushes of dawn came.

The wreckage came down in a thunderous assault. Each piece collided with Nauveena's aura and bounced backwards. Large bricks collided, and their force sent them out over the lake. She could hear their splashes high on the tower, through the wind and laughter.

None penetrated the aura. None could. Nauveena would not allow them.

The whole wreckage of the tower came — candelabras, bookcases, bed frames, pots, pans, bricks, chairs. They made impressions on the aura and bounced back into the lake. Those beneath remained safe, protected, unharmed.

The cloud thundered. It sent the rubble in different directions, looking for a weak point.

In the cloud, Nauveena could see his face. Certainly, all of Athyzia could see it.

Another brick. Another stone. None could get through.

Then, as quickly as it had come, the phantom evaporated, dispersing into the night sky.

All that remained was his callous laughter.

Then this too faded.

Chapter Eleven
Twilight of the Elves

> "The question remains: when the elves fade from this world, will the magic fade with them?"
>
> ~*Seven Years in Saphalon*
> Pitrinois
> 274 BU

When dawn came, it came quickly. A ruby-hued glow slipped over the mountains, cascading down in an avalanche of light until the night's darkness felt like it had never existed.

Nauveena flexed her aura, then relaxed. The forcefield lingered for a moment, shimmered like a mirage, and then dissipated.

The threat was gone.

The Osseomancer, despite his show of force, was still too weak. All he wanted was to escape.

Nauveena looked at the destruction of her tower. The roof and several levels had been ripped off in the onslaught. Her bedroom, her kitchen, her solar. All lost.

She had not only lost the books she had collected from her dreams, but her own private collection as well. She could replace them, but they held sentimental value. She had often retreated to those books when she had felt alone or lost. Snorri had given her many. She thought of her hand nearly closing around *Philosophies of Magic* as it vanished into the night.

Nauveena helped Venefica to her feet.

"He has escaped," the witch said.

"At least that is *all* he did."

"He has revealed himself. Next time, we will be prepared."

The two surveyed the damage: parchments, blankets, candles, the feathery down from exploded pillows and mattresses, and the splintered wood from wardrobes and cabinets.

Each had suffered injuries as well. Nauveena had a deep cut across her cheek from the crystal orb. Venefica, Pinerva, and Kitrinos had several cuts and bruises as well. Queen Yellialah's knight had a nasty gash across his forehead. Venefica found a rag to hold against it as the knight got to his feet.

Prince Javee had suffered the worst. The blow he received had fractured his collar bone. His right arm hung limply. He winced when Kitrinos touched it.

Nauveena continued to survey the damage. Her cabinets were smashed. Various plant stems and seeds and crushed leaves littered the floor. What did not appear in the shattered tower had fallen into the lake below. Cut into the mountains, the lake reached immeasurable depths. Even if these items were not ruined by the water, they would be unretrievable.

Nauveena felt as if she might cry. The tower had been her sanctuary, her home. All of her belongings had been lost. She couldn't look at the tower any longer. She turned to the shores of Athyzia.

The fight had aroused much of Athyzia. The noise had been heard by all, and they came in aid.

King Bane arrived on the shores first, leading at least twenty men at arms. Without Prince Javee to guide them, the soldiers of Qadantium fell into step behind King Bane, looking to him for command. Zufaren and his warriors came next. The elven archers kept their arrows notched to their bows as they advanced. The dwarves too rushed down without hesitation, each gripping axes and warhammers.

They came in time to see the Osseomancer in full force, his face composed of smoke and cloud, laughing menacingly. He had been massive and otherworldly, looking down on Athyzia as if it were just a model. They watched as he vanished, the dawn light fell upon the fractured tower, and Nauveena withdrew her aura.

She would need to address them all. It would not do to have everyone waiting awkwardly, watching them, looking for answers. With Venefica tending to Queen Yellialah's knight and Prince Javee standing of his own power, Nauveena picked her way through the debris towards the tower stairs. She lifted the battered doorframe away and went down.

In the base of the tower, she found the second knight, still cradling the sleeping queen. Venefica's potion had been quite strong, and the queen would sleep for some time more.

Nauveena exited the tower and went across the bridge. The causeway too was covered in rubble from the exploded tower. Broken chairs and baskets and cutlery cascaded across the bridge.

"My word." King Bane rushed down the steps to the bridge. He threw his arm around Nauveena when he reached her to help her the rest of the way. "Are you hurt, sorceress? Is everyone all right?"

"Everyone is fine," Nauveena said. "A few injuries. Prince Javee got the worse of it."

"*Prince Javee?*" King Bane looked disappointed that the prince had been involved in the fight and not him. "I imagine he gave worse than he got, though."

Nauveena smiled at the way men talked about such conflicts, as if they were nothing but jousting or rumbleball matches. She realized King Bane was looking for more, although he didn't want to ask it, not out loud. But his question was clear: "What happened here?"

Nauveena hesitated. She did not want to admit it. She had been adamant that the Osseomancer had not been a threat. She feared the hysteria she would cause if she admitted the truth. But she could not deny it. They had all seen him clearly.

The audience grew larger. Above them, on the shore, the crowd parted. The elves and dwarves and the soldiers had closed ranks in a defensive maneuver. Now they moved apart to allow others through their midst.

Out of their group stepped a cohort dressed in dull gray robes, led by the First Protector of Leem.

He always arrived at the least convenient times.

Fallou left his entourage of Protectors and Keepers of Order and followed the stairs down to Nauveena and King Bane on the bridge. He hoisted his vestments daintily so he would not trip on the slick stairs.

"Have my eyes deceived me?" Fallou asked when he reached Nauveena. "I saw a phantasm hovering over the lake, as if something from nightmares. My men whispered that our worst fears had been realized. That *he* had returned. I told them it was a mirage. But now, we have come here to find the Tower of Yalde destroyed. Tell me something else has caused such a terrible event. Tell me it was not him."

Nauveena wasn't sure where to begin. Even if she wanted to explain the events of the night, they had all happened so quickly and unexpectedly, she was uncertain how to explain it.

She knew how Fallou would react. She knew how he would twist the events of the night to his own gain. She did not want to tell him. She wished he were not here.

She remembered the dream. She remembered standing in Pravulum. She remembered what the Osseomancer had told her and how it had made her feel.

Why should she allow Fallou to twist her words? She wielded more power than him. She felt the magic fresh in her fingertips. It lingered there. She could easily expel it again.

It would be a simple thing.

Her aura could be used defensively, to deflect objects, but she could just as easily use the magic to fling Fallou from the bridge. What harm would come from that? So what if she did so in front of everyone? Who could stop her?

She clenched her hand into a fist, squeezing the magic. She could release it so easily.

But she held back.

No, she thought.

She would stop Fallou, but not with magic. She would stop him with votes. Through the council.

As Snorri would have wanted.

"Speak, sorceress," Fallou demanded. "What force wrought such destruction? What caused the collapse of this tower? What new evil threatens our peace?"

"We had an encounter," Nauveena said. "Tonight, we discovered that the dreams of myself and Queen Yellialah had been violated by — "

"By whom?" Fallou asked.

Nauveena gulped. She could not hide it.

"By the Osseomancer."

"The Osseomancer?" Fallou yelped in surprise. Those gathered above could not help but hear him.

"Let me finish," Nauveena insisted.

"It is true, then? The Osseomancer did this? That is who we saw projected against the night?" Fallou made his voice audible to everyone, while Nauveena could only whisper frantically.

"He is in a weakened form," she said. "He came into our dreams. As soon as we discovered it, we tried to capture him."

"'A weakened form?' Your tower has been decimated. You are bleeding. This is 'a weakened form?'"

"He came into our dreams."

"And where is he now?"

"We tried to capture him, but he was too strong for us. He escaped."

"*Escaped*," Fallou repeated loudly. He turned from Nauveena and King Bane to address everyone else gathered. "Tonight, the Osseomancer rose and attacked Athyzia itself. He does not want this council to continue. He does not want rules placed on magic. He does not want his supporters brought to justice. The leader of our council fought the Osseomancer off, but even in a reduced form, he was too great for her. She fought bravely, but he escaped."

A tremor of fear rippled through the crowd.

"The Osseomancer?"

"He is returned."

"He cannot be killed."

"We must remain vigilant," Fallou continued. "We must all work together to ensure he threatens us no longer. I ask the head of our council, let us have the vote I have been asking for. Let us decide, collectively, to no longer allow such a menace to threaten us. The Osseomancer is strengthened by all sources of magic but one. Let us do what is right. Let us put aside our differences and vote to ban all magics but the one the Osseomancer cannot defeat. Let us make the Magic of Order the one true magic of all."

A tremendous applause came from the Protectors standing between the elves, dwarves, and men of Druissia and Qadantium.

"We will do no such thing." Nauveena could barely raise her voice, certainly not to the level of Fallou. None gathered on the shore could hear her.

Fallou lowered his voice. "You have seen you are not enough to defeat him."

Nauveena felt very weak and small. She remembered the Osseomancer's might. She had not been enough.

"Let us vote immediately." Fallou raised his voice once again so the crowd could hear him.

"We must vote on the Elf Laws first," Nauveena said, unable to think of anything else.

"You have shifted the council schedule many times before. But maybe that is only when it is convenient to you."

"We must not rush to decisions because of these events," Nauveena said. "We must proceed in an orderly fashion."

"They have waited long for a resolution," Fallou said. "Let them have it. Then we must vote. Let us vote to uphold the only form of magic the Osseomancer fears — the Magic of Order."

"*Oh, fuck off.*" Venefica stormed across the bridge. Behind her came Pinerva. Then the still-sleeping Queen Yellialah carried by the second knight, while the first held Venefica's rag to his cut. Last came Prince Javee and Kitrinos. The oracle walked close to Prince Javee's side, holding his broken arm. King Bane looked at Javee's injury jealously.

"There will be no vote today." Venefica waved Fallou off dismissively. "How can you think of voting at such a time? We must get Prince Javee to the infirmary. Queen Yellialah will not wake until noon at the latest. You should not speak about things you know nothing about."

"Many look to me for guidance in troubling times," Fallou said.

"Well, have them look for you elsewhere," Venefica said. "Clear the way. We must get moving."

"There must be no further delay," Fallou said to Nauveena. "You denied the Osseomancer's threat until it was too late. As soon as these members can vote, we must resume the council."

Venefica ignored Fallou. Nauveena followed her lead. The witch led them up the stairs. She glared at the Protectors of Magic, and they quickly shuffled out of the way.

Once in the crowd, Nauveena saw Csandril Em' Dale behind the line of elven archers. She grabbed his arm and spoke in a quick whisper. "It is now or never. We will vote on the Elf Laws tomorrow. I cannot hold Fallou back longer than that. Not after what happened last night. We will go to Veeslau and tell him we can deliver his exception on necromancy."

"You have my vote," Csandril Em' Dale said.

"And the others'?"

"I am working on that."

"You must deliver them. I am telling him we have the votes either way."

※

While Kitrinos brought Prince Javee to the infirmary, the rest brought Queen Yellialah to her chambers, where the knight laid her down. The queen's four-poster bed with down comforter would be much more comfortable for resting. The queen continued to sleep. A look of pleasure appeared on her face, as if the events of the night had never transpired.

"We must continue to monitor her," Venefica said. "I doubt the Osseomancer would try to enter her dreams again, but I would rather be safe."

"I can watch her." Pinerva pulled a pink crystal from her sleeve. She placed the crystal on the bedside table and waved her hands over it while chanting. A faint image of an ocean slowly materialized on the crystal's surface.

"A compound of vervain, wood betony, and lilac applied to her forehead would stop any dreaming," Venefica said. "As an added precaution."

"I will work on a charm to protect Athyzia in the future," Pinerva said. "So no one else can enter through our dreams."

"That would be wise," Nauveena said. "Now, let us go speak with Skiel."

"Skiel?" Venefica asked. "To do what? Ask Veeslau to vote against the Elf Laws? Now is not the time to worry about votes."

"We might have had to deal with the Osseomancer, but Fallou has not. He is already pushing for further restrictions on magic. He is going to try to skip the elf vote, or at least rush it. I suspect he knows he does not have the votes and wants to use these recent events to his advantage. We cannot let him."

As they left Queen Yellialah's, Venefica said, "I spoke to Veeslau last night. He will only vote down the laws if we can provide his exception on necromancy."

"Csandril told me we will have the votes." *Did he?* Nauveena did not feel certain. But it did not matter. The elves would come through. They had to.

They were interrupted by someone shouting their names across the courtyard.

"Nauveena. Venefica."

Both looked as their names were called.

Malachite.

"Where have you been?" Nauveena asked as the druid jogged across the courtyard to them.

"I came as quick as I could. Gwalk has told me what happened. Are you both alright?"

Nauveena turned from Malachite to hide the gash on her cheek.

"We are fine," Venefica said.

"Is it true?" Malachite asked. "Has the Osseomancer really returned? I wish I had been there to help."

"He was too weak to be of any threat," Venefica said. "He only just escaped."

"Where were you?" Nauveena asked once more.

"Last night, after we parted, I went to Gwalk to receive news on Caeruleom. The wizard has been seen. In woods not far from here."

"It is true, then," Venefica said. "He survived his encounter with the Osseomancer."

"He most certainly did. And he is well enough to try and make his way to Athyzia. Or that is my guess, at least. Gwalk has seen him once or twice coming in this direction. He makes a slow pace, however. He is likely still weakened. Even weakened, he has taken efforts to conceal himself. The hawks and other birds often lose track of him. Still, I rode out to where they had last seen him, but when I arrived, he had already disappeared. I have sent word across the forest to be on the lookout for him. If he is found, the animals will tell me immediately. We must get him to Athyzia as soon as possible. Especially if the Osseomancer threatens us again."

"And he could be one more vote," Venefica said.

Nauveena gasped. "I thought you said now is not the time to worry about votes?"

Venefica smiled at her chiding. "No, you were right. Fallou will take advantage of the events of last night. He will try to force through a vote to ban all magics but the Magic of Order. We must not let him."

"We will not," Nauveena said. "We must control all the votes we can. Come, let us continue to Skiel. Veeslau's vote is most important now."

"How certain are you of the elves' votes?" Venefica asked. "Can we guarantee Veeslau that they will vote for his exception?"

"Csandril knows how important it is."

"Csandril knowing that and being able to deliver the votes are two different matters," Malachite reminded them.

"We will have the votes," Nauveena said, hoping she was right.

They crossed Athyzia in the direction of Veeslau's apartment. Until now, Venefica had visited the mage alone. Nauveena was glad she did. She did not enjoy addressing Veeslau in council. The mage wore a blindfold across his eyes. He was pale and thin, practically a corpse himself. She had heard the rumors of Skiel, and now had them confirmed. Their magic was used for grim pursuits, but its sources were grimmer still.

A small, hunchbacked creature opened the door, welcoming them into the apartment. Venefica stepped past him, as she had seen him many times, while Nauveena did her best not to stare at his disfigurements.

Veeslau's apartment was without personal effects. White curtains and blank walls. It appeared as if no one lived there. Nauveena felt a chill cross her body. It ran along her spine. She wished she had worn something warmer, but outside was still the beginning of a hot summer day. She felt like it had suddenly become winter.

"You have returned soon." Veeslau the Unbound sat in a simple chair, facing the opposite wall. He did not turn when the group entered.

"We believe we have the vote," Venefica said.

"You have been very busy, then." Veeslau still did not turn. From behind, it seemed he no longer wore the blindfold. Nauveena hoped he would not turn towards them. "Much has happened since we last spoke. I felt *his* presence in Athyzia."

Venefica continued to speak. "The Osseomancer was frightened off. He will not disturb us again."

"He will not be easy to defeat. He will bide his time until he can campaign again."

"Until then, we must deal with our own issues," Venefica said.

"You have brought others. The druid. The sorceress?"

"Yes — hello," Nauveena said meekly. She and Malachite were both behind Veeslau. Yet he had been aware of their presence all the same.

"We have come to discuss the council," Venefica said.

"The council continues to concern you?" Veeslau asked. "When the Osseomancer recently tried to regain strength?"

"We must continue the voting. The council has been gathered for many months. Many want to return home."

"I see."

"We have discussed the upcoming vote before. On the Elf Laws. We need you to vote against them. Let us end the injustice."

Veeslau did not speak for a long moment. His body was so still he seemed not even to breath. When he did speak, it was as a rattling whisper. Nauveena had to lean forward to hear. "They are a grave injustice, of course. But I have outlined my terms to you. Few elves reside in Skiel. I cannot concern myself with their well-being. I must think about Skiel and our way of life first."

"As must the elves," Venefica said. "They have agreed to vote for your exception."

Veeslau did not respond. He continued staring at the wall, then said, "Magdus."

Nauveena did not know what it meant. Then the hunchback slouched into the room. He held a thin length of cloth in his hand. He approached Veeslau and wrapped the bandage across his eyes.

When the blindfold had been secured, Veeslau turned around. Even without his eyes, Nauveena could sense that he looked at her.

"Sorceress, you are close with the elves. Was it *you* who secured their vote?"

Nauveena felt exposed. And not from the cold. The eyeless face looked not at her, or through her, but *into* her. She could feel him peering into her, searching for the lie.

She hesitated.

Csandril 'Em Dale would come through, she told herself. He had to.

"The elves will — yes, they will vote to continue necromancy," she said.

"I had been told they were against it."

"I admit they will vote for it reluctantly," Nauveena said. "And only in exchange for your vote in the sessions tomorrow."

"You must vote to remove the Elf Laws," Venefica said.

"The vote on the Elf Laws is first," Veeslau said. "How do I know they will honor this arrangement when it is time to vote on necromancy?"

"It is all we can do." Nauveena felt exasperated. "The Elf Laws were on the schedule before necromancy. When we vote on necromancy, we will carve out a separate vote to allow it in your capacity, in use on the Dark Sea, before a larger vote on the whole topic."

"The exception should not be an issue," Veeslau said. "It is not true necromancy. It is bought at great cost. An equal exchange has been made for it."

Nauveena shuddered at this. She did not like to think what that great cost was. All magic took something from its bearer: strength, will, intelligence. But the magic of Skiel took much more. *What had Veeslau's eyes bought?*

"You are certain you can secure the vote with the elves?" Veeslau asked. "Are their numbers enough?"

Again, Nauveena felt Veeslau's unseen eyes peering into her, searching for... what? Doubt, fear, deception. She swallowed, trying to push those feelings further down.

"The elves are three," Nauveena said matter-of-factly. "The dwarves provide another four. They will want the trade to continue. Malachite. Druissia. Dunisk. Qadantium. The oracles. Then yourself. That is thirteen. I would break the tie."

Veeslau considered this a moment, counting in his head.

"Let the elves know they are bound to their promise. I must protect the interests of Skiel, for no one else will. Do not make me to be a fool."

Nauveena went immediately to the elves' gardens. She went alone, without Venefica or Malachite. She wanted to speak with Csandril 'Em Dale by herself.

"Have you spoken to Queen Em' Iriild?" Nauveena asked.

"She is not in a state for me to talk to her," Csandril said.

"You must. I have promised Veeslau the Unbound your votes."

"You must not make promises for the elves."

"Then the laws will remain in place. We are out of options. We must have Skiel if you wish to overturn the Elf Laws."

Csandril sighed and turned from Nauveena. "You will have them," he said after a moment. "The queen has only just received terrible news. A riot in Vabia. Townsfolk claimed elven shop keepers had cheated them. The town erupted. They claimed the elves were in league with the Osseomancer."

"*No.*" Nauveena knew where the story was headed.

"They beat the elves. Then hung them from a tree."

"I am sorry."

"They did not stop there. They went through the village and arrested any elf they could find. They claimed they were all conspiring to revive the Osseomancer."

"How can they be so ignorant?"

Now, it was Csandril's turn to wheel upon her with rage flashing across his face. "Because they *choose to be*. They know we fought against him, when, by all rights, we needed not. The madness is spreading across Vabia and the middle kingdoms."

Nauveena thought of suggesting going to Malthius, the Protector of Vabia, and asking him to stop it. But she knew this would be useless. Likely, the Magic of Order had spurred the riots on.

"You know how important the vote is, then," Nauveena said. "And how important Skiel is to that vote. You must uphold your promise to them. It is a simple thing: vote for their exception, and you can overturn the Elf Laws."

"But it is not a simple thing," Csandril said. "Do you not see? You ask us to debase ourselves to be treated with respect. In order to gain a shred of decency, we must abandon our most sacred laws. We do not take magics reversing death lightly."

"But it can stop these riots and the mistreatment."

"Only at the cost of ourselves. It is a price we should not have to pay."

◆

Even after speaking with Csandril 'Em Dale, Nauveena did not feel certain. The poet understood the seriousness of the vote, but even he seemed conflicted. Could he convince Queen Em' Iriild and Zufaren to vote as needed?

Nauveena did not sleep that night. She had no appetite for sleep, even though she felt tired. She was not afraid to dream again — Pinerva had given her protective charms — but sleep seemed a waste when she had so much to worry about.

Her tower had been destroyed, so she went to Venefica's. Her mind raced, thinking of all that had happened and what might be in store for the next day. She received dawn eagerly. She only wanted to get the day over with. So much could still go wrong.

When the bells tolled shortly after daylight, Nauveena was already dressed and ready. She arrived at the terrace even before the Protectors and Keepers of Order.

She waited as each member of the council filed into their seats. She tried her best to study each, especially the Protectors. She normally had trouble reading others' facial expressions. Now, with her anxiety, she found this especially challenging.

When all had gathered, Nauveena addressed the council. She saw no way to avoid it. She needed to talk about the night before. At least now, she could retell the events as they had transpired, and not sensationalize them as Fallou had.

"Let me begin by accounting the events of the other night," Nauveena began. She chose her words carefully. She did not want to mention an "attack" or "the 'Osseomancer's return." "Events" fit much better.

"For many weeks, I had been experiencing quite bizarre dreams. Dreams which would be prophetic. They foretold — in their way — of a spy following me in Athyzia and of Snorri's fall from the tower. I understood their message too late. As many guessed the night Snorri died, the Osseomancer was responsible. He found a way to enter my dreams. He also entered the dreams of Queen Yellialah."

Nauveena heard a few gasps from the council at this revelation. A few eyes turned to the queen, who suddenly looked embarrassed — as well as still half-asleep. She was already so sickly, and the ordeal appeared to have aged her further.

"Once in our dreams, he entered Athyzia itself. It was in this way that he entered Athyzia the night Snorri died. Currently, Pinerva is working on charms to protect dreams within Athyzia so this does not happen again. When we learned that the Osseomancer had penetrated our dreams, we made a plan to capture him. We wanted to act quickly, so we only involved those who were necessary: myself, Queen Yellialah, Venefica, Pinerva, Kitrinos, and Prince Javee.

"We had the necessary expertise to transfer a dream containing the Osseomancer and capture him. For a moment, it appeared we might be successful. Only in the last, against our combined strengths, did the Osseomancer escape."

Fallou began to stand. Nauveena knew what he would say. She wouldn't let him.

"I know there are some who want to use these events to inspire panic," she said quickly, not allowing the First Protector of Leem to interrupt. "I know this council is too wise for this. We must think long on how to respond to these events. We must not act rashly. Yes, the Osseomancer has shown himself. But he is weakened, and he is desperate. Desperate enough to conceal himself in dreams and prey upon us when we are most vulnerable. It will not happen again. Let us not make mistakes in response."

Nauveena would not cede the floor to Fallou. She continued speaking. "Since I want us to continue reflecting on these events, I will not deviate from the council's schedule. We will proceed as we normally would. The interruptions of the Osseomancer will not determine the decisions or actions of this council. Today, we were scheduled to vote on the Elf Laws. These are vile laws that restrict the rights of our fellow beings. The elves live beside us. They want the same things we want. They fear the same things we fear. They fought against the Osseomancer when the hour was most grim. Let us vote to remove these wicked laws."

Nauveena wanted no delay. The council should vote immediately. She had the votes, but she knew how fleeting this could be. She had thought they had the Bogwaah, only for it to slip away. Any delay could result in Skiel or some other member changing their minds.

She moved to raise her hand and perform the magic needed to begin voting, but was interrupted. When she heard the voice, she expected Fallou. She was relieved when she saw Csandril 'Em Dale standing instead.

"Excuse me," said the elven poet. "Before we vote, I would like to speak."

Nauveena had wanted to move immediately to the vote, but she could not deny Csandril the stage. The vote concerned him, after all. If anyone had doubts on the issue, perhaps he could persuade them.

"Of course. We welcome your thoughts," she said.

As Csandril prepared to speak, Nauveena glanced around the council. She saw Veeslau the Unbound. He faced her, but she could not see his eyes with the blindfold. Once more, she felt him looking into her, searching for doubt and uncertainty. The elves would keep their word. Now that she had promised their votes to Veeslau, the elves would have to follow through. They were honorable.

"Council members," Csandril began in the eloquent speech he was known for. "Thank you for listening to me today. And thank you for listening to myself and my queen over the last few days on this issue. To many, these Elf Laws might just be a strange tradition with no real ramifications. But for the elves, it is our lives. This council has done something never done before. We have gathered the different realms of Jenor. Men. Dwarves. Elves. Beasts. And we have given consideration to how we can live together in peace. We must pride ourselves on these efforts.

"We must not only unite when threatened by terrible evil, but at all times, so each can have an equal chance of happiness. No matter what is decided here, I must thank you for giving this opportunity. The work we do here today is only the start of a long process. Let us continue to listen to each other.

"Of course, this brings me to another matter. The events in Athyzia must not overshadow those from the wider world. In Vabia, a riot has erupted against innocent elven merchants. They have been executed without trial, and the riots have extended themselves across the middle kingdoms. The wellbeing of all elves is threatened."

Nauveena noticed Malthius of Vabia preparing to say something, but Fallou steadied him.

"This hostility towards the elves is a direct result of the laws. They mark us as separate. As other. And our neighbors cannot help but see us this way. We long to live among you, but these laws do not allow us. Let these recent tragedies not be in vain. Let them show us why these laws must be overturned."

Nauveena heard the hurt within Csandril's voice. He spoke with desperation. She did not know how anyone could hear his speech and not vote to overturn the Elf Laws.

She looked across the council. A tear rolled down Lord Ferrum's cheek. Others looked equally moved. Prince Javee — wearing a sling on his right arm — wore a stern expression, while Kitrinos looked on the verge of tears herself.

Even some of the Protectors and Keepers of Order appeared affected by the words.

The moment had come.

It was now or never.

"Let us vote," Nauveena said. "The vote will be to remove any laws which do not grant elves the same rights as men, and to make it impossible to pass any similar laws in the future. If you are for removing these laws, vote 'Yay.' If against, vote 'Nay.'"

Nauveena flicked her wrist and a strand of parchment appeared in front of each voting member. She watched as each found a quill or something else to write with.

Some wrote quickly, and the parchment folded and leapt with a little flick into the fire.

Others took their time, writing the three letters slowly. But even so, in less than a few minutes, each parchment had passed into the fire.

The fire glowed violet when all the votes had been cast. Nauveena paused and looked around the council. Again, she tried reading Fallou's face, but she could not find either worry or confidence. General Dolcius appeared boastful, but such an expression normally rested on his plump face.

With all votes cast, Nauveena waved her hand.

The scale appeared in front of her.

The fire dimmed, then roared to life, emitting a soft puff of smoke. The smoke floated above the council, moving towards the scale. It landed on the left side. On the side of Nay.

One vote for Nay.

The next came.

Another Nay.

Three in a row. Nay. Nay. Nay.

Fallou had at least eight. Likely thirteen. Nauveena expected a tie, after all. The Nay votes were to be expected. The votes did not come out of the fire in the order they had gone in. Snorri had made sure of this to protect anonymity.

The sixth smoke puff fell to the right side of the scale. Yay.

Five Nay. One Yay.

Another Yay. Then another.

The scale would not tip in either direction until all votes had been counted.

Another Yay. Followed by a Nay.

Seven to five. Almost halfway.

Yay. Yay. Yay

Yay took the lead. Eight to seven.

Yays continued coming from the fire.

Nine. Ten. Eleven.

Nauveena needed two more. She caught Csandril's eye. She saw hope. Voting for some use of necromancy was a small price to pay. Centuries of injustice would be overturned.

A run of Nay.

Of course, more remained in the fire.

Nauveena kept the count in her head.

Eleven to ten.

Another Nay.

Fallou always had more than just the ten. The eleventh was Valinka. Or Aryde. Or the Bogwaah.

The vote was tied. Eleven to eleven.

Nay.

Eleven Yay. Twelve Nay.

Nay.

Thirteen Nay.

That would be all of the Nay.

Another puff of smoke. It seemed to float at a slower pace as Nauveena waited.

It came to rest on the right side. Yay.

Twelve Yay. Thirteen Nay.

The last vote.

The entire council watched the fire dim and then erupt into brightness again. They watched as the smoke rose. Even the typical birdsong on the lake had quieted with anticipation.

The smoke rose high above the council. It floated above the scale.

It came down, not choosing a direction until the very end.

The left side.

Nay.

The final count: Twelve Yay. Fourteen Nay.

It could not be.

The Elf Laws remained.

◆

Nauveena rushed to Csandril.

"I do not know what happened." The elf could not look her in the eyes. Nauveena had trouble meeting his as well. She dared not look at Queen Em' Iriild. She could kill with a glare.

Anger etched Zufaren's face. What would stop him from unsheathing his sword and cutting down the Protectors of Order? Nauveena wished he would. She felt her own hands swell with magic.

"It was always a long shot." A tear appeared in Csandril's eye.

Who had voted Nay? Nauveena needed to know. They had just spoken to Skiel.

She saw Venefica, across the terrace, standing to confront Veeslau. "What happened to our discussion last night?"

With the vote final, most had stood from their seats and begun to exit the terrace. Nauveena wanted to remain with the elves, but her curiosity was stronger. She crossed the terrace, marching towards Veeslau. Venefica had guessed right. He had voted to uphold the laws.

"I voted to maintain the peace," Veeslau said as Nauveena reached him.

"*Maintain the peace?*" Nauveena asked. "What does that mean?"

"I feared the consequences if the laws were no more."

"You said you would vote down the laws." Nauveena tried to keep her voice down, but it was impossible not to be overheard on the terrace. Out of the corner of her eye, she saw Fallou approach.

"I find it strange that in all your conversations concerning necromancy, you never asked for the opinion of the Magic of Order," he said. "*The Book of Order* offers much wisdom on the topic."

"Does it?" Nauveena did not want Fallou near her. She did not care what *The Book of Order* said.

Why had Veeslau changed his mind? Had he sensed that the elves had not fully committed to the vote? He had peered into Nauveena. Had he seen her doubts?

"Necromancy is indeed a dark art," Fallou said, "when practiced *against* those who follow the Magic of Order."

"*What?*" Nauveena did not understand. She had tried to ignore Fallou, but she could not any longer. She turned to stare at his stern gray expression.

"Adherents of Order must remain at rest after their deaths. They have followed order in life, and deserve order in death. Death follows life. It is order. However, those who have chosen *not* to follow order in their lives have shown an affinity for chaos. And they are not protected in such a way."

Venefica looked at Veeslau. "You made a deal?"

"We made no deal." Fallou spoke for Veeslau. "We only had a *conversation*."

"It's a fucking deal."

"Did you not have an agreement in place?" Fallou asked. "How is bartering votes for the Elf Laws any different? Because you have done it?"

Nauveena froze. Snorri had not wanted any backroom deals. What had become of the council? She had explicitly traded votes. She had tried to play Fallou's game and lost.

"Veeslau and I have done nothing but have honest conversations," Fallou said. "I have shared with Veeslau our interpretations on necromancy. Necromancy is dark because it disturbs the order between life and death. But those that did not practice order have already upset that balance."

"So they can... what?" Nauveena asked.

"Their bodies can be manipulated after death, since their lives already were. Veeslau took much interest in this. He now understands that the Magic of Order has no issue with necromancy as long as order is maintained."

"Which means upholding the Elf Laws?" Venefica asked.

"You promised." Nauveena turned back to Veeslau.

"How likely were the elves to keep their word?" Veeslau asked. "Once they got what they wanted. I could see their promises were hollow. I needed more guarantees."

"And following order provides such a guarantee," Fallou said.

Malachite came across the terrace. Nauveena could not turn from her conversation. She wanted to lash out with her magic and strike Fallou down. But she could see the druid had come with urgent news. She turned to him.

"The elves," he said. "They are leaving Athyzia."

Nauveena could not believe how quickly the elves packed their possessions. She had not been talking to Fallou very long. In that time, the elves had returned to their quarters and begun to pack.

Typically, the elves took much time to deliberate and reach a decision. In this instance, the decision had been made beforehand. With the Elf Laws remaining, the elves saw no place for them in Athyzia.

Nauveena and Venefica followed Malachite to the central courtyard. The gates stood open. The elves had just passed through. In front of Athyzia stood a wide meadow, hundreds of meters in length. A path led through the tall grass and wildflowers to the forest beyond.

The elves had already crossed much of this expanse. Nauveena could only see their backs far beyond, nearly to the forest.

"The elves cannot leave," she said.

"They tried everything," Malachite said. "And they have been defeated."

Nauveena ran across the courtyard and through the open gates. She hiked her dress to keep from tripping on the long hem and raced through the open meadow.

"No. Stop." She did not have a reason. She did not know what she could say that would make them return. It was another sweltering summer day. Even the short run caused her to feel hot. Sweat appeared on her brow. On the back of her neck. "Wait. Come back."

She was too far away for them to hear. They had almost reached the forest.

"*Csandril!*" she called. She called again. She paused, catching her breath before yelling it once more. On the last shout, she saw two riders break from the pack and turn their horses towards her.

Csandril 'Em Dale and Queen Em' Iriild galloped in her direction.

"I am sorry. Please do not leave."

The queen had the faster mount and reached Nauveena first. She pulled on her horse's reins to end the gallop and turn alongside Nauveena. Csandril 'Em Dale came to a stop beside his queen.

"The Council of Athyzia has spoken," Queen Em' Iriild said.

"Please," Nauveena pleaded. "You cannot leave."

"We are worse off than when we came." Queen Em' Iriild's white mount snorted against the bridle. "Before, we could fool ourselves into believing most wanted these laws overturned. But now, they have been reaffirmed. Codified for another thousand years."

"I am sorry."

"And more. We have humiliated ourselves. We have begged and pleaded and debased ourselves before you. Now, men know the elves will abandon even our loftiest ideals — our ancient laws. We have shown we are no better than men themselves."

"That is not so. You have tried to do what is right for your people."

"The elves must finish the process that began fifteen hundred years ago. We must fade from Jenor."

"Please — but the council *needs* you."

"It has shown that it does not." Queen Em' Iriild's horse reared on its hind legs, and the queen had to pull hard on the reins to steady it.

"All the other votes will be lost." Nauveena rushed closer, scaring the horse into rearing once more. "If you must leave, please give your proxy. Continue to have a voice in the council."

"Is this what it has always been about?" Queen Em' Iriild asked. "Did you even want the Elf Laws removed? Or were you pandering to us?"

"Of course we wanted the laws removed," Nauveena yelled. "How dare you say that? If you leave here, you condemn others — innocents — to the same fate as the elves."

"So be it." The queen reared her horse once more. When it landed, it immediately galloped away, leaving Nauveena alone with Csandril 'Em Dale.

"And you will leave too?" Nauveena asked.

"My queen has commanded it." Csandril bowed his head. "The elves will no longer deal in the affairs of men."

"Please, no."

"Nauveena." Csandril's voice softened. "I do know you tried. I thank you."

"Please stay," Nauveena asked once more.

"Good luck," the poet said softly. He turned his horse and rode towards the forest.

Nauveena collapsed onto the meadow floor. She wanted to sink into the earth and disappear. She had no other choice but to dissolve the council.

The council had failed the elves. They had come on the promise of being heard, but that had never been the case. Now, their numbers were threatened across Jenor, and the council had done nothing but ingrain the very laws making it possible.

The council's legacy would only be failure. Snorri's too. After all his hard work. His vision. He had not been able to steer the council, and it had failed.

Nauveena had failed. She had failed Snorri. Now, the council would be dissolved without achieving any of its goals.

But the alternative was worse. If Nauveena continued the council, upholding the Elf Laws would not be the worst outcome. Without the elves, Fallou's advantage was too great. He could pass whatever he wanted.

As Nauveena knelt in the tall grass, the damask of her dress swarming around her, she saw a hawk soar from the forest and pass only slightly above her head. She looked in the direction it had come from.

It was a different edge of the forest from the one the elves had disappeared into.

The tall pines made the figure appear small in comparison. It did not help that he was stooped.

Nauveena stood and squinted against the sun.

From Athyzia, Malachite rushed down with the hawk flying just in front of him. Venefica followed close behind.

"Nauveena, come," the druid shouted towards her. Nauveena followed him towards the forest edge and the strange figure that had appeared there.

The old man wore a ragged cloak, faded blue in color. The cloak contained many holes and patches. It was weather-beaten and stained, as if he had been traveling all his life.

His white beard unraveled to the ground, where his bare feet appeared out of the folds of his cloak. He leaned on a gnarled staff for support.

They came closer to the figure cautiously, not wishing to startle him. He hobbled closer to them.

Nauveena could not believe it. She had never expected to see the wizard again. Not when he had fallen at Pravulum.

"Caeruleom?" Malachite went to the figure.

"Yes. It is I," the wizard said. "I have come when I am needed most."

Chapter Twelve
The Penultimate

> "He may rival the wizards of old, but he remains an imposter. No true wizard would use their power in the pursuit of more."
> ~King Bane's address after breaking the Siege of Ontiphon
> 5 BU

"I had never felt such force before," Caeruleom said.

They had snuck the wizard in through a postern gate. His appearance would cause a stir, and Nauveena, Malachite, and Venefica wanted to speak with him in private first.

"He is indeed powerful. The most powerful wizard I have ever faced. I fell into a shadow world. He pursued me there. We fought through tunnels of darkness. For long, I became lost. It felt like it must have been years. I only escaped by following the Osseomancer out. He was much more familiar with the other worlds, visiting them often.

"I reentered Jenor near Pravulum, where I had fallen. But I did not know how the course of the war had gone. Soldiers came upon me, and I did not recognize their flags. I knew my powers were diminished, so I resolved to hide myself until I could understand what had happened.

"I feared the Osseomancer might have prevailed. If such a fate had befallen Jenor, my best bet for sanctuary would be found at Athyzia. If Athyzia had fallen, then all was lost. I only hoped it remained, so I made my way here — slowly, I might add, as I am still frail, and I wanted to remain careful."

Nauveena could not believe Caeruleom sat before her. She was transported back to before the council. During the war, he had come to Athyzia often. He kept her company, told her news of the world and jokes. Even though the war had been terrible, a part of her missed those times.

With Caeruleom's tale told, it was now Nauveena and Venefica and Malachite's turn.

"It is summer now," Caeruleom said. "It was the middle of winter when I fell. I have missed much, even if it is the same year."

"You have," Nauveena told him. She was happy to have Venefica and Malachite with her. It would take three to tell the full tale.

She began with Snorri's vision for the council. When she mentioned her mentor, Caeruleom, interrupted. "Where is Snorri? I had expected to find him in Athyzia."

Nauveena bowed her head. Venefica and Malachite wore grim expressions.

"What has happened?" Caeruleom asked.

"There is much to tell," Nauveena said. She would tell of Snorri's passing in time, but it only made sense in the context of the full tale.

She continued again with Snorri sending letters to all the realms of Jenor. She then explained how each had arrived and the council had begun.

Venefica interrupted to explain how Fallou had conspired to have more votes for himself and the Magic of Order. Caeruleom only nodded, now determined not to ask further questions until everything had been told.

When Nauveena reached the portion about Snorri, she faltered. Malachite finished for her. All grew sad, especially knowing such tragedy might have been avoided.

Malachite continued with the fight between the northern kings and how he had gone north to retrieve their proxy and vote. He explained how they had made Lord Ferrum their representative and then Fallou's conspiring to bribe the dwarves with the Last Mountains.

Venefica finished with their confrontation with the Osseomancer and then the vote for the Elf Laws. "They left shortly before you arrived," she said.

The story had taken them long to tell. They wanted to explain each detail and leave nothing out. Night came, and they had dinner brought to them. Caeruleom had spent so long in the other worlds, he did not have much of an appetite, but the others did, and they took turns eating and talking.

When they had finished, Caeruleom had much to say. "Snorri's death is a great loss. He was one of the wisest mages I have ever known. I counted him as a friend. He will be missed."

Having been so busy, Nauveena had not had time to dwell on her mentor recently. Now, she realized how much she missed him too. She had relied on his guidance. She had not been ready to lead the council without him.

"The Osseomancer is not completely defeated," Caeruleom said next. "He is at home in the shadow worlds, and can wait there while he gathers strength. We can never let our guard down. A shame you could not capture him."

Had Caeruleom been present the other night, Nauveena wondered if events might have transpired differently. The wizard was powerful, even if he had not returned to full strength. Perhaps he could have cast a spell to lock the Osseomancer within the crystal ball.

Caeruleom had thoughts on the binding spell and the elves leaving. Much like Snorri, he feared how the magic might interpret the oath if it were ever broken. But he understood the elves' decision to leave. "They risked much coming here. I imagine we will see them less in the years to come."

Nauveena had enjoyed her time with the elves, celebrating Midsummer and working with Csandril 'Em Dale to deliver the votes. She would hate to see the elves further isolate themselves.

As for Fallou, Caeruleom also had thoughts. "Snorri and I went to Fallou during the war. We wished to get his aid in the conflict. Even then, at the moment when we should have been most aligned, he only wanted to protect his interests. Early in the war, he saw opportunity for Faulsk to extend itself. I am not surprised he has bent the council in this way."

"We must end the council," Nauveena said. "Without the elves, he has too many votes. We cannot let him pass further resolutions to control Jenor."

"He will move to ban all magic but that coming from order," Venefica said. "Our best move is to end the council before he can."

"But with Caeruleom, we have one more vote," Malachite said. "Can we not combat Fallou?"

"One more vote, but we have only just lost three," Nauveena said. "Even before the elves left, Fallou had fourteen to our twelve. The elves set us back to nine. If Caeruleom votes, we will have ten, but this is still not enough."

"I do not think my usefulness is my vote alone," Caeruleom said. "Many took my words seriously during the war. My return will only amplify my voice. I was instrumental in bringing the Osseomancer down, after all. That should count for something. Let me address the council. Perhaps I can sway all to not take such extremes."

As excited as Nauveena was to have Caeruleom returned, she doubted even he could be so persuasive.

When Nauveena entered the terrace the next day, she noticed the elves' absence. They had taken up prominent space in the center tables. Three seats had been given to them, not to mention their retinues and attendants who had sat behind them.

Now, the council was without the elves or the northerners, and felt much smaller because of it. The six tables remained in their hexagon, and the other council members kept to their original seats as if they had been assigned, rather than filling the void. It only made the absences more pronounced.

No one else paid much attention to these absences however. They could only focus on Caeruleom. The last time many had seen him had been on the field of war, fighting the Osseomancer. Now, he had returned from the dead. He was immediately crowded with excited greetings and questions as soon as he entered the council.

He had rested the night before, and Nauveena thought he already appeared taller and less stooped.

"Boy, oh, there he is." Lord Ferrum dashed across the terrace to Caeruleom. He shadowboxed with the wizard before gripping him in a hug. "I never thought I'd see you again."

"And I you, master dwarf."

"You look *great*," the Dwarf Lord said. "Like you never fell into the shadow lands."

"Indeed, welcome back, wizard," Galena said.

"It is a relief that you are safe." King Bane held equal excitement as Lord Ferrum, but rather than a hug, he offered the firm grip of a handshake. The king, in his excitement at the wizard's return, did not let go, but continued to shake the wizard's hand furiously for some time.

Prince Javee appeared at the wizard's side. "It is good to see you old friend."

"Yes — what happened there?" Caeruleom motioned to Prince Javee's arm, still bound in a sling.

"Oh, this? It is nothing. Just got into a bit of a tussle with the Osseomancer. You know how it goes."

"I certainly do." Caeruleom laughed. He had a mighty barrel laugh for a man so old and frail looking. "I am sure it is nothing you cannot handle. And how is your father? Has he made any recovery?"

Prince Javee shook his head. He still ruled in his father's place, with the king having been gripped by a curse of madness from the war.

"I always knew you would survive," Kitrinos said so Javee would not need to speak further on his father.

"I cried for many nights when I heard you fell," Queen Yellialah said.

Others continued to greet the wizard.

"How good it is to see you."

"How did you survive?"

"We thought you were lost."

Caeruleom received them all with jovial enthusiasm. Before the war, he had been well-known for organizing parties to go on quests and adventures. He was strengthened by others, and continued to grow taller as he interacted with so many. He had been alone for many months.

Even the Protectors of Order approached.

"Caeruleom, it is a pleasure to see you once again." Fallou bowed to the wizard. "Your sacrifice did not go unnoticed. Your presence has been missed in this council."

Nauveena let the greetings continue. She could not have stopped them even if she had wanted to. It was not every day that a legendary wizard returned from the shadow lands. She would let the greetings and questions run their course.

Caeruleom was forced to recite his story to everyone. Eventually, Nauveena, sitting not far from the wizard, heard several versions of it.

The excitement naturally dwindled. Each member of the council took their seats. Caeruleom sat beside Nauveena in the seat previously reserved for Snorri.

With everyone seated, Nauveena noticed how empty the council felt once again. No northerners. No elves. The central tables were without six now: King Ümlaut, King Caron, Queen Em' Iriild, Csandril 'Em Dale, Zufaren, and Snorri.

Caeruleom now sat in the center, but his presence alone was not enough to counter the losses. Was it normal for a council to lose so many members in such a short span?

Nauveena shrugged off the thought and stood to address the council. "Certainly, Caeruleom needs no introduction," she said. "By a miracle, our dear friend has returned to us. We are indeed lucky that he has survived and has come to join our council."

"*Join the council?*" General Dolcius asked. "What does that mean?"

"I would think that would be obvious," Nauveena said. "Caeruleom is the most powerful wizard in all of Jenor. We owe our victory to him more than anyone else. We are lucky he shall have a vote in the council."

"A vote?" Dolcius couldn't believe it. "Who does he represent?"

"I represent myself, which I believe is enough," Caeruleom said.

"Wizards are an ancient order," Nauveena said. "They should have representation in this council. If Caeruleom had not been lost, he would have had a seat from the beginning."

"And what of the elves?" Malthius of Vabia asked.

"They have abandoned the council," Nauveena said bitterly.

While the news was well-known, a few murmurs rippled across the terrace.

"They did not get their way, and so they are *pouting*," Dolcius said.

"No, this council failed them," Nauveena said. "We owed them fair treatment, and instead we bartered their vote to sate our greed."

Out of the Protectors of Order, Fallou asked the practical question. "Will the elves be designating a proxy as the northern kings have?"

Nauveena shook her head. "I am afraid not." She hated the smile that appeared on Fallou's face afterward.

"If the administrative issues have been addressed," Fallou said, "I would like to add an item to the agenda. The other night, the Osseomancer revealed himself while trying to enter Athyzia and end this council. We must take steps to protect ourselves in the future."

"Excuse me." Caeruleom stood. "I am sure what you intend to say is important, but as I have recently joined this council, I would like to address it first."

"Certainly." Fallou bowed low in reverence to the wizard. "I will listen eagerly to what you have to say."

"Thank you," Caeruleom said. "When I arrived in Athyzia yesterday, I spent much time learning everything that had happened since I fell. I understand the Osseomancer revealed himself not long ago. He has shown he has not been defeated, only diminished for a time. This matter interests me greatly. The purpose of this council is to guard against his ever returning and to maintain our Great Alliance for many years to come. I know many of you feel this way too.

"One answer has been suggested to defeat the Osseomancer once and for all. This is to limit all magics but one: the Magic of Order. Certainly, the Magic of Order has many merits. It helps the common folk make sense of their lives. And those who harness this magic do so quite well.

"But the other magics also have many merits, and they should not be abandoned. Blood magic can be used to heal. Earth magic to communicate with animals and nature. Astronomy to understand our cosmos. Divination to see what is to come. These should not be shunned because the Osseomancer has used them. The answer to the Osseomancer is not any one magic, but them *all*. He does not fear the Magic of Order any more than he fears any other magic. No, what he fears is love. And friendship. This alone can hamper him.

"In the end, no single magic or individual defeated the Osseomancer. Not myself. Nor the Magic of Order. What defeated the Osseomancer was all of us coming together for one common cause. The Osseomancer fears us putting aside our differences and standing firm against him — together."

When he had finished, Caeruleom sat down. The council remained silent, contemplating his words. He was right, of course. In the end, the Great Alliance had defeated the Osseomancer, nothing else.

Nauveena hopped the wizard's words might end the debate once and for all. *Why shouldn't they?* He had spoken the truth. The Protectors of Order were bound to listen.

After a moment of silence, Fallou stood. He looked to each council member, contemplating his words. Finally, he spoke. "All those who would like to add a vote to the schedule to ban all magics but the Magic of Order, raise your hands."

Immediately, all five of the Protectors' hands shot into the air, followed quickly by General Dolcius and Balzhamy. Fallou only needed seven to add the issue. Including himself, he had eight.

"What is more," he continued, "due to the importance of such a vote, I move that we vote on the matter and decide quickly. Head of this council, I demand this item be addressed next. Clearly, we have others who feel the same way. Such a vote will have impacts on other matters."

◈

"How will you allow such a vote tomorrow?" Venefica asked when they returned to her apartment. They had chosen this now — with Nauveena's tower destroyed — as their new private area to discuss.

"How could I not?" Nauveena replied. "It will happen sooner or later. Fallou will keep pushing. And he is right on one thing. If magic is banned, all other topics become moot. They would not matter, so why discuss them? We should have this vote first."

"We may have no other option but to dismiss the council," Malachite said. Nauveena thought that might be best too.

"I hope it does not come to this," Caeruleom said. "The council can accomplish much good. Many issues remain worth discussing. To disband now would be ill indeed."

"We must gather what votes we can," Nauveena said. "To oppose Fallou. If we fail, then we can discuss the best course of action."

"He has four more than us," Venefica said. "And the vote will be tomorrow. Maybe we can delay."

"We must do something," Malachite said.

"Where does the vote stand?" Caeruleom asked. The wizard had only arrived yesterday, after all. Nauveena herself had difficulty keeping track of everything, and she had not spent the last six months in the shadowlands.

"We have ten votes we can reliably count on," Venefica explained. "Malachite can vote. That is one. We can count on King Bane of Druissia, Queen Yellialah of Dunisk, Prince Javee of Qadantium, and the oracles make five. The dwarves control four votes themselves. That puts us at nine."

"You are ten," Malachite told Caeruleom.

"And Fallou has a very reliable eight," Venefica said. "He controls all the kingdoms bound by the Magic of Order. General Dolcius and Balzhamy aligned themselves with him early. Then he has made deals with the merchants, Aryde, the Bogwaah, and Skiel. Fourteen in total."

"'Made deals?'" Nauveena asked. "More like bullied and bribed."

"Do others remain who could attend the council?" Caeruleom asked. "I was a late addition. Could we hope for others?"

"In one night?" Nauveena asked.

"Hope must come from somewhere," Caeruleom said. "In the struggle against the Osseomancer, all hope seemed lost, only to be found in the penultimate hour."

"There are the dwarves of the west," Malachite said. "Of Iron Hall. Could they not be sent for? Maybe they will see the usefulness of the council now that the dwarves have gained access to all the mountains."

"They are too far," Nauveena said.

"We can delay," Venefica said. "You did so before."

"Those dwarves chose not to come not because of the distance or because they did not see the use of the council," Nauveena explained. "The orcs in those mountains have been emboldened since the Osseomancer's reign. Travel is too dangerous."

"And is it still?" Caeruleom asked. "With the Osseomancer defeated?"

"I do not know," Nauveena said. "But it seems a long shot."

"There is the Kingdom of Rocee," Malachite said. "Snorri invited them. They never responded."

"Why would they respond this time?" Nauveena asked.

"Many shamans came from the Distant Lands to fight the Osseomancer," Caeruleom said. "Should they not have a seat at the council?"

"Snorri had decided they should not," Nauveena said. "They all returned beyond the Alcyon Sea once the war ended. They should not have a say in how Jenor is managed. And they would take far too long to arrive. We could not possibly delay for that long."

"How about the monks of Clovis?" Caeruleom asked. "Why have they not attended the council?"

"They declined," Nauveena said, but here was hope. "However, they might be an option. Clovis Monastery is within a few days ride. The monks had not been interested, but if they understood how important their vote has become, maybe they would be persuaded."

"I will write them a letter immediately." Malachite stood to rush to the aviary. The monastery was quite small and did not have a speaking stone. They would need to communicate with birds.

Nauveena steadied him, however. "They still could only provide one vote. Even if they sent multiple monks, they only represent one entity. Even to stop Fallou, I could not give them more than one and still honor the rules of the council."

"But one is still more than we began with," Malachite said.

Nauveena considered a moment. Perhaps the monks of Clovis would come to their aid. They certainly would stand against any ban of magic. They could be relied upon for that.

But they were going about it all wrong.

"We do not need additional votes," Nauveena said. "Caeruleom's arrival helped and provided one vote, but we cannot count on four more Caeruleoms arriving here. Our focus must be on gaining back those already on the council."

"We have failed in that regard," Venefica said. "We had difficulty getting the numbers before the elves left. We cannot possibly get four to turn against Fallou now."

"But we do not need four to turn, only two," Nauveena said. "Two turning from Fallou to us would be counted twice. Instead of a vote of fourteen to ten, we would have a vote of twelve to twelve, creating a tie, which I would break."

"Ahh, of course," Caeruleom said as he understood the math. "That might be an easier task."

"Who then would turn?" Venefica asked.

"The southern merchants represent three votes. Should they not be our focus?" Nauveena asked.

"Fallou has only tightened his grip on them," Malachite said. "They were originally swayed by greed and keeping markets open. The Magic of Order has further committed to these. Apparently, *The Book of Order* says that it is only proper and right to shop frequently and keep a full cupboard and to stay current on the latest fashions."

"It is part of Order to be a consumer?" Nauveena couldn't believe it.

"That's what the book says," Malachite said. "Or so I've been told. I haven't read it."

"It is similar to how Fallou secured Skiel's vote," Malachite said. "Fallou has made it known that necromancy can continue under the Magic of Order — as long as it is not done to those who follow Order. This has secured Skiel for every vote."

"The Bogwaah?" Caeruleom asked. "Why did they turn? They are close neighbors with the elves and rely on them for protection."

"They did so for greed also," Nauveena said. Her opinion of the council members kept falling lower and lower. "Fallou promised them sole production of magical items. It is a difficult proposition to turn down."

"Sole production of all magical items?" Caeruleom asked.

"Yes, all kingdoms that practice the Magic of Order will only buy their magical goods from the Bogwaah."

"And what about the other kingdoms and realms?"

"Well, I guess they can continue to do whatever they wish," Nauveena said.

"Aha." Caeruleom leapt into the air as if he were a much younger man. "There are two sides to this coin, then. Come, I think it is time we had a long chat with the Burgomaster."

The four proceeded to the Burgomaster's apartment. Nauveena remained uncertain how Caeruleom thought he could persuade the Bogwaah, but she was eager to find out.

They traveled in such a large group that if Fallou retained any spies, they were certain to be seen. But at this stage, Nauveena did not care about such matters. She only cared that they convince the Bogwaah to vote with them again.

Caeruleom thumped on the door, knocking loudly and aggressively. After several thuds, he waited, and Nauveena could hear movement inside. "Now it is our turn to try some *bullying and bribes,*" the wizard said to Nauveena as they waited. She was still uncertain what this could mean.

The Burgomaster opened the door and leapt back in surprise. Certainly, the four — a wizard, sorceress, witch, and druid — would be a surprising sight.

Wilhelm Vaah had also been in the middle of dinner, as evidenced by the napkin tucked into his collar. After the surprise settled, he only looked annoyed to have been interrupted during his meal.

Caeruleom managed to transform the annoyance, however. Throughout the day, the wizard had been gaining height as his back unwound and he stooped less. Now, in front of Wilhelm Vaah, he rose an additional foot. The Burgomaster did not possess great height, and now, the wizard towered over him. Nauveena felt intimidated by Caeruleom's sudden increase in stature. Certainly, Vaah did as well.

"Might we come in?" The wizard's voice became deep and menacing. In the moment since Wilhelm Vaah had answered the door, his expression had gone from surprise to annoyance to — now — something bordering on fear and general concern for his overall safety.

"*Caeruleom the Blue,*" Wilhelm Vaah stammered. "How wonderful it was to see you today at council. I cannot tell you how pleased I am that you survived and have joined us."

"We would like to come in."

"Of course. Certainly. Yes." Then the Burgomaster realized he must step out of the way for the wizard and his companions to enter. He stepped back in a quick shuffle. He needed to press further back against the wall so Caeruleom and the others could maneuver past him in the narrow hall.

"Hello, hello." Vaah greeted each in turn. "Nauveena. Pleasant evening, great job at council. Venefica. Umm. Hi. Malachite, how do you do?"

"I am well," Malachite said. Nauveena couldn't help smiling at how worked-up the frog-like man had become.

Caeruleom led the way into the apartment chamber. Vaah had been given one of the larger complexes, and he had made himself at home. He certainly couldn't be called tidy. Vests and dress shirts covered the furniture. Several pairs of muddy boots had been tucked into each corner.

"I have been learning about how the council has gone," Caeruleom said. "I understand you secured quite a partnership recently."

Now, Wilhelm Vaah looked confused. "'Partnership?' I am not sure."

"An exclusive trade partner? Is this right?" Caeruleom asked.

"With Faulsk and the kingdoms of the east," Nauveena said, helping to clarify.

"Oh, yes." Wilhelm Vaah slapped his forehead. "Oh, yes, of course. The Protector of Leem. You see, he explained that the Magic of Order can only use very specific ingredients in their magic. And it so happens that those ingredients must be grown and produced by the same techniques the Bogwaah is currently using."

"How great is that?" Caeruleom said.

"Great indeed." In his nervousness, Vaah rushed around the apartment picking up what he could so his guests could sit down. Even with the clothing cleared off, Nauveena had no strong desire to sit in the dirty room. She saw several crumbs on the couch.

"And to secure such a partnership at no cost to you," Caeruleom said.

"'No cost?'"

"Well, some cost. The cost of the well-being of your neighbors: the elves."

"They — umm — I had been told that order must be maintained, and the laws, as difficult as they may be, maintain order."

"You must know much about the Magic of Order," Caeruleom said.

"I am learning."

"I would suggest you learn faster."

"What — ah?"

"It might interest you to know that very few in the Magic of Order can actually practice magic. Did you know this?"

"I can't say that I did." Wilhelm Vaah's normally green features became a ruby-red color.

"Yes. Curious indeed. I've only recently learned it myself. Really, only Protectors and Keepers perform magic. And the Ultimate Defender, of course. But there is only *one* of those."

"Of course." Vaah gulped.

"And I do not believe they perform much magic involving potions and crystals or anything else you might produce."

Wilhelm Vaah looked utterly stunned. He had not considered any of these points, but now, it made his deal with Fallou look much different.

"The kingdoms of Druissia and Qadantium and Dunisk, on the other hand," Caeruleom continued, "have many magical users — sorcerers, witches, and folk mages — that do use such ingredients."

"Of course, they are some of our largest buyers."

"Let us hope they remain this way."

"Let us — why wouldn't they?" Wilhelm Vaah asked.

"You see, the mages in these kingdoms do not practice the Magic of Order," Caeruleom said. "If all magics but the Magic of Order are banned, then it will be very difficult for these kingdoms to practice magic — a magic that uses far more of your products than the Magic of Order does."

Wilhelm Vaah's mouth fell open. Nauveena imagined that Fallou had filled his head with all sorts of ideas about the Magic of Order. The Burgomaster had likely always wondered why the kingdoms of the east bought so few of his produce. Vaah had thought he had found a new trade partner whose purchases would be incremental to what they already sold. He had not realized that by gaining the Magic of Order, he would lose far more lucrative clients.

"So, tomorrow, when we hold a vote to ban magic, how will you vote?" Caeruleom asked.

Nauveena did not need to hear the Burgomaster's answer. She knew he would vote in his best interests.

◆

"Well-done, well-done indeed." Malachite thumped Caeruleom's back as they returned from Wilhelm Vaah's chamber. Nauveena could not believe it had been so simple. Why couldn't the wizard have come earlier? If Snorri had still been present, he might have made the same appeal. They were one vote closer to staving off disaster.

"To the banquet hall," Malachite said. "We should have a drink."

"It is too soon to celebrate," Venefica said. "We need one more vote to ensure the tie. We must have it by tomorrow."

"Who else could we persuade?" Malachite asked.

"Our best hope is Aryde," Nauveena said. "They are not a natural ally with Faulsk. They could be persuaded."

Fichael Porteau, the foreign minister of Aryde, had been bullied the most by Fallou and Faulsk. The small republic feared an invasion from its neighbors and would do anything to prevent it.

Nauveena led the way to Fichael Porteau's chambers. She had visited him many times in the last few weeks — unfortunately, with nothing to show for it. Tonight, she hoped they would be more successful.

This time, when Caeruleom knocked on the door, he did so more gently. Fichael Porteau did not look nearly as surprised as the Burgomaster had.

"Good evening," he said. "Should I expect another proposal?"

"I am afraid so." Nauveena could already smell the stale smoke inside.

Fichael looked around. The sun had just begun to set. He opened the door a bit more to allow the others inside.

The foreign minister returned to his cigarette as his guests entered the room. At the sight of the smoke, Caeruleom produced his own long wooden pipe from his sleeve. "Do you mind?" he asked.

Fichael waved at all the ashtrays that had sprouted throughout his apartment as response.

"I have not had pipeweed in some time," Caeruleom said as he packed the pipe. "A shame the Free Oak elves left before I arrived." The wizard sat down to smoke.

Fichael Porteau had long ago set a rule against smoking indoors. And just as long ago, abandoned it. He rubbed his eyebrows while holding his cigarette between two fingers.

"I do wish I could help you," he said. "I just fear you will be disappointed."

Nauveena remembered how close she had come to convincing Aryde to grant the dwarves access to the Last Mountains. Unfortunately, while Fichael might have agreed with her, he worked in a democracy. He needed to convince others of whatever terms they might arrive at.

"The vote tomorrow is very important," Nauveena said. "You mentioned on some matters, you might be willing to vote against Faulsk."

"I have had lengthy correspondence with the other minsters." Fichael sighed. "Only the minster of magical affairs wants me to vote against it."

"You would be the swing vote," Nauveena said. "If you vote against the ban, we would have twelve for it and twelve against. I would break the tie."

"That is more reason for me to vote with Faulsk," Fichael said. "They will not enjoy being denied this, and they will remember who denied it."

"But what of the magical users in Aryde?" Venefica asked. "Your folk mages and elves and witches?"

"We also must think of our common folk. Those who use magic might be upset, but everyone would be more upset if Faulsk and Lyrmica invaded."

"What if we could protect you from such an invasion?" Caeruleom smoked the pipe thoughtfully.

"How would you do such a thing?"

Caeruleom did not need to answer. Nauveena had thought of a solution.

"We can have a vote," she said. "As we did for the dwarves. Let us vote that all existing borders must be maintained and protected. Certainly, we could get the votes to pass that. Other than Faulsk, the larger kingdoms have no grand designs. The smaller ones would want the same protection. The merchants would endorse it. Maybe even some of the middle kingdoms."

"That might be something," Fichael Porteau said. "Can that be put to a vote?"

"I don't see why not."

"I do not see how the Magic of Order could fight it," Malachite said mockingly. "Wouldn't maintaining borders protect the current order?"

"This could get some traction from the other ministers," Fichael said.

"Please, how soon could you write to them?" Nauveena asked.

"We could delay a day, perhaps," Venefica said.

"I will write them now." Fichael ashed his cigarette and strode over to his writing desk. He leaned over and had begun wetting a quill when he paused. "Wait. No."

"What is it?" Nauveena asked.

"I already know what they will say: The plan is too risky. Faulsk will find some loophole to invade. They are bent on expanding their borders beyond even their *first* empire."

"It is worth a try," Nauveena said. "If they will invade either way, try to put in what protections you can."

"We have received word they've invaded Rocee. Faulsk claimed they harbored pirates that had been harassing their merchants. It was an obvious lie. The invasion was terrible. Faulsk was ruthless."

"The council can protect you," Venefica said.

"Can it?"

"We have put a binding spell in place," Venefica said. "Fallou knows better than to break it."

"They will find a way." Fichael shook his head. "They will claim we protect agents of the Osseomancer."

"Please write your fellow ministers anyways," Nauveena begged. "See what they might say."

She'd had so much hope a moment ago. Now it had been snuffed out.

"I can tell you their response, because it is my response too. It is too risky. We cannot provoke them."

Caeruleom had been sitting, smoking his pipe the entire conversation. He appeared lost in thought. He blew smoke rings and then sent smaller rings looping through the larger ones.

Now, he stood.

"Aryde will be protected," he announced.

"We will?" Fichael asked.

"Yes. If we have your vote, then I will come to Aryde myself and fight against any who try to invade. You have my word."

The foreign minister was lost for words.

Caeruleom the Blue had fought against the Osseomancer. He alone had challenged the Osseomancer's power. He had fallen and survived.

If he stood by Aryde's side, few could challenge him.

The Lanterns of Evening, the flowers planted by the elves in front of Snorri's statue, had bloomed. Nauveena could see their soft glow as she approached.

The others had returned to Venefica's chambers, but Nauveena continued walking. She needed a moment to herself after all the events of the last few days. It felt like she had not stopped.

She had often wandered through Athyzia's many paths and gardens when she needed a moment to think.

Now, her path took her towards the Library of Esotericism.

And Snorri's grave.

With nightfall, the flowers released a soft luminescence. Their petals had absorbed the sun's warmth throughout the day, and now they emitted it in a pale green light.

The lights lit Snorri's statue above. The dwarves had rendered him well. Their craftsmen were quite skilled.

She wished Snorri could have been there the next day. Disaster would be avoided. Now, maybe once and for all, they could proceed with the council as he had first envisioned it, and without Fallou forcing his agenda upon it.

Nauveena knew she missed her mentor beyond just this. She did not care if he saw the end of the council. She only wished to see him once again. To get his thoughts on a book or to share a joke.

Eventually, the council would end, and Athyzia would return to normal. Nauveena knew when this happened, it would not be the same.

Chapter Thirteen
The Magic of Order

> "For mages, who live longer lives, the war will soon become a distant memory, but for many common folk, it will be all they ever know."
>
> ~*The War Journals*
> Prior Whilip of Clovis
> 2 BU

Nauveena wanted nothing more than to see the look on Fallou's face. The First Protector of Leem rarely registered emotion. His face often showed a blank slate, regardless of what occurred in the council. His voice always remained steady, monotone, measured.

Now, Nauveena expected it to crack.

Fallou had shown a deftness for maneuvering the politics of the council. At each turn, he had gained the upper hand and pivoted to take advantage of each new opportunity.

From the beginning, he had been scheming. He had only reluctantly responded to Snorri's invitation to the council. He made his hesitation well-known. He remained openly skeptical of the entire premise of the council. Snorri would take any measure to keep him and the Magic of Order at the council. The First Protector had taken advantage of such eagerness.

In the council's first day, he had cried foul over the representation of the middle kingdoms. Nauveena remembered how he had complained that each should be represented, that each had their own perspective to add. Of course, that had been a farce, and Fallou's biggest victory.

In short order, he had gained six votes for himself out of the possible twenty-six.

He'd used fear to further solidify those six. Not that any ever thought of turning. They all knew their role. The Magic of Order maintained a strict hierarchy. At the council, they followed Fallou.

But at each chance, Fallou wound them tighter to himself. He used the fear of the Osseomancer's return to stoke fear in his fellow Protectors and Keepers. They had to remain with him to protect against the Osseomancer. Their fear bound them to the First Protector.

Rheum and Lyrmica soon added to his tally.

General Dolcius wanted legitimacy.

Balzhamy needed allies.

The other votes had come through trickery. Nauveena had described it correctly: bullying and bribes. Fallou knew what each council member wanted — or feared. He'd used each in turn.

He threatened the merchants and Aryde's independence.

He played on the Bogwaah's greed.

He offered Skiel the ability to continue their necromantic practices.

Each had been easy.

Also easy had been the elimination of the northern kings. Queen Breve's adultery was an open secret. It was easy enough to send an Obeyer to point it out to King Ümlaut. Fallou had done his best to delay the druid so he could not return with the northerners' proxy. Nauveena had no doubt that he had sent the riders that had hampered Malachite.

Fallou might have been thwarted by Malachite returning with the northerner's proxy, but he had seen how easy eliminating votes could be. It was not enough to gain votes. Eliminating them was a valid strategy as well.

His last triumph had come against the elves. Fallou had turned Skiel at the right time. He knew it. He knew he could land a death blow to Nauveena and her allies.

With the Elf Laws upheld, the elves had no choice but to leave the council — taking with them their three votes. The gap had become insurmountable. Fallou felt confident when he added the next item to the agenda.

It had been his ultimate goal, the goal of the Magic of Order. Their cult believed magic could only come from order. Any other magic threatened that order. It had been Fallou's goal all along.

He must have thought he was close to achieving his aims. He had added the ban to the agenda easily. He had more than the required seven.

But he had not accounted for Caeruleom's return. Fallou continued to underestimate him. Even if Nauveena and her allies went to the other members late in the night, they could not get them to flip.

Certainly not two of them.

Nauveena looked forward to seeing some emotion on the First Protector of Leem's face for once.

Normally, she would have drawn out the council. She had gotten used to taking her time. For so long, she had been set to delay. Now, she let it go at its own pace.

As she expected, Fallou addressed the council first. He had much to say about Order and the Osseomancer and the wickedness of all the other magics. But Nauveena barely listened. She only wanted to get to the vote.

Others responded to Fallou. King Bane and Prince Javee protested that magic was not evil in and of itself. Kitrinos explained that prophecies did not come from order, but from the odd intersections of past, present, and future. They served a purpose and she could not stop herself from receiving them, even if she wanted to.

Nauveena realized that if she did not give some protest, it would seem suspicious. She made an impassioned plea that surprised even herself. She had not expected to make one.

Once she began, she could hardly stop herself. Magic was her passion. She remembered her meeting with the Osseomancer. He had been right on one thing, at least.

"If it were not for magic, I would have no life at all," Nauveena found herself saying. "I would have remained a poor oyster farmer on the island of Ciri Daahl. Or I would have died in the war. But I mean it much more than this. The life of an oyster farmer is not all bad; it is simple and quaint, and the common folk feel much love for each other. It is not a love to be rejected. But that love also meant my family wished the best for me, even if it meant they could not have me.

"Without magic, I would have remained on that island, and I would have come to love its simplicity: the heat of the sun in the summer and the warmth of companionship and the hearth in the winter. But I would not have known the mysteries of the world. I would not have known about the lives of the elves, or the dwarves. I would have known nothing outside that small island.

"I would not have wondered about our meaning. I would not have contemplated our existence. I would not have a million questions about our lives and our purpose. I would not have played a wider role in the world. I would not have found a love for study and reading and wonder.

"But because of magic, I was introduced to all of this. But the magic was not just the physical movements I could make or the forces I could wield. The magic was the wonder itself. The magic was the asking of such questions and the seeking of their answers. Magic was a gift given to us so we can make our way in the universe and, maybe, eventually understand why we are here.

"For that reason, magic, like knowledge, must remain free and available to all. I was given such opportunities because of the magic residing inside me. Why should this be the case? The common folk cannot shield themselves with magical force, but they can wonder about the same questions as us. And closing off magic will not allow them to do so. Restricting magic will not allow us to continue to stare in awe at the vastness of what we do not know. We should not fear magic, but fear not having it."

If anyone still needed convincing, Nauveena felt certain she had done her job. She felt quite persuasive. A shame, she thought. Snorri envisioned the council full of speeches and debates that would persuade. Not conniving and bartering and bribing, all in back rooms, in private, far away from the open forum of the terrace.

Even though Nauveena had not tried to delay the council, discussions continued. She wanted to hold the vote today, though. She held a twelve-to-twelve decision. She did not know if her confidence would remain through the night. She wanted to vote *now*, before Fallou could learn of their plans and counter.

"We could talk until night and into morning," Nauveena said. "This topic is one of the most important the council will face. The only true way to settle it is to vote. I will open the voting now. If you are in favor of a ban on all magic but that deemed acceptable by *The Book of Order*, vote 'Yay',

"If, however, you believe all magic should remain free, and no one magical system should be superior to the others, vote 'Nay.' Voting 'Nay' will keep Jenor as it is. Magic will be shared among all. No one can dictate how it is used or where it comes from."

Nauveena flicked her wrist, and a spread of parchment appeared in front of each member. She would not vote yet. Not until the votes came out in a tie. As such, she only sat back to watch.

What would Fallou's reaction be? Would he leave, taking the rest of the Protectors and Keepers with him? The council would end, surely, but at least magic would have been protected and secured by the binding spell. The Magic of Order could not even outlaw other magics in their own kingdom.

Nauveena glanced around the tables. King Bane and Prince Javee had already stopped writing. Their parchments rolled up and flung themselves into the fire.

Kitrinos finished writing as well. She wrote in a flared cursive, and even the three simple letters took time.

Queen Yellialah had not written anything. Her quill hovered over the parchment. Had the vote been confusing? Often, she had been asked to vote 'Yay,' as with the vote on the Elf Laws.

Now, the queen turned her head to look at Venefica sitting beside her. She said something that Nauveena could not hear.

Then the queen pressed the quill down onto the parchment. Nauveena looked to Venefica. The witch waved her hands, trying to get Nauveena's attention. She mouthed the word "Stop."

Nauveena could not do anything. Snorri had constructed the voting spell so it could not be stopped once it had begun.

What was Queen Yellialah writing?

The queen finished, and the parchment rolled up and floated into the fire. The fire burned indigo for a moment, digesting the vote.

What had the queen said to Venefica? Nauveena looked to the witch. Venefica still wanted to stop the vote.

But Nauveena could do nothing.

Only a few votes remained. One by one, they flickered off the table and into the fire. The fire burned violet each time.

Each vote had been collected. The scales appeared at the table beside Nauveena. Venefica had gone very pale. Nauveena could only watch as each vote came from the fire.

Nay. Nay. Nay.

Several. Followed by just as many Yay.

Nauveena did not pay attention to each individual one as they came out. It did not matter. She could tell how the vote would go based on Venefica's expression.

Malachite had seen Venefica as well.

"What is happening?" he asked from his position beside Nauveena.

The sorceress did not respond. She only watched the scales. At the end, it would tip — or remain balanced. Nauveena only hoped for the balance. Maybe Venefica was wrong. Maybe she had misheard what Queen Yellialah had said.

But Nauveena knew this was not the case. Venefica had gone too pale.

Nauveena's heart stopped beating. She held her breath.

Nay. Yay. Yay. Nay.

Only a few more remained in the fire.

Nay. Yay.

Nauveena looked at the scale.

Eleven Nay. Twelve Yay.

Only one vote remained.

The smoke flickered out of the fire. It hovered so long over the scales. Snorri had a flair for dramatics at times. Nauveena wished he hadn't in this case.

The smoke crystalized and landed on the right side of the scale.

On the side of Yay.

Nauveena did not want to look at Fallou's face now. But, when she did, she saw some emotion.

Triumph.

The council erupted into chaos. Even though they had been voting on the issue, neither side had expected such an outcome. Many of the Protectors and Keepers of Order stood and shook each other's hands.

Prince Javee stood. "It cannot be. No. It is not possible."

"You have seen the vote." General Dolcius laughed.

"Qadantium will never ban magic," Prince Javee announced. "Binding spell be damned."

Nauveena could not focus on any of that. She rushed across the terrace, ignoring Malachite and Caeruleom as they tried to talk to her.

Venefica had stood as well to speak with Queen Yellialah. "Why have you voted this way?" the witch asked.

The queen did not respond. She did not look at Venefica. Her knights came and stood between Venefica and the queen.

"Answer me," Venefica demanded. "You promised me your vote."

"I am sorry," Queen Yellialah said. "I had to."

"*Had to?*" Nauveena could not believe it. "What has the Magic of Order offered you? Have they threatened you?"

"The Magic of Order has offered me nothing but what they offer everyone else."

"What?" Venefica was fuming. "What could they offer you that you do not already have?"

"Safety. Peace. Freedom from fear," Queen Yellialah said. "They welcome common folk into their magic. They do not use their magic against us."

"The Osseomancer cannot hurt you again," Nauveena said.

"It is not him I fear," the queen said. "It is *you*. You who claimed to protect me, but then used me as bait to ensnare the Osseomancer. You do not see the common folk as equals. We are nothing but pawns to be used as you see fit. If you will treat a queen in such a way, how will you treat anyone else?"

Venefica stepped towards Queen Yellialah, but her knights stepped closer together, blocking the witch. The queen continued to leave the terrace. Venefica and Nauveena worked to follow, but the knights blocked them.

"And what of your debt?" Venefica asked. "Think of what I have done for you."

"I have voted as you wished on every other issue. I cannot be bound to you forever."

Venefica's anger faded momentarily. Her voice softened. "I sacrificed myself so you could go free."

"Did you?" Queen Yellialah asked. "Or did you want *him* for yourself?"

"Step away from her." Fallou, the First Protector of Leem, had never embedded his voice with so much authority.

Venefica stepped away from Queen Yellialah and her knights. Fallou and the other Protectors and Keepers formed a half-ring in front of Venefica and Nauveena, blocking them from leaving the terrace. Their backs were to the lake.

"The witch will threaten you no longer, queen," Fallou said. "You do not need fear her."

"I was not threatening her," Venefica said.

Fallou nodded, and two burly Obeyers of Order stepped forward. One held a length of rope. The other drew a sword. Nauveena had never seen the Magic of Order carry a weapon.

The one with the rope came behind Venefica and grabbed her arms roughly. She struggled against him, but he was too large. He pulled her arms sharply, pressing them together, and began tying the witch's hands behind her back.

"What is this?" Venefica asked in disbelief.

"Let her go immediately," Nauveena demanded.

Prince Javee and King Bane stepped into the circle. "What do you think you are doing?" King Bane asked.

The Obeyer tightened the rope on Venefica's hands, causing the witch to grimace.

"The vote has been settled," Fallou said. "To protect Jenor from all dark arts and wickedness, magic will only be conducted which comes from order. We must move to eliminate all that would threaten order."

"How do I threaten order?" Venefica asked.

"You once served the Osseomancer," Fallou said. "You threaten us all."

"What will you do with her?" Nauveena felt magic flash into her hands. Fallou saw it too.

"Auras have been prohibited, if I am not mistaken."

Prince Javee, likewise, produced an orb of fire in his hand.

"You are willing to break the binding spell this quickly?" Fallou asked him.

What would happen if the spell was broken? Nauveena feared to find out. The Obeyer who had bound Venefica pushed her forward.

"Witch, you are under arrest," Fallou pronounced. "You have committed crimes against order and inspired chaos in Jenor. For these crimes, you have been sentenced to death."

"Death? No." Nauveena could not believe it.

Another Obeyer of Order entered the semi-circle. He carried a flaming torch.

"We are ready, First Protector of Leem."

What did they have planned? Would they burn Venefica right here?

"Certainly, she must have a trial first," Nauveena said. She could hope for something. Maybe Venefica could be saved.

"Of course," Fallou said.

"Then untie her. Extinguish those flames."

"The flames are not for the witch."

"What are they for, then?"

"The libraries."

Nauveena did not care about the binding spell any longer. She would not let Fallou continue.

"*The libraries?*"

"Yes," he said. "All the libraries of Athyzia contain knowledge on magic that comes from chaos. If we wish to live in a world of order, they must burn. We cannot allow their collections to continue."

"You wouldn't," Nauveena said. "So much knowledge would be lost."

"I would," Fallou said. "To protect order, we burned the Library of Ülme, so the Osseomancer could not have it."

"You burned Ülme?" Nauveena had been told the Osseomancer's armies had destroyed the great library. Its Protector himself had claimed it.

"Of course we burned Ülme." A spark flashed in Fallou's eyes. "The library's collections threatened us all. We could not let it continue to tempt others with chaos. We could not let the Osseomancer have it. We could not let *anyone* have it."

"You will not burn Athyzia."

"But I will — how else do we honor the promise of the binding spell? As long as these books exist, magic of chaos can be conducted. Too much knowledge is a danger to us all."

Nauveena burned with anger. She envisioned Fallou leading the Obeyers of Order from one library to the next. The Library of Reason. The Library of Songs. The Library of Enigmas.

The Library of Esotericism.

She pictured Fallou dancing as the flames leapt higher than Athyzia's highest towers.

The magic escaped Nauveena's hand. It flared out in a flash of purple. Just a momentary flash. She withdrew, restraining herself.

"Careful. Careful, now," Fallou said. "What will happen if you break the binding spell?"

It took everything within Nauveena not to flare out with her magic. How bad could the punishment be for breaking the spell? It could not be worse than the destruction of Athyzia's libraries.

She did not care what befell her. She would not let Fallou touch Athyzia's books, even if it meant she was struck dead because of it. The magic coursed down her arm. She felt the energy swelling in her fist. She would lash out in a tremendous flash, enough to strike back all the Protectors and Keepers in front of her. They would regret the day they challenged her.

Caeruleom the Blue entered the circle.

"Excuse me."

Everyone had been focused on Nauveena. They turned to the wizard.

"I have only recently learned of this binding spell," he said.

Fallou looked menacingly at the wizard.

"I would like to understand more details," Caeruleom continued. "It is my understanding that only those who made the vow are bound to it."

"And those kingdoms they represent." Fallou cast an eye towards Prince Javee.

"I also believe I was not present when the binding spell was made," Caeruleom said.

"But you are a part of the council that made the oath," Fallou said.

"I was not then a part of the council," Caeruleom said. "I do not believe I am bound by the same oath."

Fallou's mouth fell open. For once, he had nothing to say. His eyes fell on Caeruleom's staff, only recently repaired.

"Nonsense," General Dolcius said. "Of course the wizard is bound by it."

"Would you like to find out?" Caeruleom asked.

Dolcius stepped behind two Obeyers of Order.

"If you do not untie the witch and leave Athyzia immediately, we will test who this binding spell is applied to," Caeruleom said.

Fallou regained his composure. He looked to his fellow Protectors and Keepers. "This council has been ill-conceived from the beginning," he said. "At least it has accomplished one small good: banning all magic cast from chaos. We have little more to do here. Let us return to our homes, where we can be useful."

The Protectors of Order nodded in agreement.

"Obeyer, let the witch go." The Obeyer began untying Venefica. "Witch, if you ever step foot in the east, you will be made to regret it."

Venefica snarled at Fallou as she massaged her wrists.

"The rulings of the council stand," Fallou said. "Only the Magic of Order will be practiced in Jenor. All others will be outlawed on punishment of death."

With that, Fallou turned and left the terrace, followed by his fellow Protectors and Keepers and Obeyers.

Everyone left the terrace in confusion. All magic but the Magic of Order had been banned? But what could that mean? So little was known about the Magic of Order; what exactly was allowed and what exactly was prohibited? Would they just try small amounts of magic, incrementally, to see how the spell would react?

Those who had voted against such measures conferenced long into the night.

Some suggested further bargaining with Fallou and the Magic of Order. Nauveena saw no point in it, but a messenger was sent to the First Protector's chambers. They wished to ask for more details of what could and could not be practiced.

Fallou sent the messenger away with a short note: only those who followed Order could practice magic, and only magic approved by the Magic of Order. The message did little to clarify. By the end of the night, only one thing had been decided: *the council had ended.* Nauveena saw no need for it. The next morning, she sent word around Athyzia.

The followers of the Magic of Order left Athyzia first, as unceremoniously as they had come. They had few possessions and packed quickly. No one watched them go.

Shortly after, Queen Yellialah and those of Dunisk left. She tried to slip out quickly. Venefica went to speak to the queen at the gate, but the queen avoided the witch's eyes.

The merchants left shortly after dinner. They apologized for how the vote had gone and hoped it would not end any trade with their cities.

Veeslau the Unbound and his servant left in the middle of the night. They did not say goodbye. Veeslau would be protected going forward. Skiel's magic would be protected under the Magic of Order. Like his own magic, he had paid a cost for this; Nauveena wondered how steep he considered such a cost.

In the morning, all that remained were those who had opposed Fallou in the end. A defeated air filled Athyzia. Fallou had been driven off, and Athyzia saved, but Jenor had been changed forever.

News came from Qadantium that would not improve morale. "Tempests have come off the ocean," Prince Javee said. "The rivers have begun to flood. It's happened practically overnight. The entire kingdom is almost under water."

"How is this possible?" Malachite asked. Qadantium had not been known for flooding, especially in the middle of summer.

Nauveena knew what had happened. "The binding spell. You denied it. That alone has broken the spell and incurred its wrath."

Kitrinos stepped forward now to speak. "Qadantium's fate will be much worse. This is only the beginning. The magic has been ruined, and so the land must return into the sea."

"I must go immediately," the prince said. "Qadantium needs me now. They will be confused by the news coming out of Athyzia."

"Go," Nauveena said. "There is little to be done here."

The one thing they had done the night before was issue decrees warning what would happen if magic were practiced. Nauveena feared for Qadantium. How much knowledge would be lost? Not to mention innocent lives.

Prince Javee left at once. Kitrinos went with him. The Temple of Xanthous lay at the very tip of Qadantium, and they would make much of the journey together.

Wilhelm Vaah, the Burgomaster of Bogmantic, left with the others from the Bogwaah later that day. The vote had left him without any market. Few would be buying the Bogwaah's magical ingredients any time soon.

The dwarves left shortly after. Galena and Lord Ferrum both wished to return to their mountains.

"If there is ever anything we can do, please let us know," Lord Ferrum said at the gates.

"Yes, the dwarves owe you a debt of gratitude," Galena said. Indeed, the dwarves would be newly rich from the council. Gems might not be used for magic any longer, but they still held value regardless, not to mention all the gold and silver they could mine.

Nauveena watched the dwarves leave with sadness in her heart. They seldom left their mountain homes. She wondered when she would see them again. Only later did she realize they had never put back all the books in the Library of Erudition.

"I too must return to my kingdom," King Bane said after dinner. "They will need me to guide them in this troubling time. A new world order indeed has come from this council."

"Of course," Nauveena said sadly. She feared how quiet Athyzia would become once everyone left.

King Bane turned to Venefica. "Will you return with me? I will keep you safe from arrest. I can promise you that."

"No." Venefica shook her head. "I appreciate that I will always have sanctuary in Druissia, but that is not where I am needed."

"Where will you go, then?" Malachite asked.

"To the east."

"You will be arrested," Nauveena said.

"Many witches remain in the east. With this new edict, they will be hunted. I must go to their aid and help as many escape as possible."

"Let them all know they can seek refuge in Druissia," King Bane said. The issue would be getting them there before the Magic of Order found them. "They will still be bound by the spell, but at least they will not be hunted by the Magic of Order."

"But you will put yourself in danger," Nauveena said to Venefica, concerned for her friend.

"So be it," the witch said. "I have failed with this council. I must help."

"I will go with you," Malachite said. "I also was not there when the binding spell was made. I do not believe it applies to me. King Bane had my proxy to vote in the council, but not to make oaths in my name."

King Bane left with his men at arms, but without Venefica. Venefica and Malachite proposed to set off the next day. Nauveena only wished she could stop them. She spent much of the night trying to convince them to remain, but they would not reverse their decision.

When Nauveena finally retired for the night, she did not sleep, but instead, tossed and turned.

She walked with Venefica to Athyzia's gate. Over the many months of the council, they had often walked together, usually bent towards each other in conversation. Today, they only found silence. Nauveena could not think of anything else to say. It had been so long since she'd had what could be called a friend.

At the gate, they saw Malachite approaching from his quarters. As he neared, Nauveena saw that the druid carried a book. He offered it to Nauveena.

"Snorri's copy of *Philosophies of Magic*?" She couldn't believe it. Some of the pages were creased and ripped, and the binding was dented, but otherwise the text was none worse for wear. She could still read it. "It survived the destruction of my tower?"

Since that night, different pieces of debris had washed up on the lake's shore — some Nauveena recognized like the arm of a chair or a pillow case — but none of her books, neither her own nor the ones she had recovered from the dreams.

Malachite nodded. "Athyzia's stray cats found it in the garden last night. They had seen you reading it. They wished for me to return it."

Nauveena looked at the text. She thought she had lost it forever. She clutched it close to her. She felt a moment of happiness, but it did not last. Her friends were still leaving.

"You are certain you must go?" she asked.

Venefica nodded sadly. "This is not the end, though. I will return to Athyzia. I will need your guidance often in the years to come."

Caeruleom also approached the gate. He had no possessions, but Nauveena could tell he was leaving.

"You will leave as well?" she asked.

The wizard nodded. "I will go to the Republic of Aryde. I must honor my word and stand beside them. Faulsk will see their vote in this council as an excuse to invade."

Fichael Porteau approached now too. "Thank you, Caeruleom. It means much that you will offer us protection. Hopefully, we can stave off despair."

The foreign minister turned to Nauveena. "I imagine this is not how you wanted the council to go. Sometimes, politics can be even more difficult than magic. Although I cannot do magic at all. You fared quite well, all things considered."

Nauveena didn't feel that way at all.

She watched as the foreign minister and wizard rode down the road. They would head south and cut across the Pass of Giants before heading to Aryde.

With them departed, only Venefica and Malachite remained.

"You are certain?" Nauveena asked once more. Athyzia would feel so empty. For months, it had been filled. Now, she would be left with only the mages, who preferred study over conversation. She did not even have Snorri any longer.

"You could come with us," Venefica said. "Even if you cannot do magic, you will be quite useful."

Nauveena considered it. She had not left Athyzia in many years. It would be something to see the wider world, even if it was the bleak kingdoms of the east.

At last, she shook her head.

"No, my place is here."

"And what will you do?" Malachite asked.

"I will find whatever books I can on binding spells. If there is a way to undo them, I must find it."

Acknowledgements

This novel would not have been possible if it were not for the love, support, and guidance of a large number of people. Sitting down to write this has made me realize how fortunate and privileged I am to have all these great people in my life.

First, thank you to my wife Christine for giving me the time and space to write (i.e. going to bed early), and for putting up with me while I zoned out to think about my weird fantasy world. I am sorry I made up so many names you could not pronounce, but I am glad I could give us our own version of *The Cones of Dunshire*.

To my dad, thank you for introducing me to fantasy and reading. I still remember buying our first copy of *The Hobbit* together and your readings of the Redwall books. I particularly thank you for doing the accents for the moles. I wish you could read this.

To my mom, in addition to raising me and instilling in me a love for reading, thank you for being the first person to read *The Council of Athyzia*. I knew I did something right when you called one Sunday morning to yell at me about the ending.

To my sister Katie, thank you for all the feedback as well as your requests to add more maps. I will never be upset by this request. I can't wait for Norah and Henry to read this.

To my sister-in-law Katie, thank you for all your feedback, even if fantasy is not your favorite genre and you do not know the difference between a druid and a droid. I appreciated all your perspectives and encouragement.

To Kurt, your feedback has been invaluable. I will thank you, even if Nauveena might not. You have definitely left your touch on this novel and the ones to come. And also thank you for being a friend throughout this very lengthy process.

To Brian, thank you for being there from day one on my writing journey and reading much longer (and more eccentric) manuscripts. Don't worry, those will be revived some day.

Of course, most importantly I need to thank my dogs, Millie and Rufus. Millie particularly was sleeping besides me for the majority of this book's creation. I don't know how many plot holes I solved while walking you. And so far any Instagram posts featuring my dogs gets the most engagement.

There are so many others who have supported me and offered encouragement throughout this process. Thank you to Kyle, Nicole, Bridget, Dave (but not Julie), the whole Cleary family (particularly JC and Sharon), Conner, Steve, Wyzga, Mr. Hannum, Dr. Case, Eugenio Volpe, Sierra, Freddy, and Susan.

To Oren, I don't think I could have found a better editor. You helped guide me through the big things like magic systems and world building to small thinks like how to use a semicolon; which I am still not clear on. Thank you for putting up with so many of my writing ticks, such as my over use of the word 'only' and many unnecessary scene breaks. I really enjoyed working together.

To Lucy, my cover artist, I can't believe what you have come up. It is beyond my wildest dreams and really has helped bring Athyzia to life. I can't wait to work on the rest of the series together.

Also thank you to all of bookstagram. The internet is a scary place, especially for someone sharing something so dear to them. I can't believe how friendly, interesting, and supportive strangers on the internet can be. This is generally a great community and thank you for accepting me. Particularly thank you to my amazing ARC readers as well as my fellow indie authors for giving such invaluable advice on publishing.

And last, of course, thank you to you the reader, without whom, none of this would be possible.

About the Author

D.H. Hoskins probably spends too much time thinking about maps of places that do not exist. When he is not writing, he enjoys playing basketball, boardgames, hiking, and hanging with his dogs. He lives outside Boston with his wife and their two French Bulldogs, Millie and Rufus.

To keep up with future releases, follow him on instagram **@d_h_hoskins** or check out his website **www.dhhoskins.com**.

If you enjoyed this work, please consider leaving a review on Amazon, Storygraph, Goodreads or anywhere else where others gather to find reading recommendations.

@D_H_HOSKINS

Made in the USA
Middletown, DE
06 May 2024

53925963R00243